THE MAGIC HOUR

www.**booksattransworld**.co.uk

Novels with Terence Brady:
VICTORIA
VICTORIA AND COMPANY
ROSE'S STORY
YES HONESTLY

Television Drama Series with Terence Brady:
TAKE THREE GIRLS
UPSTAIRS DOWNSTAIRS
THOMAS AND SARAH
NANNY
FOREVER GREEN

Television Comedy Series with Terence Brady:
NO HONESTLY
YES HONESTLY
PIG IN THE MIDDLE
OH MADELINE! (USA)
FATHER MATTHEW'S DAUGHTER

Television Plays with Terence Brady:
MAKING THE PLAY
SUCH A SMALL WORLD
ONE OF THE FAMILY

Films with Terence Brady:
LOVE WITH A PERFECT STRANGER
MAGIC MOMENTS

Stage Plays with Terence Brady:
I WISH I WISH
THE SHELL SEEKERS
(adaptation from the novel by Rosamunde Pilcher)

THE MAGIC HOUR

Charlotte Bingham

BANTAM PRESS

LONDON · TORONTO · SYDNEY · AUCKLAND · JOHANNESBURG

TRANSWORLD PUBLISHERS
61–63 Uxbridge Road, London W5 5SA
a division of The Random House Group Ltd

RANDOM HOUSE AUSTRALIA (PTY) LTD
20 Alfred Street, Milsons Point, Sydney,
New South Wales 2061, Australia

RANDOM HOUSE NEW ZEALAND LTD
18 Poland Road, Glenfield, Auckland 10, New Zealand

RANDOM HOUSE SOUTH AFRICA (PTY) LTD
Endulini, 5a Jubilee Road, Parktown 2193, South Africa

Published 2005 by Bantam Press
a division of Transworld Publishers

A catalogue record for this book is available from the British Library.
ISBN 0593 054237

Typeset in 11/13 New Baskerville by
Kestrel Data, Exeter, Devon.

Printed and bound in Great Britain by
Clays Ltd, St Ives plc.

3 5 7 9 10 8 6 4

Papers used by Transworld Publishers are natural, recyclable products
made from wood grown in sustainable forests. The manufacturing processes
conform to the environmental regulations of the country of origin.

For Terencey
who has given me so many

Prologue

The Magic Hour is that time when late afternoon and early evening meet, when sun and moon seem set to tussle as to who is to take possession of the darkening sk. The Magic Hour is a time when it seems that the distant sound of children playing will never cease, when birds sit on telephone wires pretending that daylight will never fade, and bicyclists amble home without their lights. The Magic Hour is when night creatures are still found to be asleep, when daisies on lawns remain detergent bright, and birds sing among richly various leaves.

Then, with silent surrender, as day slips off and night's black agent sets out his stall to claim his percentage of the skies, and the burnt-out worlds we know as stars burst through the great dark curtain above – the Magic Hour is gone.

So it is with people. They too have their Magic Hour of meeting, when it seems that neither day nor night can yet claim victory, and guardian angels hold their breath, willing them to turn their backs on that devil's comedy that is the past, urging them forward towards a new dawn, where the early-morning salutations of the birds will provide the opening chorus for their joys to come.

Part One

THE PAST THAT WILL NOT GO AWAY

England Before World War II

A Mess of Pottage

Betty Stamford was a tall, big-boned woman with tightly knotted grey hair and an expression of unremitting sobriety, as befitted a widow of some long standing. Just at this moment her expression was unusually severe, even for her, which was hardly surprising, since her only son John had recently informed her that he was marrying a London girl. No matter what the girl's social standing, this news had come as a rude shock to John's mother, for in common with their country neighbours, the Stamfords regarded London at best as a foreign city, at worst as a centre of all that was bad in English Society.

To any other family perhaps, Laura Anne Millington might have seemed a catch, but to Betty Stamford, her future mother-in-law, Laura seemed flighty, suspiciously patrician, and not likely to take to the country life that the farming Stamfords all knew and loved.

'My dear, such a day! So wonderful for you!'

Betty's best friend Janet Priddy beamed at her over the top of her rose-patterned teacup. Betty nodded automatically, something that she found she had taken to doing all too often since the Millingtons had posted the announcement of Laura's engagement to her John in the *Daily Telegraph*.

'What a joy a son is to be sure, for you will have nothing to do with the wedding arrangements, it will all be up to the bride's side, and so all that has to be done is to sit back and buy a hat.'

'The reception is to be at her brother's house at Knighton Hall.'

'And a tiara will be worn, perhaps?'

This time Betty shook her head.

'No, the Millingtons have no family tiara.' Betty straightened her back. 'They are county, not aristocratic, Janet,' she reminded her friend with some asperity, and then she sighed.

What her son John, always such a sober-sides, could see in a social butterfly such as Laura Millington, she had no idea, but there it was. It must be borne.

'Such a pretty girl, she will be sure to make a beautiful bride.'

Betty nodded yet again, and put her teacup down. No one seemed to realise that because your future daughter-in-law came from a well-to-do family that did not mean any wealth passed on to her future husband's family. Laura Millington had no dowry to speak of, and little jewellery besides, and while her future husband's family, the Stamfords, might be land rich, they were certainly not cash rich. They worked for their money, tilled the fields and harvested, and grazed their animals, and always had, and always would, please God.

'Would you like another cup of tea, Janet dear?' Betty asked her childhood friend in a flat voice.

Janet nodded, but as she dutifully handed Betty her pretty cup and saucer with its accompanying apostle teaspoon, Betty raised her eyes to hers for the first time. Janet gave a sharp intake of breath, for in Betty's eyes she saw reflected nothing except misery.

*   *   *

John Stamford was besotted with Laura, as well he should be. A stocky, stout young man with a florid complexion, he could hardly believe his luck when Laura Millington set her cap at him, making it quite plain that she thought he was the handsomest man who had ever come into her life, and quite the most witty. She seemed to find anything and everything that he said funny, laughing inordinately at his attempts at humour, and even extolling his seat on his horse.

'How could you?' Laura's best friend Jenny asked her. 'I mean to say, Lala, look at him, would you?'

They were both seated at the window watching the hunt meeting in front of the Stamfords' solid, square, eighteenth-century house, observing the polished hunters, their breath steaming the air, their assorted bridles, double or single reins, snaffle or curb bits, betraying their tractability, their tightly held mouths indicating the nerves of their riders – for who knew who would come back from that day's hunting on the hard frosty ground in the English winter?

Laura stared down at her fiancé. She had become engaged to John Stamford knowing full well that she neither loved him nor saw anything remotely attractive in him. He was, to her mind, a poor sort of creature, the kind of young man who could never attract a full-blooded girl such as herself; but, as one of her aunts had told her, 'a gel must get married', and so marry him she would. She was after all twenty-two, and quite sure that she was about to gather dust on the shelf, about to become an old maid, and this despite always finishing up the last sandwich on the plate, as the old country superstition dictated.

'I just don't know how you could tell John that he looked divine on his horse. I mean, look at him!' Jenny started to shriek with laughter. 'Oh, do look!'

Laura too started to laugh, but as she did so, her hand flew up to her mouth to stop a sudden sob as she remembered how divine Gerald Hardwick had looked on his magnificent grey hunter, how elegant his figure in his beautifully cut hunting coat, how handsome the set of his head on his slim shoulders. Her eyes filled with tears at the memory. To cover this she turned quickly away, but happily Jenny was still swaying from side to side mimicking a farmer's seat. What on earth was she doing marrying John Stamford, a thick-boned son of a country bumpkin? But it was too late now.

It was a late spring afternoon in Knightsbridge and the trees in the London parks were beginning to paint the town landscape with that fine fresh green that Londoners so enjoy to see. Ellen Millington, wife of Laura's uncle, Staunton Millington, was taking tea with Laura's former fiancé's mother, Sally Hardwick. Not a happy occasion for either of them, but something upon which Ellen, for the sake of her husband's family, had insisted, for in her view the Hardwicks could not and should not be allowed to what she called 'get away with it'.

Laura might be hitched to someone else, but nevertheless salt must be rubbed into several people's wounds or she and Staunton would not be able to retire to the South of France with clear consciences.

'Of course, Ariel did actually steal Gerald from Laura, you know that, don't you, Sally?'

'Yes, of course.'

Sally Hardwick sighed inwardly. She knew exactly why Ellen Millington had called round to take tea with her at her London house. She also knew that whatever her punishment, it must be borne, as it was thanks entirely to her son Gerald. A young man breaking off an engagement was always scandalous, but when the young man happened to be your son, the backwash was constant, and humiliating.

'So what's to be done now, do you think, Sally? After all, it is plain to see that Gerald and Ariel are about as unsuited to each other as it is possible to be. This is a right mess of pottage, to be sure, wouldn't you agree?'

'I could not *but* agree, Ellen, but what's to be done with the young when they are too old to tell? Gerald is a sweet-natured boy, but weak. And Ariel is such a very beautiful creature. He had his head turned by her. It does happen, you know, really it does.'

'Too feeble-minded, your generation, that's what's wrong with you, too feeble-minded. Not strict enough. If you can't tell the young when they're taking a wrong turning you will bring up a generation of weaklings, mark my words. In our day we children were never married to whomsoever *we* chose, our parents went to the begat book and they chose *for* us. They knew better than us, and we knew they knew better than us. But what can one say? With the present Prince of Wales besotted with an American divorcée and heaven only knows what else going on, what *can* one say?'

'Well, quite, I do see, and I must say Laura has behaved awfully well and now she is safely married and settled – not too much of a trial, after all.'

'Believe me, Gerald will live to rue the day,' Ellen stated with some satisfaction. 'Ariel is not *steady*. In fact, I would say that Ariel is a bolter if ever I saw one.'

'She has been a bit flighty in the past, but such a beauty.'

'I tell you if Tasha Millington, if Laura's sister-in-law had had her way Laura *would* have sued for breach of promise, but no, she was off seconds later, on the rebound as gels who have been hurt so often are; pinging off the nearest lump of beef; in this case poor John Stamford, and all of it just to show Gerald. What a catastrophe. If Gerald had not been sent to Germany on some footling mission for his regiment the moment he became engaged to Laura, and if Ariel had not been visiting some grand friends at some schloss or another,

Laura and Gerald would now be happily married, with at least one brat on the way.' Ellen paused to sip her tea before resuming. 'But as it is she has settled for marrying *down*, and doubtless is generally making a hash of everything. Laura will not be suited to country life,' she went on relentlessly. 'A large working farmhouse is not the kind of house that will satisfy a gel like Laura. She will be forever standing in the milking sheds with the cows because the dairy maid is off; but there you are, it's all spilt milk now – and bite on the bullet she must.'

Sally found herself frowning vaguely at nothing much, probably because she was becoming a little confused with all the talk of milk and bullets.

'At least Laura is *married*, Ellen. That at least is something.'

'Exactly. And when all is said and done both Ariel and Laura have made their beds and now they must lie in them, and that's all there is to it.'

'Yes, of course, quite right. That is all there *is* to it.'

Laura looked over at her new husband. Her honeymoon had been bad enough, and it was no good anyone saying that shutting your eyes and thinking of England took your mind off being made love to by an oaf, because it jolly well didn't, and now she was about to give birth she regretted the honeymoon even more. What *had* she been thinking marrying John Stamford? But too late now to think. She gave a sudden gasp.

John watched his beautiful young wife disappearing through the bedroom door out onto the landing, prior to trying to find her way down the dark corridor to their only bathroom.

'Why are you going to the bathroom, my love?'

'Because I'm having a baby, that's why, John. Why do you think?'

Laura was gone before John's next thought, which, not unlike the sturdy steam engine that chugged into Knighton station, gradually did the same into John's head. Could it be, might it be, that Laura, his wife, Laura, was giving birth? He sat up straight in his bed. Laura was calving! He stepped out of the old oak bedstead and tripped down the corridor to his mother's room.

'Mother? Mother? Laura's having the baby. In the bathroom. I think she's calving in the bathroom.'

Gerald Hardwick allowed his best man to smooth down the back of his morning coat, and smiled at himself in his dressing mirror as he did so. His wedding day had been a long time coming, but at last it seemed it was here and he was greatly looking forward to it.

'You're better than a valet, you know that, Eddie?' he murmured to Edward Foster, and his bright blue eyes reflected his satisfaction with his handsome appearance as his old friend's long-fingered hands anxiously smoothed his beautifully tailored morning coat.

Gerald had to feel pleased with himself. He was tall and handsome, and he was marrying Ariel, who was not only beautiful, but so fascinating that he couldn't wait for the whole wedding fandango to be over, and for them to be alone.

'I'm afraid that was really rather a quiet do for a stag night, Edward,' he went on. 'But you know how it is, I did promise Ariel that I would not fetch up on my wedding day as so many bridegrooms do, hung, drawn and quartered from the night before, as it were.'

Edward nodded, checking his immaculate appearance yet again in the mirror. He really did not mind not having a hangover, and they had enjoyed a jolly good dinner at the Savoy with some fine wines, which now seemed just the job.

Edward and Gerald had been through school together, done National Service with the same regiment, and were now well set up as stockbrokers in the City having fun with their relatives' not inconsiderable fortunes. Not content with that, both young men had become engaged at the same time – although Gerald did have to go through the small matter of getting un-engaged to Laura before becoming engaged to Ariel. That had been a bit of a messy business, until you met Ariel, and then you understood, because Ariel was an absolute cracker. Not Edward's sort, actually, because he himself could never even begin to manage such a spirited girl as Ariel. Too much to handle for a simple chap like himself. You needed to have a real way with women, such as Gerald undoubtedly had, to have the slightest chance with someone like Ariel.

'Come on, time to face the firing squad.'

Gerald turned reluctantly from his satisfyingly handsome image and smiled at his old friend.

'I think I can hear the wedding bells of St Mary's, Eddie, calling me to my beauteous bride.'

Edward stepped back from the bridegroom, admiring his appearance. Gerald really did look every inch the eager groom.

'Time for the off, Gerald, time for the off. You know weddings always remind me of my confirmation, all that preparation and then everything seems to tear past one.'

The two young men made a handsome sight, and of course they knew it, as they made their way down the steep London staircase of the tall Knightsbridge house. It was as they were passing the first-floor drawing-room door that Gerald paused on the stairs, and reversed back up the last two he had just taken, while glancing at his wristwatch.

'I say, let's have a glass of champagne for the road, Eddie, shall we? Just the one. After all, you deserve it, and I'm damned sure I need it. Besides, we can drink to the old days, to the days of our youth, which are about to end. What do you say?'

Edward glanced at his watch. It was true, they were early, and St Mary's was only a step after all, only a step or two away.

'These are the only drinks I really enjoy, do you know that, dear boy?' Gerald mused as he lifted a champagne glass to his lips. 'Drinks with one's best friends, they're the best.' He opened a silver box and offered Edward a cigarette.

There was a short silence as both men drank and smoked in appreciative silence, a silence finally and annoyingly broken by the sound of the front-door bell.

'What the hell is that? You don't think Ariel's backed out on me, do you?' Gerald lifted one eyebrow at Edward. 'See who it is, dear boy, can't speak to the grocer or whoever, really I can't, spoils the moment.'

Edward leaned over the side of the banisters, halfway down the stairs, and peered at the top of the glass door.

'Looks like someone in uniform,' he called back to Gerald. 'I don't like it at all. Don't like people in uniform, not unless it's someone from one's own regiment,' he joked.

'If it's the police tell them they can't arrest me until after my honeymoon,' Gerald replied.

'No, it's not the police, I think it's a boy with a telegram,' Edward shouted up to his old friend as he took the small envelope from the nattily dressed boy and opened the front door.

'Thank you, sir.'

The boy saluted smartly and jumping on his bike he bicycled off, disdaining the use of his saddle, his bottom staying high above it, the sunshine glancing off the metal of his handlebars.

Edward glanced at the addressee on the envelope.

'Captain Gerald Hardwick. It's obviously a congratters telegram for you, old thing.'

He smiled and handed it over to Gerald to open, picking up his drink and happily finishing it off, as Gerald stubbed out his cigarette and picking up a paper knife from the table slit open the envelope.

'I hate this tradition that's growing up of sending one rude messages on one's wedding day,' he confessed. 'And then all that reading them out at receptions . . .'

'It does seem a ghastly waste of time, time better spent in swigging the in-laws' champagne, I would have thought,' Edward agreed.

He looked over to Gerald who was frowning.

'Anything the matter, Gerry?'

Gerald held up a hand.

'Got to read this again.'

'Some people's jokes one just doesn't get first time, does one?'

'No, this is not a joke, Edward. At least if it is, which it can't be, it's a pretty poor one.'

'Well, go on, try it out on me, I might get it, you never know.'

Gerald shook his head, speechless, and sat down suddenly on the velvet-covered chair behind him.

'It's Laura.'

'A telegram from Laura? I say, that's pretty decent of her – considering.'

'No, no, it's not from Laura, it's about Laura.'

Edward suddenly noticed that Gerald was a great deal paler, and he was yet again reaching into the pocket of his waistcoat and taking out his slim silver cigarette case, from which he proceeded delicately to extract one of his special mix of Fox's cigarettes and slowly light one with a shaking hand.

'It's from her brother, from Jamie Millington. It seems Laura died in childbirth – this morning.'

'I say, a bit much telling you now – doesn't he know you're getting hitched today?'

Gerald stared from the telegram to Edward's appalled face and then down at the telegram again.

'Yes, I think he does, Edward. I think he must know that all too well.'

A Question of Birth

Her Uncle Staunton and his wife having gone to live in the South of France to escape the English weather, and Laura having only one brother, there were very few of the Millington family at poor Laura's funeral, something that Betty Stamford, Laura's mother-in-law of only ten months, realised at once.

She also realised that it was not a particularly Christian thing to do – to note who was who at such a time, and how many had bothered to attend her daughter-in-law's funeral, but it was all too human. Very well, the poor dead girl's father and mother had both been killed during the last war, and her brother had a family of his own, but nevertheless she had thought that they might make a better show of it. It was as if they were ashamed of her. As if, having attended Laura's wedding and duly noting the family into which she had married, gracious, it had to be faced – it was as if the Millingtons had determined not to have any more contact with the Stamfords.

'It's not as if we're not somebody, it's not as if the Stamfords haven't some standing in the county,' she insisted to her grieving son, as she prepared to hand out plates of sandwiches at the funeral tea.

'Her brother is here, Mother, representing the family, we can't expect more. It's not as if Laura's brother hasn't come—'

'On his own, please note.'

'Well, at least he's here.'

Betty sat back down on the large, faded satin-upholstered chair and crammed a curling sandwich into her mouth. She had not known her daughter-in-law very long, but it had been long enough to realise that, try as she might to disguise the fact, Laura despised her.

'John, your brother-in-law is calling you over.'

John looked over to where a tall, fair-haired man was standing by the old carved chimneypiece.

'I think this would be a good time to discuss family business, don't you? Shall we adjourn to the library?'

John Stamford nodded, but only because he did not like to admit that he did not actually own a library, the fact being that if the Stamfords came across someone in the house reading, they would come to the swift conclusion that they must be feeling unwell, for surely there could be no other possible explanation for someone picking up a book?

However, John did have a dining room, and it did have shelves and a collection of bound volumes to which he carefully added every year. In this way he was able to imagine his formal dining room might be counted as a library.

Jamie Millington looked round the room into which he had been led, and wondered at its oak furniture, its ladderback chairs and three-leaf oval table, so different from his own old mahogany furniture, just as the people in the paintings on the walls were so different. Jamie Millington's family portraits showed gentlemen in lace cravats and much gold on their uniforms or jackets; the Stamford family portraits showed men and women in black clothes, the women's sole adornment being a cameo brooch, the men's a watch chain. The hands of the Stamford family bore no signet rings, and there were no large houses with flights of steps in the background. Nevertheless their expressions, low key in keeping with their Low Church beliefs, were those of people of substance.

'I don't really have a library, just a few books, which Mother likes to read. I am hoping to buy more books, in time, but things have been rather tight the last few years, what with having to buy new machinery for the farm.'

Jamie did not really know what to say in answer to this assertion, since he came from a background where people did not actually talk about money, or possessions, perhaps to make up for the fact that they seldom thought about anything else at all.

'The thing is, John,' Jamie began, determined to come straight to the point, 'Laura's child, yours and Laura's child, the baby. Might be better if it was brought up at Knighton Hall with us. With two girls and two boys in the nursery already, as Tasha says, a third girl won't make much difference. And Tasha's awfully good at coping with children, as you know. As the baby's uncle, I'm sure it would be a good thing for her to be brought up with brothers and sisters, rather than here, motherless, alone with you.'

Even before he finished speaking Jamie knew that his was a lost cause, and he sighed inwardly, already hearing his wife's indignant tones when he returned home, hearing her questioning him, over and over again.

'But didn't you explain? Didn't you explain that the poor little girl is as much a Millington as she is a Stamford, and just because her surname is Stamford doesn't make her wholly so? People like the Stamfords, they don't read books, they don't go to art exhibitions, they don't even go to the theatre. I mean they just don't! What will happen to the poor little girl? She will grow up ignorant of the fine things of life, ignorant of everything that makes life worth living. She will not be a Millington.'

Jamie could hear himself replying.

'I know, darling, I know, but nothing to be done. She has a father. John Stamford is her father. I am only her uncle, there is truly nothing that I can do.'

Now, as he stared into John Stamford's face, whose lower lip seemed to be sticking out ever more stubbornly, the look in his eyes reminded his brother-in-law of a farm animal refusing to budge from the middle of the road. Again Tasha's voice came into his head. *'You have to face it, Jamie, your niece will become a tousle-headed farmer's brat, not a young lady, if you leave her with the Stamfords.'* Jamie knew it to be true, but much as his heart reached out to the poor little motherless girl in the crib upstairs, much as he knew that if she was in any way like his dead sister, he also knew, as sure as eggs were eggs, that it would probably prove to be easier to move a mountain than Laura's poor little offspring. Of course Tasha was right about the Stamfords, for decent though they might be, and probably were, they were so utterly different to the Millingtons, it was almost ludicrous. Chalk and cheese would have more in common than the Millingtons and the Stamfords.

For perhaps the thousandth time Jamie wondered what had come over his sister to marry such a man as poor John Stamford. His sister Laura had been a will o' the wisp, a beautiful butterfly with gossamer wings, a piece of fine porcelain, sunlight on water. Her husband was pottery, heather on hills, rain clouds over mountains. They were about as suited as organza and tweed.

'They are not a couple, they don't look like a couple,' Tasha kept whispering insistently all through the wedding. *'No one can say that they do.'*

And that was not all that Tasha kept insisting. Her newest assertion was that poor Laura had probably died owing to her mother-in-law insisting the local midwife attend her daughter-in-law, rather than send her to a proper gynaecologist; obviously not appreciating that Laura was a thoroughbred, not a cob, and simply not up to giving birth in a field or a stable, or – in poor Laura's case – in the upstairs bedroom of a farmhouse.

'Thank you very much for the offer, but I don't think that I would like to hand over the baby. She is after all a Stamford, and besides, Mother would not like it.'

Jamie sighed inwardly, and outwardly, and then walked out of the dining room, knowing it was useless to argue, or even to try to persuade a man such as John Stamford from any course other than the one upon which he was intent.

As Jamie's wise old batman used to say about so much: 'You might as well spit in the wind, sir, as to try to change that matter. Now I come to think of it, sir, spitting in the wind might be of more use.'

Betty Stamford watched Jamie Millington leaving the funeral tea, and she too sighed inwardly, and outwardly, but with relief. *She* knew what his brother-in-law taking her John into the dining room must be about. Luckily she had warned John that this might be on the cards, that the Millingtons might come after the baby now that Laura, the silly girl, had gone and died.

'Say as little as possible. Don't refer to the birth, don't say a word.'

'I can't say nothing, Mother, either I say *something* or I don't say anything at all.'

Betty stared at her son for a second. She could never quite make up her mind as to whether John was stupid or just down to earth.

'In that case, don't say anything at all, John. Not that you're not capable, my love, because of course you are, but the Millingtons are the Millingtons, and they're bound to want to take the child over, and when all is said and done it is your child, John, and you can't allow that. Above all, don't say anything about the birth, do you hear? We don't want the Millingtons getting wind of what happened. Above all, we don't want that, John.'

John had nodded in his slow way, so broken over the events of the previous week that he found it difficult to concentrate on anything other than his sorrow.

'Such a pity the baby's a girl, she's going to be no use on the farm, a girl, is she?' Janet Priddy murmured to another of the mourners.

'No matter, John'll marry again soon enough. He'll have to, to get sons for the farm, it's his duty.'

The two women nodded wisely. They were both farmers' wives, they knew their reputations in the neighbourhood were unimpeachable: they'd done their duty, they'd had sons.

'I hear she had some sort of paroxysm, apparently.'

'Oh no, I heard she was haemorrhaging, my dear, and nothing to be done.'

'No, but apparently she passed away with the shock of the birth, at least that was what I heard; but whether that's true, I don't know.'

They both nodded, together, feeling that curious satifaction that plain women often feel when a much prettier one dies young, as if some sort of opposition had been removed from their neighbourhood.

'By the way what is she to be called, the poor baby? What is she to be called?'

'Alexandra, apparently.'

'She'll always be known as Alex, of course, which is really a boy's name, I always think. Such a waste of time, these long names. Why not call her something sensible, like Jane or Elizabeth?'

'Apparently the mother wanted her called after her grand-mother, John told Betty.'

'She would. She would want a stuck-up sort of name like Alexandra. Talk about Miss Nose in the Air! Tuppence to talk to Laura Stamford it was, and now, doubtless, her daughter's going to turn out the same.'

The infant daughter of the late Laura Anne Stamford (née Millington) and Mr John Stamford was christened at St Luke's Church, Witchampton. Mr G. Priddy and Mr W. Stanley stood as godparents.

The christening tea was if anything quieter than the funeral tea, and once again Jamie Millington attended, still without his family, and yet again inadvertently caused ruffled feelings with Betty Stamford.

'Us Stamfords are just not good enough for the Millingtons, we really are not, just not good enough,' Betty murmured. 'I'm surprised even that James Millington has come, that even the uncle's turned up. I was that surprised to see him at the church, really I was.'

Janet Priddy nodded absently at Betty while all the time staring from under her new hat at what she always called the 'goings on'. She could readily appreciate what Betty Stamford was saying. Just watching Jamie Millington standing over by the fireplace, as he had at the funeral six months before, just watching him lolling there with his cup of tea and his scone, it was for all the world as if he owned the place, as if he owned the farm, as if the Stamfords were his tenants.

'The trouble with the Millingtons is they're not just stuck up,' she said, picking up what she knew to be her friend Betty's thoughts, 'they're jumped up. The way they go on you would honestly think they were the De Vere de Veres, which they definitely are not.

'No, but they think they are, so when all is said and done, they might as well be,' Janet reasoned, and several of the women standing around, ostensibly admiring the baby in her crib, nodded sagely at this, knowing it to be only too true.

'It only takes a couple of generations of money and everyone is forced to bend a knee when the so-called quality walk by, that's what my old father used to say.'

'He's only taking John into the dining room again – look.'

Janet nudged Betty and they both looked around.

'What *now*?'

'Going to try and adopt her again, I dare say, but John won't have that. She's his daughter, John Stamford's daughter; a Stamford born here, and that's an end to it.'

Once again in the dining room Jamie Millington looked round and felt strangely relieved to see that there were two more books on the shelf. He leaned forward, curious to examine their titles, and then sighed inwardly as he read the gold letters on the new volumes – *The Family Doctor Volume I* and *The Family Doctor Volume II*. He raised his eyebrows towards them.

'It's a good twenty miles to the nearest surgery.' John nodded almost affectionately at his two new books, in a way that he might have done had they been new acquaintances at market. 'Probably more than twenty, more like twenty-five miles I would say, so I thought I should learn a bit of home doctoring, childhood diseases and suchlike.'

He sighed. Normally a farmer would have a wife, and wives, as everyone knew, would be able to diagnose at two paces any and every malaise, differentiating between measles and German measles, between chicken pox and eczema, between whooping cough and tuberculosis; but his Laura had gone, and he had no such luxury, so – despite his mother jeering at his purchase as being an unnecessary expense – he had gone ahead and bought both volumes. He stared at them solemnly now, peering forward as if to satisfy himself that they were indeed what he had ordered.

'The point is, Stamford,' Jamie began, attempting to adopt a casual tone while succeeding only in sounding patronising. 'The point is, at the moment you are simply not placed to be able to bring up little Alexandra, now really, are you? As a single man, it is not ideal, is it?'

There was a long pause while John breathed in slowly and out through his nostrils again, quite loudly, the sound reminding his brother-in-law of the sound made by stabled horses or cows on a frosty morning.

'I have a name, you know, Millington, and so do you.'

Jamie coloured. Stamford had attended a minor local private school whereas Jamie had gone to what he and his generation facetiously referred to as 'Slough Grammar School' but which the rest of the world customarily knew as Eton College, widely regarded as the most exclusive school in England.

'Very well – John.'

'Yes, James?'

John swayed slightly forward again, this time towards Jamie, who for reasons he did not like to examine too closely, immediately stepped back and away from him.

'The point is, John, and I must return to this point again, now Laura's dead, and you have no wife to help bring up your child, I really think it would be better if you let Tasha and me adopt little Alexandra. It won't mean that you can't see her. After all, Knighton Hall is only a couple of hours' drive away, and we can bring her over for the weekends, and so on and so forth. But really, in view of Laura's death, it would be better for the little girl, as I am sure you must realise. She will have company at Knighton.'

John stared at James Millington. Ordinarily in a day-to-day

situation he might have said 'bloody cheek', but try as he might he was always a little overawed by James, as overawed as he had been when James's sister Laura had consented to marry him, John Stamford of Lower Bridge Farm.

'I have to thank you for your concern, James, but Mother and I are determined to bring up Alexandra here in the country, with us. She will be perfectly well looked after on the farm. This is the family into which your sister married, and it's only right that her daughter should be brought up by her father's family. After all, she bears our name, she is Alexandra *Stamford*.'

'What if you remarry?'

'That is not something I am contemplating at the moment, and perhaps never will. As you know, Laura, my wife Laura, your sister Laura, was an angel, and angels are not easily replaced.'

Jamie was perfectly aware, as are most brothers, that his sister was anything but an angel, but seeing the look of grief reflected in his brother-in-law's large brown eyes he turned away, momentarily embarrassed by the extreme sorrow on the other man's face. After a few seconds he turned back again, nevertheless determined to try to persuade this grieving hulk of a man that the Millingtons should have some influence over his daughter, that she could not be brought up solely as a Stamford.

'I shall therefore have to ask you, as Alexandra's uncle, for regular visiting rights. In the name of my sister, your late wife, I must insist that we, the Millingtons, have some say in the upbringing of my niece.'

'I can't see that there will be much harm to that,' John agreed, after a few minutes' leaden silence during which Jamie wondered yet again what on earth his sister could have been doing even contemplating marriage to such a man. 'No, I can't see that there is much to object to in that.'

But he counted without his mother, and as Jamie said goodbye to Betty Stamford he realised that he had taken the wrong person into the dining room. John Stamford might be slow, but his mother was not, and as he drove away Mrs Stamford's 'goodbye' seemed to Jamie to hold in it a dreadful finality.

Comings and Goings

The news of Laura Stamford née Millington's death was such a shock to her ex-fiancé that although Gerald turned up at the church on time with his best man Edward Foster in tow, in his mind he could have been anywhere. He had after all been engaged to Laura for fully six months, and before that they had known each other, on and off, since they were children, remeeting in London when Gerald was on leave from his stint in the Army, so the idea that she was now dead was somehow inconceivable. Nevertheless he knew his duty. He had to put Laura's death from his mind. He had to smile and say his vows, look happy for the photographer, make a speech, remember to thank his in-laws for giving him the happiest day of his life so far – all that – he had to do it. He just had to.

Once ensconced in their Dorchester honeymoon suite, he found his smile was as fixed as a poster on a billboard. Notwithstanding, he took Ariel in his arms and kissed her as passionately as was possible given the fact that at that moment he felt drained of every emotion except the will to drink.

'I love you, darling, what a wonderful wedding.'

His voice sounded strange even to himself and he saw that

Ariel, who was now standing by the bedroom window in a pure silk champagne-coloured nightdress and matching peignoir, turned and stared at him possibly because, for some reason he could not explain, he found himself tightening rather than loosening the sash of his fashionable silk Sulka dressing gown.

'Are you all right, Gerald?'

Gerald smiled.

'Of course, Laura.'

He had not really said that, had he? He stared, panic-struck, at his wife of a few hours, wondering if he had, not knowing if it was in his head or from his lips that the phrase had inadvertently materialised.

'You look strange.'

Ariel turned back to the window staring out at the traffic in the street below.

Gerald moved closer to her, hoping that the nearer he drew to her the less she would look like Laura. Laura smiling, Laura laughing, Laura riding beside him on a beautiful spring morning in Hyde Park, both of them at ease with the day.

Ariel turned from the window and walked back past her husband.

'I think before we go any further we should both have a brandy, don't you?'

In the morning Gerald's head was as thick as the carpet upon which he placed reluctant feet. He could hardly remember anything of his wedding night, and Ariel was certainly no better. Happily they both realised that there was only one thing that could pull them together and that was a glass of champagne, which Gerald promptly ordered to be brought up with breakfast.

'You've heard, have you?' he asked her as they met in

the adjoining room, each unable to look the other in the eyes.

'Yes. Suki told me as I was changing for the honeymoon.'

'Suki would—'

Gerald poured them both a glass of champagne and shook his head. He could just see Suki bursting through the door with the appalling news. He looked across at Ariel, wondering if she was feeling as he did: wretched and at the same time defiant. It wasn't his fault that he had fallen out of love with Laura Millington and into love, if that was the word, with Ariel. Happily it seemed that despite everything, Ariel had other things on her mind.

'Blasted hairdresser ruined my hair yesterday,' she was complaining as she brushed her hair in the mirror above the chimneypiece. 'After all that rehearsing of my hairstyle, he still managed to make me look as if I had a haystack on my head.'

Gerald considered this for a moment.

'Not a haystack, darling, no, more a cottage loaf!'

Gerald laughed humourlessly, and as he did so his eyes slid towards the small ormolu clock on the hotel mantelpiece. It was hours before they had to catch their plane to Kenya for their honeymoon, hours and hours. Hours that he had to spend with Ariel avoiding the topic of his ex-fiancée. He knew that Ariel too had drunk too much the previous night for the very same reason as himself. She must feel horribly guilty about Laura, about how she had pinched Gerald from her, quite ruthlessly really, now he looked back on it. That was why she was going on about her hair, her stupid hair, about how awful it had looked, which it had really.

'It wasn't even as good as a cottage loaf,' Ariel continued, moaning. 'I wouldn't have minded looking like a cottage loaf if it had been a good one, but it was terrible. My big day ruined by a wretched two-bit hairdresser. It's just not fair.'

Ariel shook out her hair. It was her crowning glory. She loved her hair the way other people loved their own hands, or their eyes. Her hair was thick and dark and she was proud of the Titian lights in it. The fact that it was fine and thick, that too was a source of pride.

'I'm not going back to him, I'm not going back to François when we get back from Kenya, Gerald. I am definitely going to change my hairdresser, no one does that to me and gets away with it.'

Gerald, feeling slightly sick, tried to stifle a yawn.

'I say, Ariel, is it going to be in the gossip columns, do you think?' he asked, attempting humour. 'Mrs Gerald Hardwick is changing her hair torturer?'

'How anyone could fail a bride on her big day the way François failed me yesterday, I don't know.'

'I am afraid it wasn't just your hairdresser who failed you on your big day, Ariel, darling.'

Gerald gave a short laugh. At this Ariel stared at him.

'You had a bit too much to drink last night, Gerry, that's all.'

Gerald looked rueful but gamely started to tackle his cooked breakfast. All too late he realised he hated Ariel calling him, 'Gerry'. Laura had never called him by a diminutive, it had always been 'Gerald'.

It seemed to him now that he could see how happy and carefree his life had once been, until he saw those words on the telegram, and then he had known immediately that his life would never be the same again.

It wasn't just that Laura and he had been childhood friends, and then drifted into adolescent love and from there to being engaged, it was the fact that Gerald had ditched Laura so precipitously, not even giving her a proper reason. Now he had no idea what he could have been doing, what he could have been thinking, most especially since he knew now that everyone would somehow blame him for Laura's death.

'What would you like as a real opener, darling?'

Ariel turned momentarily from staring at her reflection in the mirror.

'Bloody Mary – with plenty of Lea and Perrins in it.'

Gerald started to fill two large glasses. Drink had never really been a mainstay in his life, but just at that moment, drink seemed to be the only answer to the way he was feeling, because Laura was dead.

When they returned from their honeymoon Gerald's mother was the first to telephone them.

Ariel answered the telephone sounding as if she had only just woken up.

'Ariel, my dear, how are you? How was everything?'

'Everything was fine.'

There was a small pause as Ariel did not add anything more.

'If you don't mind me saying so, you sound just a little monosyllabic for someone just returned from their honey-moon, my dear.'

'No, just a bit tired, Sally, that's all. The train was very hot.'

Sally waited for a few seconds, wondering whether this was the right moment to remind her daughter-in-law of the dinner-dance she and Gerald had promised to attend with her, and then decided against it, determining instead to let a few days pass, to let them both settle in to their new life together, before she herself went to Baden Baden to take the waters, travel the continent, and generally behave as all widows do who have been left a sizeable income and do not know quite how to spend it.

When she returned after some weeks, she felt it perfectly acceptable to remind Ariel gently of the date they had made to go to the dance together, before once more sitting back to wait for the next few weeks to drift by again, as all her days seemed to do since her husband had died.

And when at last the day did arrive, she dressed slowly and carefully, and was ready long before it was necessary, because she had to admit that she enjoyed sitting about her drawing room in a long, glamorous, albeit old evening dress, waiting for her maid to bring her a drink on a tray.

At last it was time to walk round to Gerald and Ariel's house, from where they were all due to take a taxi to meet Sally's friends for the dinner-dance.

'Oh, Mama, there you are.'

As he opened the front door to her Gerald's smile was as crooked as his bow tie. Sally stared at her son in his otherwise smart dinner jacket. She had not seen him for weeks, which possibly made the shock of his appearance all the worse, for it was immediately quite obvious to his horrified mother that he was not just drunk, he was incapable. She felt her mouth go dry as she assimilated the state he was in. He would be lucky to get as far as the taxi without passing out.

'Where's Ariel?'

'She's gone out.'

'Gone out? But we're all meant to be going to the dinner-dance, Gerald. Did you not remember? I reminded you both, before you went on honeymoon, you were meant to be going to the dinner-dance at the Berkeley with me. We're joining the Goslings and the Griffins, remember?'

Gerald shook his head, leaning against the doorway of his house, his right arm holding on to the doorframe. Despite the fact that he was taking up most of the doorway Sally pushed impatiently past him, the skirts of her silk evening dress rustling against the doorway.

'Don't mind me, Ma!'

Sally stalked up to the first-floor drawing room, and once

there turned and faced her son, who had walked all too slowly and over-deliberately up the stairs behind her, catching on to the banisters every now and then to steady himself.

'Gerald, I don't mind people getting a big tight, really I don't. God knows I've been tight enough in my time, but when you're as drunk as you are now, it's too awful, darling. More than that it's such an insult to your hosts. How could you get like this when you knew we were all meant to be going out? The Goslings, everyone who is coming, they are all old friends of mine who were not able to come to the wedding, so they were all looking forward so much to meeting Ariel and seeing you again, and now look! She isn't here, and you're as tight as a tick. I can't tell you how disappointed I am in you, really I can't. And you know, they are frightfully well heeled, and would be only too glad to put business with you and Edward, really they would. I can't think what's got into you lately.'

'Nor can I, Mama, nor can I. Can't think, but I will soon, really I will, I will see what has got into me soon.'

Gerald smiled fatuously, staring into space, and Sally immediately realised it was useless to go on at him, about as useless as she herself felt to deal with the situation. She went to the white telephone in the corner of the room.

'I shall telephone to the Goslings and the rest, and tell them that you have been taken suddenly and inexplicably ill, which you have, and that Ariel has to stay behind and look after you.'

'Jolly good.'

Gerald sank down on one of the old chintz-covered sofas that had once belonged to Sally's mother, but now looked as they would never have dared to look in her day, worn and dirty, their poor colours faded. Sally thought briefly of her mother, as she always did in times of crisis, and sighed to herself. What would she make of Gerald? She stared down at her son who had now fallen into a reverie, his head subsiding beneath a clutch of cushions, which half obscured his face.

Sally turned away from her disappointment and tele-phoned through to her friends, who immediately made the best of the inevitable gaping hole in their evening that her news had caused. Then, feeling thankful that she had at least paid for their tickets to the wretched thing, she finally left Gerald to his drunken stupor.

Later, after the dinner-dance, Sally stepped out of a shared taxi and waved goodbye to her friends, before walking back up the steps to her house, letting herself into the hall, and thankfully taking off her earrings and pulling off her evening gloves. The evening had been vaguely disastrous, as evenings always are when some of the guests do not turn up. She walked up the steep stairs of her Chelsea home to her own first-floor drawing room and went to the drinks tray in the corner, thinking as she did of the disappointment that her friends had done their best to try to hide from her, of how much they had been looking forward to meeting Gerald's new wife. She leaned forward and sunk her head into her hands. She had never thought to feel so low. Everything could have been so different – if only Gerald had not thrown Laura over in such a peremptory manner, if only poor Laura had not died on his wedding day.

Ariel had not known what to expect from marriage to Gerald, but she knew now that she had definitely expected him to change. She realised now that she had thought of marriage as being some sort of beautiful doorway through which you drifted to meet this new reformed man – your bridegroom – and that after that nothing would be quite the same.

She had actually imagined that husbands would be quite different from fiancés or boyfriends, in that once they had married their brides they would become instantly responsible and kind. They would not only open doors for you, give up seats for you, but also manage everything from the paying of bills to the lighting of your cigarette. She sighed, thinking of how wrong she had been – and all this before raising her eyes to the doctor's face, waiting for his verdict, half hoping that she had something really wrong with her.

'You are expecting a child. You are pregnant, Mrs Hardwick.'

Ariel tossed back her head and instantly lit a cigarette with a slim gold lighter taken from her chic leather handbag.

'Don't be silly, Dr Stillman, I can't be.'

Dr Stillman could not prevent himself from smiling at that.

'Why are you so certain you can't be, Mrs Hardwick?'

'Because . . . Well, if you really want to know because my husband is out most of the time, I have hardly seen him enough to become pregnant. I must have caught pregnancy off a chair.'

She gave a short laugh.

'In my experience babies are sometimes determined to be born, Mrs Hardwick, as if perhaps God has them in His mind's eye, long before we ourselves have them in ours.'

Dr Stillman smiled at her again in his kindly old-fashioned way and his eyes turned towards the leather-framed photographs of his own children and grandchildren.

'If you don't mind my asking, had the idea never occurred to you that marriage might bring children?'

Ariel shrugged her shoulders over-elaborately, and blew smoke across the doctor's surgery while her foot encased in its chic leather shoe swung backwards and forwards restlessly.

'I can't say that it had, Dr Stillman. As I say, my husband is rarely home of late, sleeps through most of the day, and only gets up in time to go to a nightclub. Between all that, I can't say that it had ever occurred to me that he could have made me pregnant. No, I can safely say it had never occurred to me. As a matter of fact, I was sure that since my honeymoon, my sickness was due to something I had *caught* on honeymoon, which I obviously did, if I'm that far gone.'

Once again she gave a short cold laugh.

'You will have to try to eat more you know, Mrs Hardwick. The fact that the baby is so small means that he might be born underweight if you do not eat more. And drink plenty of milk.'

'I hate milk—'

'Milky drinks are best for baby, you know. And plenty of meat and chicken. Soups are good, full of nourishment. Babies do not take care of themselves, not even in the womb, we do have to look out for them, take care of them, from conception.'

The doctor paused. He had a smart, thriving practice with many well-to-do patients, but looking at this young lady he, like so many people who knew Ariel Hardwick, could not help feeling a mixture of compassion and impatience towards her. She was an attractive enough young creature, but from his many years as a family doctor, he could see there was an inner worm of self-destructiveness that seemed to be eating away at her, making her wayward and hard, despite her youth and beauty.

Nevertheless, he continued to smile warmly at her from the other side of his red leather-topped desk.

'Well, at any rate, however this has come about, there is no doubt that congratulations on the little chap will certainly be in order—'

'Why did you say "little chap", Dr Stillman?' Ariel asked, interrupting him.

'*Did* I say that?' The doctor looked innocently surprised, despite the fact that he was perfectly aware he had said exactly that. 'There was no reason, no reason at all, just a generality really.' He smiled and adjusted his half-moon

44

glasses. 'I'm afraid I tend to call a baby in the womb the "little chap", until I know better, that is.'

There was a long silence during which Ariel smoked and he pretended to study her notes.

'The baby should, all being well, be arriving around about Christmas. Just don't call him "Noel" will you, so cruel I always think, calling babies Noel or Noelle, and then expecting them to like having their birthdays at Christmas, only receiving one set of presents, and all that.'

Ariel was not listening to him, as Dr Stillman was well aware, instead she was wishing to God that Dr Stillman had not said 'little chap'. It meant that the doctor had instantly created a picture of a small boy in her mind. It meant that her blacking out at that cocktail party, and feeling sick when she smelt coffee, were not just vague symptoms of some horrid bug that she had been harbouring since her honeymoon, but that a real person was inside her: a little chap.

She felt faint with fear. She could not have a baby, for all sorts of reasons. She was not old enough. She was not good enough. Besides, people who had babies did not fall in love with men like Gerald who were only interested in amusing themselves, going out to cocktail parties, socialising, being in the right places. They married other men, decent men like Dr Stillman whose desk and filing cabinets were festooned with photographs of little girls in smocked dresses and boys in silk romper suits, men whose faces lit up with delight at the idea that Ariel was lucky enough to be a parent.

'Do you go to cocktail parties, Dr Stillman?' she asked suddenly.

The doctor removed his glasses and laughed.

'I have been to cocktail parties, Mrs Hardwick. But you know, since the children were young our habit has always been to take them away to our cottage by the sea at weekends. Plenty of fresh air and good food is what I prescribe both for myself, Mrs Stillman and our young. Most especially fresh air, so good for growth. Not that Mrs Stillman and I need to grow,' he joked, 'rather the reverse.'

'My husband hates going to the country unless it's to socialise, in which case he will be indoors all the time, and really you might as well be in London.' Ariel paused. 'I – I know that you will find this difficult, Dr Stillman, because you have children and grandchildren, but really, I really should not be having a baby. Really and truly, I am not suitable, and nor is my husband, particularly not my husband. This is not a good moment for us to have a baby.'

The telephone on the doctor's desk rang. He picked it up, not dropping his eyes from his patient's face, determined not to let her out of his surgery until he had persuaded her that there was never a good moment to have a baby, and never a bad moment.

The voice at the other end, as if being directed by some power from above, was that of yet another of Dr Stillman's patients, requesting a repeat prescription of her sleeping tablets.

'What a wonderful coincidence, Mrs Hardwick, I am only now seeing your daughter-in-law, and she has some very exciting news for you – yes, very, very exciting.' He smilingly held the telephone across the desk for Ariel to speak into, nodding encouragingly to her. 'No, no, let her tell you herself, Mrs Hardwick.'

As she took the telephone receiver from him Dr Stillman had the feeling that, despite the fact that he was not a religious man, the angels above had indeed been smiling down on his surgery that afternoon, if only for a few seconds, before passing on their way to greater matters.

He started to shut Ariel's medical file, as if the matter they had been discussing was now happily resolved, when he heard Ariel say mechanically, 'Yes, isn't it exciting, Sally?'

Ariel put down the receiver a minute later, and if looks could kill Dr Stillman was sure that he would be dead.

'My mother-in-law is very excited at the news,' she said in a flat voice, and having stubbed out her cigarette against the side of his metal wastepaper basket, she promptly and defiantly lit another.

'Yes, well, she would be. She is after all a widow, and it will be so exciting for her to be able to help you and your husband bring up a Miss or Master Hardwick.'

There it was again, the baby was no longer a baby in either of their imaginations, instead he or she had become a small tousle-haired person zipping about on a fairy cycle, bringing with him or her happy shouts of laughter, arms held up to be carried.

'I can't have this baby, Dr Stillman. My husband, Gerald, is just not suitable to be a father, and an alley cat would make a better mother than myself, really. I just can't have it.'

It was as if she had not spoken. Dr Stillman leaned back in his chair.

'The thing is, Mrs Hardwick,' he began again, clearing his throat at the same time as he tried to get Ariel to pay attention to him rather than the tip of her cigarette at which she kept staring, as if it would provide her with some sort of answer. 'The way you are feeling is perfectly normal. Everyone feels a certain amount of panic when they know they're pregnant for the first time. I know my wife and I did, but childbirth methods have come on in leaps and bounds after all. We are no longer in Queen Victoria's reign. It's perfectly normal to feel anxious, what is not normal is not to adjust to the fact, not to bring yourself to understand – and you're an intelligent young woman – that the gift of a healthy baby is one of the wonders of this world. It truly is. When the doctor lays the baby in your arms there is no emotion to compare with it. Even for the doctor, however many babies he delivers, the emotion is one to which he can look back with eternal joy. And I mean that.'

He smiled, but only because Ariel had at last turned her eyes to look at him, rather than her wretched cigarette. He paused as she stubbed out yet another of her cigarettes.

'I'm not a religious man, Mrs Hardwick, but I do believe in life, the miracle of life. Having children changes us so much for the better. It makes us more rounded, but of course, some people don't want to change, do they? Maybe you don't want to change?'

The expression on Dr Stillman's face was so kindly, so paternal, so understanding that Ariel found herself leaning forward and putting her face in her hands, if only to get away from the sight of it.

'I want to change so much. You have no idea how much I want to change . . .'

'If you want to change you must go ahead and have your baby. He will change you; within seconds of holding him in your arms you will become a different person, it's just a fact. That too is one of the miracles of life.'

Ariel wanted so much to believe in the doctor's words, in what he was saying, but supposing he was wrong?

'I think I will go for a walk in the park,' she said finally, standing up at the same time.

Dr Stillman also stood up.

'Splendid. What a splendid idea. Go for a walk in the park, good for baby, good for you.'

Ariel walked slowly through Hyde Park, well aware that she was in a state of turmoil. Somehow she had never thought to consider what would happen if she became pregnant. Her wedding and honeymoon had seemed to pass in such a blur. Gerald in such a state over Laura's death, everything not at

all how it should be. After a while, as she walked slowly
around the park, not really seeing the horses trotting by, the
Guardsmen from the barracks, or the dogs fetching and
carrying balls for their owners, she at last became aware
of being passed by beautifully uniformed nannies pushing
beautifully groomed babies. She stopped by one and smiled
at him, and his nanny.

'He's beautiful.'

'He certainly is.' The young nanny smiled proudly at her
charge. 'Most beautiful baby in the park. Everyone says so,'
she added.

Ariel nodded. He was beautiful. A beautiful baby.

'*I'm* having a baby – my first,' she confided suddenly.

'You are?' The nanny nodded. 'Well I dare say, looking at
you, that yours will be as beautiful as this young man.'

Ariel stared long and hard at the pram, realising as she did
so that she had already made up her mind to believe Dr
Stillman. She would have the baby. She would let him or her
change her. She would take the chance, and hope that she
was doing the right thing. And after all, if she changed, so
might Gerald. He might get over Laura. He might stop
punishing himself.

She knew that telling him their good news would not be
easy, but she imagined that, like herself, he would come
round to it, that pretty soon he would realise their foolish
pre-marital vows not to have children were hollow and
childish and, as Dr Stillman had said, they would both quickly
come to understand how lucky they were.

She had hardly taken her key out of her handbag to open
their front door when she found Gerald downstairs facing her
in the hall.

'Good God, Gerald, is something the matter?'

She glanced at her slim gold watch.

'What do you mean?'

49

'You're up, darling, it's only five o'clock in the afternoon, and you're up!'

'Shut up, would you, Ariel? Just shut up.'

Gerald looked terrible, even for Gerald, unshaven and darkly furious. As a matter of fact at that moment there was little about Gerald that was not dark. Dark lines under his eyes, dark hair sprouting from the top of his dressing gown, a trembling hand covered in dark hair reaching for his first drink, his first cigarette, his first view of the day that was even now becoming night.

'Where've you been?' he asked her thickly, preceding her up the stairs to the first-floor sitting room.

'To the doctor, darling.'

'Been to see the croaker.'

'Yes. Did your mother telephone you?'

'No idea, she might have done. I took the phone off the hook—'

'So she hasn't told you?'

Gerald stared at her through bloodshot eyes.

'No. She hasn't told me anything, and I haven't told her anything, which is probably just as well, because when she hears what I have to say she is not going to be very happy.'

He gave a huge juddering sigh.

'She hasn't told you that I'm pregnant.'

Gerald lit a cigarette and poured himself a drink in one swift and faintly terrible movement before turning to his wife.

'Good God, Ariel. You can't be. I've hardly been near you.'

'Well you must have been near me enough, Gerald, enough for me to become pregnant.' She went on quickly before he could say anything. 'And before you say anything, I must tell you that whatever happens, I've decided I am having the baby. I am going through with it, Gerald.'

'Babies and you, Ariel? They are surely about as likely as, well – beer and salmon!'

Ariel nodded, sitting down suddenly and staring ahead of her.

'I know, I know, I thought you might say that, or something like it,' she admitted.

'You hardly knew your own mother, what makes you think you'll be any different?'

'I don't know.' Ariel fixed her eyes on something in the distance, something that Gerald could not see, but which seemed to him to be something that he should see, if he were not feeling so lousy. 'The thing is, Gerry, Dr Stillman has just persuaded me what a wonderful thing it is to have a healthy baby. He has just explained to me how much you and I will change in our ways, how we will become different, less selfish people. And I think it's true. So, Gerald, I think we must have this baby. And I'm sure you will agree, when you have thought about it.'

Gerald stared at her.

'I don't think you will want to have a baby, when you hear what *I* have to say.'

He refilled his glass. 'I've lost everything. We're ruined.'

Part Two

MANY YEARS LATER

Alexandra

When she was young the feeling that there was always silence downstairs would come to Alexandra as she dressed in the mornings, already longing to be standing with her best friend, Frances Chisholm, waiting to answer her name at the roll call held in the small village school that had been founded by local farmers in thanksgiving for the defeat of Napoleon at Waterloo. From an early age Alexandra had always dressed herself, not liking to be fussed over. For this reason she was always up and washed long before Gran came into the old oak-beamed room that was her bedroom, making sure to have laid out her school clothes in strict dressing order on the round-backed cane-seated oak chair the night before.

Once at school the silence of the first hours of her day was broken, never to return until evening. Hurry, hurry, hurry, the voices in her head would command her as she brushed her hair under an Alice band and cleaned her teeth with a Mickey Mouse toothbrush; hurry to friendly noise and no more tick tock of the old Grandfather clock in the hall, no more hearing her own footsteps ringing out across the old wooden floors as if she was the only person in the house, which of course she was not, but she always felt that at any moment she might well discover herself to be.

Sometimes she thought that she had quite forgotten what her father looked like, until he would suddenly appear in the kitchen when she was having her supper, eye her with the look of a man who had not expected to come across such a creature as herself, only to back out again through the kitchen door, thankfully leaving her with Mavis, his old cook, and Charlie and Michael, the boys who helped him on his farm, and who were fed three times a day in the kitchen by the ever maternal Mavis.

'*Three gypsies stood at the garden gate, they sang so high and they sang so low, three gypsies stood at the garden gate – I've gone with the raggle taggle gypsies oh!*'

The first time Alexandra sang that at school she felt a frisson of excitement, and a feeling rose up inside her that she would like to find gypsies at her garden gate, and that when she did she would run off with them, to become barefooted and wild, her hair tangled, her food cooked on an open fire, her hands ungloved, her body browned by the sun and the wind; but when she did see gypsies on the road, she always thought better of it, because they looked careworn and worried and their ponies thin and miserable.

She picked up her school bag every morning, and walked the long route through her father's farmland to the top of his drive, some three miles long, until she would find herself standing on the corner of the sign that read 'Lower Bridge Farm' and eventually, usually very eventually, along would come her best friend's mother, driving in the middle of the road in an old van with the mud and the rain, as it was this morning, splashing generously up the sides.

'Hop in!'

Mrs Chisholm always said that, her careworn face looking momentarily eager, and at the same time concerned, because they all knew that if the van paused too long and stalled, she might not ever get it started again.

Alexandra was always grateful to hop in, but never more so than on half-days at school – Thursdays and Saturdays – days when the other children did sport, and Mrs Chisholm had stopped by the fish-and-chip shop in town, and the most delicious smell imaginable was rising from under the old copies of the *Daily Mirror* and the *Sunday Pictorial*, in which old Mr Peters the fishmonger had wrapped the food.

Although food rationing had hardly touched their part of the world after the war, and the village fish-and-chip shop had been doing a brisk trade for some years, Alexandra's gran would have had a fit if she knew what was being offered her granddaughter for lunch. But to Alexandra, the smell of that fried fish wrapped in newspaper was the best smell in the world, most particularly when it was raining outside and the windows of the car were steaming up with the heat of everyone's bodies, not to mention the two retrievers who were usually found to be lying protectively across the precious parcels.

Mrs Chisholm was slim and blonde, with a permanently vague smile, which her daughter, Frances, always maintained masked at least one completely deaf ear.

'You have to run round the front to talk to her,' she would remind Alexandra, and then she would add, 'That's why she shouts, but she won't wear one of those big brown leather hearing aids because she thinks they're not elegant. If they made them look more like Dior handbags, she would wear them, but because they look like binoculars in a case, she won't.'

Alexandra didn't mind Mrs Chisholm's shouting in the least. In fact she liked it, the way she liked everything about Mrs Chisholm, probably because she knew that Mrs Chisholm liked her.

'It's a good thing that your grandmother can't see you now!'

She would shout something like that at Alexandra when Alexandra was in the middle of happily stuffing her face with chips, and then she would wink and turn away, half running, half walking back to the stable yard where she kept horses at livery for Londoners who came down at the weekends to hunt.

Alexandra's grandmother would never let Alexandra ride horses, maintaining that it was too expensive and anyway only snobs rode. Mrs Chisholm could never afford to keep an animal that didn't make her money in some way, so she would never keep a pony just for Frances, on account of the expense, so this meant that as they were growing up a great deal of Alexandra and Frances's holidays were spent on the Stamford farm trying to ride cows.

Unhappily the cows proved less than satisfactory, at first ignoring the girls' efforts to scramble on to their backs, then cantering off in the opposite direction the moment they threatened to be able to get a leg over them. Sometimes as they sat on a gate staring at their recalcitrant potential mounts grazing away in the field, more well-off local families would trot by on smart horses and ponies, and smart riding people who came down from London for the weekend would often stop to chat to the two girls. This enabled Alexandra and Frances to admire their crisp white stocks, their shining black boots, and their beautifully cut hunt coats; but that was as close as the two growing girls would ever get to being able to ride horses.

And so sweet, warm, vaguely boring summers drifted by, followed by over-long, harsh, brazen winters; until finally Alexandra and Frances left their childhood, and their longings for horses turned to other things; and they started to notice not riders on horses, but elegant ladies stepping in

and out of beautiful motor cars, and pretty dresses in magazines which they knew they could never afford, but could at
least dream about, while all the time being permanently
confined no matter what to their school uniforms, their long
grey or white socks, and their felt or panama hats according
to the seasons.

'What are you reading?'

Alexandra tried to hide the book under her eiderdown.

'Give me that!'

Betty Stamford leaned over the bed and took the offending
novel from under the eiderdown. Alexandra found herself
blushing as if the book was improper, which she knew very
well it could not be. After all, the lady who had lent it to
Frances Chisholm was a very smart lady, who rode out twice a
week on a beautiful bay mare whom she called Cherrypan.

'What is this, young lady?'

Alexandra stared at the title that her grandmother was
tapping accusingly before she started to flick disapprovingly
through the pages.

'It's a book. It's going to be a classic, Mrs Chisholm says.'

'She says that, does she? What have I told you, Alexandra?
I have told you time and time again you are not to read
novels at night, or at any other time for that matter. Novels
are full of bad ideas. Girls who read novels end up in
hedgerows with their stockings tied round their necks. They
bring home trouble, because they've read about trouble in
just such a book as this. This is going straight back to whoever
gave it to you. I'm having none of that sort of nonsense at
Lower Bridge Farm, and that is quite certain. We don't have
books in the house unless they're about farming. Reading
novels turns girls into fly-by-nights, and we all know where
that leads to – gin lane, that's where that leads to. You must
read nothing but the Bible before you go to sleep. I expect it

was that Chisholm girl who loaned it to you. They're worthless those Chisholms, really they are. Always did live high, wide and handsome before the war, and now they're down on their luck, letting out liveries and scratching around to find a penny in the straw, all they can think of doing is pulling you down with them.'

'The-the-the lady who lends books to Frances, she owns Cherrypan at the stables,' Alexandra finished, finally speaking at a gallop, which was her usual way of overcoming the hesitation that had dogged her since she was a toddler.

'If she owns Cherrypan then she's a snob. I've told you time and time again, horses are for snobs. You're a Stamford. You're not from a family that keeps horses. We're a proper farming family, not nose-in-the-air gentry types like those Chisholms. Your grandfather always thought of them as being jumped up, people like the Chisholms. They should keep themselves to themselves as we have always done. From now on you're not stopping off at tea with them. I don't want you getting ideas, really I don't. And nor does your father.'

She switched off the light, and closed Alexandra's door a little too noisily behind her.

Alexandra lay in the dark, tears forming behind her closed eyes. All the time she was growing up she had never thought of the Chisholms as being anything but kind. And she didn't see how they could possibly be nose-in-the-air types when they were always so friendly to her. She wished, oh how she wished that she was not a Stamford, with only Gran and Father as relatives, especially Father who never spoke to her except when he had to, who passed her in the garden with just a nod, and never took her on picnics as Mr and Mrs Chisholm always did as soon as summer came, giving them chicken with a delicious mayonnaise that Mrs Chisholm took such a pride in making, not to mention her home-made lemonade, and the soft sponge cake that she made with a double filling of cream from the cows and strawberries from the garden.

As she lay there feeling sorry for herself it seemed to Alexandra that nothing cheerful had ever happened at Lower Bridge Farm, not even when Father won a prize with one of his bulls at the County Show. It was always just the slog, slog, slog of farming life, then church on Sunday, followed by tea, when her grandmother's friends came and went, and that was that: nothing else to relieve the unvaried pattern of the farming week with its early mornings and early bedtimes gauged to the light outside.

'Rather good,' was all she remembered Father saying when he had won a prize for his bull, nothing more, and then he had put the cup and the rosette up on the mantelpiece in the dining room, right opposite his bound copies of *Farmers' Fayre*.

'And about time too,' was all Gran had said.

Alexandra stayed awake, waiting for her grandmother to go away so that she could put on her light and go on reading the novel, which was exciting and emotional in all sorts of ways.

The following morning for some reason Alexandra could not fathom, her grandmother seemed to have forgotten all about the wretched novel lent to her by the Chisholms, so that when Alexandra walked out of the house pulling down her hat, her head bent against the east wind, her grandmother did not appear in the least bit interested in the book. As a result of this Alexandra arrived at the top of the drive, all set to wait for Mrs Chisholm's van to come into view and feeling vaguely as if she had got away with something, although quite what, she could not have said.

'Hop in!'

Alexandra opened the back door and climbed in beside the inevitable medley of dogs and lead ropes, bailing twine and faded newspapers.

'All aboard the Skylark,' Mrs Chisholm sang out, and the rest of the children she had picked up replied in kind as the van chugged on to the next pick-up point.

Back at Lower Bridge Farm the reason for Betty Stamford not paying much attention as to whether or not Alexandra had returned the notorious novel to Frances Chisholm was becoming rapidly clear, if not to Alexandra, at least to her father.

'There's nothing I can do about it, Mother. It's just a fact, her mother had a family, Alexandra has relatives. They will be sure to drag us through the courts if we drag our toes any more over this business.'

'Who says?'

'Haimish Dunbar, Mother, that's who.'

'That Dunbar, he knows nothing, he knows less than nothing. He's just like his father – useless.'

'He's been in the habit of looking after our affairs really quite well, Mother, and we have to face it, it's ten years now, must be ten years, over ten years since Alexandra last visited Knighton Hall. We have to bite on the bullet and let our Alexandra go and visit her Millington relatives, or it will be the worse for us. Can't honestly see much harm in it myself.'

'Course you can't, John, course you can't, you're a man, aren't you? Course you can't see any harm in it. I'll tell you what harm it will bring, and it's this. Once over there, we'll lose her to the Millingtons, sure as eggs is eggs, and that'll be that, particularly now that she is growing up – nearly grown up, if you happen to have noticed, which I doubt. Your daughter has matured, John, and once girls mature they get funny ideas without any help from us, but we can at least try to make sure they don't get the wrong funny ideas.'

John turned away. He still couldn't see any harm in Alexandra visiting her relatives. More than that, he could only see good. The girl needed to get out from under her grandmother's skirts, all girls did, he knew that now, not least because a little birdy had told him so.

'My own idea is that she should go and stay with Brother-in-law at the end of term, after Christmas. It's always a bit of a dull time for her here, on her own, in the New Year, seeing as she's an only child.'

'She needn't be an only child, John. If only you would settle down she wouldn't be on her own, would she now? But you won't. If only you would, how much better life at Lower Bridge would be.'

'I want to settle down, Mother, you know that. We've talked about it, time and time again. But at the moment my life is my life, and that's all there is to it. I just have to cross my fingers that things will change for me.'

Betty Stamford's constant reference to 'settling down' was her euphemism for 'remarrying', but constant though this theme was in her conversations with John, he never seemed able or willing to respond to her despairing encouragements. He wouldn't go to any farmers' dances, nor would he take any notice of young women, pretty young women too some of them, whom she was in the habit of inviting to tea on Sunday afternoons.

'Your father never laughs, does he?' Frances once said to Alexandra, and Alexandra, knowing this to be true, ran off in the other direction, but when she was alone with Mavis in the kitchen, after the two farm lads had scoffed their tea, she made the same comment to their old cook.

Mavis had her back turned to her, and she kept it turned, until finally, just as Alexandra thought she might not have heard her, she turned slowly away from the sink and faced Alexandra.

'Your father was that devoted to his Laura, your mother, he's never laughed since the day she died.' She paused, a look of reverence on her face as she wiped her hands on her flowered apron. 'I give it as my opinion, Miss Alexandra, that after she died he imagined that if he allowed hisself to laugh he would cry; and once he started to cry he would never stop. That's why your father never laughs, and I dare say he never will.'

'She looks pale, I think she might be sickening for something.'

Betty stood back from Alexandra's side, but John Stamford shook his head.

'She's not pale, Mother. She's just normal. Let her alone, for heaven's sake.'

'How's she getting to the station, then? You can't take her, and I can't drive.'

John nodded. His mother always mentioned that she couldn't drive as if it was some kind of virtue.

'Mrs Chisholm's very kindly said she would take Alexandra to the station and put her on the train for us, Mother.'

'I could do without that Mrs Chisholm. Always interferring in our lives.'

'We can do very little without the kindness of the Chisholms, Mother, most especially since you have always refused to drive.'

Betty turned away and leaving Alexandra's bedroom, slammed the door behind her. John looked across at his daughter.

'Time to go, Alexandra,' he said, half apologetically.

Alexandra nodded. Over the past few days she'd seen just how upset her grandmother was about Alexandra having to go to stay with her cousins, and just how upset her father was that his mother was so cross, but try as she might she could not help her feelings of bursting excitement. The last time she had been on a train was to visit her Millington cousins, but it was so long ago, she could hardly remember it, only that her father had sent her in the charge of the guard, and so the prospect of going all the way to Knighton Hall on her own was intoxicating.

'Hop in!'

Mrs Chisholm leaned over and undid her van door.

'Hope you don't mind, Frances's in bed with the flu, so she can't come, and you're stuck with me.'

'It's ve-ve-very kind. So-so kind of you to take me to the station, is what I mean.' She handed over a brown paper parcel. 'The-the-the book. That's the book the Cherrypan lady lent me.'

Mrs Chisholm who, ever mindful of the eccentricities of her van, had kept the engine running all through the proceedings, now crashed gaily through all the gears and the van shot forward.

'You're a good girl, Alexandra, do you know that?' Mrs Chisholm yelled over the sound of the engine. 'I've always liked you, and although I know that your grandmother is so against you going to Knighton Hall, I have to say that I think it will do you the world of good. You're not just a Stamford, you know, Alexandra, your poor dead mother – whom I have to say I only met once but I do remember – she was a Millington through and through, quite different from the Stamfords. For myself, I really think that it is about time you met up with her family again, got to know the other side. I've never met them myself, but it is the principle. Your Stamford grandmother can't keep trying to bar the Millingtons from taking an interest in you, and frankly I think it's quite ridiculous that she has tried, and what's more succeeded. Really, she has taken the whole situation right to the wire. Thank heavens that your father has finally seen reason and allowed you some independence, and about time too, I have to say.'

Alexandra stared at her feet. She knew at once from what

Mrs Chisholm was shouting at her above the sound of the engine that the events at Lower Bridge Farm must have been the talk of the neighbourhood, and that everything Mrs Chisholm said was true. She had overheard too many conversations between her grandmother and Mavis, and between her father and her grandmother, not to realise that she herself had always been the subject of a tug-of-war between her dead mother's family and her father's family, although why she was the subject of such a tug-of-war, she had never quite understood. Surely everyone had cousins? Certainly everyone who lived around them seemed to have ever so many relatives, but none of their grandmothers or other relations ever seemed to stop them from visiting each other.

'Well, here we are,' Mrs Chisholm yelled, keeping the engine not just ticking over, but raging. 'I can't put you on the train, but the porter there will help you with your bags. Have a good time, and don't give a thought to anything else.'

'Than-k you very much, Mrs Chisholm. Than-k you ever so much.'

Alexandra took her two suitcases from the back of the van and stepped back to allow Mrs Chisholm to circle just as the station porter hurried up to her. He took her cases and, having helped her buy a ticket, led her up to the quite empty station platform to wait for the expected train.

'Come on, Miss Alexandra, got to get you put on the right train, haven't we? Mrs Stamford warned me to put you in the Ladies Only carriage, most especially she did. My life won't be worth living if I don't do as she says.'

Her father had not said anything about her travel arrangements. He had simply handed her what seemed a great deal of money and told her not to spend it all at once. Perhaps because of this Alexandra suddenly felt quite alone. To hide her vague feelings of trepidation she pushed her Alice band higher up her head, and smiled at Bob the station porter as brilliantly as she could. Bob's dog had won first prize for looking most like his owner at the Hunt Dog Show, but now that Alexandra stared up into Bob's large brown eyes, it seemed to her that it should have been the other way round.

'There you are, my dear, there is the Ladies Only carriage.'

Both Bob and Mr Fudge the stationmaster stood on the still-deserted station platform and waved Alexandra off.

'You sit there, my dear,' the train guard told her, 'and these good ladies will keep an eye on you all the way to Knighton, and I'll be coming by all the time to make sure you're not feeling train sick nor nothing, so don't you fret about a thing.'

Alexandra smiled around at the older ladies in the carriage, all of whom were knitting, but she said nothing because her grandmother had always told her not to dream of opening her mouth in front of someone she did not know unless they had said something to her first.

As it happened, the ladies in the carriage must have all been brought up by people with similar ideas to her grandmother because not one of them exchanged a word with her all the way to Knighton. The train guard came by every now and then and with a kindly expression waved to her through the glass door. Finally he opened it and called, 'Luncheon in the refreshment car is ready.'

Alexandra had her lunch money in a special purse, also given to her by her monosyllabic father, so that while the other ladies remained seated, she was able to follow the guard down the swaying train to the refreshment car.

She read the menu presented to her by the waiter, who she could see was trying to pretend that she was just as old as everyone else around her, and then pointed to the first set menu.

'Than-k you. Thi-this one.'

He whisked the menu back and smiled at her.

'Gin and tonic to start with, miss?'

The waiter's face had assumed a mock-innocent expression, and Alexandra knew he was making fun of her, but did not mind in the least. In fact she responded in kind, pretending to consider the order, but finally deciding against it.

'Ner-no – just an orangeade, please.'

It was magical to look out of the window and see the towns and villages posed on the landscape and know that no one was going to come along and interrupt her thoughts, so that the daydreams of previous years when she had been growing up at Lower Bridge Farm were able to take on a reality that was almost breathtaking. No longer did the fields and trees, the hedges and the lanes serve only one purpose: to get to school and come back, to pass on the way to visit a friend. Now they lay scattered about the countryside with no evident logic, sometimes so near to each other that they might well have been embracing, at other times sprawling carelessly in a wanton manner, a cottage here, a house there. Everything was quite untidy, but so exciting, so new, so full of promise that it seemed to the fascinated Alexandra that each place, however small, must house someone or something that she had never seen before and yet (she was somehow completely certain) by which she might well become astonished.

Her arrival at Knighton station filled her with a secret anxiety that she was keen not to show to the other much older passengers. Long before the train drew to a noisy, groaning stop and the porters pulled open the carriage doors for the passengers to alight, despite the fact that she had faithfully counted each stop – since she had been told by Mrs Chisholm that hers would be stop number ten – she nevertheless looked round anxiously for the name of the station before stepping carefully down, and leaving her suitcase behind her on the luggage rack. Realising her mistake she turned as the whistle was blown, flags waved, and the train drew away from the platform.

I've left my suitcase on the train, I've left my suitcase on the train.

As so often happened with Alexandra, the words would not come out, and she found herself staring dumbly into a strange face.

'Anything the matter, miss?'

The porter leaned so near to her that Alexandra could smell the tobacco on his breath and see that he still had a light white stubble under his nose where he had missed shaving that morning.

I have left my suitcase on the train, I have left my suitcase on the train.

Still the words would not come out.

'Buck up, miss, can't stand here all day.'

Before Alexandra could finally speak she saw a board with her name on it being carried by a man in a peaked cap and long, pale rubberised riding macintosh that reached down well below his knees.

'MISS ALEXANDRA STAMFORD', the board read.

'Th-th-that's me!' she finally spluttered, and ran towards the man with the board before he too, like her suitcase and the train, disappeared. 'That's me!' she shouted from behind him, pulling at his arm as he started to turn away. 'That's me!' she said again, pointing at his chalk board. 'I-er – I am Miss Alexandra Stamford, from Lower Bridge Fer-fer Farm.'

The man stared down at her from beneath his peaked cap.

'Oh, so it is you. Good heavens you have grown up,' he stated slowly, and then he smiled and took off his cap. 'Welcome once more to Knighton,' he said, shaking her hand slowly up and down. 'It's been so long, don't suppose you could possibly remember me? I'm the estate manager, Douro Partridge. So glad you made it. Where's your suitcase?'

Alexandra stared up into his handsome face with its thick blond hair and kind blue eyes, and coloured furiously, for the good reason that she had, just for a second, thought it might be her Uncle Jamie, whom she could hardly remember.

'It's-it's-it's on the train, my suitcase. I left it on the train. I am so sorry, so very sorry,' she managed finally.

'And the train's gone?'

She nodded in an agony of embarrassment.

'Don't worry, Miss Stamford, we'll soon fix that, really we will.' He turned to the stationmaster. 'Mr Blaize? Miss Stamford here has left her suitcase on the train. Telephone through to Gilcombe, will you? Ladies Only carriage, was it? That's the ticket.'

Alexandra nodded while at the same time shifting her weight from foot to foot. How could she have been so stupid? She had been so worried in case she would miss the stop, she had missed her suitcase instead.

'Ladies Only carriage mind, Mr Blaize. Mr Blaize here will take care of everything. Your cousins are always leaving things on the train, he's quite used to it, as you can imagine.' He nodded towards the white-haired stationmaster and then smiled down reassuringly at Alexandra. 'Your suitcase will come back to you via the station taxi at Gilcombe. Besides, you can always borrow some jim-jams from the other girls, can't you?'

Alexandra, who had only ever been allowed to wear night-dresses of the most formal nature, felt delightfully shocked – not just at the notion of wearing pyjamas for the first time, but also because Mr Partridge had mentioned them so casually. At Lower Bridge Farm no one mentioned under-clothes, or night clothes, or anything like that. People went to the 'aunt' or 'visited the cloakroom' or had 'unmentionables'.

'Want to hop in beside me?'

Outside the station stood an old battered pre-war motor

car, very like that owned by Mrs Chisholm, although perhaps not so old as Mrs Chisholm's, because this one started up first time, and they were able to sweep out of the station yard in splendid style, and so on to a country road, the first of many that finally led to the gates of Knighton Hall.

'Nearly there!' Mr Partridge nodded up at the two lead greyhounds that were poised on the stone gate pillars, before changing gear and shooting between them, and so up the beech-lined drive.

Knighton Hall lay before them, its many windows reflecting the setting sun. To Alexandra it looked larger and even grander than she had remembered it, grand to the point of being daunting, whereas to Douro Partridge, who never confronted its façade without a feeling of being privileged to help look after it, it merely looked what it was: a beautiful gem.

The house itself was set calmly against a backdrop of rich pastureland, of fields sprinkled with sheep, the distant acres beyond them finally ending with the sea, which on this particular calm winter's afternoon looked as if someone had taken a brush and colour-washed it into the far horizon, especially for Alexandra's coming.

She stood and stared at the scene before her, and without realising it became so exalted by the beauty of what lay before them that she put both her gloved hands up to her face in an artless gesture of delight and joy. Douro glanced at her, smiling, but perhaps understanding how she felt, he too stood and stared at the loveliness before them, and it was a few seconds before he himself turned to go up to the front door, closely followed by the new visitor.

'Hallo, Jeffryes,' said Douro, as a black-coated butler opened the door to them.

'Good afternoon, Mr Partridge.' Jeffryes's gaze slid from the estate manager's face to Alexandra, who was now feeling nervous all over again. He walked towards her and bowed slightly, which made Alexandra feel both silly and awkward.

'May I have the keys to your luggage, please, miss?'

Alexandra went to speak, but Douro intervened.

'Miss Stamford's case was sent on in error by the porters at Knighton station, Jeffryes,' he said, his hand moving to Alexandra's shoulder to which he now gave an avuncular pat. 'There's hardly a day goes by at the moment without this happening.'

Alexandra stared at the butler's expressionless face, still overcome with shyness. She knew that Mr Partridge was lying on her behalf, so that she would not look stupid in front of the butler, and she felt so grateful to him.

'May I take your coat, please, miss? And then perhaps you will care to follow me to the library, would you, please? Mrs Millington is taking tea there with Miss Jessamine and Miss Cyrene.'

Alexandra made to step behind Douro, but he gently put his hand into the small of her back and indicated for her to be the first to follow the butler down the short, dark corridor lit only by a vast brass Gothic lantern, before he finally opened one of two double doors and announced them.

'Miss Stamford and Mr Partridge, madam.'

'Ah, Douro. Here at last, we have been waiting tea for you.'

Tasha Millington nodded from the library fireplace where she was seated in front of an elegant silver teapot, hot water and milk jugs, a pair of King Charles spaniels at her feet, her two daughters seated opposite, seemingly sunk so deep into a button-back sofa that at first all that could be seen were their long white lacy-stockinged legs with silvered shoes. They were both wearing mauvey-silvery-coloured dresses that showed off their beautiful blonde hair, and holding plates with scones perched on them. Both also turned as one when Douro and Alexandra came into the room.

'Girls, girls, look, here is your cousin Alexandra,' Tasha cooed, and she patted her unsurprisingly immaculate hair, which she went once, sometimes twice a week to London to have styled, and which she was careful never to allow to become rain-sodden.

Alexandra looked across at the fireplace and instantly became conscious that she was dressed in a jumper and skirt that she was well aware were far too young for her, not to mention heavy stockings and shoes; and that was all before it came to the hem on her skirt, which, although it had been let down some time ago, still showed the lines where the previous hems had been, and which their cook Mavis had said never would come out.

Tasha stared at the new arrival, taking in the visitor upon whose shoulder Douro had once again placed a reassuring and avuncular hand. They had only once had Jamie's niece to stay and that was many years before, when she was quite small. Now she could not help staring at the daughter of poor silly Laura who had married in such haste and never even, poor girl, had time to regret at leisure – since she had died in childbirth barely ten months after her wedding to John Stamford.

'Hallo, Alexandra,' she went on to Alexandra in as kind a voice as it was possible to use without sounding either accusing or patronising.

Alexandra looked up at Douro as if to confirm that she was indeed the right girl, and then across at Tasha.

'Ye-s.'

'Come and sit down in front of the fire. I expect you'd love a cup of tea and a scone, wouldn't you?'

Alexandra walked across the old polished boards that led up to the cosy scene placed so securely in front of the chimneypiece. She was aware that her shoes were making a clumping sound and her thick lisle stockings looked as heavy as chain mail compared to the lacy white stockings of the other two, that her wool skirt and jumper were bulky and hot compared to their mauvey-silvery dresses, and her long dark hair pulled back under her black velvet Alice band, although washed and clean, was nothing compared to their perfectly ordered blonde hair drawn carefully back at the sides and tied at the back with matching mauvey ribbons, the whole set above ringlets tumbling down their backs.

'Shake hands with your cousin, girls – do.'

Two pairs of greenish eyes turned on Alexandra, and two white hands whose wrists were identically decorated with seed pearl bracelets were obediently extended. Alexandra held out what looked like a brown paw, for her hands were still tanned from helping with the harvest in the now long past summer.

'How are you?'

'Hallo, Alexandra, years since we met, isn't it?'

The taller one was Jessamine, and her sister, younger by two years, was Cyrene. Alexandra knew this all too well for whenever a Christmas or birthday card for Alexandra had arrived at Lower Bridge Farm her grandmother would say, over and over again until Alexandra could have screamed, 'Did you ever hear the like? I mean, *did* you? I've had cows with more sensible names than those.'

As if to make up for the girls' high-flown names the next visitors to the teatime scene were the two Millington boys, Anthony and Rufus, the last named being inevitably red-haired.

They were tall like their sisters, and judging by the sober cut and hue of their clothes undoubtedly older by a few years. In fact they were so tall that when they walked across to shake hands with her they seemed to Alexandra to be staring down at her as if they were two Irish wolfhounds, and she some sort of small farm terrier.

'We've met you before, haven't we, cousin? We've met her before, haven't we, Douro? We've met Alexandra before.'

Anthony Millington turned back to his father's estate manager for confirmation while his brother stared in some fascination at their countrified cousin in her cumbersome clothes, so different from those of his sisters.

'Yes, I believe you have,' Douro agreed, carefully returning his teacup to the silver tray in front of the fire. He looked across at the two boys as if to say, 'Behave yourselves, you understand?' and then he said to Tasha, who was once more sipping a cup of tea with lemon and no sugar, 'Alexandra's suitcase was sent on by mistake to Gilcombe, so Mr Blaize at Knighton is having it sent back here. If the suitcase doesn't arrive in time I think she will have to borrow some clothes for dinner tonight, and some night things too, of course.'

There was a small silence lasting only a few seconds while all eyes seemed to Alexandra to have focused not just on her, which was bad enough, but on her woollen jumper and skirt, on her thick stockings and her chunky slip-on shoes.

'How vexing for you for the suitcase to go on without you. Nevertheless, I am sure we can manage something for you, can't we, girls? Yes, we can lend her some clothes,' Tasha agreed, smiling with sudden relief at the idea that she could take what Alexandra was wearing off and replace the clothes with something a great deal more in keeping with her surroundings. 'We will take her up to the day nurseries and find her something charming.' She smiled effortlessly at her husband's niece, hardly able to contain her impatience until Jamie came home, already imagining what she would say to him on the subject of '*poor little Alexandra Stamford*'. Meanwhile the four Millington children tried not to stare at their cousin and ask the question, '*Why is she so different from us?*'

Later Tasha was able to attack her husband on the subject of his impoverished-looking niece.

'It was just as I said it would be if we left her to be brought up at Lower Bridge Farm, *just* what I predicted. The poor girl has no clothes. She is in rags, Jamie darling, but rags. And as for her lisle stockings and clumpy shoes, well, it makes you wonder, really it does. I mean, the arrogance of the Stamfords in thinking that they could bring up your poor sister's child in keeping with her Millington background. If it weren't so tragic it would be funny, really it would. As it was I was in an agony of embarrassment all the time we were having library tea, in absolute agony thinking all the time that one or other of the children would come out with something appalling, but they were very good, I have to say, they truly were. Not that they could help staring. You can't blame them. The poor girl looks so *rustic*.'

'Well, that is only to be expected, after all.'

They both enjoyed having these sorts of conversations every evening, usually as they were busy changing for dinner. When at Knighton and dining only with the family Jamie compromised, changing into a richly coloured velvet jacket rather than evening dress, one of three or four that he kept for informal dinners at home. Tasha's choices were also informal, usually some sort of decorous evening skirt, worn, as on this particular evening, with a long-sleeved lace blouse underneath a black velvet waistcoat.

'How are her manners?'

A small silence followed in deference to the fact that Tasha was applying a softly pink lipstick. Finally, after staring at her upper and bottom lip solemnly and separately, she pressed them together, before turning to face her husband.

'What did you say, darling?'

'I asked how her manners are. Is Alexandra nicely mannered? We don't want her infecting the other girls with bad ways.'

'Oh. Her manners? Oh, they are fine. No, she seems

really very well mannered, her manners are perfect, she is courteous to a fault. It's just that she has a pronounced hesitation. Not a stammer, no, just a small hesitation, but still I can see it makes it difficult for her. She seems to find it hard to start up sentences but once she has she is perfectly all right, and she has certainly not gone feral like your poor cousin Ashton who, really, one would not know from the man who lives with a pig down the lane, would one?'

Jamie stared at himself in the mirror. He had to admit that he would have given up the fight to see his sister's child long ago, if it hadn't been for Tasha. She had been stalwart, to say the least, battling on, no matter what, determined to get her way, not letting up; above all not letting the Stamfords have it all their own way. It was quite something to have the poor girl under their roof at Knighton Hall, if only for a week.

'I must go and find a dress for the poor young woman. She left her suitcase on the train. Not that it matters, because judging from her clothes it does not look as if the arrival of the suitcase is going to improve matters very much – I mean she would have had to borrow something suitable for dinner anyway. We're going to have to buy her better clothes, Jamie. If it's the last thing we do, we're going to have to do that. Not to beat about the bush, she looks *frightful*.'

'So you said, darling, so you said.'

Jamie nodded again at himself in his dressing mirror and watched Tasha giving a final brush to her shoulder-length blonde hair. They were really very lucky, most especially compared to his poor sister Laura. Awful for her dying like that, just as she was having a baby too. If only she had not married on the rebound, which when all was said and done was one of the worst reasons for getting hitched. He sighed, and finally shut the intervening door between their two dressing rooms before going slowly down the shallow steps of the beautifully carved staircase to the library, where Jeffryes was waiting to mix him a perfect cocktail. He never did like to think of his sister being dead, but she was, and nothing to be done about it except try to bring her daughter more into line, make her more sophisticated, as Tasha had just indicated.

Alexandra reappeared behind Jessamine and Cyrene wearing a black velvet dress that was one of Cyrene's discards. She now also sported white stockings with gold pumps, all also discards. She felt strange, as if she were not herself, as if she had fallen down a rabbit hole and turned into someone or something else. She was also painfully aware that no matter what, she would never be able to display the sophistication of the other two girls, both of whom had declined to talk to her, except when their mother had appeared on the scene, at which point they had talked to their mother over Alexandra's head.

'Sit down over in the window and Jeffryes will bring you a drink, darlings,' Tasha now commanded them. All three did as told, sitting demurely in the bay of the window on slim plum-coloured velvet cushions.

Alexandra was grateful for the glass of iced lemonade offered to her by the butler, because she felt hotter than she had ever felt before and it wasn't just because of the immense fire burning in the grate filled with vast logs from around the estate. It was because she was afraid that her Uncle Jamie would ask her a public question, and that because of her hesitation, she would take an age to answer it. Happily for both of them he seemed more interested in hearing about the girls' recent trip to London, the play they had seen, the friends they had visited. Alexandra listened attentively, knowing that their conversation echoed a life that she might never know.

Finally when her uncle did turn round he came straight

across to her and said abruptly, 'Hallo, Alexandra. Don't get up, and don't say a word.'

He kissed her lightly on the cheek and stood back smiling, yet as he did so Alexandra knew at once that Aunt Tasha must have warned him that Alexandra had a hesitation. Her uncle was relieving her of embarrassment, and that was very nice of him, but at the same time it was terrible too, and made her feel hotter and more awkward than ever. Now she felt quite sure that she would never, ever be able to open her mouth again, that her hesitation was going to be all too evident for the rest of her stay at Knighton Hall.

The Oik

'Thomas O'Brien?'

Tom looked up from sawing yet another log for their cottage fire, the only form of heating that he and his mother were able to allow themselves.

'Yes?'

Tom turned to see another, older young man standing watching him. He knew at once from his long white apron and striped trousers that he must be the new under-butler at the house.

'It's your mother, Mrs O'Brien. She's fallen down again. Them up at the house, they wants you to come and collect her.'

Tom flung down his saw and ran outside to the yard where his truest friend, his bicycle, lay propped against the water pump. It was only as he was standing up on his pedals cycling as fast as he could up the drive towards the great house that he realised he had nothing in which to bring his mother home.

Crikey!

Nevertheless, he pedalled on, circling the beautiful exterior of Knighton Hall and finally arriving at the entrance that served the servants. He flung himself down the steps, ignoring the elegant iron railings, bursting through the half-glassed oak double doors at the bottom, along the boot room, which always smelt of a pleasant mix of damp clothing and horses, through the gold-studded green baize door and into the large, well-lit kitchens, the main one of which was where his mother reigned supreme every day of the week, except Sunday afternoon.

'Ma? Ma?'

The other staff looked up from mixing bowls and drying cloths, and one of them nodded towards the door that led to the flower room. Slowing only so that he did not jog the arm of someone intent on whipping up a soufflé or drying a cut-glass decanter, Tom half ran, half walked through the door indicated, and finally into the relevant room.

It was a room lit from above to enable the all-important matter of 'flowers for the house' to be done with maximum attention to colour. A pair of butlers' sinks with old brass taps stood in the centre of one wall, flanked on either side by wooden draining boards; opposite these was a chair. In the chair lay his mother; her thin body sprawled against the headrests, her grey hair falling back, her eyes closed.

'Ma? Ma?'

Tom leaned over knowing all too well what to expect, and having had his expectations amply fulfilled, he went back through the doors to the main kitchen.

'Black coffee, please, if you wouldn't mind?'

There was complete silence as one of the staff peeled away from the big wooden table and went towards the place where kettles were boiled and coffee and tea made all through the day, and sometimes, when the family were entertaining, part of the night.

Mary, who acted as housekeeper as well as undertaking many other unofficial personal and domestic duties for Tasha Millington, passed Tom a large breakfast cup of black coffee.

'Get that down her soon as you can, Tom,' she told him in a kindly voice.

Tom nodded and turned away. He would actually have liked to run back to the flower room, but the coffee made it difficult, so he walked as fast as he could, and as he passed through the far-end baize door using his backside in the accepted manner to propel himself through to the other side, he could hear his heart beating, a positive bongo drum of a sound in his ears. He had so, so hoped that this time, this situation at Knighton Hall would put an end to his mother's drinking. It was not just for her sake, it was for his sake too. If she got the push from Knighton Hall, it would mean that Tom too would get the push, and God knows she would probably never get another position as good, and nor would Tom.

'Ma? Ma?'

The third time he bellowed '*Ma!*' he put his hand into the small of her back, trying to force her to sit up, but to no avail. Ma was intent on remaining unconscious.

'Passed out again, has she?' asked a voice from the door.

Tom turned slowly and, seeing who it was, he paled.

'Look, sit her up. I'll help you. If we can get her walking, walking, walking, it will start to bring her round.'

Anthony Millington, the eldest boy of the house, was not as tall as Tom, who was already well over six feet, but with him on the other side of Ma, they were able to force her to walk, despite the fact that her head was sunk on her chest, and her feet seemed to be paddling the air rather than the floor.

'Come on, Mrs O'Brien, come on!'

Anthony stopped walking and yelled at her.

'Black coffee time, that'll do it. I swear I saw consciousness in her eyes.'

They propped her up in the chair once more and started to try to pour the black coffee down her. Unfortunately most of it ran down into the collar of her prim navy-blue white-collared cook's frock.

'Stay there, I'll get some more.'

Anthony hurried off while Tom, taking ruthless advantage of his absence, promptly started to slap his mother gently round the face while yelling into her ear, '*Ma!*'

Tom was not a coward and he did not lack grit, but as he sat back on his heels waiting for Anthony Millington to return with yet more coffee he could have burst into tears. He had so hoped that his mother would now be on the straight and narrow, that she would have taken note, finally and for ever, of the fact that she suffered from a medical condition that meant she must never, ever taste alcohol again.

Anthony came back with not just a fresh cup of coffee but a whole tray laid with a full pot, and after patiently feeding the slowly galvanising Mrs O'Brien, it seemed that she was finally able to recognise not just Tom, but the room in which they were both crouched around her chair.

'What am I doing here?'

Anthony could not help feeling amused that Mrs O'Brien, in common with most cooks, spoke with a patrician accent, although unlike most cooks she was neither fat nor even plump, but alarmingly thin.

'It's all right, Mrs O'Brien, you just passed out. All the heat in the kitchen, I expect. Best if you had the rest of the night off.'

Anthony caught Tom's eye, giving him a significant look as if to say, '*Get her out of here quick if you know what's good for either of you.*'

'Tom here's going to take you home now, and he will tuck you up with a hot-water bottle and a couple of aspirin, and in the morning you will be quite back to your old self.'

Tom stood up and walked with Anthony to the door. They hardly knew each other, and they would not expect to know each other, seeing that Tom was merely the cook's boy, boot boy, lad of all work and heaven only knew what else.

'Take her home, Tom,' Anthony advised, 'and no more to be said about it, eh?' He leaned forward and whispered in Tom's ear. 'I shan't say a word. Can't do without Mrs O'Brien's chocolate cake, let alone her haddock soufflé, know what I mean?'

Tom smiled nervously, at the same time pushing his hand through the front of his thick dark hair.

'Thank you, Mr Anthony.'

Anthony patted him on the arm.

'She'll be fine in the morning, you'll see.'

Tom looked after him as he swung back through the gold-studded baize door and the look of longing in his eyes was speaking. What must it be like to be part of a family that never had to deal with a drunken mother? What must it be like to be upstairs laughing and talking, not trying, as he would be in a few minutes' time, to hold his mother up as they walked home in the rain to the workman's cottage that was their home, to a cold bare room that had few tokens of wealth, only a calendar, a brass vase filled with limp leaves, and a rug of indeterminate colour?

'I'm sorry, Tom, there must have been some tiddly in the sauce. I had to taste it because Joan, who as you know normally does the tasting for me, was off with a cold. But, well, you know what Dr Bradley said the other day, it only takes a little bit, and I'm off again. I really and truly must be more careful.'

It was the next morning and Tom was standing by the door that gave on to the small road up which he would now be bicyling to work once more. Pedalling up the long drive towards the Hall, pushing his bicycle round to the sheds where he would once again start chopping logs and clearing leaves, doing all the tasks that the other gardeners were in the habit of passing off on him, simply because they knew he depended so much on staying employed, seeing that he had no credentials, that, as everyone on the estate knew, he was only employed as a dogsbody and second groom because his mother had recently arrived as the cook at the big house.

'Don't worry, Ma, you'll be all right now, see if you're not.'

Tom turned and looked at his pale-faced mother. Sometimes he felt as if he knew what it was like to be St Christopher, fording an everlasting river of life with his mother on his back.

'I must hurry, so much to be done – the stock for the soup.' She rushed back to her own tiny kitchen where, from early dawn, she was in the habit of preparing stocks for the big house. 'Mary will be calling in to fetch me and there'll be nothing done, must hurry.'

Tom cycled slowly up the long drive back to his workplace feeling strangely light without his mother. As he did so he gazed around him at the beauty that was Knighton. In the early-morning light, with the mist rising, it presented itself in a manner so magical that it made his young heart turn over. As he passed a bird sang out from some almost leafless tree, and a robin hopped near to the hard gravel of the drive. Soon the light would grow much stronger, and he would not need his bicycle lamp, but at the moment the small spill on the already visible road ahead of him was a warming sight. With his thin trousers and socks that nowadays reached only a little way up his legs, his chapped hands, and his icy-cold cheeks, just the sight of that yellowy-pinky-whitey light was a comfort, just as his breath on the frosty air was a signal that despite being half asleep and frozen, although his heart felt leaden after a night spent worrying about his mother, at least he was still alive. And, greatest of all good fortunes, there was a whole day of work ahead of him, a day when he would be paid, when he would be fed, when his mother would be paid, when his mother would be fed, and no more of that untamable animal known as hunger would be allowed to gnaw away at his insides.

It was when she was passing their bedroom door as they were dressing to go for a ride that Alexandra overheard the girls talking.

'Have you asked poor Alexandra to tell the oik to get the horses ready for us?'

First she heard Jessamine's voice followed by her sister's gentler tone.

'You know I did. I told you that. I asked her just now. She's just gone. By the way, Jess, what is an oik exactly? And why do you always call the new boy that?'

'An oik is someone who is not one of us, someone of the lower orders, someone just like Tom. They will never be asked to dinner by people like us because they are common.'

'Oh poor oiks, how horrid. I should hate not to be asked, it would make me feel so—'

'*Oiky!*'

They both laughed and as they did Alexandra, who had doubled back to her own bedroom to snatch up a scarf and gloves, pelted down the stairs away from the sound of their mockery.

Once outside she found herself running towards the discreet green-painted sign that indicated where the stables lay, as Cyrene had directed, feeling all too excited at the prospect of seeing the horses. As she ran through the archway that led to the yard she stopped, suddenly silenced, for if Knighton Hall was impressive, its stable yard was awe-inspiring, as beautiful as anything she had yet seen: a large cobbled square with stone-built boxes dominated by a clock tower. It seemed to Alexandra that it must be a paradise for both horses and riders. She gazed round her, momentarily forgetting that she was meant to be finding the unkindly named oik, and instead walked towards the thoroughbreds that were now turning their beautiful heads towards the sound of her footsteps as they echoed across the ancient cobblestones. Summoned by their interest Alexandra began to visit each one in silent reverence, and as she stroked their necks with tender care, a voice spoke from behind her.

"Im there, that's Merryman, and 'im there, that's Tobias.'

Alexandra turned to find herself facing an old groom, tweed cap set straight on his head, small, shrewd blue eyes staring out first at her and then at the horse. Despite his great age and bowed legs he was dressed in excellently cut jodhpurs and half-boots, and a tweed jacket that even Alexandra knew was always described as 'rat-catcher'.

'Do you ride?' he asked in a pleasant North Country voice.

Alexandra shook her head.

'No-o, not really, but I love horses.'

'I'm Westrup.' He held out a gnarled hand. 'I've looked after 'orses 'ere, man and boy.'

His expression was proud, which Alexandra could well understand. She turned back to the shining head and neck that was reaching towards her over the door breathing out smells of sweet hay, bran and corn.

'The chestnut is such a lovely colour, I love liver chestnut. They want the lad to get them ready for them, Miss Jessamine and Miss Cyrene that is, and as soon as possible, please. They are going for a ride,' she added quickly, and rather unnecessarily.

'Oh aye.'

Westrup turned quickly back towards the tack room, Alexandra following him. Here was another breathtaking sight: a large wood-panelled room, the sides steeped with racks of shining saddles and pegged bridles hanging alongside rows of brass-studded halters, leather lead ropes, and every other kind of tack, each item seeming to be beckoning to the people below to admire their shining rows.

'Cou-could I help you?'

It was back, the hesitation, but not so noticeable, she did not think, that Mr Westrup would be embarrassed by it, as so many people could be.

'If you like – but our Tom should be 'ere any moment, probably running errands for one of those benighted—' He stopped. 'Doubtless 'e'll be 'ere any moment, like, meanwhile we'll get on with 'is job, shall we?'

He nodded at the tack and then at Alexandra to stand closer to help carry the bridles, his expression disinterested, as if he was quite used to people coming into the stables to help him. After that she gave a little sigh of happiness and held out her hands to help carry the bridles and martingales.

She stood behind Westrup as he laid the saddle on the back of each horse, sliding it carefully from the neck to the centre with tender care, noting how both horses seemed to open their mouths long before he proffered them their bits, bits which he had carefully pre-warmed between his two hands.

'I'm always telling our Tom, you can tell a well-broken 'orse from the moment you go into his stable,' he said con-versationally. 'That's why Knighton 'orses are so easy to 'andle, not like some you can come across,' he added, a little darkly.

Alexandra nodded, her eyes still wandering round the yard, too shy to be able to think of a suitable reply. She had often helped tack up Cherrypan and other horses, but watch-ing Westrup do it in such a careful, unhurried manner was a small revelation. She was just about to try to say this when she heard the girls' voices coming towards them.

'I must go now. Thank you for letting me help you. I love horses, although I've never owned one. Goodbye.'

She turned on her heel and ran back a different way to the

house so as to avoid seeing her cousins, just as Tom entered the yard, only slightly ahead of Westrup.

Westrup stared after the slender dark-haired girl who had run off so suddenly, before turning to Tom.

'Ah, there you are, lad. Never around when you're wanted.'

'Sorry, Mr Westrup. Mr Anthony wanted me to help him with—'

'Always summat with Mr Anthony, 'bout time he went into the Army and got some common kicked into 'im, 'ands of a lady he 'as.'

Westrup turned to see Miss Jessamine and Miss Cyrene, dressed in immaculate tweed jackets, pale lemon polo-neck sweaters and fawn jodhpurs, walk into his yard.

'You can deal with this lot, young Tom,' he muttered. 'I want nothin' to do with 'em, spoilt poodles both of 'em.'

As always just the sight of his new employer's daughters made Tom's heart sink, knowing as he did that they would do anything to be able to compromise him in some way, simply because they thought of him as nothing more than a servant.

'Horses ready, Tom?'

Tom nodded, eyes firmly turned towards the stables.

'Well then, don't be all day about it, bring them out, would you?'

He led out Tobias.

'Come on, give us a leg-up, Tom,' Miss Jessamine commanded, holding out one elegant leg.

Tom avoided looking at her, not because she was not pretty, but because, owing to his mother's employment problems, he needed her sort of trouble about as much as he needed a kick in the head.

'There's the mounting block, Miss Jessamine,' he indicated.

'You know I hate using the mounting block, Tom. You know I prefer a leg-up.'

Tom said nothing but merely led Tobias to the side of the

mounting block, and held his bridle on either side of his head. Happily the horse stood as still as a rock, only moving his bit gently from side to side in his mouth. It was always the same with Miss Jessamine. She liked to cause trouble, and for no better reason than it amused her.

'Tobias isn't near enough to the mounting block,' Jessamine moaned, smiling in a conspiratorial manner round at Cyrene, while furtively pushing Tobias away from her, but Tom was ahead of her.

'Allow me, would you, Miss Jessamine?'

Tom pulled gently on the bridle and the beautifully schooled animal once more side-stepped carefully up to the mounting block, standing ramrod still, as Tom knew that he would, while Tom pulled on the stirrup nearest to him, waiting patiently for Miss Jessamine to place her booted foot in the opposite stirrup.

'Oh really, Tobias, you're such a pig.'

Jessamine smiled down at Tom.

'Adjust my leathers, would you, Tom. You know you do it so much better than I—'

Tom sighed inwardly.

'They're at your usual length, Miss Jessamine,' he said in a calm voice.

'And what's that?'

'The length at which you feel most comfortable, Miss Jessamine.'

'I don't think they are, Tom.'

'I think, with the greatest respect, you will find they are.'

'Count them.'

Tom did as he was commanded, before turning back to Cyrene, who proceeded to try out the same old tired tricks on him.

As Tom held the bridle and pulled on the opposite stirrup, as he did everything he could to help Miss Cyrene while doing everything he could to avoid eye contact, Merryman pressed the side of his head against his tweed cap, his nostrils flaring imperceptibly, his sweet-smelling breath a tribute to the fodder that came off the carefully tended Knighton fields, his large, all-seeing eyes staring ahead, perhaps at dreams of summer fields, at the sounds of skylarks overhead, at the slow tread of warmth to come. As always Tom found himself fleetingly wondering why it always seemed to be the wrong people who ended up owning horses like Tobias and Merryman and living at places like Knighton Hall: spoilt brats like the Millington sisters, at last riding out of the yard on their immaculate thoroughbreds. The wrong people seemed to have everything.

Tasha Millington liked to invite her children and her friends, all sorts of different people, into her dressing room to talk to her in the mornings. It was an enjoyable moment in the day when she would pen the menus for the evening, even suggest wines to go with them, but most of all choose the clothes for her various social engagements in a leisurely fashion.

And it was here where the opinions of children and girl-friends, of all and sundry, were so valuable, for as she gossiped and laughed with them she would wrap a scarf around her waist, or around her neck, or drape it around a hat, and ask whoever it was who had been organised to amuse her to tell her what they thought, following which she would inevitably ignore everything they had just said.

The point being that, as all Tasha's guests knew, they had not really been asked up to her dressing room to give their opinions, but to tell her news of themselves, or someone else, to pass on gossip, generally to entertain the lady of the house while she was at play with her clothes and her menus.

Shoes were often tried; small- or tall-heeled shoes were walked up and down and dresses held against her long, slender body, while her eyes flickered from the mirror to whatever it was that she was showing off and back again. Jewellery too would be brought out of leather boxes of all shapes and sizes and put up against yet more items of clothing. Lapels had brooches held against them, and necklaces were poised above the cut of décolleté evening dresses. All in all, although mornings were a busy time for Tasha Millington, they were also blissful, for they were *her* time. A time when she could put herself before her husband, a time when luncheon with him seemed far off, and dinner, happily, even further.

For, as she often said to her trusted friends, 'It sometimes seems to me that men want nothing more than to *eat*! And when they're not eating, they're talking about eating. Nothing else seems to interest them as much as food.'

While in a way this statement was as true of Jamie Millington as it was of the rest of his sex, Tasha was wrong in another way. Something else did interest Jamie Millington, or was interesting Jamie, in the shape of a new tenant in the village, someone down from London for the hunting season, only foxes were not the only prey she had in mind to chase.

Alexandra was glad to be back at Lower Bridge Farm, glad to be home, until she unpacked her suitcase.

'What are these, may I ask?'

Betty Stamford turned from the contents of the suitcase, the expression on her face as hard and furious as when she had found her reading the book that Frances and Mrs Chisholm had lent her granddaughter.

'Ther-ther-those are clothes, Gran.'

'I can see they're clothes, Alexandra, I have eyes in my head, don't I? What I want to know is what you are doing with these clothes?'

'The-the-the *Millingtons* gave them to me. Their mother, that is Mrs Millington, she gave them to me.'

'Oh she did, did she? Well, they can all go back to where they came from, my girl. I am not having you wearing fancy and frivolous clothes like that at Lower Bridge Farm, I'm not. Not for all the tea in China.'

She picked up the cardigans, the dresses, the satins and the silks that had been carefully pressed and wrapped in tissue paper for the delighted Alexandra.

'You are not going to go flouncing round the house in these, Alexandra *Stamford*. These are going to be parcelled up on Monday and sent right back to where they came from, and that will be that. You are no poor relation of the Millingtons. There'll be no crumbs from the rich man's table here, at least not if I have anything to do with it.'

She shook out the tissue paper and emptied their contents all over the bed in a horrible muddle, and as she did so Alexandra stared from them to her old relative's face. Up until that moment when she saw the expression in her gran's eyes Alexandra had wanted only to come back to the farm, to resume being a Stamford, to go on as before, to run to the top of the drive and wait in the wind and the weather for Mrs Chisholm's old motor car to come roaring along the highway, stopping only for Alexandra to fling herself and her satchel into the back before roaring off again. Now as she saw the deep-seated resentment in Gran's eyes, she wanted to run straight back to Knighton Hall, she wanted to sit and watch Mrs Millington in her dressing room as she tried on an endless succession of dresses and tops, of jackets and skirts, of coats and hats. She wanted to be back in the dining room gazing secretively round at the paintings of her dead mother's ancestors, at the silver on the sideboards, and the gold carved frames surrounding the paintings on the walls. She wanted to be walking slowly down the shallow wooden stairs towards tea in the library. In a few seconds it seemed to her that compared to her grandmother her Millington cousins were everything that everyone should be: graceful and glamorous, artless and light-hearted, not heavy-handed and resentful, sarcastic and caustic.

But all this happened in a lightning flash, and only as result of Alexandra seeing the look in Betty Stamford's eyes, of seeing how she cast aside the beautiful frocks and cardigans that Tasha Millington had so kindly given Alexandra, as if they were dirty or ugly.

'You are not to wear any of these, do you hear? I do not want our neighbours making fun of you in these *nobby* clothes, do you hear?'

Alexandra stared at her grandmother, her face expressionless. She knew that Janet Priddy was coming to tea that afternoon. She knew it because Janet Priddy always came to tea on a Sunday afternoon. The moment Alexandra heard the dog barking, the moment she heard Mrs Priddy's voice raised in the hall, she would carefully close her bedroom door, and start to undress. She would try on every single one of the cast-offs she had been given, she would twirl in front of the mirror wearing cashmere cardigans and silk-lined skirts, and as she did so she would smile at herself and whisper, '*I'm a Millington now, and nothing you can do about it, Gran!*'

'Westrup is really too sick to ride, O'Brien, do you want to lead up second horse for me?'

Jamie Millington, immaculate in his hunting clothes, his stock tied with artless elegance, his boots shining as if they had just left the hands of a military batman – instead of Tom's eager hands – looked questioningly at Tom.

The prospect of leading up second horse for the first time for Mr Millington made his new groom burst with an excitement he was careful not to show. Happily he was already dressed for the role, smart as paint in his second-hand clothes, as he now took care to be on a winter's morning when Mr Millington was setting out to join the meet.

'Very well, it's only two miles to Alfred's Point, you follow as soon as you can, and be smart about it, I don't want to be looking round for you all the time.'

Tom was on the old cob that usually served as Westrup's conveyance when leading up Mr Millington's second horse of a winter morning. Now it was Tom's turn to do the same, and he was ready to do so in fine style only minutes after his master had left the yard. He was proud to say that he had learned to saddle up so quickly that even old Westrup could not do it faster; as fast, but not faster. Such was his hurry to keep up with Jamie Millington he was still tightening his girth when he was turning out of the gate, while at the same time leading up Mr Millington's favourite hunter, Prospero. A natty Welsh cob crossed with thoroughbred, Prospero already had his ears pricked eagerly forward as he heard hounds ready and waiting at the meet, and realised that it was going to be one of his favourite days. Tom smiled across at him.

'You lot don't need a telephone, do you, Prospero my lad?' he asked the big shining bay as they trotted smartly along. 'You just point the old ears towards where you know you want to go, and there we are.'

They completed the couple of miles to the meet at such a fast trot that they finished by catching up Jamie Millington some few minutes later, Tom's heart singing all the while, as he realised that poor old Westrup's illness had released him from the normal duties of the day: the cleaning, the chopping, the fetching and the carrying. For once Tom had drawn the long straw and would be able to follow Mr Millington across hill and dale until his first horse tired, and Tom led up second horse for him, and took first horse home.

What a pleasure it was to sit back and watch the mid-week riders arriving, some like Mr Millington accompanied by their grooms, some by horse box, all of them giving every appearance of being up and raring to go. It was a fine sight, and one that never failed to thrill Tom. He himself had learned to ride from an early age by dint of mucking out horses in return for lessons from whichever groom was in residence at whatever house his mother had been currently, if not lengthily, employed to cook. Learning to ride had been one of the many things upon which he had always been determined, and yet he could never have said why. He had always known that while his formal schooling was non-existent and his mother's and his lives hand-to-mouth, to say the least, if he meant to get on, he had to learn to ride.

'Meet me at the county boundary by the beeches,' Mr Millington called back to Tom as ''ounds please' was called, and the day's sport had begun.

The sun was breaking through and the morning well ahead of itself when they found for the first time, and Tom led up Prospero for Mr Millington to change horses.

'Thank you, Tom. You can take Bezique back now. I'm not going to stay out the whole day. Oh, and I'll rug him up myself when I get back. Just leave the feed out, will you?'

Tom set off back to Knighton Hall in the best of spirits, for leading the old hunter was no trial, and the late-morning sun meant that he finally clattered into the old yard feeling warmer than he would have thought possible on such a winter's morning.

'Mr Westrup, you're up and doing after all, then?'

The old groom looked awful, white in the face and hardly able to speak without coughing, but he grabbed Bezique's bridle from Tom.

'I'll put him away, you do the cob.'

Tom smiled wryly. Nothing could persuade old Westrup

that Tom could do a good job, nor that Tom was not after *his* job.

'Mr Millington says he will rug up Prospero when he gets in, we're just to leave the feed out.'

Westrup raised his eyes to heaven.

'Not in my yard, 'e won't.' He turned away, still coughing horribly. 'I put my 'orses away, not Mr Millington. Now be off with you and back to your other jobs before I 'ave a word with you about those 'ay wisps I found in water buckets this morning *and* the straw not 'eaped up to the side of Merryman's box the way I like.'

Tom sighed inwardly. There were days when Westrup was just a little difficult to take, and this was one of them.

'Look, Mr Westrup, I don't actually have any other jobs this morning, the family's all out for the day, no logs to be chopped or fires to be laid, nothing like that, so why don't I go and get you some cough medicine from the chemist in town?'

Westrup was just about to argue with him when yet another paroxysm of coughing burst from him. When it finally left him holding on breathlessly to the water pump, he must have finally seen sense, because he nodded.

'All right, Tom lad,' he said in a more conciliatory tone, 'but nothing fancy, mind? I just want a linctus. Something to clear this up.'

'I'll take my bicycle, once I've rubbed this lot down, and I'll be back in a jiffy, see if I'm not.'

Westrup nodded, unable to speak for fear of bringing on another fit of coughing. He hated being ill worse than sin, particularly during the hunting season.

'If you go the back way to Kennard the Chemist, it's much quicker, lad, you know that, do you?'

Tom hesitated. The back way was his least favourite bicycle ride since it took him by so many of the old tenanted cottages whose back gardens and alleyways housed bicycle-chasing dogs; but he knew Westrup was right, it was quicker.

'I'll do that,' he agreed, before starting to blanket up the cob.

Without bothering to change from his treasured riding clothes, he bicycled off towards the village. The sun was still shining, the sky was an unbelievably clear winter blue, and he was sure he could see leaves of a fine light green on every tree that he passed. Finally, deciding that discretion was the better part of valour, and he would go the long way to Kennard's rather than risk getting his backside bitten, he began to push his treasured bicycle across an empty field, through a gap in the hedge, and so finally past a barn that was sometimes used by Douro Partridge to store Millington hay after a particularly good summer's harvest.

He had actually swung his leg over the saddle and was cycling along the path that led past the barn when he heard voices. Mr Westrup was always on about keeping his eyes open for travellers on the road, for strangers and 'undesirables' as he liked to call them, so, thinking to do his duty by his boss, Tom dismounted from his bicycle. Laying the precious vehicle against the barn wall, he was able to slide the old wooden door open just enough for him to be able to fit his head through the gap.

If he could have taken back those foolish seconds, that moment of rash curiosity, of over-zealous loyalty to Mr Westrup and Knighton Hall, there's no doubt about it, Tom would have done, and instantly, but he was halfway through the barn door before he saw Mr Millington.

'I'm sorry, so sorry, sorry, sir!'

Even as he scrabbled with nervous hands to pull the old door back into place, plucked his bicycle from the barn wall and started to cycle furiously towards Kennard's and the village, Tom knew with cold certainty that his days at

Knighton Hall were numbered, and, of necessity, those too of his poor mother in the kitchens. He had just seen Jamie Millington in a position in which no married man would want to be discovered with someone who was not his wife, and not the hasty sliding back over the old wooden door, nor the fact that he had hardly taken in the scene before him, nothing could save him now.

'My dear, I'm afraid the O'Briens will have to go, you know?'

Tasha, once more enjoying her morning in front of the mirror, turned and stared at Jamie.

'I'm sorry? What did you say, Jamie?'

'I said, my dear, I'm afraid the O'Briens will have to go, you know?'

'Don't be silly, Jamie darling, they've hardly arrived and we're all thrilled with her cooking.'

'Mrs O'Brien has a drink problem, as you were warned, Tasha—'

'Most cooks have, darling,' Tasha told him gaily. 'I know because Maudie Little always tells me if any of hers ever dropped off the wagon she would just throw a bucket of iced water over them, pour black coffee down them, and that always did the trick!'

'I was going to say that we knew Mrs O'Brien had a drink problem when we took her on but we were willing to risk that since she has such high standards, but it's not her, my darling, it's Tom, I'm afraid. Westrup found him *in flagrante delicto* yesterday, when he was meant to be going for cough linctus for the poor old chap.'

'Tom? You don't mean it! Tom O'Brien? But – but he's not old enough to be found whatsit in whatsit.'

Jamie smiled slightly, and sighed.

'You're very naïve, darling. I'm afraid most teenage boys are old enough, if willing enough.'

'But Tom is such a good boy, so willing, never given any trouble.'

Tasha turned away, chewing her lip, upset to a degree that she could not explain.

'Besides, the girls will be so upset if Tom goes, surely we can turn a blind eye to such a lapse? I mean, really. Of course he shouldn't have succumbed to – to that kind of thing, but even so, he's only a boy still, just give him a clip round the ear and tell him not to do it again.'

'The girls will get over his leaving. Besides, Westrup's not been particularly happy with his work lately. He has someone else in his sights already. We won't be long without a lad, don't worry, darling.'

Tasha sat down on the satin quilt that covered her bed.

'Jamie, to my certain knowledge Tom has never put a foot wrong before. Hand on heart, I would have sworn he was the last person to do anything like that. I mean, he's always been so proper, quite the old man, and you know how the girls both like to tease him, push him too far, and he's never put a foot wrong.'

'Well, he has now. And so I'm afraid it is curtains for him.'

'Have you told him?'

'Oh yes, and his mother. I've paid them up for the month, only fair, really. They're packing up now, even as we speak.'

'Jamie! You can't, you can't possibly sack Mrs O'Brien. She's the best cook I've ever taken on.'

Tasha stood up, pulling on her chic tweed jacket that owed nothing to a country tailor and everything to a modish London couturier.

'Where are you going?'

'I am going to find Mrs O'Brien and tell her to ignore everything. I cannot possibly lose Mrs O'Brien, Jamie. You must be mad. We have a house party of fourteen next Friday, and where am I supposed to be finding a cook before that, may I ask?'

'Best if you leave them be, my dear. Nothing to be gained from going to see them.'

Jamie tried to block the door to prevent Tasha from leaving.

'No, Jamie, no. After all, I employ Mrs O'Brien. You must allow me to go to her at once. Now please, let me pass, Jamie.'

Tasha's tone was so firm that Jamie was forced to step aside, but as he did so he murmured, 'Don't be surprised if Tom denies everything, will you? I insist that he has to be dismissed whatever happens to your cook.'

'Silly boy,' was all Tasha said.

But for some reason he could not have explained, Jamie was not quite sure whether Tasha was referring to him or Tom O'Brien.

As it turned out, happily for Jamie Millington, young Tom O'Brien denied nothing. He merely stood white-faced outside their now former home, with his mother and their pathetic-looking luggage, staring past Tasha as she arrived in her new convertible Morris, at the same time as the station taxi was drawing up.

'I'm so sorry about what's happened, Tom, about your silly mistake. And Mrs O'Brien, I'm sorry that you have to bear the brunt of Tom's foolishness, really I am, but you can't leave me now. As you know I have a house party next Friday, how will I ever replace you by then? Besides, it wasn't you that was caught out, it was Tom here. So, please, you must stay. Please.'

Tom looked across at his mother. It made sense. He must go. She must stay. At least that way she would have a salary, and a place to live. If he had copped it, well and good, but for her to cop it because of him was stupid.

'She's right, Ma, you should stay. It's none of your fault, what's happened is none of your fault.'

Tom noted the look of relief on his mother's face.

'But how will you manage, Tom?'

'I'll find another dogsbody job, Ma, see if I don't. I've got a month's wages in my pocket. I'll find another position in a jiffy. I'll ring you, soon as I'm settled.'

He stepped into the station taxi that was now waiting for him, and closed the door firmly after himself. He wound down the window to wave goodbye to her, and as he did so he felt his mother's hand over his.

'I know you didn't do what they said, Tom. I know you wouldn't do such a thing.'

Tom nodded, solemn-faced.

'No, I didn't, Ma, but someone has to take the blame for what happened, and I'm afraid it's me that's drawn the short straw this time. Doesn't matter – not really,' he lied. 'Face it, it wasn't much of a job, Ma, mucking out, chopping logs and that, not much of a job if you're going to be a man to be reckoned with. It's fine for you, cooking is what you're good at, Ma, but I would have to move on sometime soon anyway. Now go back to work, and don't give it another thought, Ma, really.'

His mother hesitated, and then, seeing the determination in her son's eyes, she finally gave in, her spectacled face grim.

'Very well, but be sure to let me know where you are, and I'll send you on some money, until you're fixed up. Just let me know, promise, Tom?'

Despite her scrabbling about in her old, worn handbag and handing him some of her precious wages, his mother could not help looking relieved, so much so that Tom could see that she was only too happy to believe what he was saying. Although in their heart of hearts they both knew he was only braving it out, there was no other decision that they *could* take. For the sake of any future security, he had to be the one to go.

The taxi moved off down the back drive that led from the small row of tied cottages to the main road, and as they did so Tom watched his mother and Mrs Millington in the driver's mirror staring after the old cab until it was out of sight, after which he knew Mrs Millington would drive back to the big house leaving his mother to follow on foot carrying in large straw baskets whatever stocks and soups she had been up brewing since dawn. What a stroke of luck that Tasha Millington had been giving a house party the following Friday. If it had not been for that, they both might have been yet again out of a job.

'Can you stop by the main gates, Mr Bosworth? If you wouldn't mind, that is?'

'Of course I don't mind, Tom. Do anything for you and your mum.'

Tom looked momentarily surprised at Mr Bosworth's warm tone, until he remembered that Ma had given the Bosworths, all six of them, Christmas in their cottage, and what a Christmas it had proved to be, despite the fact that they had to celebrate it six days early, on account of Ma being on duty in the kitchens of the main house for the whole of the Christmas holiday. And, what was more, she had made sure that each one of those children had been given a present, not to mention both the grown-ups. But then Ma always did have eyes too big for her wallet when it came to other people.

The taxi drew to a slow, reverential halt in front of the main gates of Knighton Hall and, as it did so, Tom climbed out of the passenger seat and went up to the vast black intricately wrought-iron gates with their large old-fashioned pillars supporting two sleek lead greyhounds.

'Listen to me, Knighton Hall, and listen well, because one day I am going to come back and I'm going to buy you!' he whispered to

the old house that he could not quite see, but whose façade he knew so well. *'And one day it is going to be you who will be packing your bags, Mr Millington, sir, and me who will be unpacking mine, because I'm never going to forget what you did to me and Ma today, not ever.'*

'Saying goodbye to the old place, were you, Tom?'

Tom stared for a few seconds longer out of the back window of the car as the elegant entrance started to grow smaller and smaller.

'Not goodbye, Mr Bosworth, more . . .' He sat forward once again. 'More, well . . .' He coolly considered the point for a few more seconds. 'More what you might call, *"See you again soon."*'

Mr Bosworth now glanced at young Tom's thin, anxious young face, taking his eyes momentarily from the narrow country road, because there was something in the young man's tone, some look to his eyes, and to the set of his mouth, which made him stare at him in surprise. He sensed that from today – whether Tom himself knew it or not – young Tom was not going to be someone that anyone would want to cross.

New Brooms

The reason she had finally been allowed to go off and visit her Millington relatives at Knighton Hall soon became very clear to Alexandra. It was evident in the fact that her father went off whistling after eating his usual hearty breakfast, it was evident in her grandmother's uneasy smile every time the telephone rang and a husky female voice asked to speak to *John*, it was evident in the fact that Janet Priddy kept telephoning and her grandmother would carefully close the sitting-room door so that no one could overhear her conversation.

Her father had what everyone on the farm called a 'lady friend'.

'More like a lady fiend,' Betty grumbled when she thought Alexandra was not listening. 'All red nails and tight skirts, lipstick and cinched waist, not at all suitable. He met her at some wedding or another.'

Tea every Sunday became a ritual torture as John Stamford insisted on asking Kay Cullen to join in what was usually only an occasion for close friends and farming neighbours.

'More tea, Miss Cullen?'

'Oh thank you so much, Mrs Stamford. So delicious. Really lovely. So refreshing. How do you manage it?'

From the first Sunday tea at Lower Bridge Farm that her father's new love interest attended, Alexandra became acutely aware of the fact that Miss Cullen was overdoing it, and that her compliments about her cup of quite ordinary Indian tea, or the lightness of the scones, or the deliciously different Victoria sponge, were only earning looks of spite from the other teatime visitors to Lower Bridge Farm.

'I seem to remember that they grow their own tea here, in the greenhouse, at least that's what I heard.'

Janet Priddy looked around the room, careful to keep her face straight, although her tone was mocking. Her statement was greeted with half-smiles and sly looks as the assembled company took in Kay Cullen's high-heeled shoes and the long red talons that were reaching out with feigned gratitude for a sardine sandwich to go with her cup of tea.

'Poor John's taste has always been for London girls, it seems,' Janet said later to her husband, as they were driving home. 'Why he can't find someone in his own neck of the woods, the Lord, and the Lord alone, knows. There are enough good country girls in the villages around for him to choose from, but no, he had to go for a swimwear model, or whatever she is meant to have been.'

'Knitwear, John told me, knitwear. Quite respectable.'

'Nothing respectable about modelling, Mr Priddy, and you know it. And if you think there is, then you should be taken away in a plain van, and that's the truth.'

'You're not fixed on this one for a wife, are you?' his mother finally heard herself asking John.

'Let us put it this way, I have proposed to Kay, and she has accepted me, Mother. I am a very lucky man, and I think you should agree with that.'

John looked round to see his poor mother looking as if he had just shot her through the heart.

'Never say so, John, never say that's true.'

'It is, Mother, and since this is my house, and mine alone, she will, once we are married, be coming to live here with us.'

There was a long silence. Finally his mother turned her chignoned head and, staring across the room at the boy she had once loved more than life itself, she breathed in and out deeply before making her announcement.

'In that case, if Miss Cullen will be definitely moving in, I will be definitely moving out, John.'

Another silence followed this, and if Betty Stamford had hoped that her statement would bring about a change of heart she was mistaken.

'So be it, Mother, so be it. If you can't live here any more, in all conscience, then so be it. As you know I have long prayed for a replacement for my Laura, taken so soon after our marriage, and now I have found Kay nothing will induce me to do anything except marry her, and thanks be, she accepted my proposal only last night after I had walked her back to her cottage—'

'Her cottage? Your cottage you mean, but now you've put her into it, heavens only knows what else will follow.'

'What else is that next week, Mother, we are to go to Chapeltown to buy the ring.'

'Going to Chapeltown to buy a ring?' His mother's voice at once rose in indignation. 'They'll scalp you for every penny you have in Chapeltown they will, really they will. Besides, what is wrong with my old engagement ring, may I ask?'

'I put it back in your box, Mother, many years ago. Let's face it, I don't wish to be hurtful, but as Kay said, it brought my Laura nothing except bad luck. That's why I'm taking Kay to Chapeltown. And—'

His mother quickly interrupted him, at the same time leaving the room in as dignified a manner as was possible for someone who knew her heart was breaking.

'I will be moving out of here as soon as I find somewhere else, John. And taking Alexandra with me,' she told him, the finality in her tone surprising even herself.

John did look momentarily taken aback by this news before, after some time spent in thought, nodding his head slowly in agreement at his mother's proposed plan.

'Well, now I come to consider it, it probably will be best. Now that she's older, it probably would be best if you take Alexandra with you. I mean I don't suppose my Kay will want a step-daughter hanging around the place. Besides, she can always come back here on a visit – Sunday tea, that sort of thing – Alexandra can come back here on a visit, any time.'

But Betty was gone long before John could have time to consider the real implications of losing his daughter from his house, or perhaps even from his life.

To give her some credit, Kay Cullen did her best to try to make up to her future stepdaughter for the loss of her home and status.

'Would you like to be a bridesmaid at our wedding, Alex dear?' she cooed.

Alexandra stared at her.

'I don't think my gran-gran-grandmother will allow it,' she stated finally, with complete truth. 'Be-be-besides, we are moving out so soon, it will make it a bit awkward, wer-wer-won't it? Spe-spe-specially since my grandmother is not coming to the wedding.'

Her hesitation was back with such a vengeance that Alexandra could see by the way Kay Cullen's foot was moving up and down in irritation that it was all she could do to stop herself from finishing Alexandra's sentences for her.

'You don't have to be ruled by your grandmother, you know.' Kay stared at herself in the mirror in front of which she was now seated slowly brushing her hair, and as she did so it occurred to Alexandra just how many hours women seemed to spend in front of looking glasses staring at themselves, before finally leaving them looking much as they had before.

'I know your *father* wants you to be at our wedding,' Kay went on, now applying a light powdering to her already pale face.

It was difficult for Alexandra, steeped as she was in family politics, to make the right decision without offending just about everyone. Her grandmother's insistence that she herself would not be attending the wedding was ranged up against Alexandra's own loyalty to her father. On the other hand, she was too honest not to know that if left to herself she would really rather be helping out at Mrs Chisholm's stables, polishing Cherrypan's tack, grooming one of the many hirelings that were kept for hunting, rather than watch her father being married to Kay Cullen.

It was not jealousy, because she could not remember her own mother – not even the photograph that she kept of her by her bedside seemed to stir her emotions as much as she knew it should – but on the other hand, remote though her father might seem on occasion, he had always been very kind to her, never uttering so much as an impatient phrase, always at pains to seem pleasant and caring, while silently suffering; so much so that it sometimes seemed to Alexandra that she could actually see him bleeding inwardly, sighing heavily in sorrow at the loneliness of his widower's lot, emotionally unable to move back into the past, or forward into the future.

'Of course I-I will come to your wedding,' Alexandra heard herself saying, although not quite believing. 'But I-I think I am—' She stopped for a second. 'I-I think I am a bit old to-to be a bridesmaid now, and I-I would look a bit funny. My grandmother thinks I am a – bit too old,' she confided in a rush.

'Your grandmother seems to know best about everything.'

'My grandmother brought me up – because of my mer-mer-mer—'

'Because of your mother dying, I know that.'

Kay shut what they both knew was about to become her dressing-table drawer with some force.

'We'll see about what your grandmother says, and does not say about you being a bridesmaid, or about anything else for that matter. After all, it is my wedding, not hers. Mine, to do as I like, and I want you and my goddaughter as my bridesmaids, so that is what I will have,' she added crossly, slamming down the silver-backed hairbrush that still had the initials *LM*, for Laura Millington, engraved on the back.

As soon as she sensed the war that was about to break out between Kay and her grandmother over the wedding arrangements, Alexandra knew that it might actually be impossible for her to go to her father's wedding. It had to be faced that the battle lines had been drawn long ago. To attend the wedding would be to be disloyal to everyone at Lower Bridge Farm who had helped to bring her up.

'Kay has told me that she is to have you as her bridesmaid . . .'

Her grandmother was seated by the kitchen window staring out at the same inner courtyard where she had so delighted to watch her hens peck and scratch for the past forty years.

'I know, she wants me and her goddaughter as bridesmaids, Grandma, so perhaps it would be better if she did, because after all it is her wedding. And she really should have what she wants, don't you think?'

'She wants everything her own way. She is a London madam. Mark my words, it won't just be the wedding she takes over, it will be the house soon, every inch of it, and we will not be wanted here any more. Mark my words. She's even got you calling me "Grandma", hasn't she? Mark my words, this is the end.'

Alexandra ignored this, and since Betty did not turn as she spoke, it seemed to her granddaughter she was speaking not just quietly, but with awful finality, as if she herself knew she was standing by a door through which she must pass and which she knew must soon close behind her, for ever.

'I-I don't think that's true, Gran, I-I – er I ther-think she just wants her goddaughter and me for bridesmaids, that's all, ber-ber-cause it is her wedding.'

'No.'

The old lady stood up, still staring out at her courtyard at the familiar sights and sounds of her days, and shook her head.

'No, Alexandra, this is it, I'm afraid, the thin end of the wedge. I will be out on my ear very soon, and not much to be done, I'm afraid. I knew this day must come some time, but I always hoped that it wouldn't; or at least I hoped that your father would choose a country girl, someone who would understand the old ways, who would keep the house the way the house likes itself to be, someone I could work in with. But that would be too much to ask. No, I realise that very soon this will be the end for me, dear, and nothing to be done, for as that Dunbar keeps saying to me, "A widowed mother has no status, Mrs Stamford, no status at all, not in castle nor cottage." Much he knows about being a widow, or anything else for that matter, feather-bedded all his life that Dunbar, and like all feather-bedded sons he's turned into a fly-by-night with thoughts only for enjoying himself. No, the end has come for me, Alexandra, and I know it.'

But before the end could come as her grandmother had so gloomily predicted there had to be a wedding.

*   *   *

It was strange for the now even slimmer, and certainly more sophisticated, Alexandra to dress up in a long pink dress and put rosebuds in her glossy dark hair and stand beside another younger girl, also dressed in a long pink dress with rosebuds in her hair, and watch her father being married to Kay Cullen. Perhaps the whole event was made stranger because she had never seen photographs of her parents being married, or perhaps it was strange because it was John Stamford, Alexandra's father, saying 'I take thee to be my wife' or whatever it was that they were saying in front of all the locals in the village church. Whatever else it didn't do, it made Alexandra realise that he was going away from her for ever, and he was going to lie with this tall dark-haired woman from London, in a hotel somewhere, and that they would probably have babies together. This thought made her turn away from what was happening in the church and try to think only of other different things, things that were a million miles from church and weddings: of Knighton Hall and the beautiful stable yard, of the old groom who had led her round the boxes, of hay-making in the fields when she picnicked with Frances and her parents; anything rather than what was happening in the church where she was standing feeling much younger than her nearly seventeen years and a little stupid too, what with the rosebuds in her hair that made her look about twelve, and the pink of the dress which suited her skin tones about as much as the awful stockings that her grandmother had always insisted that she wore in winter.

'Do you think Kay is having a baby?'

Her fellow bridesmaid stared round at the chic proud bride seated with her older husband at the top table. As her words hit home Alexandra blushed scarlet and put down her fork of delicious chicken.

'Oh-oh-oh I der-der-don't think so!' she stammered quickly. 'Ner-ner-no. At least I der-der-der-don't think so.'

'I do, or why else would they have married so quickly, my mother wondered? I don't care, but she wanted to know. She thinks she is or else they would never have married so quickly.'

Alexandra stared at her fellow pink-dressed bridesmaid who was gazing at her with delighted malevolence, knowing that what she was saying must be hurting the daughter of the bridegroom. They were isolated below the top table, like two children being punished for bad behaviour, and perhaps it was because of this that Alexandra found herself struggling not to seize the tablecloth that was covering the stupid table at which they had both been placed, and throwing everything that was on it at the wretched girl opposite her with her fat hands and tiny eyes and her overt enjoyment of Alexandra's evident discomfort.

'My fer-fer-father would never marry someone for that reason.'

'That's all you know.'

Alexandra knew that however vague this statement the truth was that the wretched girl was right. It *was* all Alexandra knew, and what was more for all she knew Kay Cullen *could* be pregnant; she and her father *could* already have lain together, as she and Frances Chisholm always called It.

Alexandra turned away. She did not want to be there when the happy couple drove off for their honeymoon, but she knew she would have to be, and indeed she was, smiling inanely as Kay purposefully threw her bouquet at her god-child, as her father forgot even to say goodbye to his daughter; and so it was that through all the hustle and bustle of the end of the wedding, all Alexandra could do was to struggle against the thought of her father and Kay lying together.

'Cheer up, dear.' Janet Priddy leaned forward and tapped Alexandra on the shoulder as the wedding car finally disappeared round the end of the hotel drive. 'They won't be back for a fortnight and by that time the world may have come to an end.'

The world did not come to an end but in the weeks that followed all too swiftly one upon another, Alexandra could not believe how quickly her life changed. There were no rows, no arguments, just a subtle change from day to day as, newly returned from honeymoon and brown as a berry from the sunshine in the South of France, the all-too-confident second Mrs John Stamford gradually took over the reins of the house.

She began by encouraging Mavis to retire – a retirement that Mavis bravely pretended was what she had wanted all along.

'Why is Mavis going, may I ask?'

'Because she wants to, Mother-in-law.'

Kay's eyes gleamed as she turned to stare at the old lady. As she watched her Alexandra had the feeling that the gleam in her eye meant a great deal more than her actual words. The gleam in her eye meant, *'And what are you going to do about it, Mother-in-law?'* The gleam in her eye finally also meant *'got you'*. Because the truth was that as much as Kay had got her man, she had also got herself a substantial living, and the unshakable position of mistress of Lower Bridge Farm.

'She never said anything to me about wanting to go—'

Alexandra had never heard such hopelessness in her grandmother's voice.

'Really? Well, she told me she wanted to retire to the seaside and enjoy her last years without ever having to cook another steak and kidney pie!' Kay laughed. 'She could not *wait* to leave.'

This was a stinging blow not just to Betty's organisation of the kitchens but also to her long friendship with Mavis, a friendship that had lasted through the war, through all kinds of upheavals, and many a culinary disaster, and Kay must have known it, must have known what a bitter blow it was for Betty to find Mavis there one minute and gone the next, when Betty returned from market.

'I expect she'll send you a card, Grandma,' Alexandra said, slipping her hand into that of the old lady. 'I expect she will, when she gets to her cottage.'

But her grandmother just shook her head, tears in her eyes.

'No, dear, I know my Mavis. She will think this is something to do with me, she's always been that thin-skinned. Whether it was over a fallen soufflé or burnt chutney, Mavis has always had a skin as thin as gossamer. No, she'll think it was me, dear, because Kay did it when I was out, she will think I wanted her to go, I let her go without so much as a goodbye.'

'You could write to her – *explain*.'

'Yes, I could.' Betty looked down at her granddaughter with sudden hopeless despair. 'I could if I knew where she'd gone.'

The news of the turmoil at Lower Bridge Farm spread around the village.

'Apparently that Kay's hired someone who's better with the kind of London food to which she's more used,' Janet Priddy told her husband with barely disguised relish, because other people's troubles are seldom discomforting. 'Yes, Betty is heartbroken, and Mavis gone in a moment, and not a word said to poor Betty. And . . .'

Janet stopped, waiting for her husband to put down his newspaper, which, hearing the silence around him, he promptly did with a sigh, knowing that if Janet had a mind to talk that was what he had to let her do. It was after all his solemn duty, particularly if he wanted supper.

'What else, my love?'

Janet nodded appreciatively, realising that she now had his full attention.

'Well, it seems the new Mrs Stamford's taken over the running of the house in every way. She did not even like the kind of furniture polish that they've always used, won't have a washing line, doesn't like the plain white of the walls, nor the way the dining room is situated in the library, too far from the kitchen. Oh, and she doesn't like the kitchen table under the window, she wants it in the middle of the room. She doesn't like her bedroom curtains, nor the rugs in the corridors.'

George Priddy let all this information sink in, before speaking.

'Sounds to me as if the new Mrs Stamford likes very little at Lower Bridge Farm.'

'No, she doesn't, George, but I have to say, I think she's right about the kitchen table, it's never been right under that window, I've never thought, blocks off one side, not sensible.'

Janet nodded with satisfaction, and her husband, sensing that she had come to the end of her news bulletin from Lower Bridge Farm, returned to his newspaper.

The house had always been in Betty's sole charge, and as she saw it being changed, her old cook fled, and most of her loved furniture being set aside, Alexandra saw a sense of hopelessness creep over her relative, until finally, after what seemed hardly any time at all, she was following a grim-faced Janet out of the front door of Lower Bridge Farm and climbing into her car, followed closely by her granddaughter.

'Bound to happen,' Janet Priddy had kept saying, over the previous weeks when she and Betty met for tea at Janet's house, 'new brooms, dear, bound to happen.'

And of course it had been bound to happen, but not as quickly as it had. Even Alexandra had not thought that Kay would take charge so quickly, or so ruthlessly. 'Mrs Hitler' they had nicknamed her behind her back, but it did not make the pain of the new reign any less, until finally Betty took down their suitcases and, having dusted them off, began to pack up those things that she knew were hers.

The silence in the car was profound as Betty Stamford stared grimly ahead of her and the car made its way as slowly as any funeral cortège down the drive to the dear familiar old gates. It would not be Betty's way to make a fuss or cry, but Alexandra saw that her lace-gloved hands were gripping the overnight bag on her knee as if it were a ledge from which she was now dangling, as if should she let go of it she would fall into a ravine below.

'Oh look, Cherrypan!' Alexandra pointed through the car window as they passed the elegant chestnut trotting back to the Chisholms' stables.

But her grandmother said nothing, staring ahead in grim silence, as Alexandra turned round to watch horse and rider through the back window of the car. It was a fine sight on an early summer morning, but it was obviously not one in which her elderly relative could delight. As both horse and rider grew smaller and smaller, so small that they could have been ornaments on a chimneypiece, Alexandra became aware that what her grandmother had stated only a few weeks earlier was true, her life at Lower Bridge Farm was finally and completely at an end. Nothing could restore Alexandra to her father's affections again. Nothing could restore John to his mother's life. They were all being cast adrift, and, as her grandmother had kept insisting while the wedding arrangements had forged ahead, a new woman was coming into the house, a new woman who would change everything, a new woman who already had.

*   *   *

Upon agreeing to marry John Stamford it seemed that Kay had at once marked out the small black and white thatched former workman's cottage that her fiancé had bought for her to use on her weekends from London as an ideal Dower House for her mother-in-law. Perhaps it was the news of this purchase by her son that had first brought home to his mother that his intentions were to marry Kay Cullen. Whatever the original aim behind the purchase, it certainly proved to be an almost unnaturally convenient place to deposit a teenage daughter from a previous marriage and an elderly, obstinate relative.

Certainly it was obvious from the moment that Alexandra and Betty stepped into the little house that for the short time of her occupancy Kay must have tarted it up London style, for although small it was surprisingly chic inside with new black and white tiles throughout the downstairs rooms and a scarlet tweed sofa, not to mention a purple Eames chair. They had hardly put down their suitcases when, after looking round, Alexandra's spirits rose and she turned to her grandmother smiling her delight, but her elderly relative had already turned away, seating herself in the smart new chair in a way that spoke more of despair than cheer.

'This is rather ger-ger-good, don't you think, Grandma?' Alexandra asked, once more looking round appreciatively, while not really expecting a reply. 'I mean, it's lots better than I thought it would be.'

'It's got a roof, Alexandra, that is the best I can say for it. It's got a roof.'

Alexandra left her staring ahead at nothing at all, her suitcases still in the middle of the sitting room, and, determined to keep looking on the bright side, started to explore the other rooms, all of which she discovered Kay had painted the same white that she had told everyone she so hated at Lower Bridge Farm. Nevertheless, despite the low ceilings and dark beams, the moment she lifted the latches on the other dark wooden doors, Alexandra appreciated that all the interiors did at least look bright and inviting.

As soon as they had both set out their now surprisingly few possessions and lit the fire, it seemed to Alexandra that they were going to enjoy living at Pear Tree Cottage. In fact she could immediately see that their life together could be a great deal better than they had both at first thought. She could see herself cooking new things for them both, the kind of things that Kay was busy demanding of the new cook up at Lower Bridge Farm. She could see herself asking Frances Chisholm and her mother to supper. She could see that they could be cheerful together, setting about making the garden as bright and inviting as the cottage interior.

'I say, Gran, I think we're going to be happy here, really I do.'

She turned round to the old lady, but she had, for some reason that Alexandra could not fathom, instantly fallen fast asleep.

'A-are you all right, Grandma?'

There was no sound from the chair, so Alexandra walked quickly over to her. Frightened to wake her from what seemed like a state of near unconsciousness, and realising with sudden, anxious maturity that her grandmother might be taking refuge in sleep, Alexandra put a guard in front of the fire she had just lit, before tiptoeing out to the kitchen to make herself a cup of cocoa, which she took upstairs to her new bedroom and drank in solitary splendour, staring round her at the Victorian prints on the walls, all of which on closer examination seemed to be peopled by young women whom, she imagined, would have been just as grateful as she for such things as hot cocoa and a Rich Tea biscuit, filched from a tin found at the back of a kitchen cupboard. It was difficult not to feel not just lonely, but completely alone. Nevertheless, before long she too fell asleep, curled up under a heavy eiderdown, and not waking until morning, when she discovered Betty Stamford still asleep in front of a now cold, grey fire.

'How is your grandmother?'

Frances Chisholm was staring at her with such quiet awe that Alexandra knew at once that she must have heard all about the scandal of the power struggle that had gone on at Lower Bridge Farm, of how Mavis had been made to retire, and Betty Stamford encouraged to move out of her home of over forty years.

Alexandra looked up from her careful grooming of Cherrypan, at the same time standing back to admire the satisfying polish that her hard work had brought about on the horse's quarters. She was silent for a minute.

'I-I – don't know, not really. I-I don't know how she is feeling, but-but she-she-she seems to be like a plant without water. She just sits staring in front of her, and-and then she falls asleep.'

'Perhaps she's ill?'

Frances looked bright-eyed and at the same time practical, which was one of her many attractive expressions. Alexandra stared at her for a minute before turning back to Cherrypan's quarters.

'Ner-no. She's not ill.' She started to move the brush over the horse once again, determined to be able to see her face in its shining quarters. 'Ner-no, she's not ill. That's what I mean about being a plant. You ner-know how you can water it, and all that, but it doesn't do any good. Well that's what my grandmother's like, she's like a per-plant without water.'

Frances stared with interest at Alexandra.

'I think you ought to call a doctor, you know. If old people stop eating and sleep all the time, they can be not just ill, but very ill. Sometimes you find them in their chairs frozen to death, because they haven't moved for days. I know because I heard it on *Mrs Dale's Diary*.'

Although Alexandra had never heard *Mrs Dale's Diary* except once at Frances's house, she was nevertheless impressed.

'Do you think she could be dying too, then?'

Frances looked oddly excited by the idea that she might have diagnosed correctly the state of the older woman from listening to her mother's favourite radio serial.

'If I hadn't heard it, I wouldn't have thought of it.'

Alexandra put down her grooming brush, her mind made up.

'In that case I am going to call Dr Frobisher, because Gran likes him. It might help to keep her awake, if she knows the der-der-doctor is coming.'

When he arrived at the cottage Dr Frobisher was already looking serious. He knew all about the new situation that had come about at Lower Bridge Farm, all about Betty Stamford refusing to stay on with the new wife, and leaving without any of her possessions, except her clothes in a suitcase, and not wanting to attend John's wedding. He knew too that although the village gossip was none of his business, it would have every bearing on the declining health of his older patient. He was also uncomfortably aware that no one except the dark-haired young woman with the bright blue eyes standing in front of him was in the least bit interested in the old lady's wellbeing. Now that John Stamford had a new woman in his life, now that he was getting his oats again, he would be less than interested in the poor old girl. Indeed the good doctor was all too aware that if Betty had been an animal on her son's farm he would doubtless have had her shot, but since she was not an animal on his farm, indeed since she was no longer living in or near the farm, it would seem that her demise would be nothing but a relief to John Stamford. The truth was that decent though John was, his life had now taken on a whole new brighter turn, and he could not be blamed for allowing it to take him on a new road, even if it did mean cutting with the past – a past that included his mother and daughter.

'I am going to give your grandmother a vitamin tonic, and some brewer's yeast. There's nothing physically wrong with her, at least not that I can find,' Dr Frobisher told Alexandra, who was staring up at him with large anxious eyes as they both conversed in quiet tones in the small cottage porch. 'No, what has happened is that Mrs Stamford has lost her interest in life. This happens in old people, but doubtless' – he continued quickly, because finding himself faced with such patent anxiety as he saw in Alexandra's eyes, he suddenly knew he could not be as honest as he might perhaps have been with someone older – 'doubtless as soon as she starts taking the vitamins she will perk up.' He gave Alexandra a kind smile as he clipped his suitcase smartly shut. 'And let's hope that, like the horses in the meadows over there, as soon as she has some sun on her back, she will spring back into working order again.'

Following the doctor's visit Alexandra dutifully dosed her grandmother with the required vitamins, every day before and after school; but although she hoped with all her heart that with the ingestion of the tonic the old woman would turn back into her usual crusty self, in her heart of hearts Alexandra soon came to realise that if the vitamins were having significant results, they were not, as yet, visible.

Even so, every evening, as she lifted the latch on the old oak door, she could not help hoping that she would soon be hearing the dull thud of her grandmother's wooden spoon vigorously mixing up a cake, or the kettle hissing on the old cottage range as she waited to make tea for them both.

Instead, as the daylight from outside momentarily lit the old oak-furnished room, she would see her grandmother still seated in the same chair, still seated in front of a now dead fire, fast asleep, not even turning at the sound of the latch lifting, as if she was determined that if she slept long enough and deep enough, friendly death would soon come to her aid.

In the kitchen the daily sight of shiningly clean unused china proclaimed the same lack of interest in life, but pride stopped Alexandra confiding in anyone except Frances, and finally Mrs Chisholm.

'She's quite given up on life, I saw that in her eyes,' Mrs Chisholm announced when she returned from her own regular weekly visit to Betty Stamford. 'I really think you will have to call the doctor in again. You can't be expected to cope, Alexandra, really you can't.'

She gave Alexandra a kindly look, touched her briefly on the arm, and strode off towards her house, her riding boots making a sharp, clear sound on the cobbled stones of the yard.

After she had finished helping Frances to hay up the horses and freshen their water buckets at evening stables, Alexandra found herself half walking half running home in panic, Mrs Chisholm's words ringing in her head louder than her own footsteps. She pushed open the cottage door, still panting, and walked quickly into the sitting room, expecting to see the old lady fast asleep in her own preferred armchair. On seeing the chair was empty her heart soared with sudden delight. Grandma must be awake! The vitamins must be working. She must be getting better.

'Grandma? Gran? Yer-yer-yer-who-hoo, Gran?'

Receiving no reply Alexandra ran excitedly up the steep cottage stairs to the two upper rooms they used as bedrooms, hoping all the time to see the old woman once more as she had always been throughout her granddaughter's childhood: busy, vigorous, full of what she always referred to as *gumption*.

But there was no Betty Stamford, not in either of the small bedrooms with their flowered wallpapers and white counterpanes, not in the oddly large walk-in linen cupboard, nor was she in the small garden into which Alexandra peered from the upper windows.

She ran down the stairs again, a feeling of suffocating anxiety coming over her, for the cottage was undoubtedly empty, and what with the road so near, it quickly came to her that the old lady might have wandered off on her own, perhaps still half dazed from sleep. Or she might have decided to return to the farm, or set out on some mission to find Alexandra, so it was only when she returned to the sitting room, that she found the note.

Have taken Mother to the old people's ward at the cottage hospital, as Dr Frobisher was worried about her condition. She will be put in a side ward, that is a room on her own, and they will look after her until she is better. Kay will come by to see that you have everything you need until we can all make plans for your future, for I don't suppose you will want to go on living at Pear Tree Cottage on your own, now Grandma's gone. I will talk to you about this tomorrow some time. Father.

Alexandra stared at the note. It was curt and to the point, and in her father's handwriting. She glanced up at the old cuckoo clock on the sitting-room wall with its long brass chains. It was well past teatime, she had a mountain of homework, her sausage and bacon supper was waiting on the sideboard to be cooked, and it was raining hard, nevertheless she grabbed her grandmother's old flowered umbrella and headed back towards the village, and the cottage hospital.

*　　*　　*

The cottage hospital was divided into two. One section was devoted to young mothers, pregnant women and children, and those in a younger age group. There was also another smaller section, now taken up with the elderly and infirm, with those who found it too difficult to cope, or were thought to be too dangerous to be allowed to care for themselves.

'Families handing over their old to be cared for by other people, did you ever hear of such a thing?'

Alexandra had grown up with the shocked tones of Betty Stamford and Janet Priddy discussing the treatment of the old people in the village, old people who before the war would always have lived on with their families, revered for their farming knowledge and useful for the young who loved them with that unreserved affection that children feel for the old.

But of course the conversations that she had overheard had meant little to Alexandra at the time, so that it was only now that she was walking up to the reception desk with a leaden heart that she realised their import, and the words came back to her as if they were something that had been read in church, or a quotation from the Bible. It was only now that she realised what they actually meant. They meant that someone whom you had once loved took over your life and made a prisoner of you, put you in a place where you did not want to be, shut you away, left you to die.

'I have come to see Mrs Stamford, Mrs Betty Stamford.'

'We're just making your grandmother comfortable,' she was told as a young nurse in a crisp uniform walked ahead of her to the main ward. 'You sit there, my dear, until we call you. Matron likes to get to know her elderly on arrival, doesn't want to treat them like they are just a number, which of course they are not to us, my dear, I do assure you, they are not just a number to us.'

She smiled brightly and was gone, leaving Alexandra to look around the area in which she was seated, an area that was currently occupied by several old people, one of whom was clearly unable to recognise her surroundings, and the other of whom was singing to herself in a low voice. To Alexandra the whole scene was reminiscent of a painting in one of the art books at school. The low lighting of the seating area, the darkness outside that was beginning to fall, the nurses' starched white hats glimpsed every now and then through the window of the ward opposite, the sound of the warbling from the other side of the room, her own school dress and white summer sandals, all carefully picked out by all the available light. She knew that her grandmother would hate to be even a visitor to such a place, that she who had so loved fresh air and the farm, who lived and breathed the rhythms of the seasons and the countryside, would sink into despair at being put in such a place.

Despite every effort not to look at the two old ladies seated opposite her, there must have been something about Alexandra that attracted attention, because the one who had been singing stopped suddenly and, standing up, came towards her. Putting out longing hands to the young woman's cardigan-clad arms, she pulled at her in desperation.

'My name's Mary Laughton, you don't know me dear, not really, but I haven't done anything, not anything. It's my daughter that put me in here – says I've gone mad, but I'm not mad, really I am not. Please, please, help me get out. Have you a car, can you take me away? I'm no trouble, they all said I was trouble, but I'm no trouble, really I'm not. Take me away, please, take me out of here!'

The words stopped in Alexandra's mouth as she found herself staring into the old lady's desperate eyes. How terrible to be put away by your family, abandoned to a dull cream-painted room, no familiar voices, nothing to comfort you with its easy familiarity, no piece of furniture or painting to evoke tender memories, no young people to need you.

'I-er-I . . .'

Although she left the despairing hand on her arm Alexandra found herself desperately searching around in her mind for what to say by way of an excuse.

'I-er-I don't have a cer-cer-car, I'm sorry, I-er cer-can't drive.'

Another old woman on the other side of the room stopped rocking herself as she heard Alexandra's young voice. It was as if the sound of younger tones had somehow reminded her of something cheerful and happy, something from her past.

'Miss Stamford?'

As Alexandra turned in answer to the nurse's voice she could not help feeling an overwhelming relief, could not wait to leave the room and follow the nurse quickly down the hospital corridor.

'Grandma?'

She went up to the bed. Her grandmother was staring ahead of her, her hair swept back in a pristine unflattering medical fashion, as if the nurses had wanted her quickly to achieve an anonymous look that they themselves found proper to her age; as if like at some over-strict school, on admission, they had wanted to make her look uniform, the same as all the other old ladies in all the other beds.

'Grandma?'

Betty turned slowly on the pillow and stared at her grand-daughter. She knew she must now look like a frail old lady to Alexandra, not the vigorous old woman that she had once been, but something pathetic, and yet strangely . . . she could not find it in herself to mind. She just wanted to be on her way, to get out of it now.

'Alexandra,' she stated.

Alexandra put out a hand and held that being now held out to her.

'I'm here, Grandma.'

'I know, dear, I can see you; and very nice of you to come.'

She turned her head away and lapsed into silence, staring ahead, unable to continue.

'You'll be out of here soon, Grandma, see if you aren't. I'll get you out of here, really I will.'

Alexandra was struggling to keep the panic out of her voice, but knew she was failing miserably. She should be more grown up. She should be more mature. For heaven's sake, she was seventeen!

'If only you could get me out of here, dear.' Her grandmother turned her head to look at Alexandra once more, a mixture of resignation and despair in her eyes. 'But you see . . . you see, John, your father, has committed me. Says I can't live on my own with you any more, must stay here for the moment, until I start to eat again. Lost too much weight to be responsible for myself. I might have an accident, or set the cottage on fire, or some such.'

'You-you-you can get out of here, Grandma. Get dressed, get up and get dressed and I will take you back to the cottage with me, we'll have tea together, and I'll make you a-a Her-Her-Horlicks the way you like it.'

'No, dear. He has committed me. John has committed me. My own son has committed me.'

Tears rolled down the old lady's now sunken cheeks.

'See those things at the side, dear?' she said finally, when she could speak. She patted the sides of her institutional bed with her old hands. 'Well, these, these are the things they lock you in with at night. Can you see them? See, dear? They're like a child's cot. They lock you in here, and they leave you so you can't creep out at night and find your way home.'

Alexandra stared at the iron contraptions on the side of the bed, her emotions boiling over as she saw the tears once more rolling down her grandmother's face.

'I won't let them do this to you, Gran, I wer-wer-won't!'

The words burst out of her, and later as she walked and ran back through the rain to the cottage, she thought with murderous hatred of her father and Kay Cullen, of their new, smug life together, with Kay calling all the shots, her father going along with everything, Mavis being made to leave; and as she neared the front door of the little thatched house she realised that much sooner than she cared to think her grandmother would be dead, and she would be left quite alone.

Tom knew that it would be hard for him to find another position in a house such as Knighton Hall. Without his mother to apply for a position as a much-needed cook, he quickly became just another young lad desperate for work, wanting nothing more than some sort of roof over his head, some kind of wage, one of many in the long queues staring up at boards, or running to be the first to fetch the earliest edition of the local newspaper, newspaper that he would later wrap around himself to keep warm at night in what passed for lodgings at the run-down house where he was staying.

Grooms' positions were highly prized and few and far between, so he began to apply for any or every situation that might fit him. Assistant gardener, footman, under-butler, but even if he was seen, which was rare, the response to him was always the same. He was too young, too inexperienced, and there was not enough time to train him.

He had never felt lower, or hungrier, not even when, during the war, his mother had been sacked from two positions in a month, and she had finally ended up cooking for a rich old lady who liked to have food set in front of her, which she promptly left, and then expected to be reheated for her, again and again, before she finally and generously donated it to Tom and his mother.

That had been one of the worst places. There were others that had been bad, but none quite as bad as that damp old house with its mouse-infested kitchens and its furniture that seemed to drip with moisture.

Although he tried to keep his spirits up, Tom was all too aware that it was not only inexperience that was keeping him from employment, it was the way he looked. It seemed that the hungrier he felt, the less he had eaten, and the more he had grown, so that for all he was certain that he was intelligent, and his manner appropriately deferential, nevertheless, he no longer looked what his mother would call *suitable*. His old third-hand hacking jacket that had been handed to him as part of his uniform at Knighton Hall was now so short it looked ludicrous. Passing shop windows and trying not to look at himself, he was nevertheless well aware that he looked more like a scarecrow than a hard-working likely young lad who could make himself if not indispensable, at least useful.

'You know your trouble, don't you?' his landlady said to him one day. 'You're going after jobs what have already gone. What you want to go after is a job that's not yet come up. As it happens I know that there's a job coming up, at the nursery up on the hill out of town – it's some walk from here, I tell you, but I know the man who runs it. Mind you, you'll be lucky if you get in there either, seeing it's owned by the Duke of Somerton. They don't take just anyone; even with so many acres of garden to look after, they're strict as can be. Still, if you tell them that Muriel Posnet sent you, and ask for Jim Blakemore, you might be lucky. Mind, I only said "might". Here's the address. And remember, you go in the back gate. Don't dare go up the main drive, not that I think you would.'

She had hardly finished scribbling down the address than

Tom had left her, shooting out of her front door and starting to run and walk along the road that led out of town to the great estate owned by the Duke of Somerton, one of three great estates in which Mrs Posnet had told Tom that the Duke liked to pass his time, but which was nevertheless rumoured to be his favourite.

Muriel Posnet stared at her now closed front door. She had grown quite fond of young Tom O'Brien in the weeks and days since he had first arrived. And, although she herself was hardly rich, having seen that the boy was all but penniless despite his brave airs, she had been careful to pass on any leftovers from her kitchen, leaving them under covered plates in his downstairs windowless room, and allowing him to use her bathroom to wash: trying to give him some sort of chance, which, following his arrival at her house one rainy evening, she had soon realised few people would be prepared to do. And yet, to his credit, he was never late with his rent, and did without sheets and pillowcases on his narrow bed in order to save on the expense of laundry, sleeping instead in an old Army sleeping bag.

'People are still a great deal poorer than the government likes to make out, despite what they say on the wireless,' an old lady remarked out of the blue to Tom as he passed her on the road to the Duke of Somerton's garden. 'A lot poorer. Never mind the war, never mind that farming's on its feet again, there are still people going hungry.'

'I dare say.'

'No, young man, *I* dare say, not you. You're too young to have a say.'

Tom smiled wryly to himself as he walked faster and faster towards what he hoped would be a job. The old woman must have known just how poor he was. Not that he had not become really rather used to hunger in the past weeks: the feeling that his stomach was not part of his body, but a wild animal writhing inside him, longing for just a scrap to chew on. The familiar rack of anxiety, the sleepless nights as he waited for the post to arrive and his mother's precious, hard-earned postal order enclosed with a quickly handwritten note hoping that he was well and would find a good position *soon*. Tom would have liked to have written back to her, but he would not, and could not afford the stamp until he had some kind of work, because not just every penny counted, but every halfpenny, every farthing. His mother would have to wait to hear from him, and the good thing was that the poor soul would know that until he had found another position, stamps and the telephone were out of the question.

He found the back gates to the great estate with ease, and walked up the drive, admiring the beautiful old silver birch avenue, the informal planting of the flowers beneath them, the brightness and calm of this beautifully tended world, a world whose splendour he could sense, even before he came across it.

'Come for the job, have you?'

Mr Blakemore stood six feet four inches in his stockinged feet, so that Tom, six feet two in his cheap shoes, now raised his eyes to him.

But Mr Blakemore was not just a tall man, he was a big man, in every sense. Everything about him was large. His head large beneath a faded tweed cap, his ears like wings either side of large eyes, his nose vast and sporting a large wart, his lips large, which when he parted them showed large teeth.

At that moment Mr Blakemore was standing outside his favourite demesne, somewhere that Tom would very quickly come to realise was most definitely Mr Blakemore's own little kingdom, namely the gardening sheds and buildings, green-houses and cottages that housed him and many of the other workers on the estate.

'Have you had any experience of this work before, lad?'

Tom considered telling a lie, and then rejected the idea, but only because he shrewdly realised that his landlady might well have told Mr Blakemore that he had none.

'Not with young plants, no, sir. What I have done is to work on country estates in stables, in woodsheds, wherever needed, that's what I have done.'

'You're a Hampshire lad, judging from your accent.'

'It's where I was born, sir, but I have migrated a great deal since then, my mother being a widow woman and cook, we have worked in many different places. Derbyshire, Surrey, Yorkshire, many places.'

'Oh yes?' Mr Blakemore looked uninterested. 'My father was a Hampshire man. Any references, lad?'

Tom's heart sank, but once again, after a fractional pause, he opted for the truth, the whole truth and nothing but the truth.

'No, sir. No references, and not likely to get any from my last position, I am sorry to say.'

At this Mr Blakemore looked more interested.

'Not likely to, lad, and why would that be, may I ask?'

Tom looked straight into the older man's eyes.

'Because, sir, I had the misfortune to catch the master of the house in a place and position that I would not have wanted to catch anyone, sir, seeing that the master is a married man, sir.'

There was a short silence during which Tom had the feeling that he could hear birds from around the estate singing louder than before, that the warm spring breeze, unnaturally warm for the time of the year, was in fact tropical, and that the quiet of the moment would soon be shattered by Mr Blakemore's voice. He'd ask him to walk straight back down the long avenue of silver birch trees, and so on to the old country road which would lead Tom eventually to his ground-floor room, to his army surplus sleeping bag, to yet more long treks around the town in search of work.

But then came the sound of a rumble from deep inside the big-boned man in front of him. It was a sound that seemed to come up from a wall of tweed-covered flesh, making its way to the top, to the large head that was suddenly thrown back with a ferocious force as Mr Blakemore laughed. It was a thunderclap of laughter, and Tom stared at him in astonishment as the laugh seemed to rumble on and on, reverberating between the cottage walls opposite, bouncing off the greenhouses and sheds, until like a real clap of thunder, it finally rolled merrily away towards the outer reaches of the estate.

'Well, lad, my, my, my!' Mr Blakemore wiped his eyes. 'My, my, my, you have given me the best laugh of the month, surely you have. You have a way wiv you, I would say, and that's the truth, and I like a lad wiv a way wiv him, I do. So, when would you like to start, lad?'

'Right now, I'd say, sir, if you want me, right now.'

'Follow me. You know hours, do you? Six in the morning to four in afternoon, an hour for dinner, and hop off home for tea, and that's that until next morning. Saturdays same, Sabbath is off, naturally. After one year continuous, you have a week's holiday of your choice, but taken in parts is preferable for His Grace as he has a mind to thinking plants can miss you if you turn your back on 'em too long.'

All the time Tom was walking behind Jim Blakemore he was observing the plants either side of the paths, the generous borders filled with spring colour, the espaliered trees, the statuary.

Mr Blakemore stopped suddenly, in the manner of a horse who has suddenly spotted something suspicious. He pointed at Tom's shoes.

'Shoes is no good for this work, lad. You need good thick

boots, is what you need, and good thick socks and a water-proof jacket.'

They were standing in what was obviously the gardening office. Seed catalogues, lists, pencils on string, accounts books neatly stacked on shelves, with dates in gold on their spines, 1931, 1932, 1933, and so on until the war years when they grew slim as reeds and lacked gold spines, only to start again in 1946, growing fatter and fatter as more men returned to their previous occupations and the estate once again came back to life.

'Here is an advance on the year, and nothing to be said, please. Get yourself some good thick boots, and socks, and a waterproof jacket, as I say. Don't want you freezing to death. His Grace doesn't like his gardeners suffering. He always says suffering gardeners lead to suffering plants.'

Tom stared at the money that Mr Blakemore had just handed him, realising that the older man must have guessed from the state of his clothes just how skint he was, and at the same time unable quite to believe the amount of money he had just been handed. It was untold gold to him.

'It's all right, sir. I can manage till wages day,' he said stiffly, handing back the money.

'Course you can, lad, but I don't want His Grace coming by and giving me a wigging when he sees you pricking out seedlings and blue with cold. He's particular like, is His Grace. And likely to remain so, seeing he is unmarried.'

Mr Blakemore nodded his dismissal, while at the same time making sure to fold Tom's hand around the precious five-pound note.

Tom turned, his hand still clasped around the paper money, realising as he did so that his stomach was telling him what his mind was only just beginning to believe, namely that he would be mad not to take the munificent advance on his wages.

It was only when he was halfway back down the silver birch avenue that his pace started to quicken to a slow trot, and then to a fast trot, until eventually he was running faster and faster towards the back entrance to the estate as he realised that if he reached his lodgings in time he would be able to tell Mrs Posnet that he would be in for supper, and what was more that he could pay her for a full dinner, not just depend on leftovers. And what was *more* dinner might even be steak and kidney pudding, it might even be roast lamb, it might even be boiled gammon with parsley sauce; any of those dishes might be on the menu. But whatever was on the menu, Tom knew that he was going to relish every mouthful, that at long last he was going to be able to gallop into Muriel Posnet's kitchen and, whatever she was cooking, he would be able to inform her for the first time: '*I shall be in for dinner.*'

After that he could go into the town and buy himself a warm jacket, and a pair of thick wool socks, perhaps even two, and that being done, he would turn back to Mrs Posnet's bed-and-breakfast establishment knowing that provided he was careful, hard-working and honest, life could actually start to get better for Tom O'Brien.

It was not getting better for Alexandra. Her grandmother, as Alexandra had dreaded she would, had died after many months during which she neither raged nor moaned at her granddaughter but lapsed into an awful silence which no visit seemed able to alleviate.

'It was peaceful, dear, very. No doubt about that, very peaceful. And not at all inappropriate considering she was of such a good age.'

They were all standing about in desultory groups as people do after funerals. Alexandra nodded in agreement at grandmother's oldest friend, Janet Priddy, at the same time realising that she must also be of a good age because she and grandmother had been thick as thieves for as long as anyone at Lower Bridge Farm could remember. Yet Mrs Priddy was still living in her own home, still had her own furniture around her, her hens and her ducks; she had not been shoved aside by her family, put into a hospital ward, and left to die.

'I just wish I had been at her side, been with her, held her hand.'

Alexandra stared miserably around her. Seeing her palpable sadness Janet touched her on the arm.

'You had just seen her, dear, that is all that matters. People who love you never want you to see them die, they wait for you to leave the room. It's an old country saying that is, and I've never known it not to be true.'

A great shuddering sigh came up through Alexandra's body. She did not know what was going to happen to her. She knew even less than when she had left the farm and moved into Kay Cullen's cottage with Grandma.

Perhaps Mrs Priddy understood this because she went on, 'Well, I dare say not much has changed for you, as far as I can see, dear. I mean you can just stay as you are, I should have thought, for you certainly can't move back to the farm, not now that your father's expecting a baby with this new wife. With her.'

Mrs Priddy gave a disparaging jerk of her head towards where Kay, now proudly and very evidently pregnant, was standing beside John Stamford, one hand slipped possessively through his arm, her stomach protruding through her grey flannel spring coat.

Alexandra turned back to Janet Priddy, looking reflective. It was true she could not go back to living with her father and Kay, but neither did staying on at the cottage hold much appeal, especially since her grandmother had gone. The whole point of the cottage had died, and now she had no one to visit daily, no one over whom she could try to fuss, making her scones and little biscuits, cakes and fresh sandwiches, all of which would be barely touched. Pear Tree Cottage seemed less appealing than ever, however cheery its furnishings.

'I-I – er I ther-thought perhaps I will go and stay with my Millington cousins for a little, until I can make up my mind what to do. Grandma left me a hundred pounds, you know.'

'Yes, I do know, dear, and how she did it on the money her son gave her, heaven, and heaven alone, must know. She scrimped and saved as she worked and slaved for that man, and in the end she was set aside as if she had never done anything to help him. I don't know how she didn't take his shotgun and shoot him, really I don't. All those years without a holiday, all those years scrubbing and polishing, helping with the milking and that, and what did she get to show for it? Nothing, that's what Betty got – nothing.'

Perhaps because Alexandra had heard this speech before she now pretended not to hear it at all.

'The last time I was at Knighton Hall, the last time I was the-the-there, Mrs Millington said I was welcome at any time.'

'Yes, but that was then, dear; some time ago. She might not feel so welcoming now. Besides, what about your studies? Shouldn't you be thinking of staying on at school and taking your matriculation, or what they call A levels now, and such like? They all do nowadays, you know, even some of the girls.'

'Ner-ner-no. I left school long ago, in my head, you know I did, Mrs Priddy.'

They both smiled at the truth of this.

'Ner-no, I thought I'd join my Millington cousins, now that Grandma's gone. Maybe I could help out on the estate and things like that, but it would be good to see Knighton again, wouldn't it?'

'Yes, but as I say, will they want you, dear? Will those Millington cousins of yours want you, do you think?'

'Oh yes, I ther-think so. After all, my mer-mother was a Millington,' she reminded Mrs Priddy with sudden pride.

'Yes, dear, but that doesn't always count for as much as you think, not in reality, at least that is what I've always found.'

'My uncle too ter-told me I could cer-cer-come back at any time.'

'Well, that's all right then,' Janet agreed, trying to leave the doubt out of her voice, because as she knew invitations were always fast and loose when no dates had been fixed, but something quite other when a hopeful guest tried to follow them up.

'I think my uncle likes me to visit.'

'Well,' said Janet, still sounding doubtful, 'that's all right then. If you're quite sure.' She turned away, looking sad.

Invitations

Tom's first gardening season had passed swiftly, a season during which he had become accustomed to the routine nature of the work on the old estate, when suddenly there was a flurry of activity up at the big house, and the gardening staff were warned to be on their best behaviour – the Duke's family were coming down to spend the Easter holiday on the estate.

'You must never look up, lad, not when they pass with their guests,' Mr Blakemore reminded Tom. 'Just keep your eyes down. No one likes being gandered at, least of all His Grace and His guests.'

Tom was glad to have been reminded of this, for the big house had hardly been occupied than His Grace, followed by a straggle of his guests, passed after luncheon one day. Tom stared hard at the weeds in his barrow, careful to put it between him and them; but he need not have worried for the guests wandered by him without so much as a glance, and as they did it occurred to Tom that had he been made of stone, as were so many statues in the park, they might have stopped to admire him, but because he was human, they politely ignored him.

'And how is your Orchid House coming along, Bundle?' a

clear English voice asked as His Grace stopped to point out the newly planted arboretum in the distance.

The owner of the voice was so near to where Tom was once more stooped to his work that he could smell her perfume on the clean country air, and hear the rustle of her silk-lined skirt as she passed him.

'I hope your men know how to be hard on them?' the voice went on, laughing lightly.

'Blakemore knew nothing about them when he started, now he knows everything. I told him charcoal, they love charcoal. Like dogs and their biscuits, the black ones are their favourites.'

More light-hearted laughter, then the fashionable party was gone, and walking in such a leisurely fashion that Tom was able to stare after them, mesmerised by the sudden strangeness of their rich clothing, of the women's beautifully cut tweed suits, their hair carefully coiffured, their dogs trotting after them, never letting their mistresses' well-heeled shoes move too far ahead of them.

Of course over his years of growing up he had seen photographs of such women, their perfect profiles staring from the magazines that had lain about the houses in which his mother had cooked, but he had never been so close to them, never realised how different they were even from pretty women such as Tasha Millington, the sort of women for whom his mother had cooked delicious meals, ever since he could remember. These women were something quite other, the ultimate in svelte sophistication, Europe their playground, wealth their ticket on the train of life; they exuded a kind of gloss and patina that Mrs Millington had never achieved. More than that they exuded confidence. It encircled them as if it were some sort of special grace, which perhaps it was.

'His Grace would like it to be known that he is very pleased wiv all the improvements,' Mr Blakemore announced later that Saturday, as the gardening staff all queued up for their wage packets.

Tom, who had always been careful to keep himself to himself, looked up as he heard the general murmur of satisfaction around him, and registered that this was something for which everyone waited with some eagerness to hear; they waited to know how His Grace appreciated their work, waited for news of his appreciation.

'Do we gather from that His Grace is not always pleased?' a pleasant voice from beside Tom asked.

Tom looked round.

'I'm Bob Atkins.'

Bob thrust out a hand for Tom to shake, at the same time staring at Tom with an amiable expression from under a mop of fine blond hair. Tom nodded absently and turned back, determined as always to be taciturn, collected his wage packet from Mr Blakemore's large hands, but said nothing, before finally preparing to walk off towards the town and his lodgings.

'Coming into town? Can I give you a lift?' Bob Atkins persisted, nodding proudly towards a brand-new Morris convertible as he followed Tom back out past the sheds and greenhouses and into the waning light of the early evening.

'I should walk, really—'

'Oh come on, don't be such a goody goody.'

Tom shrugged his shoulders.

'No, I just think that I should walk, that's all.'

'Look, I know I'm not like the rest of you chaps, but I wish you weren't all such snobs about us temporary fellows. It's like being back at school, being put in Coventry, and all that.'

Tom coloured. It was true. There was a line drawn between the temporary people – students on their university holidays like Bob, young men taken on for a few weeks during the spring and summer months – and the permanent staff. He was only observing the unspoken rules.

'Come on, hop in, it's a grand little motor this, you know. Specially with the roof down.'

Tom stared at the green paint, the red leather seating, every aspect of the dapper little car. The offer was irresistible.

'Oh, OK. If you're sure.'

'Sure I'm sure.'

It was grand to lean back against the leather seat and push his cap to the back of his head, feel the breeze blowing into his face through the open car window, listen to Bob crunching through his gears and singing at the top of his voice, before finally stopping some minutes later outside the side entrance to Tom's lodgings.

'Coming on to the pub?' Bob looked round from his driving seat nodding waggishly down the street to the pub sign. 'Best bitter in town, you know, at the Fighting Cock.'

Tom hesitated, not wanting to spend his hard-earned on beer, and then, noting the good-humoured expression on Bob's freckled face, the eager look in his eyes as he stared up at his new companion from under his fringe of straight hair, he relented once more.

'Wait while I leave my boots off and change into my shoes.'

He had no intention of inviting Bob into his plain cream-painted room with its one bed, one chair and the inevitable shared toilet facilities down the garden. Bob seemed to sense this, because he nodded affably at his passenger.

'I'll wait in the pub for you, but get your skates on, won't you? My tongue's getting the size of that gargoyle on the side of the town church.'

The pub was already full when Tom pushed his way towards Bob, so that all of a sudden it seemed to be the jolliest of places.

'Two pints, please, and my mug's the one with the lion on it.' Bob turned and once again grinned at Tom as he started to undo his pay packet to contribute towards the round. 'Don't be daft, Tom. This is my round.'

As Bob picked up his own pewter mug and started to swallow his beer with large grateful gulps, Tom's eyes moved from his own ordinary pub glass to Bob's Adam's apple that seemed to be moving up and down at an incredible speed as he drank. The pint of beer in his own hand suddenly looked much larger and its liquid contents vast. Nevertheless, he picked it up and started to drink.

Alexandra's eyes moved from the wooden dashboard in Douro's car to stare out of the window. Douro had met her at the station, just as he had before, but now he no longer seemed the easy-going, charming man who had been so helpful before; now he seemed strained and anxious, hurrying her out of the station and into the car as if he dare not be late in returning her to Knighton Hall.

They were not far out of the town and heading for the house when he stopped the car and turned to her.

'I am afraid you will find a great deal changed at Knighton Hall during the past year, Alexandra. Your uncle has moved into a cottage on the estate, and only comes up to the house at weekends, for the sake of the children. You see, your uncle is in the process of divorcing your Aunt Tasha, after which she will be leaving Knighton and moving back to London where she is buying a small flat. It is all very sad but, as you know, these things happen, I'm afraid.'

Alexandra dropped her eyes and stared in front of her. She wished he would go on driving while he talked. There was something rather irritating about people stopping a car to talk. Perhaps he realised this, because he turned the key in the ignition, and they proceeded on their way.

'Per-per-haps I shouldn't have come . . .'

'On the contrary, Jessamine and Cyrene, they need some distraction. No, you are all too welcome, I'm afraid. You see, everything must go, your Aunt Tasha will not be very well off after this, however good her lawyer. And new wives, well ·. . . new wives of rich men do not feel very disposed towards the children of the previous marriage. I doubt that any of the children will be very welcome at the Hall at all in a few months' time, or however long it takes. No, not at all welcome. It is just a fact.'

Alexandra stared ahead of her, feeling guilty at having written to her uncle asking herself to stay, or rather taking up his permanent invitation, and at the same time – despite the fact that her own life had changed so suddenly on the remarriage of her own father, not to mention the death of her grandmother – feeling shocked.

As soon as they arrived at the beautiful old house, the changes were evident. No Jeffryes to open the door in his black coat and striped trousers, no sudden sighting of a uniformed maid bearing a basket filled with cleaning materials, no vast flower arrangement on the hall table. No sounds of a bustling household, doors opening and shutting somewhere everywhere, only an odd sort of silence, as if everyone all over the house, even the staff, had gone to their rooms and were lying staring at the ceiling, wondering what would become of them. Perhaps Douro Partridge sensed her surprise at the sudden feeling of emptiness around them, at the bareness of the hall table.

'I'm afraid all the servants have gone, Alexandra,' Douro murmured. They all went, almost as one. It happens, you know. A scandal scares them off, they see change coming, and suddenly they disappear.'

Alexandra turned round and stared at him, realising at once that this was one of the many reasons he himself looked so different, harassed and older, his shoes not polished, his shirt collar frayed at the ends.

'Oh, Alexandra, how kind of you to come, my dear.'

Tasha Millington was sitting beside a dead fire in the library, her hair held back in tight combs, her tweed suit looking tired and creased, as if it had been worn for too many days at a time on far too many consecutive occasions, her face as tightly drawn as her coiffure. She was a sad contrast to the woman to whom Alexandra had said goodbye on her last visit; the woman who had so enjoyed having people come up to her prettily festooned dressing room as she tried on the latest fashions, gossiped and laughed, looking forward to a full social diary, to being not just the centre of her husband's world, but the star of it.

Alexandra stepped forward and kissed Tasha Millington's cold cheek. She herself took one of Alexandra's still-gloved hands and held on to it tightly, both of them realising that Alexandra now looked more suited to their surroundings.

'It is so nice to see you, my dear, so very nice. You were such a bright presence here on your last visit, truly you were. Now everything's changed, so much, too much; so we need your bright presence even more, a great deal more.'

She tried to smile over Alexandra's head at Douro who tried to smile back in his old relaxed way, but also failed. They were neither of them wearing black clothes, neither of them much older, neither of them ill, but as she stepped back from embracing her aunt by marriage, Alexandra had the feeling that perhaps the two older people between whom she was now standing were actually both in mourning, so laden with sadness was the atmosphere in the library.

'I dare say Miss Millington would like a glass of lemonade after her journey, Douro,' Tasha stated, talking to him in the same way that she had been used to talking to the now departed Jeffryes, something which poor Douro seemed to accept as part of their new way of life.

The telephone started to ring, and Tasha was now moving towards it, answering it by bending towards it, almost grabbing it, as if she could not wait to hear who it was, or as if she knew exactly who it might be. Meanwhile Alexandra followed Douro Partridge to the kitchens, which now seemed vast and deserted.

'As you can see not only have the staff all gone, but so has the food and drink. No more of Mrs O'Brien's home-made lemonade, no more of her elderflower champagne, d'you see?' Douro called back to her as he opened and shut endless cupboards in search of drink. 'Ah, here we are.' He produced a bottle of lemon barley water and poured it into a glass before filling it with water from the tap, and handing it to Alexandra.

Alexandra was undeniable thirsty, but unfortunately Douro had poured too much barley water into the glass, and the tap water was tepid, so the drink was by no means thirst-quenching. She sipped at it, remembering with sudden nostalgia exactly how Mrs O'Brien's home-made lemonade had tasted and how delicious it had been, tasting of proper lemons and not too much sugar.

'Mrs O'Brien had to go, along with Jeffryes, and all the rest, well, they went too; everyone's gone, except the dailies, they still come in to clean the place twice a week, but as you can see . . .' Douro looked round the kitchens, his eyes wandering towards the deserted sculleries. 'As you can see, the life has gone out of the place. We miss Mrs O'Brien greatly, especially her roasts and her pastries. Mrs Millington has never cooked, can't even boil an egg and so the meals are pretty scratchy affairs at best, nowadays. She does her best . . .' His voice tailed off. 'Happily the boys are both off in the Army, which is probably just as well. Anthony's so cut up about it all, he won't come home. All happened so quickly really, that was the trouble. One minute we were literally just one happy family, the estate, the house, everyone, and the next . . . well, you can see.' He glanced round the kitchens once again, an expression of sad resignation on his face. 'I shouldn't be saying this to you, but I dare say you will find out anyway. You see' – he looked at Alexandra – 'you see, the worst of it is, your uncle is not allowing Tasha to divorce him for adultery, despite his being quite obviously the guilty party.'

In order perhaps to accompany Alexandra and her barley water, Douro had opened a bottle of whisky and poured himself a glass, which seemed to loosen his tongue.

'Yes,' he continued, 'despite the fact that . . . well, despite obvious evidence to the contrary, Tasha is having to divorce your uncle on grounds of mental cruelty. If she does not it seems she will be even worse off than she is going to be anyhow. Trouble is, as she says, she has never had any money of her own: her parents both died after the war and every-thing went to her brother in the Bahamas, and he is a hopeless alcoholic. She is, as she says, defenceless – has to go along with whatever your uncle says, pretty much. But your uncle is buying her a flat, she will at least have a flat.'

Alexandra now found herself staring around her, wonder-ing if the house too would be sold, or if new people would be found to come in and look after her uncle and his new wife.

'My fa-fa-father ter-too has just remarried.'

'I heard.'

Douro looked uninterested, too preoccupied with the state of play at Knighton Hall to be even vaguely interested in life at Lower Bridge Farm.

'My father's new wife's ex-ex-ex-pecting a baby, so I won't be going back to the farm, I shall have to find a job, perhaps go to London,' she finished hurriedly, before her hesitation could cause her even more embarrassment.

This admission also failed to arouse Douro's interest. He merely stared ahead, his eye focusing on a future devoid of Mrs O'Brien's cooking, perhaps a future devoid of all the benefits to which he had grown so accustomed over his years at Knighton Hall. Seeing this, Alexandra felt a fleeting impatience, for knowing as she did from her grandmother that the Millingtons thought the Stamfords were beneath them socially, she quickly realised from Douro Partridge's indifference that he too must consider the Stamfords not really worthy of his attention.

'Your father's new wife is not the only one to be expecting a new baby, so is your uncle.'

Alexandra dropped her eyes, remembering suddenly that Douro Partridge had a house that he rented on the Knighton Estate, and realising that he must be in fear of losing it. He must be worried that when and if the new woman in her uncle's life moved into the Hall, a new man might be moving into Douro's house. Wives were not the only people who were replaceable.

'Shall we . . . shall we ger-go and fer-find Jessamine and Cyrene ner-now?' she asked suddenly as she saw Douro's hand reaching out once more for the whisky bottle.

'Yes, yes, of course. We must. They will be so pleased to see you.'

Since her cousins did not even bother to stand up and greet her when Alexandra eventually found them lying about their interconnecting bedrooms listening in a desultory fashion to the radio, it was difficult to tell how pleased or displeased they actually were at seeing their cousin.

'I'll bring your suitcase up later,' Douro told Alexandra as he left her at the door to their suites of rooms, once more seeming to take on the role of the butler.

'Shut the door, Douro!' Jessamine shouted from her half-prone position, but as the door remained half open she was forced to go to it herself and slam it. 'Bloody man!'

'I don't know why you're here, really,' Cyrene told a now bewildered Alexandra. 'They should not have let you come, Mummy and Douro should not have let you come. I mean, can't you see everything's changed?'

'Yes, yes, of cour-course I ca-ca-can.'

'Everything's gone,' Cyrene continued, seeming not to hear her reply. 'All the servants have fled. Frightened they were going to get caught up in the divorce, I say. Frightened they were not going to be paid, I should think. They just grabbed their wages and a lot of the silver spoons and some of Mummy's jewellery she'd left lying about, and got the hell out, and you can't blame them, not with all that was going on, all the shouting and screaming. Mummy trying to take an overdose, the doctor being called, and I don't know what.'

One of Cyrene's long, tanned legs moved up and down on the bed constantly, up and down, up and down, restlessly, so that finally, seemingly in response to its demands, she too moved, and started to walk up and down the room.

'Oh do shut up, Cyrene! Shut up that walking! Shut up, I tell you!'

Jessamine, on hearing her pacing up and down, sprang off her own bed in the next-door room, and walking through pushed Cyrene back down on to her four-poster bed.

'Don't do that!'

Cyrene sprang up, and they started to punch each other, and pull at each other's hair making both their Cavalier King Charles spaniels run round them, tails wagging, thinking it was a game.

'Ster-ster-stop it, stop it, both of you!' Alexandra tried to push her way between them. 'Ow! Wer-wer-wer-will you both stop that! Please!'

Eventually, reluctantly, they parted, both panting, both unrepentant, waiting only to start again at any moment.

'This is ner-ner-not going to help!' Alexandra stared from one to the other of them. 'Really. It's ner-ner-not going to help. I know you're ber-both pretty angry at what's happening ter-ter-to your parents, at what's happening to you, but hurting each other is not going to help, really it's ner-ner-not.'

'What do you know about anything, Alexandra Stamford? You know nothing, you know less than nothing, you're just a country bumpkin who likes to hang up her hat wherever she can.'

Jessamine spat out the words, but in the end walked unwillingly back to her own bedroom, and lay down on her bed looking flushed and miserable. Alexandra followed her.

'Look, I ner-ner-know, it's true, I don't know mer-much, and I der-don't mind what you call me, but I do ner-ner-know a bit, because mer-my father has just remarried, and I had to leave home with my grandmother and live in his girlfriend's cottage, and then he per-put Grandma into an old people's ward, which broke her heart, and so she der-died. And now my stepmother is having a ber-baby, and they don't really care what happens to me, because people who get mer-married and have ber-babies together forget all about everyone else, my grandmother ser-said. She said when people get married and have ber-babies they go off into a different land, and only cer-come back when they're quite old, and the children have grown up, and all the ner-nesting is over. So I know what it's like to have to leave home, leave everything behind and start again, really I der-do.'

But Jessamine was not listening, and neither was Cyrene, they were both crying.

'They've taken the horses and sold them, the stables are empty, and Douro says our dogs may have to be put down, because Mummy absolutely won't have dogs in London, she says it's too cruel, and anyway we will all be out all day, and she won't do that to them; and she won't pass them on to anyone else who might be cruel and try to sell them. So they may have to be put down.'

Alexandra stared at the younger girl's tear-stained face as she hugged the small brown and white Cavalier King Charles spaniel, which was now on her knee.

'Who are *they*?' she asked with sudden pragmatism.

Cyrene sat up.

'Everyone. Mummy, Douro, the lawyer people. Everything has to be sold, before Daddy can start again with his new – his new person.'

'Thing!' Jessamine shouted. 'His new *thing*.'

'She won't have anything around that has to do with us. Anthony and Rufus have had to choose anything they want, and Mummy and us too, and everything we can't use will go into storage, and then she will move in after the divorce, when they're married, and nothing is to remind her of us.'

'Lucky Daddy is so rich, isn't it?' Jessamine added in a sarcastic voice. 'Otherwise what would he do? He might have to get a job or something. He might not be able to get rid of us all at a moment's notice, and ruin Mummy's life, make us all go and live in London in a beastly flat, so isn't it lucky he is so rich?'

'No, it's ner-not lucky at all, it-it's very *unlucky*,' Alexandra agreed. 'And I don't think you should have to leave your home, I think that's terrible. It's terrible for you to have to go and live in London, and terrible to have the horses sold. And terrible for the stable staff too, they will mer-miss the horses so much. What will happen ter-to them, I wonder?'

'Oh, they've gone anyway. Westrup died, you know. And the oik got the sack. Poor Oik, Daddy said he was found misbehaving in a barn. Like master like servant, Mummy said. Mrs O'Brien was given the sack ages ago, and has gone to work for a lady in Norfolk, lucky woman her. God, Mummy is such a rotten cook, all we have is either a boiled egg and fingers, or bacon and cabbage, she doesn't seem to know how to do anything. She can't even make Yorkshire pudding.'

'Oh her-her-heavens, really? Well, that's one-one thing I can do, I can cer-cook, and I can cook quite well.'

There was a short pause while two pairs of reddened eyes stared round at Alexandra.

'How do you mean?'

'I was ter-ter-taught to cook by Mavis, my grandmother's old cook; she taught me to cook every rainy day there was, and on Sunday mer-mornings after church I would always der-der-do the vegetables and help with the puddings. Queen of puddings, roly poly pudding with treacle on top, I can make them all. I could make per-pastry when I was knee high to a grasshopper. Mer-Mavis used to stand me on a chair, eight ounces of flour, four ounces of fat, a per-pinch of salt if it's for steak and kidney pie, a per-pinch of sugar and a squeeze of lemon if it's for apples, or apples and blackberry. Deliciously light, plenty of air, and not a thought of it der-doing anything except melt in your mouth.'

Without realising it Alexandra was mimicking Mavis's voice as she had heard it when she was a child, and as she did so she imagined she was back in the old flagstoned kitchen at Lower Bridge Farm – a floor that Kay Cullen had already had removed in favour of black and white lino tiles. But as she finished speaking it seemed to Alexandra that she could hear the rain flinging itself against the diamond-paned windows, and feel the warmth of the old cream-coloured Aga behind her, as she watched Mavis, her thin gold wedding ring carefully removed and hanging on the dresser hook, her large-boned hands sifting carefully through the flour before she nodded to Alexandra to add a little water from the jug to the mixture they were both watching so carefully.

'Come on, coz!' Cyrene was off her bed and had started dragging Alexandra after her. 'What are we waiting for?'

'What do you wer-wer-want? What do you *want*?'

Alexandra stopped, standing stubbornly facing Cyrene.

'We wer-wer-want you to cook for us,' Jessamine commanded, at the same time mimicking Alexandra, 'and we-we're going to eat what you cook, and you can stay here as long as we der-der-do, no matter what Daddy or his stupid lawyers say, because if you can cook we aren't going to let go of you, Alexandra Stamford, and that is certain.'

Alexandra started to laugh because she always tried to take people mimicking her in good part, but also because she knew now that she was wanted at Knighton Hall, and that was terrific.

She followed both her cousins down the wide staircase to the marble-floored hall, and so through the green baize doors to the kitchens and the sculleries, where they proceeded to dart about trying to find flour, and lard, and every other kind of ingredient.

Later they would watch Alexandra cooking them a steak and kidney pie, baked potatoes and chopped cabbage, which they would not eat, but would wolf down, as if they had not had a decent meal in weeks, which it seemed they had not, because – '*Mummy can't even boil an egg*'.

Changes

Tom stared up at Mrs Posnet. She was looking sanguine, amused, afffectionate even.

'Here, you'd better have these, and then drink this,' she commanded, putting a large cup of black coffee, a glass of water, and two aspirin down on the side table beside his bed.

She stood back and stared at Tom, her expression unchanged.

'You stuck one on with young Bob Atkins last night,' she continued as Tom sat up feeling sicker than he'd ever felt in his life. 'And now you're paying for it. Luckily, happily, you passed out before you could wolf down my steak and kidney pie, so that was God smiling down on both of us, weren't it?'

Tom sat on the side of the bed and put out a trembling hand for the aspirin, which he took and duly swallowed.

'Now for the coffee,' Mrs Posnet went on in a maternal voice, 'and after that I should lie back down again while your head clears. You want to watch that Bob Atkins,' she went on, 'he's always been a bit of a lad, specially now he's been at university. Students. They learn everything except what they should at those places. I don't know why anyone bothers with them, really I don't, but I do know you're a sober-sides, so just watch him in future, and steer your boat past his of a Saturday night. He's got a stepfather indulges him with motor cars and the like and you've got nothing but what you stand up in. That's the difference between you two, and always will be.'

Tom nodded as he sipped the dark sweet coffee, not paying much attention, wondering only if he would ever again be free of pain.

Later Mrs Posnet looked in on him and, seeing him dressed and shaved, asked him in for Sunday lunch.

'And no charge. Today you're my guest, young man. All the other lodgers are out, and seeing that I'm on my own, I'm grateful to have you for company.'

She cooked them a splendid roast lunch followed by a magnificent lemon meringue pie, all of which – in the light of how ill he had felt earlier – Tom was surprised to find that he relished.

'You'll be better for that.'

They both sat back after the last piece of pudding had been demolished and Mrs Posnet smiled as Tom sighed with satisfaction.

'You sound like a horse, young man.'

Tom looked across at her.

'I used to look after horses, perhaps it's catching.'

Mrs Posnet nodded.

'Perhaps it is. My late husband, his mother fed him goat's milk when he was young, because cow's milk brought him out in a rash, and blow me if he didn't look like a goat. Everyone said so. I used to say on Monday when I hung out the washing that I wouldn't have been shocked to find him eating the socks off of it.' She smiled. 'And he was as nimble as a goat too. No, there's a lot to be said for what's in a baby's bottle, and more to be said for what's in the soil. They say that round here. "*It's all in the soil.*"'

Tom smiled at that. He was used to hearing Mr Blakemore

saying, 'It's all in the soil,' at least once a day, if not twice. Mr Blakemore would murmur it in passing, half to himself, and half to anyone who happened to be near by.

'Do you know, young man, that's the first time I've seen you smile since you arrived here?'

Tom stared at her.

'And it's no good you staring like that. You're that serious, not like a young person at all. But doubtless with a full stomach and a job to go to we'll see more of that smile, but less of Bob Atkins, eh?'

She started to clear the dishes, and Tom stood up at once to help her.

'Your mother trained you well, didn't she?'

Tom dropped his eyes. His mother. He had only heard from her once since she had been dismissed from Knighton Hall and gone to Norfolk. She had sent him a card hoping that he was all right and reassuring him that she had found a good new position in Norfolk with some people called Stirling-Jones, and would keep in touch, which of course she had not, because Ma always did have trouble writing letters. Once she was in a new position it was as if the writing of a letter reminded her of yet another change of address, of yet another new position which she would have a hard job holding down. So she just sent postal orders and scribbled on the back of envelopes.

Tom resolved he must write to her; he had her address. He *would* write to her. He would write and tell her there was no need for her to send him any more money. He hurried through the drying up knowing that he should have done as much weeks ago, but he was too busy holding down his own job. He suddenly knew he had to hear her voice, had to know how she was exactly, that a letter would never do.

*   *   *

'I wonder if I could speak to Mrs O'Brien, please?'

'Mrs O'Brien no longer works here . . .'

Tom pushed some more money into the coin box.

'But she must work there.'

'Not any more she doesn't.'

'Have you any idea where she might be? Have you any forwarding address for her, please?'

'Whom am I speaking to?'

More money spluttered into the box before Tom could continue.

'Her son. Thomas O'Brien. I'm her son.'

'Oh yes, she said she was going to stay with you, that's what she said. More than that I can't say, I'm afraid. And Mrs Stirling-Jones is away in the United States, so that's all I can tell you, I'm afraid. They terminated their relationship somewhat abruptly, if one can say that? Something to do with broken dishes at a dinner party, and more than that I won't say.'

'Thank you, thank you very much.'

Tom replaced the receiver and burst out of the public telephone box feeling numb, his headache of the morning swiftly returning, despair and bewilderment jostling themselves for position in his heart. Why hadn't his mother let him know she was leaving Mrs Stirling-Jones's employment? Why hadn't she searched out Tom at Mrs Posnet's house? She knew where he was. They could have talked about everything. He could have helped her find a new job. Instead she had just disappeared.

He walked slowly back to his room, knowing now what must have happened, knowing that his mother must have fallen off the wagon. That's what 'dropped dishes' always meant: if she was dropping dishes she must have succumbed to tasting some sauce with wine in it, as she had that last time when she actually passed out when she was first at Knighton Hall, and then again when the second cook was off sick and she had tasted the sauce by mistake. Anything could set her off, he knew that as well as anyone.

'*Just don't taste anything, Ma. Get someone else to taste for you, really. Just don't taste anything.*'

When he was a little boy following his mother round England, listening to her passing off her drinking problem and frequent dismissals as mere misfortunes or twists of fate, when he was traipsing after her, pretending to like always being at new lodgings, forever moving in and out of new staff cottages as Ma took on yet another job, Tom, young as he was, had soon come to realise that his mother's constant problems could not be entirely due to the war.

'Your mother actually has an allergy to anything with alcohol in it,' a kindly doctor had at last taken the time to explain, as the war, and with it his mother's frequent excuses for their equally frequent moves, had at last come to an end. 'A violent allergy. One taste and it will always have a terrible effect on her. You must see that your mother never even has cough medicine, young Tom, not even a mouth rinse, nothing with alcohol in it, or she will become unstable. It's not her fault. It's a disease, an allergy, nothing to be ashamed of, just a fact, and as long as you look out for her, she will be fine, really she will.'

Tom had looked out for her, but since he was occasionally forced to attend some local school or another, looking out for his mother was not always possible. And now it had happened again. Because he had not been able to look out for her, had forgotten to ring her, she had disappeared, but to where? Suddenly the world seemed so damned big, so vast and so empty, the despair in him deepened into panic.

'What's the matter, young man?'

Mrs Posnet eyed him from the door. She was not so stupid that she had not noticed his reaction to his mother being mentioned, and how, soon after, he had disappeared to the telephone box on the corner, and now was back looking as if he had lost his job.

'It's nothing.'

Tom went to walk past her, but Mrs Posnet stopped him.

'Not nothing, not nothing at all, young man, I can see that. Is your mum not well?'

'My mother's left her job again, disappeared, not left any new address. I don't know where she is, where I'll find her. She must have been given the sack again,' he ended bitterly.

Mrs Posnet felt embarrassed for him, and perhaps because of this she picked up her old pre-war kettle and quickly filled it, which was always the first thing she did when she had to think of the right reply.

'Don't worry, young Tom, if she needs you she'll be back to you in a trice. No news is good news, eh? We must always assume the best until we hear to the contrary.'

Tom turned away, nodding, despite the fact that he knew in reality this was far from being the case. But he could not say as much to his landlady, could not tell her that his mother was an alcoholic, that she might be insensible somewhere, anywhere, lying in a ditch unconscious, as he had once found her, or in some bus shelter or on a railway station, passed out.

'There we are, tea with two sugars, get that down you, and stop looking like the world's come to an end, because it hasn't, at least not yet. Your mother may have found love, she may have gone for a new job, she may have tried to write to you and the letter got lost. Cheer up. Down in the mouth does no one any good, eh?'

Alexandra could not look her uncle in the face, so she found herself staring instead at the top button on his waistcoat. When she did manage to raise her eyes to his face, when he was not looking at her, she saw at once that he had the same look that her father now seemed to sport. It was strange, because outwardly they both seemed unchanged, both wore the same clothes, both had thick heads of hair that were greying at the sides, both wore country tweeds, albeit of very different designs, but the look on both their faces was precisely the same, and there was an increased swagger to their walks.

'Just as if no man has ever got a young woman banged up before. No reason for a divorce, nothing to do with love, everything to do with conceit,' Alexandra had heard Douro saying bitterly to someone on the library telephone only the previous day.

Douro would not be caught saying such a thing now that Jamie Millington was once more occupying his house, pouring the drinks, generally dispensing bonhomie while, by prior arrangement, until Monday morning once more dawned, his soon-to-be ex-wife Tasha was forced to spend the weekend ignominiously holed up in one of the tenants' cottages on the estate.

'You see, darlings, your father and I are trying to keep everything as normal as possible,' Tasha could be heard saying hopelessly and helplessly, over and over every weekend, as she dutifully packed her overnight bag and prepared to retire to a vacant cottage on the estate.

But of course nothing could be kept remotely normal, least of all the formal meals where the three girls were encouraged to sit silently at the long mahogany dining-room table, at the foot of which, in their mother's place, sat Miss Jennifer Langley-Ancram.

'Miss wher-wher-whatie whatie what?' Alexandra had heard herself asking when she was first told the full name of Knighton Hall's Public Enemy Number One.

Miss Jennifer Languorous-Anagram was what Jessamine and Cyrene called their father's mistress, which was not at all funny, but somehow seemed to cheer them up every time they repeated it, which they did all too often.

Jennifer Langley-Ancram was dark-haired and of medium height. She spoke with an accent so affected that even Alexandra, brought up in far less grand circumstances than at Knighton Hall, could not help observing after first meeting her that it was as if she had swallowed not just a plum, but a whole orchard.

'Well now, and what did you all get up to today?'

Silence as Jessamine and Cyrene stared up the table at their future stepmother.

'We went for a walk,' Alexandra volunteered. 'And we saw pheasant—'

'And we let them out!'

Jamie and Jennifer both stared at Cyrene as if she herself were a pheasant that they would jointly like to shoot.

'You what? I hope that's not true, Cyrene?'

'No, of course it's not. Someone else had let them out.' Jessamine smiled first at her father and then at Jennifer. 'So there was nothing to do but watch them run about, poor things. Once they're in the wild again they just don't know what to do with themselves.'

'See to it in the morning, would you, Douro?' Jamie turned to his estate manager, reproof in his eyes.

In return Douro nodded, his eyes firmly on his soup plate. With the advent of Jennifer to the house at the weekends, had also come the hiring of a weekend cook, and a good cook at that.

Jennifer stared down the table at Jamie.

'There is a great deal to be done at Knighton Hall, it seems,' she said, over-enunciating her words in such a way that it was as if she were speaking down the table to her husband-to-be in some sort of code.

Jamie smiled appreciatively down the table back to her,

but his smile disappeared as Jessamine suddenly and with surprising and dextrous accuracy threw the contents of her wine glass in her stepmother's face.

No one would ever quite know what occasioned such barbarity. Perhaps it had been the annoyingly smug expression on Jennifer's face, perhaps it was the way she had said 'Knighton Hall' as if she had mentally already moved into the house, and was setting about making it hers, but whatever it was, there was one undeniable fact: the wine was sticky. It was a type of ginger wine that Mrs O'Brien had been in the habit of making for the older children, a recipe she had copied from a very old book that had a comforting amount of sugar: good for long winter days spent outside, good for tucking into your saddle bag before you set off on a ride.

'Oh my God! You little bitch! Oh my God!'

Jennifer, her face and carefully styled hair covered in the sticky liquid, fled the room as they all stared open-mouthed at first Jessamine, and then her father.

'How dare you! How dare you! Go to your room! And don't come down again, not ever, do you hear? I don't want to see you again.' As he looked round the table and realised that the rest of the assembled company were quite obviously struggling not to dissolve into hysterical laughter, he added, 'Any of you. I don't want to see any of you again. You can all get the hell out of here. And that includes you, Douro. All of you. Go!'

One by one they all put down their heavy linen napkins and trooped out of the dining room, leaving only Jamie who sat on by himself staring down the table to the place where his wife-to-be, only minutes before, had been presiding so happily. He would not stand another moment of such behaviour. Jennifer was the love of his life, and the only way to get the message through to them all was to rid Knighton Hall of the lot of them, even Douro, even his old friend and estate manager must go. He had lost his touch, Jamie was sure of it.

Upstairs, back once more in their suites of rooms, all of which had a strangely desolate air, as if they had already packed up and left, the girls sat about their beds knowing that they had nothing to do now but climb into them. No one moved, only stared round at each other, all of them feeling and looking over-dressed for that time of day, but for once unable to think of what to say to each other, wondering all the time what was going to happen next, while at the same time knowing that whatever it was, it was definitely not going to be good.

'You shouldn't have done that, Jessamine . . .' Cyrene said at last.

'No, I shouldn't,' Jessamine agreed, but then, looking across at Alexandra, she smiled suddenly and gloriously. 'But, you must admit, it was really fantastic, wasn't it? I mean, Languorous-Anagram's face! It was funny, wasn't it?'

There was a small silence as the three of them remembered the look of total shock on Jennifer's face, and then they all burst out laughing. They laughed until their sides ached from laughter, they laughed because it had been such a splendid moment, and finally they laughed because their hearts were breaking. It was the end, and they knew it. The old regime, the remains of the first family were about to be split up for ever, making way for what in time would become the more important second family. They had all had it long, long ago, and really Jessamine's brave gesture of defiance had only precipitated the inevitable.

Two days later Tasha announced that they would all be leaving the Hall as soon as possible. She spoke in a low, flat, expressionless voice, as if she had been through an emotional mangle so many times that even she could recognise that she was quite flattened, dried out, ready only to be shelved. In other words she was now without hope, and seemed to know it.

'We must all go rather quicker than we had thought.' She turned to her eldest daughter. 'Jessamine's silly behaviour at dinner the other day has rather speeded things up, I'm afraid. Not that it matters particularly, for really, what *does* it matter? We would all have been booted out some time soon anyway. It's poor old Douro I feel sorry for, he's been at Knighton ever since he was quite a young man. Started on the estate, working for Jamie's father, and now Jamie. But there you are, these things happen. Nothing is for ever, particularly since the war and the wretched government bringing in all those death duties and taxes, as if the country has not endured enough. I will be in London, at the flat, until I can find something else, but there are only three bedrooms, so no room for Alexandra or the poor dogs, I'm afraid.'

She turned sadly to Alexandra who nodded sympathetically. She would not have expected to go with Tasha to London.

'It-it's all rer-right, Aunt Tasha, I've fer-found a job anyway.'

They all three stared at her as if she had suddenly announced that she was becoming a nun. No one in their family, three sets of eyes seemed to be saying, had ever had a *job* before: she was quite obviously the first.

'You already have . . . you already have a – job?' asked Tasha, uncertainly.

'Yes.' Alexandra tried not to sound proud, but knew she would fail. 'Yer-yer-yes, I ler-looked in the *Der-Daily Telegraph*, and I rer-rang up the number, and I have fer-found a job in Sussex, working for a very ner-nice old lady. She wants somebody—' Alexandra stopped, knowing that she could not say 'to live in and clean for her' because to do so would be to risk shocking Tasha. 'She wer-wants somebody to help her arrange fer-flowers, and check in her guests. She runs a private her-hotel, I ther-think, something like ther-that,' she added, quickly inventing something that she thought would not sound too servile. 'Remember when I went to London? We-well, that's when I got the job.'

'A private hotel? Is that quite nice, Alexandra?'

Tasha looked alarmed.

'Oh, very ner-nice. Her ner-name is Mrs Smithers, and she used to have horses, until her husband der-died.'

This information seemed to soothe Tasha's evident fears for Alexandra, particularly the mention of horses, and the fact that the lady in question had a nice English name like 'Smithers'.

'Well, that is good, Alexandra. Well done. I only hope that when we get to London, when we leave, that Jessamine and Cyrene will be as quick off the mark as you have been. Imagine – we all thought you'd gone to London to enjoy yourself. What a good girl you are.'

Alexandra smiled. She wanted desperately to hug Tasha for saying such a kind thing, but she did not because she knew that Tasha would not like it. It would not be the kind of thing that she understood. Instead Alexandra turned away from the sight of Tasha's cashmere twin set with its missing button, from her hair that she no longer went to London during the week to have styled, her fingernails that were no longer manicured at one of the top salons, but were now plain and unvarnished and cut short like those of a child.

'Now, I think we should all go and cheer Douro up, don't you?' Tasha suggested, sighing. 'Poor fellow's leaving later today. I think we should take him a bottle of champers and make sure that he has a jolly good send-off, don't you?'

Having raided the wine cellar, they all trooped dutifully off to Douro's house where the removal men had already packed up his possessions of years, where his guns stood ready to go, where his dog, perhaps for the first time in years, was wearing not just a collar, but a lead too.

'I say, jolly good of you, really very good of you.'

Douro's smile was such that if he had not been smiling with such determination, his face might have broken in pieces.

'We've robbed the cellars for you, Douro!'

Tasha seemed to have got back some of her old zest, because she bounded determinedly up the steps to meet him in the hall. The girls followed her, all three of them clutching a bottle of champagne in each hand.

'Not only are we going to drink all this champagne, but, Douro, we have brought you some of the old man's best claret, best port, best vintages. He'll be furious when he finds out at the weekend, but by that time, we will all be gone, so what can he do about it?'

Douro started violently as he saw two of the men from the estate pushing wheelbarrows of wine.

'Oh, no, Tasha, no!' He looked from her to the wheel-barrows and back again. 'No, no, you mustn't bang them about, you'll ruin them!'

Tasha stared at Douro and then gave a sudden shout of despairing laughter, her once pretty face distorted with bitterness.

'Who cares? For God's sake, Douro, who cares whether or not we ruin the wine? We're all ruined anyway!'

Before she left for her first job, Alexandra had one more duty to perform which she did with the same assiduous care that she had demonstrated before leaving Kay's cottage for Knighton Hall. She helped Jessamine and Cyrene smuggle their dogs away from the Hall.

'Mummy says we must take them to the vet tomorrow and have them put down, because it's kinder than giving them to someone who wouldn't treat them well or who would pass them on to someone who would be cruel to them, perhaps starve them and beat them.'

Alexandra looked down at the two brown and white spaniels.

'Wer-wer-well I asked Mrs Smithers and she says it is fer-fine for me to bring them, because they'll be in the ber-basement with mer-me. I will look after them for you, and when you're ber-both able to have them, I will ger-give them back to you.'

'Yes, but you mustn't tell Mummy, she wouldn't understand.'

'Wer-wer-what do you mean?'

'She honestly has a real thing about lending horses or dogs. Better to have them put down, *always, always, always*, she always says that. She has made the appointment with the vet, Douro says.'

'In that case I had ber-better leave wer-with them now – ber-before she comes back, hadn't I? Get an earlier ter-train to Deanford.'

They could all see the sense in this, but because the moment of parting was coming a day earlier than they had expected, Jessamine and Cyrene looked at each other, and then down at their beloved dogs.

'I suppose you'd better. I'll call a taxi, before Mummy comes back from seeing the lawyer. Oh, *why* she doesn't fight for herself better—'

'You know very well, Jess, it's because she has no money. She has to do what Daddy says, or he told her he will go and live abroad in the Bahamas or somewhere, and she will not get any money out of him, ever. She *keeps* telling you that, so do shut up about it.'

'I just don't understand.'

'Because you don't want to, that's why; you just don't

want to,' her sister told her, turning away, shrugging her shoulders.

The sisters helped Alexandra fetch her suitcases from her room, and then they all stood about awkwardly in the deserted hall waiting for the taxi to arrive, none of them knowing quite what to say to each other.

'Goodbye, Rupert, goodbye, Rodney.'

They handed the two spaniels into the taxi cab to sit either side of Alexandra.

'Don't forget that Rupert likes to have a Rich Tea biscuit every night—'

'And Rodney likes the black ones from the Spillers' bag—'

Alexandra looked back at her cousins standing forlornly in the drive as the taxi pulled away from Knighton Hall. In an effort to cheer them she held each of the dogs in turn up to the back window waving their paws up and down, but Jessamine and Cyrene had both turned back into the house, and she knew from the way they were hurrying up the steps to the front doors, not looking back, that they must both be crying.

Tom was turning over the earth in the Long Border when he heard a woman's voice behind him. The owner of it seemed to be sighing as she spoke, as if despite the warmth of the day, the flowers, the blue sky, she was unhappy.

'I do love delphiniums, there's something about the blue of them that is like no other.'

Tom turned and found himself gazing into a pair of eyes staring up at him from under a straw hat. They were so beautiful that even the superb herbaceous border, currently at its summer best, seemed to pale beside their perfection. Their blue seemed to out-blue the very flowers their owner appeared to be admiring. But it was not just the beauty of the young woman that was making him a prisoner in the place where he was standing, it was the mirror she was holding up to him.

For the first time Tom was seeing himself reflected in a young woman's eyes. There was nothing teasing or provocative in her gaze, as there had always been in Miss Jessamine's eyes, nothing flirtatious, as there had been occasionally with village girls, or maids that worked in his mother's kitchens; instead as he stared down at her, Tom saw himself as she was seeing him.

For the first time he found himself staring at a tall, muscular young man with a firm set to his mouth. Hours of working in the heat of the sun had tanned his skin to a rich brown, setting off his large grey eyes and emphasising the auburn streaks in his dark brown hair. For the first time too he understood with a sense of shock that someone was looking at him as if he were not just some gardening boy, but a beautiful young man. For some reason at that moment who he was in the pecking order of the estate did not seem to matter, and the realisation momentarily took the breath from his body, as if he had been punched.

'Florazel? Florazel?'

It was a male voice calling, deep, resonant, insistent, but Tom stood on against his will, mesmerised, for the mirror had turned from his image to hers. He had never, ever seen such a beautiful woman, not even in pictures. It was not just the cold, clear blue of her eyes, which did not match but vied with the colour of the delphinium that she seemed to be sighing over, it was the delicate tones of her white skin, which he knew, should he have the nerve to lean forward and stroke, would have a slight, soft down on it, like the fruit in the Peach House. The nose was classically straight and set above lips that were beautifully shaped, the sides tilting upwards above a chin that was perfectly proportioned.

Of course he did not know, and perhaps would not even

have been interested in the fact, that Lady Florazel was a famous beauty. He only knew that, in a matter of seconds, he had become impassioned by her aura, by the mirror she was holding up to him, by her intoxicating difference. He also knew exactly what was going to happen next, long before they started to kiss.

'You're up earlier and earlier, young man.' Mrs Posnet turned at the kitchen range, her hand as always ready to reach for the old-fashioned kettle. 'I don't know why you bother to go to bed if you're going to get up this early of a morning,' she added, smiling.

'Don't worry about breakfast for me, Mrs P.'

Tom turned at the door trying to look and sound innocent.

'Not skipping breakfast yet again?'

'I'll get something on the way, and it means I can get on quicker. In this hot weather if I don't get there and open the vents there'll be a disaster.'

Mrs Posnet stared at the back door, which had now closed quietly behind Tom.

'He's a good lad,' she told the kitchen. 'Too handsome for his own good, but a good lad.'

Meanwhile, Tom, once more the proud owner of a second-hand bicycle, flung his leg over the saddle and pedalled hard. It was true that he wanted to open the vents of the greenhouses and make sure of all the temperatures. It was also true that over the last fortnight he had taken to eating breakfast at the estate, and that it was indeed much quicker. As he cycled along he was satisfied that he had not told Mrs Posnet anything except the truth.

The sun was up and, as it always seemed to do, warmth appeared to produce a pleasant muffled sound, so that not even his footsteps sounded so harsh against the path that led to the Orchid House. The largest and most elaborate of all the Duke's glasshouses, it was already filling up with rarities of which His Grace was most proud. Orchids were once more in fashion, being pinned to the lapels of tight-waisted jackets, carried in clear plastic boxes to the theatre as gifts by rich men for the women they were escorting, or worn with evening dresses. Tom knew that the Duke himself, although unmarried, delighted to give them to his lady visitors to wear on their evening dresses.

'Already here? And I was so hoping to surprise you for once!'

Lady Florazel came into the Orchid House carrying a gingham-covered basket and a rug. She gave a little sigh as she closed the door behind her, after which she smiled up at Tom. As always there was a trace of becoming sadness in her eyes, while as always Tom found himself wordless at just the sight of her beauty, which seemed all the more pure and English compared to the Chinese charms of the exotic flowers ranged behind her on the wooden staging.

'Lady Florazel—' he began, determined to put an end to their meetings at last.

But before he could say any more she had put her arms up to him and kissed him long and sensually, and Tom, realising with reluctance that whatever she was or was not doing she was certainly making a man of him, found himself responding with all the eagerness of a lover who has not been kissed for fully twenty-four hours.

'Now what was it you wanted to say, dear, dear Tom?'

Tom caught her to him, longing to taste the sweetness of her mouth. He had no idea what he had been going to say. It must have been something, but as always since they had met, words seemed such a waste of time, only love mattered, until they both heard the sound of heavy gardening boots on the path outside.

Delicately Florazel withdrew from his love-making and,

swiftly doing up the pearl buttons on the front of her chiffon dress, she turned calmly to one of the orchids. As the door opened, she pointed to it, laughing gaily.

'It is that one that I want to take with me on my picnic breakfast, Mr O'Brien,' she stated. 'I insist that I take that one.'

'I will ask Mr Blakemore for you, Lady Florazel, meanwhile might I suggest that perhaps you take this one for your corsage this evening?'

Tom indicated one of the finer hybrids recently arrived on the estate.

Lady Florazel laughed up at him, her eyes crinkling at the corners, the blue of them quite as startling as the white of the orchid which Tom was now indicating.

'I'm sorry to interrupt your ladyship, but there is an urgent message for young Tom O'Brien here, from Mrs Posnet. She sent her neighbour's child up to find him.'

'Ah well, I must be on my way.'

She passed them both, moving with delicate grace, her picnic basket still packed, her hair only slightly less arranged than it had been when she first entered the glasshouse.

Mr Blakemore stared after her, but once he had closed the door behind her he turned on Tom.

'You stupid young arse! Didn't you learn anything from what happened at your last position? Didn't you learn nothing from that sacking?'

Tom tried to look surprised and failed miserably.

'I – she—'

'You, she, me and the gatepost! And every other darn thing. Wipe that lipstick off your mouth and get back on your bike, back to your lodgings.'

'I'm sorry, Mr Blakemore, really I am—'

Mr Blakemore had never looked bigger, his features never so large, his hands seeming quite ready to strangle Tom for his stupidity.

'No, you're not, but you soon will be if you don't keep your hands off of her ladyship.'

Tom stared at the Head Gardener, bewildered by the ferocity of his fury.

'Lady Florazel's the Duke's sister. You start taking off your trews wiv her and you'll find yourself in the bottom of the lake. Now get back to your lodgings. There's an urgent message waiting for you.'

Gentlefolk

A warm breeze was blowing across from the sea when Alexandra walked up the area steps from her flat in the basement of Mrs Smithers's house dressed in a sober black dress and carrying a mixture of freshly washed aprons, some floral, some starched white. She turned her key in the Yale lock of the door and walked ino the main house, ready to do battle with the household chores.

'Ah there you are, Alexandra. Good morning to you, and a very lovely morning it looks to be.'

Mrs Smithers' small, precisely suited figure always seemed to be coming downstairs to greet Alexandra as she came into the house. More than that she always seemed to be paused on exactly the same step as the one from which she had last greeted Alexandra the day before, and at exactly the same time, giving her maid-of-all-work the impression that she must wait there purposefully posed, perhaps listening for the BBC announcer on her old pre-war large mahogany wireless set to announce the time of nine o'clock, thus enabling her to catch Alexandra out, prove that she was late by a few seconds.

Thankfully Mrs Smithers had never yet caught her maid-of-all-work arriving late, for Alexandra always made it her business to be ahead of time, having first walked the spaniels along the front to the beach, and from there, in and around the many garden squares that made up the seaside town of Deanford.

'In Deanford people expect pre-war standards. We all do, just remember that. Deanford still has standards, unlike other places. It is something that I could never get into the previous maid's head. Standards. That is why the house went to rack and ruin under her aegis. She had no standards. So few people do nowadays.'

Mrs Smithers always made this same speech as she watched Alexandra dusting and hoovering, or struggling to cope with the cobwebs that nestled among the intricate plasterwork bordering the high ceilings of her tall, many-floored Regency house with its sea views and elegant, palely painted exterior.

This particular morning Mrs Smithers yet again stated her maxim about Deanford and its pre-war standards before settling herself on a ruby-coloured mock-eightenth-century damask sofa, one of a pair set each side of the unlit fire, but not before she had taken care to switch off the wireless, as she always did the moment Alexandra entered the drawing room, as if she was afraid something might be broadcast that would not be suitable listening for a youthful maid-of-all-work.

'Alexandra, I have to tell you something of importance today.'

She cleared her throat, holding a heavily ringed hand up to her mouth, preparing for what was obviously going to be a new announcement. She stared down at the jabot of starched lace that she always wore in the top of her jacket and then carefully flicked it to make it sit up, indicating with a slight nod of her head that Alexandra should leave her dusting and come over to her side of the room. This Alexandra did, her heart sinking, as she imagined from the grave tone being used by her employer that she must in some way have fallen below the now famous pre-war Deanford standards.

'The time has come to tell you, I do not think that I can go on calling you *Alexandra*. The name is not suitable for a maid-of-all-work, for many reasons, but most of all because, as you know, there is a statue of dear Queen Alexandra in the centre of our gardens here. It just does not seem right, therefore.' She paused. 'It is confusing, to say the least, for myself and my friends to have you, the maid-of-all-work, so obviously from a genteel background, also share the same name as the square, so I have decided to rechristen you with a more suitable name. I toyed first with Maggie, and then with Tilly, but have finally settled on *Minty*. A nice fresh name for a maid, I think you will agree.'

Alexandra accepted this statement in silence, the way that she found she had come to accept all Mrs Smithers's announcements.

'Yes, my dear friend, the Honourable Martita Hooper-Spenser, she and I decided yesterday when she took tea with me here – and by the way she much enjoyed your Victoria sponge – yes, we decided that Minty would be a very good maid's name for you. So Minty you will be, and I hope that you will be happy to be so called while living under my roof at number thirty-two.'

Alexandra nodded. She really did not care if Mrs Smithers called her Fishface, just so long as she paid her on Saturday mornings and gave her a half-day on Sunday afternoon so that she could take the dogs up to the Sussex Downs, for although her initiation into keeping house for Mrs Smithers had been just a little too real, she was now, after many weeks of hard labour, getting some sense of order not only into Mrs Smithers's household, but into her own life.

It had not been easy. Starting in the basement into which she had been consigned, she had had to struggle with mouse-traps, grime, evil-smelling drains and windows that had probably not been washed since the Crimean War.

Working her way up through the house she had made constant use of a pair of old-fashioned stepladders, placing a plank between them so that she could, in the manner of decorators, wash and clean areas that would otherwise have been well out of her reach. At last – after hours and hours of cleaning, taking down lace curtains that were repellent with the claustrophobic smell of the dust of too many years, removing heavy velvet and brocade curtains and taking them to the dry cleaners, and scrubbing covers and rugs – at last the main house had started to appear as clean as it had always been beautiful.

Meanwhile her employer, as always immaculately dressed, sat by watching with evident fascination the daily grind, the flurry of activity, the energetic wielding of the mops and the dusters by her maid-of-all-work. She watched with such detached interest that Alexandra, now Minty, had the feeling that Mrs Smithers did not hold herself at all responsible for the terrible state of her house. It was as if the spiders and the mice, the flies and the woodlice had held Mrs Smithers at gunpoint during the past months, and that she had been forced to sit by watching a foreign army march all over her kingdom while she, poor defenceless old lady that she was, could do nothing until she had found a new and more energetic maid-of-all-work.

'So, *Minty* it is from now on,' Mrs Smithers stated, half to herself, and then she glanced at the clock. She liked to have her coffee served to her on a tray at ten-thirty, silver pot polished and shining, a doily under the biscuits on the plate. Unfortunately there was still an hour and a quarter to go.

Alexandra continued to dust, moving every ornament carefully, and then equally carefully replacing it without making a noise. Mrs Smithers hated noise of any kind. Mrs Smithers liked to be able to part the long net curtains at her drawing-room windows and watch the people who passed by in the square, undisturbed by the noise of Alexandra at work. The hoovering must always be done after eleven o'clock in the morning when Mrs Smithers took her morning constitutional around the square, cautiously breathing in the healthy ozone of the sea air, while not venturing too near to the briny itself.

The post always came at ten o'clock and was served half an hour later on the coffee tray. For this daily ceremony Alexandra changed her workaday flowered apron for a starched white lace-trimmed one, being sure always to pick the post from the wire box on the other side of the handsome front door and take it up to her employer in a neat pile.

It is just like being in a play, she had written to Frances Chisholm, *but more a comedy than a tragedy I would say! You should see me in my black dress and pinny, and on the days I serve lunch I even have to wear a little starched hat.*

It was one of many long letters that she had written over previous months to Frances Chisholm, longing to hear her news, and news of Cherrypan and the other horses, of life at the stables; but Frances never replied, so that finally Alexandra gave up, realising that she must no longer be of any interest to her old friend.

She also wrote to her father, being sure to mention Kay, but he too never replied, which was hardly surprising since he had never been a letter writer and found it hard enough even to pen a postcard.

'Like the Mer-Mer-Mer-Millington girls, I am not interesting to my father any more, I'm from the fer-first marriage,' she told the two dogs as she stroked them, 'and we all ner-ner-know what that means – ner-nothing.'

Today she served the coffee punctually as usual, the letters propped against the silver pot, and stood back to await further orders. Since there were none she slipped gratefully out of the room, and went to the dining room where she proceeded to lay lunch for two. Yesterday Mrs Smithers had entertained the Hon. Martita, today it would be some other lady of indeterminate age and grand or genteel manners who would be eating her way delicately through Alexandra's fish pie and queen of puddings.

She began to lay out the requisite fish forks and knives, the dessert spoons for the apple tart, and small knives for the cheese and celery, when there was a sound from the first-floor drawing room above. A cry that could only be described as suppressed, but not suppressed enough for Alexandra not to be aware that it must be her employer, and she must be in some considerable distress.

'I am ruined, I am ruined, my shares worth nothing, my husband's company has gone bankrupt. I am ruined Alex— Minty. I am quite ruined, Minty.'

Alexandra hurried into the room to find Mrs Smithers standing holding the mantelpiece and breathing in and out too hard and too quickly, her hand to her chest. The moment she saw her maid-of-all-work she stopped and immediately turned to the mirror above the fire to check her hair and her lace jabot, before sinking back on to one of the plum-coloured brocade sofas.

'What to do? What to do?' she moaned to Alexandra who, actually not knowing quite *what* to do, took one of her hands and started patting it gently, which she imagined was what might be necessary in the circumstances.

'Sal volatile, in my handbag,' she murmured after a few seconds.

Alexandra handed her the old black gold-initialled crocodile bag, which Mrs Smithers always kept close to her side. Then, feeling as if she was robbing her, Alexandra reached dutifully into the handbag and finding a small phial held it out to her employer who promptly and quite elegantly sniffed at its contents, before carefully replacing it and snapping the handbag shut.

'What's to be done?' she asked Alexandra, a most pathetic look in her eye. 'What's to be done? I will have to sell the house, my home will have to go, the place where I have lived for over forty years. Housing has not recovered, nothing has recovered, and now I too will not recover, and all this with the Dowager Lady Inisheen, late of Muldover Castle, coming to luncheon. I shall hardly be able to give her a glass of sherry without breaking down.'

Since Alexandra had twice had to escort the Dowager home very much the worse for wear on account of too much sherry from Mrs Smithers's pre-war glass decanter – not to mention the Hon. Martita who was more than partial to too much gin – she knew their various lodgings to be places that were, at any rate from the outside, shockingly down-at-heel. So, all in all, Alexandra was well aware that Mrs Smithers's concern was not without foundation.

'We mustn't tell anyone.' Mrs Smithers was now rallying. 'You know that, Minty? It must be strictly between ourselves. Until such time that I can pull myself together, no one must know, but no one.'

'No, of cer-cer-course not,' Alexandra agreed, feeling very much as she had done when she had been left to look after her grandmother. 'We will ter-ter-tell no one, no one at all.'

There was a long silence, and then remembering the awful last days of her beloved old relative, her mouth set. She would not, must not, let such a thing happen twice.

'On the-the-the other hand, Mrs Smithers, mer-mer-ma'am, we could make sure that we der-der-do think of something, der-der-double quick.'

In keeping with the look in her eyes the tone of Alexandra's voice must have changed because Mrs Smithers stared at her, surprised. She had never thought to hear dear Minty speaking with quite such quiet authority, despite her poor old hesitation.

'Do you think we can, Minty?' she asked, faintly.

'I ner-ner-know we can. You are not to be ter-ter-turned from your house of forty years,' Alexandra told her. 'No one should be ter-ter-turned out of their house because of some-one else's fer-foolishness. Obviously your husband's company has been mismanaged, and that is ner-ner-not your fault. You will stay in your own home, no mer-matter what. I will see to it,' she finished with a flourish.

Mrs Smithers went to say something and then stopped.

'Do you think we *could* think of something, some way to cope?' she finally asked.

'I ner-know we can,' Alexandra told her briskly, straighten-ing up the cushions on the sofa opposite her, and as she did so suddenly remembering the awful sides of the bed in which her grandmother had been locked every night, and in which she had finally died. 'Stop worrying, mer-ma'am, you will ner-not have to leave your home. It is not going to happen to you, ma'am, really, it is ner-not.'

Mrs Smithers gave a small smile. She loved being called *ma'am*, and they both knew it.

'I suppose there might be a way,' she said, sadly, but the look in her eye was not one of conviction, and she sat back to wait for her friend the Dowager to arrive, which she did, almost too promptly, at twelve-thirty.

Lady Inisheen always arrived wearing precisely what she had worn for luncheon at Mrs Smithers's house the previous week. Her permanent costume was a pre-war shaved-beaver coat, and matching beaver hat, which resembled an RAF cap, worn perched slightly forward, touching her forehead. From under her hat it could be seen that her eyelids were made up with transparent Vaseline that gave them a becomingly shiny look, and her eyelashes combed black with mascara. Her startlingly white face was heavily powdered and her cheeks, in contrast to the powder, heavily rouged. Her thin lips were made up over their natural line, apparently in an effort to give them a fuller look.

While Alexandra took the shaved-beaver coat from her and draped it over the hall chair with appropriate reverence, Lady Inisheen, as always, checked her face in the mirror, adding more lipstick to her mouth, lipstick that, Alexandra knew, would then decorate everything from her cigarette to her drinks glass with a scarlet bow.

'If my ler-lady would cer-care to follow me upstairs?' Alexandra asked.

Lady Inisheen nodded briskly and maid and guest both travelled smartly up to the first-floor drawing room as if there was so much business to be done in the next two hours they must hurry to it.

'My dear.'

'My dear.'

Mrs Smithers and Lady Inisheen, as was their custom, kept their lips intact, avoiding any intimacy other than a very slight kissing sound either side of each other's heads, before sinking down onto the damask-covered, gilded sofas, placed as always either side of the now gently flickering coal fire.

'Any sign of you-know-who?'

Mrs Smithers always said this, every week, but only after allowing some minutes' desultory conversation to pass. Even Alexandra, handing round glasses of sweet sherry on her highly polished silver salver, now knew that when her employer said this she was referring to Lady Inisheen's elderly, widowed ex-lover whom both women deeply suspected might have gone off in search of pastures new, instead of, as all widowers are meant to do, doing his duty by his long-time mistress and marrying her.

'Not a note from him, not a telephone call either, but then the old devil never was any good at writing or telephoning.

He is, to say the least, on the careful side. I have known him spend hours erasing traces of a Post Office mark on a stamp in the hopes of reusing it. He was born wealthy, as a result of which he has always been very money-conscious, not to mention careful to the point of insanity, as so many are.'

'He'll ask you up to London soon. He's bound to. Any minute now you will hear from him, I am quite sure.'

This part of their weekly discussion always ended with Mrs Smithers attempting to console her friend, but so far as Alexandra could gather the call to Lady Inisheen from her lover had not yet been made, as a result of which her ladyship, like some ghostly figure on a far-off shore waiting for a friendly ship to pass and hear her shouts for help, never quite lost hope.

Lunch on this particular morning proceeded at a brisk pace, so brisk in fact that Alexandra began to suspect that Mrs Smithers wanted to get through the whole business as quickly as possible so that she could return to her drawing room, sit in front of the fire, and pick Alexandra's brains as to how best to cope with her disastrous financial position.

'Coffee?'

'Thank you.'

Lady Inisheen started to open and shut her aged handbag, making an irritating and constant clicking sound, which was almost worse than a dripping tap. This too Alexandra was used to, knowing that it always preceded her ladyship plucking up her courage to ask Mrs Smithers for the use of her writing desk and, by happy coincidence, her writing paper too.

'Sweet of you, so sweet of you, Audrey; saves me the boredom of going home,' she murmured as usual, having quickly seated herself at Mrs Smithers's elegant little writing desk and written a number of notes to various acquaintances in London and the South of France on Mrs Smithers's writing paper. 'I can post them on the corner, and then take a constitutional. You are a dear, Audrey, really you are.'

Alexandra showed her out, and promptly returned to the drawing room where, as was her habit, Mrs Smithers, net curtains parted, was watching her friend walking to the post box on the corner of the square.

'That,' she said, with some satisfaction, 'is the last meal the poor soul will eat until she comes here next week.'

She dropped the net curtain into place and went back to seat herself beside the fire.

Alexandra cleared the coffee tray but did not wash it up. instead she quickly returned to the drawing room, eager to confront her employer before she nodded off into her usual post-prandial snooze in front of the small coal fire.

'Mer-Mer-Mrs Smithers?'

Mrs Smithers looked up at her, surprised to see her back in the drawing room so quickly.

'Yes, Minty?'

'I-er-I have had an idea.'

'Yes, Minty?'

Alexandra cleared her throat.

'I was ther-ther-thinking about Lady Inisheen, and about the Honourable Mer-Mer-Martita, and Mrs Kelmsley and Mrs Jones-Melhuish, and how they all come here and use your writing per-per-paper.'

'Yes, Minty?'

'Ber-ber-but . . . how you never go back to their houses.'

There was a small pause before Mrs Smithers replied.

'Well, I don't want to use *their* writing paper, I have perfectly good writing paper of my own, Minty, so I don't expect to be asked back to *their* homes. More than that, I would not wish to be asked back to their homes. They have all fallen on hard times, which is one of the reasons they use my writing paper. They don't want to let the side down. After all,

some of them have been left very badly off by the Army, some
of them by taxes and death duties, others by their husbands,
or some inadvertent stroke of bad luck over which they had
no control—'

She stopped suddenly, looking cast down as she realised
that since the awful news of her late husband's company
going bankrupt and the imminent cessation of her annuities,
she could be talking about herself.

Alexandra saw this.

'I don't mean to be imp-imp-impertinent, Mrs Smithers,'
Alexandra put in quickly. 'Ber-ber-but this is what I have
been thinking. All your friends and acquaintances come
here not just to see you, if you don't mer-mer-mind me
saying, but also ber-ber-because, unlike them, you have a
good address, and me; a mer-maid, and so on. I mean
besides liking to see you, they like to use your address,
don't they?' Just as Mrs Smithers was about to interrupt
her, Alexandra quickly finished with a flourish. 'So, well,
supposing . . . you cher-charged them?'

Mrs Smithers looked genuinely shocked.

'Charge my friends to meet each other for lunch? I hardly
think that is a good idea, Minty.' She flicked at her lace jabot.
'I hardly think that would be any solution to our present
difficulties.'

'I understand from something I rer-rer-read once, that
Lady Johns, who has never had any money, has always
charged for the luncheons and dinners she gives, and no one
mer-mer-minds, because everyone is so charmed to meet all
her rich and fer-fer-famous friends at her lovely house.'

'Well, I dare say, but Lady Johns is titled, and titled folk
can get away with anything they choose, because people will
do anything to share even a cup of cocoa with a lord or a
lady,' Mrs Smithers stated. 'Besides, none of my friends are
quite grand enough now, and I don't think they want to meet

each other, and they are certainly not famous, so they would not have much interest in each other; and they have no money to speak of, so they would soon tire of the idea.'

'No, not to meet each *other*, ner-no, to meet their fer-fer-fer-friends and fer-fer-family, and so on. I-I-er-I-er . . . I mean—'

Mrs Smithers looked up sharply as Alexandra's stammer suddenly started to become worse.

Alexandra gritted her teeth. She would *will* it to go away. She paused.

'You ser-ser-see, if you ter-ter-take Lady Inisheen, I ner-ner-noticed that she always uses your writing per-paper after lunch, before she leaves.'

'Well, she can hardly write to her friends, people such as her friend Lord Harry and so on, from her own address, can she? She can hardly write from number two the Railway Cuttings, or wherever it is the poor woman has been forced to reside. She can hardly do that now, can she? And I don't suppose she can afford anything more than her rent, so she certainly would not be able to afford writing paper properly printed in a raised manner on which to write to Lord Harry, could she? If she has any letters they come here. To keep up the pretence to her London friends, so necessary, as you know.'

'Exactly.' Alexandra looked excited. 'Exactly, ther-ther-that is what I der-der-do mean, she can't, can she? Nor can she invite them to two the Cuttings, nor can she afford restaurants or her-her-hotels, but if she cer-cer-could hire your elegant dining room and drawing room, if all the people in Deanford who are down on their luck coud ask their friends here, as if this were their house, instead of hiding away, they could have a social life again. They cer-could see their family and friends, and they would stop feeling lonely and ashamed, and people they haven't seen for years, because they were so ashamed of their hard luck, they could see *them* again. And I could cook for ther-ther-them for much less mer-mer-money than it would cost them if they went to a restaurant or an hotel.'

Since the catastrophic news of her late husband's company going bankrupt, the truth was that Mrs Smithers had been juggling with only two ideas. The first was that she would have to sell her beloved home, and the second was that she would have to open it to lodgers of all kinds, all of whom were certain to have nasty private habits and irregular methods of payment.

She now stared at Alexandra.

'Sit down, Minty,' she snapped.

Alexandra sat down quite suddenly, as she had been commanded, at the same time straightening her starched hat and putting her feet in their shining black strap shoes together, while remembering not to cross her ankles, which Tasha Millington had always told the girls was 'beyond the beyonds'.

'Minty.' Mrs Smithers breathed in and out, and her small black eyes seemed to have more sparks flying from them than the equally small fire now burning in the grate. 'Minty, you have just come up with the answer to this old body's prayer.' She leaned forward. 'I *could* charge for the use of my rooms, to nice people, genteel folk, and they *could* go away at the end of the afternoon or evening, leaving me with a delightful cheque. It is a grand idea, Minty. Perfectly grand. And it would mean . . . it would mean I would not have to sell my home.'

She paused, and such was her emotion she quietly blew her small, retroussé nose on a lace-edged handkerchief.

Alexandra shook her head slowly as her employer finished.

'No, I der-der-don't think that they should ler-ler-leave a cheque, Mrs Smithers.' Alexandra paused as Mrs Smithers stared at her, and as she did so Alexandra remembered the phrase that the old butler at Knighton Hall had always used to Tasha Millington when he was tactfully trying to steer his mistress in the right direction. 'If you der-der-don't mind the suggestion, Mrs Smithers, *ma'am*, if you don't mer-mind it, what I think wer-would be a good idea would be if you asked them for the cheque some weeks in advance, and that way you might fer-fer-find they honour it ber-ber-better, and you can cash it long before you've been to any trouble on their behalf.'

Mrs Smithers stared at Alexandra, and yet again it seemed to her maid-of-all-work that there were sparks flying from the small black eyes set in the lightly powered face. She went to speak, but first, she flicked her lace jabot.

'Minty,' she finally said, sighing with some satisfaction, 'you're a maid in a million. We will put your plan into action straight away. We will not go under, will we, Minty?'

'Ner-ner-no, whatever happens we will not go under,' Alexandra agreed, standing up. 'Shall I bring you the *Daily Telegraph*, ma'am? I have ironed it.'

Mrs Smithers nodded happily, staring round her drawing room as she did so, knowing that if their plan worked she would never have to leave it. Alexandra also found herself smiling happily, but for a different reason. She could never now make it up to her grandmother for what had happened to her, for being thrown out of her home of forty years, leaving her beloved hens and her settled way of life, but she could at least help to stop it happening to Mrs Smithers.

Later that day when she went down to her basement flat and was being greeted by the spaniels in grand fashion, Alexandra found herself sighing contentedly. She might be alone in the world now, but she was at least needed, and not just by the dogs.

*   *   *

Tom stared first at the note in his hand, and then at Mrs Posnet.

'I'm sorry, Tom, to have to be the person to tell you this, but your mother has died. You left so early this morning that when the boy first arrived with the telegram I'm afraid I had gone back to bed, and so he had to come back. As soon as I received it I went straight to the corner and telephoned to the lady in question, and a nice woman she sounds, but it was too late by then. Although I don't suppose you could have got there in time, not really. I mean this place Deanford, it is hours away, by train.'

Tom turned. All right he had never heard of Deanford himself, but Mrs Posnet was making it sound as far away as New York.

'I'll have to get the next train.'

'You can probably make the midday fast train if you hurry, but you'll have to change your clothes, Tom. I will lend you my husband's, my late husband's, black tie and a mourning band.'

Tom nodded and went straight to his ground-floor bed-room.

All he could think of as the train pulled its way through the serene, pale English countryside was that if he had not left Mrs Posnet's house so early he might have been able to reach his mother before she died. But why hadn't she *ever* tried to reach him after she left Norfolk? Why had she disappeared?

He knew what the answer must be, and long before the landlady of the down-at-heel bed-and-breakfast establish-ment opened the door to him. His mother had not just fallen on bad times, she must have returned to her bad old ways.

'I've laid her out as best I could,' the landlady told him in flat tones. 'But I have no idea what arrangements she would have wanted. Seeing that she is called O'Brien, I naturally assumed she must be Roman Catholic. I'm afraid she died

from lack of eating,' she added tactfully. 'Just wasted away.
She died before I could call a priest.'

Tom shook his head.

'It doesn't matter, she's not, she wasn't Roman Catholic.
She's Church of England, I think.'

'Funny that, with an Irish name you would have thought
she would be Roman Catholic.' The woman paused, considering. 'In that case I'll ring our undertaker,' she stated. 'My
undertaker,' she reiterated, sounding strangely proprietary, a
vaguely proud look in her eyes.

It was not a pride that Tom could have understood until he
saw the age of the inhabitants of the run-down bed-and-
breakfast hotel, and then it seemed to him that the landlady,
if she had any business sense, would have been forgiven for
investing in the funeral business, or at least for taking a cut of
the considerable trade she must send him.

'Do you want to see her? As I say, the doctor and I have laid
her out, and the death certificate is signed.'

'No, no, really. I'd rather not. Rather remember her how
she was.'

Tom turned away.

'I can understand how you feel, Mr O'Brien, but don't you
think perhaps you should? After all, she might not be your
mother. It does happen. I have known it to happen, more
often than you would think too. It has happened quite a few
times, here in Deanford, particularly when a surname is the
same – Smith, Brown, O'Brien, that kind of thing.'

Looking at Ma confirmed to Tom that she was indeed his
mother; but as Tom stared down at her, although frightened
to do so at first, he found that his first feeling was one of
relief, because she looked so beautiful. With a shock he saw
that in death she was not just his mother, but that she was
actually beautiful, and that she must once have been a
beautiful young girl, not the always-anxious, put-upon cook,

not the woman whose constant battle with alcohol had meant that his childhood had been spent following her from job to job, in an endless and finally pointless quest for some sort of security.

'It's got too dangerous, all the bombs dropping too near,' had been one of her many wartime explanations whenever she had been summarily dismissed from some domestic position.

When he was very young Tom had readily accepted her explanation, but by the time he grew older he found he had not only given up on school, he had given up on his mother. Every night he would pray for one thing only, that Ma would somehow hold down a job for more than a few weeks, that he could count on having a regular hot meal, that life would get better for them both.

'Ma.' Tom knelt by the dreary little bed and put his handsome dark head on her cold hand. 'Oh Ma, where did you go? Why did you leave Norfolk? You could have come and lived with me. I have a job. A good job, I have a good job now.'

But his mother was gone to somewhere much better, and Tom knew it. Hearing what must be the solemn, respectful tread of the undertakers' footsteps on the stairs outside, he quickly stood up, and turned away, one question now haunting him. How would he pay for the funeral?

Having instructed the men to lay her out as she was, he left the two sober-suited men to their work, measuring and scribbling, and walked down to the hall. He had his watch, which he could hawk, and some cash that he had saved in his Post Office account, but he hardly thought that would be enough to cover the expense of a funeral.

'Are you worried about the funeral expenses? Well, don't be quite yet. There's a deposit box key here. I don't know why, but Mrs O'Brien, poor woman, she gave me the key, in the early hours, when we both knew she was slipping away.'

Tom stared at the landlady, realising instantly how honest she must be.

'They always say landladies are a race apart. I say "they"; what I really mean is that my mother always believed that landladies, particularly in the North of England, were kindness personified,' he said quietly, looking at the key she had just handed him. 'And she was right.'

The landlady ignored his compliment.

'She said to tell you the box is at the National Bank in the High Street, that she was sorry that it was all she had, she wished it was more, but that she wanted you to have it, and to say sorry. Those were her dying words, that she was so sorry.'

Sorry?

Tom turned away. Why should she have said sorry? It was not her fault that she had a weakness that she had always tried so hard to fight. And yet. Yes, there was a great deal for which to be sorry, and he and Ma had both known it. It hadn't meant that they hadn't loved each other. It hadn't meant that they had not both depended on each other, but sorry as far as he was concerned was not one word, just five letters long, sorry was a lot longer than five letters.

Sorry, Tom, for not having been anywhere long enough for you to attend school, sorry for you finding me collapsed against walls, on bathroom floors, in other people's kitchens. Sorry for never meeting you at the school gates, never going to sports days the few days or weeks you did manage to be at school. Sorry for no hot dinners when we were so down on our luck that all I could give you was a tin of beans. Sorry that you were always the poor boy in the basement in an endless succession of grand houses. Sorry that I never could give you what you wanted most. A father.

The landlady touched him briefly on the arm.

'I should get down there and see if what you hope is true,

that there'll be enough in that box at least for the funeral expenses.' Sensing the confusion of his feelings, she moved her hand up and patted him on the shoulder. 'It's all right, son, her rent was paid up, right until the end of the week. She always paid on time, never missed.'

Tom walked out into the street, and then he started to run towards the High Street. He knew now that he needed money badly, not least because he was sure that Mr Blakemore was going to sack him for making love to Lady Florazel, not least because of that.

'Name of O'Brien.'

He showed the manager not just the key, but his Post Office book, to prove his identity, and then followed the bank clerk through to the vaults where he watched him undo the cage, before leading Tom to the appropriate box, which he then laid out on the table.

Tom opened it.

As the landlady had uncannily predicted there was indeed cash inside the box, rolls of it done up in elastic bands, and that was not all, there were many small boxes, which when he opened them he found contained jewellery of various kinds: rings and lockets, gold bracelets, pearl earrings, items that he would never in a million years have associated with his mother, Mrs O'Brien the cook.

There was also an old pre-war passport whose photograph proved to him that the owner was indeed a younger version of the woman he had always known as his mother. There was only one difference, and that was the name in the front of it. The name on the passport was not Heather O'Brien, or anything like it. It was something quite other. There was also a letter.

'Minty!'

Mrs Smithers was calling down the stairs to Alexandra in

her usual sudden fashion, and Alexandra was rushing up to the first-floor drawing room to do whatever was necessary, when the doorbell rang.

'Leave it,' Mrs Smithers told her as she reached the drawing room. 'It will be Lady Inisheen, but we must not let her in until we have seen to this disaster.'

Alexandra looked round expecting at the very least a fallen vase or a broken ornament.

'Missing lightbulb!'

Since it was broad daylight on a sunny day it hardly seemed the disaster that Mrs Smithers felt it to be; nevertheless, Alexandra ran to the landing cupboard, plucked a lightbulb from a box, changed it, and then flew back downstairs to the front door, which she opened in an unhurried manner, having first made sure that her cap was as straight as it was starched.

In the event it was not just Lady Inisheen, locked as always into her shaved-beaver coat and hat, despite the warmth of the weather, but also a gentleman in an old-fashioned coat and Homburg hat, and behind him in the road, a station taxi driving slowly away.

'I've just met Lord Harry off the dirty old train, Minty, so I think we should take him straight to wash his hands in the gentleman's downstairs cloakroom, don't you?'

Lady Inisheen darted a stern look at Alexandra, and Alexandra, understanding straight away from her tone what was needed, took Lord Harry's coat and, smiling calmly, led his lordship to the downstairs cloakroom.

By arrangement Mrs Smithers had now disappeared to a newly rearranged suite on one of the upper floors. This was to be her permanent refuge when her paying guests were entertaining their friends at her address. It had a new radio set, freshly cleaned curtains and nets, a group of easy chairs and a bookcase. When Alexandra left her shortly before Lady

Inisheen's arrival, she seemed to be enjoying it more than her grand first-floor drawing room.

'What a perfectly charming reception room, Beulah,' Lord Harry murmured as Alexandra with now practised ease offered him a choice of sherry or gin, before leaving the two of them to catch up on the considerable time they had been apart.

Lady Inisheen turned in front of the large, gilt mirror over the mantelpiece and smiled fondly. What she could never tell Harry was that she had sold a ring to hire the rooms to help her friend, and, of course, herself.

'Do you think so, Buffy?'

'Charming, charming,' Lord Harry murmured as, with equally practised ease, he turned and pinched Alexandra's bottom as she went to leave the room.

Alexandra gritted her teeth and half closed her eyes. When it came to men there was something about a maid's uniform that was just not funny. A perfectly normal man like Lord Harry, a man who must be used to mixing in the highest circles, could be turned into the worst-behaved old monkey at the mere sight of a starched apron and hat. If it were not for the fact that both Mrs Smithers and Alexandra so wanted the newly widowed Lord Harry to marry Lady Inisheen and take her to London to enjoy the lifestyle she undoubtedly craved, Alexandra would have been tempted to step smartly back onto the old devil's foot.

'The luncheon was a ger-ger-great success, only for one ther-ther-thing, I just wer-wish that Lord Harry would keep his hands to himself,' an exhausted but triumphant Alexandra later reported to Mrs Smithers.

Mrs Smithers sipped her evening sherry and giggled.

'Minty dear, as far as gentlemen are concerned, maids are like snacks on a hotel bar – there for the taking. But how do you think it *really* went?'

'Like cer-cer-clockwork, actually. Lord Harry laughed and ter-ter-talked and ate every scrap of his lunch, and then they went off in a cab, and I der-der-dare say he will be back in a couple of weeks, and we will have to go through the whole ther-ther-thing once again.'

'We must get him up to the point where he will propose marriage, Minty, if it is the last thing that we do. He has no wife now, and needs someone in London to run his house and to entertain for him. Lady Inisheen has no money and needs someone to keep her; it has the makings of a perfect marriage. Each of them needs the other for a practical reason and will settle for what the other has without too much fuss, if *we* have anything to do with it, Minty dear.'

'I just pity the mer-mer-maids they employ, they will have to wear ger-ger-girdles reinforced with steel.'

This time they both giggled.

'Who else have we got this week? The Honourable Martita, naturally?'

'Yes, the Honourable Mer-Mer-Mer-Martita.' Alexandra reached for the appointments book. 'No one on Wednesday, but on Thursday a lady called Mrs Atkins.'

'Ah yes, Mrs Atkins, we don't know her, do we? Still, I don't suppose it matters, after all her cheque didn't bounce, did it? As long as the boodle is banked we're happy, aren't we, Minty?'

Alexandra left Mrs Smithers to read the evening paper in front of the fire and went down to prepare her supper on a tray for her. Unexpectedly, but delightfully, Mrs Smithers was becoming positively raffish in her new role as the sometime landlady who rented out her reception rooms for entertaining. She no longer seemed to mind at all about any mention of cheques bouncing or bottom-pinching, whereas before her change in luck, she would have minded terribly.

Alexandra removed her white apron and hat before

retiring to her basement. Mrs Atkins was the first lady to book who wanted to give a dinner party for six. It would be an exciting change.

As Tom emerged from Deanford churchyard where his mother had just been buried, he noticed a large Bentley Continental parked in the quiet street outside. It was already attracting interest, and that was before its driver stepped out on to the pavement. As the long legs and elegantly shod feet of Florazel emerged from the car, more passersby stopped and stared. Deanford might once have been a rich resort, once peopled by the wealthy and the powerful, but since the war it had fallen down on its luck, and so the sight of such elegance and wealth was astonishing. Old men and young boys, envious girls and their mothers, once the car had finally driven off, would be sure to hurry back to their families and discuss what they had seen over their tea and sandwiches. *A Bentley Continental with a great grand lady stepping in and out of it wearing London clothes and covered in gold.*

'Tom.' Florazel crossed the road and went up to him, making sure that she spoke with sympathy and evident sensitivity. 'I was so sorry to hear about your mother, Tom.' Tom stared at her. 'Mrs Posnet, your landlady, she told me what had happened, so I came at once.'

Tom frowned, bewildered.

'Lady Florazel—' he began.

'No, no, please call me Florazel,' she begged. 'After all, we are more than we know to each other already, aren't we, Tom?'

Tom stared at her, even more bewildered. Lady Florazel was the Duke of Somerton's sister. What was she doing in a back street in Deanford, standing outside a run-down churchyard where he had only minutes before buried his mother?

What was she doing waiting for him, asking him to call her by her first name?

'Lady Florazel, I have just buried my mother,' he stated. 'I am sorry if I seem rude, but I really can't say more than that. She was all I had. My whole family, and she is dead. It is not a good time to come here and tease me, ma'am.'

'Oh Tom, I would never tease you. I am dressed in mourning, out of respect for you and your mother. I came here to bring you back to my house, to look after you, to make sure you do have someone in your life now, to make sure you won't be alone.'

Tom shook his head.

'But that is just it, I do want to be alone, just for the moment.'

'You think you do, Tom, but believe me, I know, you don't really. Why not come with me, and we can have a drink together somewhere, and make a plan. Please?'

She guided him across the empty road, and opened the door of her beautiful motor car. Tom stepped in and sat back, dazed; as he did so, and despite his state of shock, he knew at once that he would never forget that first taste of real luxury. The quality of the leather seating, the wooden fascia of the dashboard, the sense of calm that pervaded the luxury of such a car; and all that before it started to weave its way through the streets of Deanford towards the seafront, towards the elegant squares and the white-fronted hotels.

'We could go to the Palace, couldn't we? We could go there for a drink, which I am sure you must badly need, and we could make a plan. I have told my brother that you will not be back for a while, and he has told Mr Blakemore, so you must not worry.'

Mr Blakemore? Tom thought dazedly of the head gardener. He seemed so far away now, so far away that he might as well have been one of the boats bobbing about on the distant horizon, or one of the fishermen on the end of the pier; or he could have been someone that he, Tom, had once worked for. Tom found himself trying to remember how Mr Blakemore had looked: his large ears sticking out from either side of his faded tweed cap; his large nose that used to disappear into a red and white spotted handkerchief when pollen brought on a sneezing fit; his large hands that seemed to make the handle of even the largest spade shrink into insignificance.

'Mr Blakemore said I was to have nothing more to do with you, Lady Florazel. You are the Duke's sister. It is not – suitable.' Tom realised that he had found himself using a word that his mother sometimes used.

It's not suitable for people in our position, Tom. We are servants now.

'Oh, dear old Blakie, he would. I can just hear him. *Not suitable*, that would be Blakie all right.' Florazel's voice oozed tolerance.

She parked the car outside the Palace Hotel.

'Let's go inside, shall we? Let's go and have a drink. You must need one so much, you poor – you poor, poor boy.'

Tom looked down at his suit, checking to see if it was clean, checking to see if it was suitable. Florazel obviously appreciated this, because she touched him on the arm.

'It's all right, we're only going to the foyer bar, you look perfectly fine.'

Tom wanted to say, And after that? And after *that*? What will happen after we have been in the bar? But he was too numb from the funeral, too much still the servant to tell Florazel that the last thing he wished was for her to take him for a drink, that all he really wanted to do was to go for a walk on the seafront and watch the white tops of the waves making asses of themselves, dancing and flirting with each other before finally sinking into the newly blue water – for just at that moment the sun had come out and the sky turned cloudless. More than that he wanted to allow the sound of the seagulls' cries to drown the leaden sorrow in his heart.

None of this could he tell *Lady* Florazel, as he still thought of her, because, when all was said and done, it was a truth never to be forgotten that if you came from below stairs, you were like a good child, you were seen and not heard, you were obedient, you kept your eyes down, and your mouth shut, no matter what had happened in the early mornings at the Duke of Somerton's estate.

Reluctantly he followed Florazel into the Palace Hotel and as he did so he thought he could smell a new and extra-ordinary life, a life of expense-account living, rich food and plentiful alcohol. And like the drumming sound behind a good band it beckoned to him, if not to dance, at least to tread carefully across the thick carpet towards the bar, but not before Florazel had discreetly slipped a five-pound note into his suit pocket.

'Mine's a gin and tonic.'

Tom went up to the bar.

'Two gin and tonics, please.'

The mirror behind the bar was pink, thirties-style, and flattering. As he waited to be served Tom stared at his reflection. He was tall, tanned and perhaps because of the solemnity of his clothes he suddenly looked older, even to himself, but not so old that he would not have been surprised if the barman had refused to serve him, for all sorts of reasons, so when he leaned forward and spoke to him, it was not unexpected.

'I'll bring the drinks over to you, sir.'

He nodded at Tom and, perhaps because he had observed Tom's black tie and armband, and the discreetly dark clothes of his beautiful companion, the look in his eyes was one of sympathy.

Tom backed away from the bar. He was going to be served. Someone was going to serve *him*. Of course, that was what happened when you were not a servant. He sat down opposite Florazel.

'Florazel,' he began, but she stopped him.

'Don't speak until you've had your drink. You've had a terrible shock, what you need now is a stiff drink. After that we will talk.'

Tom stared into Florazel's startlingly blue eyes and sighed. It was true. The shock of finding his mother dead. The shock of finding the deposit box, knowing that there must be some secret which she had kept from him all those years. Yes, it had all been very shocking.

The menu for Mrs Atkins's dinner party at number thirty-two was considered so important by Mrs Atkins, Mrs Smithers and Alexandra that Mrs Smithers decided to write out the card in French.

She wrote with her best Parker pen:

Consommé en gelée
Couronne d'agneau avec les petits pois en beurre
et les pommes de terre en chemise

'What does *"en chemise"* mer-mer-mean?'

Mrs Smithers looked up from her careful writing on the card, and smiled.

'I have no idea, Minty dear, but I always think *"en chemise"* looks so cosy, like bedsocks and camisoles, so when in doubt put it. Besides, I don't think anyone else has the least idea, certainly not anyone in Deanford, so we will be quite safe.'

Alexandra considered this for a few seconds.

'Mrs Atkins does seem rather er-er-er-educated. I think she was once a headmistress of a ger-ger-ger-girls' school.'

Mrs Smithers looked up sharply at this, and promptly tore up the card.

'In that case I will do another card, and put . . . as a matter of fact how is it you *are* doing the potatoes exactly, dear?'

'Mer-mer-mer-mashed potatoes piped into little mer-mer-mer-mounds and painted with egg ber-ber-ber-before being put into the oven and cooked at a medium temperature.'

'How delicious, but what are they called?'

'How about pom-pom potatoes?'

They both laughed, but finally Mrs Smithers wrote in her special menu writing, '*pommes de terre duchesse*', which was the correct name, and then '*Tartes tatin*' and '*Les Fromages*', even though they were only going to serve one cheese. After which Mrs Smithers disappeared up to her suite, and Alexandra put the elegantly written card at the top of the dining table.

Perhaps Mrs Atkins was aware of the trouble to which Mrs Smithers and Alexandra had gone for her dinner because at the appointed time she appeared looking bandbox fresh, and wearing a charming black dress with a gardenia pinned at the neck.

'Do smell it,' she said to Alexandra, but as she prided herself on knowing her place, Alexandra only pretended to do so, darting her head forward in a way that would not interfere with the set of her small, white starched cap, following which she picked up her service tray and offered Mrs Atkins a sherry.

Mrs Atkins was so nervous she did not take the sherry from the tray, she grabbed it and drank it far too quickly, so that her cheeks quickly became flushed.

'It's the first time I have given a dinner party since before the war, and seeing that this is not home, I feel just a little anxious,' she announced.

'Mrs Atkins, mer-ma'am, you must not be ner-ner-nervous, really you must ner-ner-not. You ner-now know the house nearly as well as I do. Remember we rehearsed everything that I shall der-der-do, and everything that you will der-do.'

'Yes, but supposing no one turns up?'

'That is someone ner-now, even as we speak, that is someone ringing at the der-der-door.'

'I do hope it's my nephew, Bob. He always helps make things go whenever I visit his mother and stepfather. He's quite a lad, really he is.'

But it was not Mrs Atkins's nephew Bob, it was her prospective beau, a Mr Albert Chamberlain.

As Alexandra opened the door to him she immediately felt reassured. Mr Chamberlain was the proprietor of a number of gentlemen's outfitters, so unsurprisingly his evening dress was everything that it should be.

'May I take your coat, sir?'

Mr Chamberlain's coat was actually an evening cloak with a red satin lining, very new, and very snazzy. It reminded Alexandra of the smart clothes that her uncle always wore, although she instinctively knew that James Millington would never wear such a thing when out to dinner with friends, he would always only wear it to a ball, or the opera, or a theatrical first night.

Nevertheless Mr Chamberlain looked most respectable, and his smile and manner were such that she felt sure that he must help make the evening go with a swing.

'Please follow me, sir. Mrs Atkins is waiting upstairs for her guests.'

Albert Chamberlain followed her upstairs and as he did so Alexandra had high hopes for the success of the dinner for the front doorbell was ringing and there was already a feeling of gaiety about the evening, as if everyone sensed that they were in safe hands, and that was all before Bob Atkins arrived.

Last, and very much not least, Bob bounded through the

front door, his bow tie crooked, his long blond hair flopping into his eyes, but only after leaving his car parked outside the front door with two wheels on the pavement.

'I say, Aunt Aggie is going to be ever so cross, isn't she?'

He flung his coat down on a hall chair and galloped ahead of Alexandra before stopping halfway up the stairs.

'Is it this way, by the way? I've never been to her house before . . .'

'Quite right, s-s-sir. Straight up the s-s-stairs, and then ahead. If you would like to follow mer-me, sir.'

'Oh, crikey. Bad habits die hard, don't they? It comes of being dragged up not brought up in good old genteel Deanford.'

He grinned at Alexandra as she carefully passed him to lead him up into the drawing room, which now echoed with the quiet conversational exchanges being made by the other four guests.

'You wouldn't like to come and work for my stepfather and my mother, would you? They could do with someone as pretty as you,' Bob Atkins murmured from behind Alexandra.

Alexandra gave him a reproving look.

'Only asking!'

He winked and, finally passing her, went into the drawing room, Alexandra following him after first picking up her tray of drinks from the table by the door. Bob Atkins might be a bit of a character, but she had to say that he had won marks: he had at least kept his hands to himself.

Putting on the Ritz

'Sir would obviously now like to go on to our "brother" street, as we here call it.'

Tom turned slowly in front of the full-length mirror, the tailor standing behind him. Within twenty-four hours of leaving Deanford for London and his new life with Florazel, she had bought Tom what seemed to him then to be enough clothing to last him a lifetime, and yet Florazel had made it perfectly plain that it was by no means enough.

'My darling Tom,' she had explained, lying back and luxuriating in a vast bed, which dominated an ornate bedroom and was part of her permanent suite at the Ritz Hotel. 'A gentleman has to have an array of clothing to suit all occasions. All we have bought so far is *un petit rien*.' On Tom turning back to her with a mystified expression, she added by way of explanation: 'We have bought only enough for a few informal occasions. You have to have a gentleman's wardrobe, Tom. You have to have properly tailored suits, hand-made shirts, hand-made shoes, a morning coat, evening dress. A gentleman is his wardrobe.' She had paused to take a cigarette from a heavy gold cigarette case and light it with a slim gold lighter. 'And after all you are a gentleman now, Tom, and if I have anything to do with it, you will always be a gentleman.'

Tom did not now want to remember how beautiful Florazel had looked in that vast bed. It was not the moment, instead he smiled at Mr Cooper the tailor.

'Yes, you must show me where to go to your "brother" street,' he agreed. 'For I have no idea. I am quite new to London.'

Mr Cooper smiled back at him, even managing to bring a vaguely astonished look to his eyes, as if he were surprised that such a customer did not know where to purchase shirts of a first-rate quality suitable for a gentleman of some standing. If he were not quite sure that Lady Florazel, famous beauty and sister of the Duke of Somerton, was one of the few aristocratic ladies who always paid her bills on time, he might not have been looking so relaxed. But knowing Lady Florazel of old, he was more than relaxed, he was purring.

'Yes, of course, sir, it is just around the corner, most convenient for our customers. Shirts are crucial, are they not? The cut of the collar of a shirt is most particularly important, it has to be most particularly right, for there is nothing worse than a collar cut too small, too mean, too large, or too exaggerated, the collar after all is what is most noted . . .'

Mr Cooper stood back and regarded Tom gravely, so gravely that Tom, who had actually thought the shirt he was wearing was pretty fine, now reddened slightly and looked back at the famous tailor from the dressing mirror with some uncertainty.

Tom knew that he had not yet acquired what someone like Mr Cooper would call taste. He was already aware that the shirts to which he would be attracted might well be the wrong style, the wrong colour, the cut of the collar not suitable for the expensive suits that Mr Cooper and Florazel had chosen for him: the cloths picked from books of cloths, the linings held up to the chosen cloths and taken to the light to make sure that they were neither too vulgar nor too dull, for Florazel hated dull linings, and said so repeatedly.

Naturally no one needed to tell Mr Cooper that the aristocracy favoured stronger colours, even down to the linings of their jackets, in the same way that they enjoyed bright colours in their homes.

There was a sound reason for this love of colour, for colour, whether in paint or materials, had traditionally always been vastly more expensive than the staples of black or white, grey or brown. The less wealthy could only run to whitewash or black serge, not having the money, or the means, to be able to choose anything more sophisticated. It was just a fact, in the same way it was a fact that the aristocracy never bought furniture, only wine and paintings, for the very good reason they always had far too many furnishings handed down to them already.

As it happened Tom would have liked to have asked Mr Cooper to accompany him round the corner to his 'brother' street, but fearing ridicule he asked instead to see some of his more recent fashion books. Mr Cooper, understanding only too well what was required, once again produced large books, which Tom studied. As he flicked through the glossy pages illustrating the fashion of the day, Tom saw at once that here were depicted men wearing casually elegant clothes, nothing too defined, everything understated; so it was really understatement that made up the elegance of the English gentleman. This was the man into which he was being turned by Florazel, and he suddenly realised that he did not mind a bit. More than that he could not wait to note the cut of the collars and the ties, by turn regimental or club, patterned or plain, or countrified to be worn with tweeds.

'Thank you very much, Mr Cooper,' he told him eventually and, turning on his heel, he left the tailor's establishment for the foreign field of the shirtmakers, and ultimately for the wilder shores of the shopping arcades beyond Mr Cooper's Savile Row shop.

He knew now what he should look like, and look it he would, although he did take care to promise himself that he would not, at any point, kid himself that he was not still plain Tom O'Brien, just a better-dressed version of the same person.

'Tom!' someone was calling but, not expecting anyone in London to know him, since he knew no one except Florazel, Tom did not turn but continued staring at an array of white shirts all of which seemed perfect to him, but all of which the salesman was going to considerable lengths to point out were actually appreciably different, not only in the cut and style of the collar, but in the materials used.

'There are no buttons on the cuffs of these shirts,' he pointed out to the salesman. 'Shouldn't they have buttons?'

'No, sir, they are left buttonless, for your cufflinks, sir.'

For a second the salesman stared sorrowfully at the buttons on the shirt that Tom was wearing, before reverting his gaze to his customer's face.

'*Our* shirts never have buttons, sir, as you can see. Doubtless you have let your cufflinks at home, sir. We can provide you with some temporary cufflinks to slip into one of these, so that you can see the look of the cuff.'

The shop asistant was expertly pulling a pair of cufflinks through the cuff of one of the shirts when Tom was tapped on the shoulder.

'Tom! You old goat!'

Tom looked round, mystified as to who in all of London should know him by name.

'Look, it's me! Tom! Bob!'

And it was not just Bob, any old Bob, it was Bob Atkins, smart as paint, with his long blond fringe flopping into his eyes, eyes which as usual wore a permanently mischievous look.

'Bob.'

Tom stood back feeling embarrassed, although for what reason he could not have said, until he realised how odd and how different he must look to Bob. But Bob, effortlessly optimistic and open-hearted, did not seem to notice the change in Tom, or if he did, he did not register it, for he quickly urged Tom to finish his transactions and come and have lunch with him.

'Smashing little place just round the corner,' he told Tom, while gaily nodding to the man behind the counter. 'Sir will take all of those,' he told him, heaping a half-dozen of the shirts up in front of the stiff-faced assistant while at the same time winking round at Tom. 'And he'll have a pair of those blue and gold cufflinks, while he's at it too, won't you, Mr O'Brien?'

Tom, unable to think of why he should not have the shirts, or indeed the cufflinks, since he already had the suits, after a second or two nodded in agreement. After all, Florazel had *ordered* him to have whatever he wanted.

'Where would sir like the order to be sent?'

Tom turned from Bob back towards the counter.

'The Ritz. Care of the Ritz, please. Thomas O'Brien, care of the Ritz, Piccadilly.'

Bob reacted to this with his usual, suddenly familiar, soundless whistle before taking Tom's arm and guiding him out of the shop.

'I say, Thomas old boy, has a great-uncle turned up his toes and left you his fortune? Have you just won the pools? Is there something you should tell me? If so, keep the story to yourself until after we have had a spot of lunch in the Strand.'

Tom stopped.

'Stay there for a second, will you, Bob? I've forgotten something. Won't be more than a moment.' He turned and darted back into the shop. 'I forgot to say that the account is also to be sent to the Ritz, care of Lady Florazel Compton.'

'Of course, sir. Thank you, sir.'

The shop assistant stared after the handsome young man, half admiring, half resentful. Some people had all the luck. But for a pair of sparkling grey eyes, a tall, slim figure, and tanned face, he too might be sending his shirt bill round to the Ritz. Life was very unequal.

Over plates of rare roast beef, Yorkshire pudding, and any amount of roast potatoes, all of which slipped down surprisingly easily considering that he had already eaten a hearty cooked breakfast at the Ritz, Tom listened as Bob talked non-stop.

Bob liked to talk about himself, having an artless belief that other people were as interested in Bob Atkins as he was himself. It seemed he had fallen in love with the maid at his aunt's house, but that the maid continually refused to have anything to do with him, for reasons he could only imagine.

'After all I am a catch, I have a car, I am at university, that is not nothing, Tom.' He looked across the table at Tom, and sighed. 'She's such a beauty, Tom. You should see her, dark shining hair, the bluest eyes, but will she have anything to do with me? Not on your life. I have written to her from university, sent her flowers, but it seems she wants nothing to do with me. Now if you were a pretty little maid, wouldn't you want to come out with me? After all, I have a car,' he repeated proudly. 'I mean, wouldn't you want to go out for a picnic on the Downs, or take tea on the beach with just such a fellow as I? But no.' He sighed. 'It is such an agony, being in love is such an agony, really it is.'

'When did you first meet her, did you say?'

'A few months ago. My aunt gave this dinner, and asked me

because I think she wanted to set me up with the daughter of a rich gentleman friend of hers, but I am afraid I only had eyes for the maid *serving* dinner.'

'Perhaps she just doesn't like you. Perhaps the maid doesn't like you?'

Bob looked momentarily put out. He did not like to think that anyone could dislike him.

'Come, come, Tom, that is going too far.' He laughed suddenly. 'Everyone likes me. It's a well-known fact.' He leaned over the lunch table. 'But how about you, old boy?' He eyed Tom's clothes for the first time with genuine appreciation. 'How *about* you? Fine clothes do a gentleman make? But how come the sudden reversal in fortunes, mmm? Bow-wow! Doggie's dinner! Come on, tell, do!'

Tom reddened for although he knew that he did look quite the part in his fine new clothes, he also realised from the look in Bob's eyes that to an undergraduate like Bob he must look a little too old, a little too got up, too much the newly made young gentleman.

'I too have fallen in love, Bob,' he confided suddenly, as if this might explain the newness of him, his richly upholstered façade, his complete transformation.

Bob was careful to look casual although Tom knew he must have heard about his sudden departure from the Duke of Somerton's estate, and indeed from Mrs Posnet's lodgings.

'Have you, by Jove? Anyone nice? Anyone you might like to introduce me to? Anyone who might have a beautiful friend who will help take my mind off the entrancing Minty?' He sighed, already slightly bored by having to discuss someone else's feelings for the opposite sex. 'A maid called Minty.' He looked dreamy. 'Doesn't even her name sound mouth-watering, Tom? And that's before you set eyes on her lovely dark hair shining beneath her little starched cap. At least my aged aunt is marrying her haberdasher beau soon, so I will have every sort of good excuse to see Minty again, I should have thought.'

With a look Tom signalled to the waiter to bring their bill, which he promptly paid with a five-pound note, leaving a generous tip and pocketing the change. As he did so in the discreet manner that Florazel had been at pains to demonstrate to him, Bob was still happily waxing on about the little maid he had met at his aunt's house.

They both stood up, walked from the restaurant with its stiff white tablecloths and sides of beef covered by great silver covers, and so out into the low hum and pleasant relaxed friendly pace of a London afternoon in the early nineteen-fifties.

As they walked towards the Ritz, Tom, now quite recovered from his embarrassment, began to think about Florazel, about the way her hair tumbled down her slender white shoulders, about the tender way she had already been at pains to teach him so much, to be so generous to him, to change his life in a thousand ways, when his pleasantly sensuous thoughts were interrupted.

'By the way, Tom old boy, you never did tell me how you came to have such a change in fortunes?'

Tom looked at him.

'I told you, I fell in love with a beautiful woman, who loves me.'

'Name of . . .' Bob looked waggish. 'Name of someone one might know, old thing?'

Perhaps it was the sunshine, perhaps it was the deliciously filling lunch they had just scoffed, perhaps he was not just thinking straight, but Tom heard himself saying really rather promptly, 'Lady Florazel Compton.'

Bob stopped dead.

'You are teasing me, aren't you, old boy?'

Tom too stopped, staring at him.

'No, I am not teasing you, Bob,' he assured him, his voice sounding suddenly more rural, even to his own ears. 'No, I am not teasing you.'

'But you know who that is, don't you?'

Tom nodded.

'Of course I do, Bob. I am not daft, even if I am not at university like you. Of course I know who she is. She is the Duke of Somerton's sister.'

'She certainly is, Tom, and that's not all she is.' Bob managed to look both sad and compassionate as Tom stared at him.

'What do you mean? What else is she? I know she's a widow, but what else is she?'

Tom felt his heart lurch. There was no other word for it. It lurched and at the same time it also seemed to stop beating, for he knew from Bob's face that what he was about to tell him he would not want to know. He knew it, and yet he could not stop Bob. Bob was going to tell him what he did not want to know. He was going to tell him something that Tom had known all along, but which he simply did not want to be told.

Alexandra refused Mrs Atkins's kind invitation to her marriage to the wealthy proprietor of the gentlemen's out-fitters. Obviously, given her status as a maid-of-all-work, Mrs Atkins could not ask her to the reception, and indeed Alexandra would never have expected to be asked.

As it was, Alexandra had many reasons for not wanting to go, all of which she refrained from confiding to Mrs Smithers, but all of which she felt were valid. Mrs Smithers seemed to understand this; she even seemed to approve.

'You are a good girl, Minty, and what is more you are a very sensible one too.'

They both knew that it was Alexandra's business to avoid socialising with anyone who had or could have anything to do with renting the rooms. After all, if Mrs Smithers's maid started rubbing shoulders with their customers, lines would be crossed and their business affected, and that would not do, not now they were beginning to get a succession of bookings, the result of which were pleasant, gossipy luncheons, old acquaintances renewed and, most importantly for Mrs Smithers, money in the bank.

They had also notched up two recent and very notable successes. Lord Harry had at last taken off Lady Inisheen to London, and as a result of the successful dinner given for Mrs Atkins, the highly strung widow was now marrying into a richly cushioned existence.

'Two maids and a chauffeur,' Mrs Smithers had told Alexandra, with justifiable pride, for had the dinner party not been such a success Mrs Atkins would still have been sitting in her semi-detached house sighing for a better life, and only able to afford a station taxi to go shopping.

Now it was Mrs Smithers's turn to sigh as she pushed the letter she had been reading back into an envelope with a London postmark.

'How very satisfactory, Minty. Lady Inisheen has just written to say that she and Lord Harry are to live abroad, in Tuscany. He has bought her a villa just near to that of the famously late Mrs Kindle.'

'Why famously late?'

'Because . . .' Mrs Smithers straightened up her highly modish hat prior to walking out of her front door and on to the church where Mrs Atkins was about to be married for the second time. 'Because Mrs Kindle was even late for the late King George's late father; so late that she became known as the "famously late Mrs Kindle". But of course she had such charm, she could get away with it; and did. After all, kings loved her. It must be so good to be loved by kings and princes rather than ordinary men.'

Mrs Smithers gave a little sigh, and then she closed the front door behind her.

Alexandra, as she always did when left alone in the house, started to inspect the place, floor by floor, taking a pride in seeing that everything was to rights, in the same way that her grandmother had used to do at Lower Bridge Farm: changing the angle of a cushion here, a vase there, making sure that all the fringes on the Persian rugs were running in the right direction, that all the chimneypieces were free of dust, before finally arriving in the kitchen to start cooking.

As she took down the old tin flour bin and put the kitchen scales in the middle of the table, a soprano was singing on the radio. Her grandmother had often mentioned that she had been in amateur musicals when she was young and giddy, before her marriage to Arthur John Stamford, a man of substance, a farmer with a fine house and acres, and not a musical note in his body, she would always add – almost proudly.

As she mixed the ingredients for pastry Alexandra remembered going to village concerts with her, and how she had used to whisper pithy comments such as: *'Not enough puff'* or, *'Missed three notes there, dear.'* It was only now that Betty was gone that Alexandra had come to realise what a character she must have been when she was young. Not always a farmer's wife, a farmer's mother, a grandmother: once a young girl who perhaps even read novels rather than the Bible, who would go skating on the Thames or bicycling in Richmond Park, who would paint watercolours and play jokes on her friends.

A couple of hours and some three recipes later and there was a scratch on the basement window that set the dogs barking. Alexandra looked round and up the area steps to see the over-smiling face of Bob Atkins. She immediately put her mouth to the window glass and mouthed, 'Go away, would you?'

But Bob sat down on the area steps, his top hat well to the back of his head, a bottle of champagne in one hand and a glass in the other.

'You didn't come to the wedding, so I brought the wedding to you,' he said, when, seeing the rain tipping down, Alexandra eventually relented and opened her basement door to him.

'You are not meant to be here.'

'I've come round to bring you a cheering bottle of champers—'

'I don't drink,' Alexandra stated with complete truth.

Bob put the bottle down on her kitchen table.

'In that case it's high time you did,' he announced. 'As Frank Sinatra famously said, "Is that really the best you're going to feel all day?"'

'Drink is not something I've ever wanted to try.'

'How do you know you don't like it if you've never tried it?'

'I don't like the smell.'

Bob ignored her, instead he sniffed the air.

'Speaking of which – what *have* you been doing in here?'

'Baking.'

'I can tell. Delicious.' He put his head on one side. 'Any chance of tasting one of the recipes? So far the wedding reception has been nothing if not liquid and only one canapé for yours truly.'

'Not a hope. Now if that's all, sir.'

'Don't say that, don't say "sir" please. It's so – sexy.'

Alexandra stared at him. Sex was not only an experience that had not occurred in her life so far, but it was also a word that she had hardly ever heard said. The visitors to number thirty-two, Mrs Smithers, her Millington relations at Knighton Hall, Douro Partridge, they all talked about money and inheritance, about the aristocracy, about hunting, about farming, about dogs and horses, but not sex.

'Have I said something to shock you?'

For a second Bob himself looked shocked at her reaction.

'No,' Alexandra said, slowly. She frowned. 'As a matter of fact, now I come to think of it . . . Now I come to think of it, I think you're right, I think it is silly not to try a glass of champagne, just one, just for fun. After all, just for once I do have Saturday afternoon off.'

Bob started to take the gold paper off the champagne bottle, his expression gleeful.

Tom had left Bob to walk alone in Hyde Park, for hours. The confusion of his feelings was such that it seemed to him the people he passed were somehow distorted, in the same way that Florazel had become distorted to him. He had always known she had been married, that her husband, a much older man, had died after barely eighteen months of marriage, but he had not thought any further, as young men who are in love do not. What he had not known was that he was only one in a long line of young men.

He castigated himself for his stupidity. He cursed himself for his naivety. He hated himself for going to her so willingly, and straight after his mother's funeral; but what he could not deny was that he was in love with her. She fired him in a way that he had never thought he could be fired, she made him laugh, she shared her status with him, and that was all before she dressed him, taught him how to order from a French menu – made him feel as he had never felt before.

Finally, after many hours during which he sat incongruously on park benches beside smartly dressed nannies in over-correct uniforms, walked past the Serpentine noting the many boats, and watched other lovers strolling in the warm air through the trees, he realised that he could not give up Florazel, and for a very good reason – because just the thought of her melted him. Just the memory of her scent sent his head spinning. The thought of her long, slender legs encased in their silk stockings trotting up the Ritz staircase in front of him made him feel faint with desire. She was irresistible. She was everything that a man could dream of, and really what did it matter if he was one in a long line of young men, as Bob Atkins had stated. He would be different; he would be the one that would remain. He would never leave her. She would never leave him. They were passion personified. They were love as it should be. When they were together life was more beautiful, more rapturous, more magical. Nothing should come between that. The past after all was the past, and he could shut that door for her for ever, by giving himself to her in such a way that she would never need anyone else. He would make sure that he was all that she had ever wanted.

Eventually he let himself back into their suite to find a note waiting for him.

Tom darling, I am at the Spencer-Churchills tonight. It is evening dress (white tie). Do come. The desk will call a car for you, and they know where to go. Please come. It is a dinner-dance and you will be a hit, I know you will.

Tom read the note and reread it, but although the tone of the note was so sweet and generous, and although the writer was so obviously in love (for why else would she sign her name with hearts and kisses?) he knew that, despite being now the proud owner of a white tie and tails, he could not go.

Hours later, having lain on the vast, ornate bed in a well of misery, not to mention jealousy, imagining Florazel dancing and flirting with any number of better-versed, better-looking, more elegant, wittier men than himself, he heard the door of the suite open.

She stood in front of the bed, smiling down at him.

'Did you have headache, darling Tom?'

Tom sat up and, getting off the bed, went to her.

'No,' he said, firmly. 'I did not have a headache, Florazel.'

'Then why couldn't you come, darling?'

Tom gripped her hands. She was so beautiful. More beautiful than he had remembered her while he walked round the park agonising over their relationship, wanting to reach back into her past and wipe out her previous lovers, like the teacher wipes a duster across a blackboard. He stared down at her evening dress. It too was beautiful. He did not know the material, would not have known that it was draped rayon jersey, only that it clung to her beautiful figure, making her tiny waist look smaller by its tight cut, making her small, rounded breasts look more desirable by the fact that the bodice was heart-shaped and the sleeves cut and gathered so they were set slightly off the shoulder. The train fanned out in a fishtail behind her, giving her figure a strange formality and, because it was lined with silk, making a slight swishing sound as she dropped her hands and walked towards her dressing room.

'Oh Florazel, you're so beautiful,' was all he could murmur hopelessly, before he followed her and, catching her by the shoulders, turned her, and they started to make love.

'So, why didn't you come to the dinner-dance, darling? You would have loved it. There were so many amusing people there.'

It was the following morning and, after a night spent making love, Florazel was brushing her hair in front of a long dressing mirror, and Tom was watching her from the bed.

He hesitated before replying, not wanting her to laugh at him, but knowing that she had every right to do so. Through their love-making he had been able to drown out the sound of Bob Atkins's voice saying, not once, but several times, 'But didn't you know Lady Florazel Compton is easy? Everyone knows that. She's easy, all right, can't get enough of it, from anyone and everyone, really she can't, it's well known.'

'There was a good reason why I couldn't have come to dinner last night,' he admitted.

She half turned from the mirror, staring at him, waiting, so that for a fleeting second he had the feeling that she was about to ask him if he had been told about her, and he could not help wondering if she would deny the rumours, if she would tell him that what was said about her was nothing but vicious gossip, and that he must not listen, that she only loved him, no one else, only him.

'The reason you did not come to the Spencer-Churchills' was?'

She was still half-turned, and waiting, definitely waiting; almost as if she had been through this particular scene before, was too well versed not to choose her words carefully, not to know she shouldn't hurry anything, she shouldn't jump in too quickly, say something in haste that she might regret. He sensed a certain hardness, but saw only her beauty, a beauty that would melt hearts of lead.

'The reason I did not come to the dinner-dance is that I cannot dance, that is why I did not come to the dinner-dance.'

At that Florazel did go to say something, but then she stopped, a most tender look to her eyes.

'Well, Tom, that was a very good reason, really it was. A very good reason. But did you not think that you could have come to dinner, but not – um – danced?'

She was not mocking him, but prompting him to a new thought.

He smiled suddenly.

'I never thought of that.'

He sprang off the bed, and twirled her round, her night-dress flowing out behind her.

'I am so thick, I never thought of that at all. But now you point it out, that would have been quite an idea, wouldn't it?' He stopped. 'And what is more I have another idea.'

'What Tom, what?' She held out warning hands, laughing. 'No, no, not *again?*'

Tom laughed at her expression.

'No, no, not for at least another hour or so. I shouldn't have thought.'

He caught her to him, feeling the silk of her nightdress in his hands, wondering at how beautiful she looked even in the early morning.

'No, I want something quite different from you, my Lady Florazel.'

'And what would that be?'

'A dancing lesson, my lady.'

'Clear the floor, young sir, roll up the carpet, and let us begin.'

Alexandra waited until Bob's back was turned and then she swiftly poured the glass of champagne into a nearby pot of parsley, after which she made a show of finishing the glass up far too quickly.

'I say, Minty.' Bob looked at her with admiration. 'You have taken to champers in quite a way, haven't you?'

He topped up her glass, and as he did so he smiled what she imagined he must think was flirtatiously at her and at the same time filled his own now empty glass.

Alexandra watched him with fascination. She had at

least learned the ways of older men via the upstairs rooms, learned how to anticipate the wandering hands, the pressing of the body against the side of her bust as she leaned forward to serve, the come-hither winks behind the other guests' backs, and even sometimes the little notes left on the drinks tray.

All in all she had come to find the ways of older men at worst cunning, and at best pathetic, and so far no visitor to number thirty-two had remained immune to the charms of a maid's uniform, not even Mr Albert Chamberlain who, to the satisfaction not just of Mrs Smithers, but of Minty, had only a few hours ago married the highly strung Mrs Atkins, aunt of Bob Atkins presently standing in Alexandra's kitchen looking more than a little half-seas-over.

'Minty . . .'

'Yes, Mr Atkins?'

Alexandra had become quite adept at looking, if not feeling, the ever-obliging, innocent maid-of-all-work.

'I was wondering, Minty, I was wondering.' Bob paused, reaching for his next words, which was not that surprising since he had already put away a few glasses at the wedding reception. 'I was wondering, Minty, if you would like to go for a walk? You know, since you have dogs, we could go for a walk, couldn't we?' He frowned. 'I've always wanted to go for a walk on the Downs with a girl as pretty as you, and her dogs. It's something of which, I have to tell you, I have dreamed.'

Alexandra stared at him.

'You're not quite as sober as you're pretending, are you, Mr Atkins?'

He shook his head.

'No. And please call me Bob, Minty. Just Bob.'

He was managing to look more pleading than her spaniels.

'In that case, how come you're thinking of going for a walk?'

Bob shook his head.

'Don't know.' He started to fall forward as Alexandra rushed to catch him. 'Don't know. Just know that ever since I saw you at dinner I thought you were the prettiest thing I'd ever seen, Minty.'

'And I think you'd better be going home, Mr Atkins, before you pass out.'

Seconds later, as Bob's head crashed onto the kitchen table, Alexandra realised that whatever was going to happen to Bob next, it would not be a walk on the Downs.

Although Tom had endured a childhood of hastily packed suitcases, and lean, mean meals – despite his mother's uneasy method of earning her living as a cook – the one thing of which he was quite certain was that he was a countryman, and not just at heart.

From an early age owing to lack of help in wartime, his mother's various employers had roped him in to help bring in cows, muck out horses, and, happily for him, had even taught him to ride them. So when one day in late summer Florazel mentioned that she would like to go riding in Richmond Park, he knew that at long last she had invited him to do the one thing he could do well. Florazel might have been at pains to teach him etiquette, dancing and innumerable other subtleties of behaviour and attitudes, but the one thing, thank God, she would not have to teach him was how to ride.

His riding clothes came round by special delivery, not tailor-made, but beautifully cut even so. Florazel unpacked each item lovingly, and when Tom finally stood in front of her, his long legs encased in tight-fitting jodhpurs, highly polished boots and beautifully cut hacking jacket, she sighed appreciatively.

'I think I will cancel the hirelings, such a pity to take you out riding now, the way you are looking I think I would really rather stay in with you, darling.'

But they drove out to Richmond Park anyway, and when Tom held out his hands in the correct way, fingers locked ready for her to place her riding boot in them and threw her lightly into the saddle, Florazel realised that here, in the stable yard, he was in complete command, and the way she turned and looked down at him from the saddle made him grow a lot taller than the six feet two inches, which was his declared height on the new passport he had acquired.

'You ride beautifully,' she murmured later when they pulled up at the top of a hill after a stiff, controlled canter. 'Have you always ridden?'

'Yes.'

Tom looked across at her from under his cap. After a half-hour's riding Florazel's hair was blowing in what looked like carefully arranged blonde tendrils about the brown felt of her hat, and what with her slim figure sitting to the horse in a way that was almost too perfect, she made up a picture that was really, in Tom's mind, a painting; and it was a painting that he was suddenly aware would stay with him for ever.

Lady Florazel Compton Riding in Richmond Park on a Sunny Day.

And there would be other paintings of her that he would keep and hang on the walls of his memory.

Lady Florazel Compton Rowing on the Serpentine.

Lady Florazel Compton Dancing.

Lady Florazel Compton Before the Famous Bennington Fancy Dress Ball at Rymans.

They had been passionate about each other for months now, and they went everywhere together, accepted in the crowded cocktail parties, the restaurants and on the dance floors of private houses, where Tom was finally able to mingle as if he too had been born on the Duke of Somerton's estate and left to the care of nannies and maids. Where Florazel told him she had been allowed to play in the vast kitchens while servants toiled to make soups and broths, preserves and bread, and every kind of jam or chutney. Where cooks like Tom's late mother roasted pheasants and crumbled bread-crumbs to the right degree of brown, whipped soufflés and distilled and reduced stocks for exquisite sauces.

'But that was all before the war,' Florazel would say, some-times looking a little sad. 'Now everything is so reduced.'

Tom had to accept that this was true, yet to his young eyes Florazel's life seemed hardly to be reduced, it seemed exotic to a degree, and he swiftly learned not just to address servants and staff, waiters and butlers in a low courteous tone, but to realise that people such as Florazel always took the time and trouble to appreciate what had been done for them. To go downstairs and thank the cook, to ask after a sick mother or a son who was off doing his National Service.

As it happened Tom's National Service papers had followed him around first to Knighton Hall, then to the Duke's estate from where they were dropped into his old lodgings; so it was some time before they somewhat in-congruously turned up at the Ritz, sent on by Mrs Posnet who enclosed a note thanking him for his rent money, which had arrived some few weeks after his sudden departure. The letter enclosing the papers also said that she hoped he was enjoying London. Since she carefully underlined the word 'enjoying' Tom knew that she must be aware of the very changed circumstances of his life.

Florazel snatched up the papers and stared at them.

'Don't worry about these, Tom, with my connections I can make sure that you don't have to waste your time square-bashing.'

She gave him a dazzling smile and swept off to her dressing room. Some hours later she came back, small blue leather notebook in hand.

'Ever had anything wrong with you, darling? Say like fallen arches, a bad back, anything useful, or silly, like that?'

Tom looked across at her, feeling instantly uneasy at the notion that Florazel could get him out of something that was after all to most people a moral obligation.

'I did have a tubercular gland, a few years ago. I was off work with a fever for a bit.'

'Splendid, that's all we need. You write to the doctor who treated you, and I'll tell old Perry Harborough and he'll get your papers stamped not-eligible because of TB.' She leaned forward and kissed him sumptuously. 'Can't have you wasting your time when you could be profiting from it, can we, Tom darling?'

Florazel swept back to her dressing room, her long satin housecoat making a pleasant sound as it trailed behind her on the carpet. Tom stared after her. He knew that she was making plans for both of them to go to America, which was exciting to say the least. He knew that, as the Duke of Somerton's sister, Florazel was what his mother would have called 'fabulously connected', so he was not surprised at her ability to pull strings. What surprised him was the ease with which people like her went about getting their own way. For a second he knew he should feel shocked, but then the thought of going to America with her took over and feelings of excitement replaced any latent guilt.

He turned away to write to the village doctor at Knighton to ask for the necessary confirmation. As he sat down at the ornate writing table with its paper headed *The Ritz, London*, he remembered how kind the old village doctor had been to him, knowing as he must have done that so much depended on Tom being able to carry on working. He had calmed

Tom's mother, reassuring her that the painfully throbbing gland was nothing more than an adolescent condition that with fresh air and a warm summer would be sure to pass. And it had. But as he picked up the hotel pen and started to write his letter Tom found that what had not passed was his hatred for Jamie Millington. Just writing the word *Knighton* brought back the memory of his dismissal.

Tom sealed the envelope and set it to one side as Florazel swept into the room wearing a white satin evening suit, the jacket and collar cuffed with plain white in contrast to the rest of the suit, which was lightly patterned. The skirt hung in soft folds that set off Florazel's tall, slender figure, and her hair was caught back into a diamond slide, which winked in the light as, having kissed Tom lightly on the mouth, she happily turned to the drinks tray.

'Time for you to change, darling. We are giving a dinner downstairs tonight, remember?'

Tom went quickly to his own dressing room. A few months before he was certain that he could not have coped with hosting a dinner party, but now he knew he could, and had proved that he could over many evenings together, for not only had Florazel instructed him in the niceties of social behaviour, but he had been able to observe and absorb from other men. Nowadays he was at such pains to appear relaxed and at ease in whatever social situation he found himself, he did not think anyone would guess who or what he had once been.

Mind you – he gave a wry look to his perfectly tailored evening jacket – no one could deny that clothes maketh if not a man, at least a gentleman. He stared in the mirror as he slowly and expertly tied his black bow tie. No, there was no doubt at all, the right clothes certainly helped.

Later he followed Florazel downstairs to the private dining room, his heart singing. He was in love, he was correctly dressed, he was certain that he was no longer an oik, and no one would know that he had once been referred to as such by the Millington girls. He was certain of it, until he faced the last of Florazel's dinner guests.

These guests walked into the private dining room with all the ease and assurance of a couple who knew that they were rich. They walked in with all the confidence of a couple who were now accepted in the less straight-laced upper echelons of patrician Society. They also knew that their hostess, besides being brilliantly born, relished the society of pleasantly raffish company like themselves, and they could not wait to meet the handsome new young man that it was rumoured she had in tow. In common with the rest of the guests they could not wait to meet him for no better reason than that they could then say that they had done so, that they had given him their approval, admired or not admired his looks, and enjoyed or ridiculed his conversational abilities. It was an undeniable truth, after all, that Society was all about mixing with one's equals, and sometimes even one's far from equals, in order to be able to go away and ridicule them.

Tom was talking to an Austrian Countess whom he had actually met before and been charmed by. He had just said something to make her laugh when Florazel touched him lightly on the arm.

'Tom darling, new guests.' She turned to the couple standing behind her. 'Mr and Mrs Millington, may I introduce Tom O'Brien?'

Tom turned and stared at the fabulously dressed new Mrs Millington – gold lamé evening coat worn with a straight, brocade dress.

'Well, well, well,' he said, slowly. 'This is a bit different from the last time we met.' He looked coolly at Florazel and then back at the frozen faces of the Millingtons. 'You know the last time I saw Mr and Mrs Millington, Florazel? They were in a barn, without a stitch on.'

From behind him came the sound of the Austrian Countess laughing, but there was an altogether different note to the sound she had been making only seconds earlier.

Sweet Sorrow

Mrs Smithers was standing by the door that led to what she, and Alexandra, now both thought of as 'Minty's basement'.

'Have you a young man down there, Minty?'

Alexandra nodded gravely.

'I am ver-ver-vastly afraid so,' she said with simple truth.

Mrs Smithers stared at her, vaguely astonished by her reply, since just for a moment it seemed as if it was Lady Inisheen speaking, not her maid-of-all-work.

'You know the rules, Minty. No gentlemen callers, especially not after six o'clock in the evening.'

'Yes, mer-mer-ma'am, I ner-know the rules, and if I could have shifted him from my kitchen some hours ago, ber-ber-believe me I would have der-done. If I could have kicked him awake I would have der-der-done, for a greater ner-ner-nuisance I have not come across in many a long day.'

Alexandra folded her arms across her chest in the manner of a village woman by her back door, or a cook pausing to gossip in a grocer's shop. It was, all in all, most definitely the gesture of an older woman, of a below-stairs sort of person, and she knew it would convince Mrs Smithers, who immediately stopped looking as if she was about to be cross and looked interested instead.

'Who is it down there, then, dear?'

Mrs Smithers gave a small hiccup and took a lace-edged handkerchief from her handbag with which she promptly covered her mouth in case it should happen again. She too, after all, had been to the wedding.

'It's Mer-Mer-Mrs Atkins's nephew. Remember Ber-Ber-Bob Atkins?'

Mrs Smithers nodded.

'Of course I remember Bob Atkins, Minty. He is Mrs Atkins-that-was, Mrs Atkins-that-used-to-be, that is, the Mrs Atkins-that-was, he is her nephew, that was or is.'

'Yes, and he arrived a sher-short while ago, from the wedding reception, and has fer-fer-fallen asleep at my kitchen table. His snoring is something ter-ter-terrible.' She held the basement door open wider for Mrs Smithers to hear. 'Ler-ler-listen.'

Mrs Smithers gave a stifled hiccup.

'Terrible,' she agreed from behind her handkerchief. 'Quite terrible.'

'He arrived without a ser-ser-say so, and insisted on interrupting my baking afternoon.' Alexandra looked and sounded indignant. 'What der-der-do you think I should der-der-do with him, ma'am? I mean, just listen to that snoring.'

'Do with him? I don't know, dear, really I don't. I've no idea how to deal with men who snore, I don't think there's a woman invented who has ever had an idea what to do with a man who snores.' She started to walk away. 'If I were you I should do what the rest of us have always done, just try and ignore it. In the end they do stop, you know. Really they do.'

There was a small silence as Alexandra watched Mrs Smithers walking more than a little unsteadily up the stairs to her suite of rooms. Alexandra finally sighed, once she was safely out of sight.

'It must have been a very liquid wedding,' she muttered to the dogs as she returned to the basement.

Happily perhaps for her sanity, Bob Atkins was now stirring from his collapsed position at the table.

'Now is the hour for you to go away,' Alexandra told him crisply as he slowly registered first her presence, then his own in her kitchen.

Bob stared at her and he immediately assumed a lap-dog, sad, please-forgive-me expression.

'Go? Oh no, surely not?'

'Oh yer-yer-yes, surely yes.'

'But I have only just arrived.'

'You have nearly just had mer-mer-me sacked. Mer-mer-maids are not allowed visitors to their quarters, never, ever, not if it was ever so.'

'You're not really a maid, are you, Minty?' Bob's look was now conspiratorial. 'And my aunt told me this is not really her house, just hired to impress, yes?'

'I certainly am a mer-maid,' Alexandra told him proudly. 'And I'm a ger-ger-good one too, now be off with you, as maids always say in plays, be off with you, ber-ber-before I get handed my cards.'

Bob stood up and smiled at her, his smile full of lazy charm, warmth and kindness.

'You speak too well to be a maid,' he announced with the confidence of a man who, on the strength of too much champagne, felt he could speak his mind.

'There have been mer-mer-maids who speak with all sorts of accents, Mr Atkins. Now, as I say, be off with you, and no coming back, please, or I really will be given the ber-ber-boot. Luckily for me Mrs Smithers is in about the same state as you.'

She handed him his top hat.

'Is she?' Bob looked intrigued. 'Weaving all over the shop, is she?'

'She certainly is, but any minute now, knowing her, she will be ringing the ber-ber-bell for her evening paper, her glass of sherry and her spectacles. So, be off with you!'

Bob walked slowly up the area steps to the street, and then, leaning over the iron railings, his top hat set to the back of his head, he called down to Alexandra.

'You have not heard the last of me, Minty. I shall be calling again, tomorrow, and the next day, and the next. I shall be calling so often that in the end you will have to marry me, see if you don't!'

Alexandra shot up the steps with his perfectly rolled silk umbrella which he had left leaning against the back door and handed it to him.

'Shoo, ber-ber-be off with you, Mr Atkins, please!'

She glanced around the square, convinced now that curtains would be twitching everywhere, curtains owned by so many of Mrs Smithers's long-time acquaintances and friends, older, genteel women who were jealous of her maid-of-all-work, and who would not be able to wait to tell her that the so-called always perfect Minty had been receiving a gentleman caller.

'Look, I'm quite serious. I do want to marry you. I do want to call on you again, for just that purpose. So where can we meet?'

He looked so pleading that Alexandra hesitated. It was a mistake, and she knew it. She knew in her heart of hearts that one hesitation can lead to a lifetime's confusion, and yet still she allowed herself to hesitate, to look into Bob Atkins's eyes and enjoy a few seconds of the warmth and sincerity that she saw there.

'Ler-Ler-Look, I have Sunday afternoon off. I'll meet you on Empire Road, and we'll walk the dogs up on the Downs. That is all I will promise. See you outside Lyons, on the corner of Eastern Road.'

'You have made me happier than I can possibly tell you. And after that, after we have walked your dogs, you will marry me, Minty, will you not?'

Bob swayed forward, his eyes half closed, his lips mimicking a kiss.

'That is my last offer, Mr Atkins, a walk with the dogs, not marriage,' she added dryly. 'Half per-per-past two tomorrow afternoon, outside Lyons Corner House. Ger-good evening to you.'

Alexandra closed the basement door and leaned against it, sighing. What with one thing and another this particular Saturday had proved just a little tiring. Even so she smiled as she started to cook herself a small meal, a meal that she would hastily eat, before having to run upstairs and cater to Mrs Smithers's needs. It would be nice to go for a walk on the Downs with someone else. It would be nice to have someone besides the dogs with whom she could talk about silly things. Nice to have a friend, really.

Tom looked across at Florazel. She was undressing. She always wore the most exquisite underwear, but at that moment she could have been wearing potato sacks, her stockings held up with gardening string, for all he cared.

'If you want us to go on being together, you will never ask those Millingtons here ever again.'

He was surprised by the authority in his voice, as well he might be, since his announcement had been enough to see the Millingtons hurrying out of the private dining room, and had been the cause of a resetting of the dinner table, not to mention a crescendo of amazed conversation, swiftly to be followed the next morning, without any doubt at all, by a flurry of the most pulsating rumours, as everyone present telephoned each other in swift succession.

'I'm sorry, Tom. I never realised that there was something

between you. I should have gone through the guest list with you.' Florazel stopped before adding, '*Never thought someone like you would know anyone that I knew, really.*'

'Never mind all that,' Tom told her. 'It is of no consequence to me who you ask to your dinner parties, they're not my friends, but just remember if you ever see or hear from those Millingtons again, you will never see or hear from me again, and that is my last word on it, Florazel.'

Florazel nodded with surprising meekness.

'Of course I won't ask them again. The last thing I would want would be to upset you.' She sat down suddenly on the bed, and her head tilted forward into her long-fingered, ringed fingers, loosening her hair. 'I never, ever want to upset you, darling boy. Never. You are the light of my life. I mean, to see Jamie Millington of all people looking as if he had just had a bucket of iced water from the wine cooler thrown at him. It was . . .' Her shoulders started to shake, as she sobbed into her fingers.

'Florazel!' Tom knelt beside her. 'Florazel!' He parted her fingers with some difficulty only to see with relief that she was laughing. 'You minx, you little devil!'

They clung together, laughing hysterically, and moments later started to make love.

At tea the following day, after a long, leisurely walk in St James's Park, Florazel decided to dig a little deeper.

'What exactly did Jamie Millington do to make you hate him so much?'

Tom dabbed his mouth with his thick, white linen napkin, and lit a cigarette.

'My mother was a cook to him and his wife, at Knighton Hall. I don't know whether you know Knighton Hall?'

'I know of it,' Florazel replied carefully.

'She was a very good cook. More than that, she was a

brilliant cook, but she had a flaw. She was a perfectionist, so if things went wrong, she took to the bottle. Well, as it happened, at Knighton Hall it didn't matter, because there was an under-cook, not as brilliant as my mother, but good enough; so if my mother collapsed she could take over from her. And that was how she came to last more than a few weeks in the position, because of this other woman. And I too had a good situation, general dogsbody, riding out, looking after the horses under old Westrup. We were fine, until that woman, until Jennifer Langley-Ancram came into the picture. Moved into Knighton village, looked round the neighbourhood for a likely victim, found one in the shape of James Millington Esquire, joined his hunt, set her cap at him, and . . . '

'You found them in flagrante delicious, *n'est-ce pas?*'

Tom looked momentarily amused at the memory.

'Yes, I was bicycling to get old Westrup some linctus for his cough, heard something suspicious in the barn as I was passing and looked in. For my sins.' He laughed shortly. 'Well, soon as I saw them I knew I had to be for the chop – in case I went and told on them – but I didn't want my ma's position to be affected. She'd been so happy at Knighton Hall, for once she'd seemed so happy. First time I'd seen her settled.' He shook his head. 'James Millington was clever though, you have to give it to him, he was wily. He accused *me*, quick as that.' Tom snapped his fingers. 'Said he'd found *me* in the barn *in flagrante delicto* with a local girl, but Mrs Millington, the first Mrs Millington, she didn't want to let her cook go, because she had guests that weekend, so the last thing she wanted was a social shambles. So I left to find a new position, and Ma stayed on. Eventually, as you know, I got a job working for your brother, and . . . '

'And?'

Tom fell silent. And.

'And.'

'And?'

'I fell in love with you,' Tom stated, finally, a little flatly.

Florazel smiled.

'Now,' Tom said slowly, 'how about your husband, about your marriage? You've never really told me anything, except he was much older, and he died.'

For the first time since he had fallen in love with her Tom saw Florazel looking vulnerable; more than that he saw her actually looking emotionally raw.

'We never actually married. Besides, you don't really want me to tell you about him, do you, Tom?'

'I want to know everything about you, Florazel. You know, I love you. When you love, you want to know everything about that person.'

'I was very young,' she began, after a short pause in which she lit a cigarette. 'I had led, as the joke goes, a very sheltered life. I had not had the war to grow me up, free me, if you like, not like girls now. My father and mother died so young, both from typhoid – you know, the drains in those old houses are lethal, and no one had done anything about them at Brindles, where we mostly lived. At any rate, the end result was that my brother being much older, and a bachelor, there was no one to help me grow up. It was inevitable, I suppose, that I should fall in love with a much older man, a jokester, a man who seemed to light up every room when he went in, for it only to become darker when he left.'

Tom looked puzzled, but said nothing.

'I ran off with him. Not a good thing in our circles, to run off aged eighteen with a *married* man. He was in fact a monster, a master of charm in the drawing room, and a master of cruelty at home, and of course he had only ever been after my money, as everyone had warned me.' She stopped, giving a wry smile. 'No one will ever know, who has not experienced it, what it is like to be belittled day and night, night and day. I cried in every capital in Europe. He spent my money and of course he never did marry me. Why should he? Over and over again I tried to leave him, but something always held me back, some foolish idea that I could change; or he could. Finally I did run off, to Italy, to Venice, to Rome, to join large circles of people who did not know about me, or care, and so gradually I did rid myself of him. And finally, thank God, he died suddenly of a heart attack, and I came back to England.' She paused. 'Anyway, enough of that, Tom. I have said quite enough. The past is the past, and in my opinion should be locked behind a door, and the key thrown away.'

'How could anyone be cruel to you, Florazel? What a bastard he must have been, a hateful cruel bastard.'

'Oh I'm afraid he was hateful, but I was a silly ignorant young girl, so we made quite a pair.' She laughed. 'By the way, Tom, apropos of nothing we were talking of, your call-up papers? The good doctor did write to my contact, a dear old general, great friend of my brother's actually, and it seems your dear little tubercular gland does mean that they have deferred any National Service until further notice. You are not suitable to be an officer, and since you are already a gentleman, we now know where we are with you, don't we?' She stood up and kissed him lightly across the tea table. 'Do you realise that this means that we can sail to New York as soon as may be? I have booked tickets on the *Queen Mary*. You will love it.' Her expression grew dreamy. 'Cut off from the whole world, one sails along in a whirl of luxury. It is something you have to know or you simply haven't lived.'

Tom stared at her. There seemed no end to the wondrous

life she had opened up for him, and perhaps as a consequence no end to his desire for her.

'What are you thinking of, Tom?'

'I was wondering what would have happened to me if Mrs Posnet, my landlady, hadn't sent me up to your brother's estate that day. What would I be doing now? That's what I was wondering. What would have happened to me?'

'You would be waiting for me to come along, which I would have done, sooner or later, because you needed me, Tom. You would be waiting for me; you need me, as much as I need you.'

As Tom caught her hand and kissed its smooth, white surface, and as he reluctantly gave her back her hand, having admired her beautiful rings and her perfectly manicured nails, he turned away from the sudden memory of Bob Atkins's voice, which would recur at such odd moments. What did it matter if Florazel had enjoyed other affairs? She was a beautiful woman, for God's sake. He would make her life, as she had made his, as beautiful as it could be. He would give her anything she wanted.

Perhaps it was thinking of this that led him to go in search of the box that contained his mother's final gifts to him: the touchingly few pieces of jewellery, her passport, the letter, everything – besides a few hundred pounds in the bank – that she had left in the world, which she had left to him. When he eventually found the cheap cardboard box, he could not help feeling almost repelled by its drab appearance, so incongruous did it appear among all the luxury of his surroundings, so out of place in his new life; and that was all before he opened it and reread her last letter to him, written with such difficulty in cheap biro on lined, narrow, blue writing paper. Mrs O'Brien and her son Tom, they had been everything to each other, no matter what, and they had been so happy at Knighton. If only he had not gone for

Westrup's medicine, if only he had not opened that barn door, she might perhaps be alive now. He might have been able to help her, find her a pretty cottage somewhere, give her everything that he had ever wanted for her: a happy life, money enough to buy a new dress or a winter coat, expensive shoes – money to have her hair done properly, things that could have transformed her back into the girl that he could see in her passport photograph.

He looked up as Florazel returned, humming in time with a tune that was playing on her dressing-room radio. She was dressed to go out for the evening in a black lace cocktail dress with a small silk bolero jacket over the top. Her whole allure, the way she wore her clothes, everything that she suddenly seemed to stand for – sophistication, good manners, and elegance – was in such sharp contrast to his mother's few possessions in their small box, that looking from the contents of the box to Florazel was like a blow in the solar plexus.

Little surprise therefore that Tom felt overwhelmed with love for this new older woman in his life who had lifted him into another world, a world where power and influence were taken for granted, where life's small luxuries were a permanent suite at the Ritz in London, a convertible Bentley in the garage, and a wardrobe of couture clothes.

'What would you say are the great luxuries in your life, Florazel?'

She was standing in front of the mirror over the chimney-piece, so she now eyed him in it.

'My great luxuries?' She sounded puzzled, as if she had never before thought of her life as having any luxuries. She frowned. 'My greatest luxuries,' she repeated. 'Oh, love, of course, love is one of life's greatest luxuries. And quiet, and – oh, and privacy. After that, maids and valets and so on, which of course all come with living at the Ritz.'

'Don't you ever think of having a house of your own? A garden. Somewhere only you went, not owned by anyone but you?'

Florazel shook her head and laughed.

'Gracious, Tom, you're beginning to sound just like my brother. No, is the answer to that. I do not dream of owning a house and garden. For the very good reason I could not bear to deal with servants and gardeners.' She stopped, looking vaguely embarrassed, remembering Tom's previous profession. 'You know what I mean.'

Tom laughed as she coloured.

'You mean you'd rather take the gardener to bed than have to tell him what to plant?'

At this they both laughed, and Tom, having replaced his treasured box on the desk, caught at her hands and pulled her to him.

'You are outrageous, Florazel Compton, did you know that?'

She nodded happily.

'I certainly hope so, goodness knows I have worked hard enough to be so.'

Tom, his heart flowing over with love for her, turned back to the desk.

'I have something in here for you, Florazel . . .'

He carefully opened the box, and took out first his mother's letter, and then her passport.

'These were my mother's,' he said with reverence in his voice. 'Her last letter to me, and her passport, from before she was married.'

'Oh poor lady, how she must have loved you.'

Tom nodded. His mother had loved him. He had been all she had. He opened her old passport and stared at the photo of the slender, pretty young woman and shook his head.

'She changed so much in her life, once she had me, she even changed her name. She always seemed so frightened in case my father might catch up with her. She never would talk about it much; except to say that my father was cruel and that she prayed to God every day that I would not turn out like him. And that's how it stayed until one day she told me that she'd heard that he'd died, but that she could not even bring herself to feel sorry. That was what she dreaded most, I think. Sometimes it wasn't easy for her, because if she was cooking in big houses, she never really knew who might turn up at any time, she was always dreading that someone might recognize her from her former life. "You never know, Tom." She always said that, she was always suspicious, always listening, waiting, in case one of my father's family caught up with her, took me away from her. Never would tell me my father's name. "You're Thomas O'Brien, and that's all you need to know," she would say. And now I suppose, in respect to her memory, I don't want to know about him either. I will always stay, as she wanted me to be, plain Thomas O'Brien. And proud of it too.'

'May I see?'

Florazel stretched out her hand and took the passport from him and stared first at the front page, and then the page containing the photograph.

'She was very pretty, Tom,' she stated, after a long pause during which she continually turned the first pages of the passport, examining them closely, before flicking aimlessly through the rest. 'Didn't travel much, though, did she?'

She turned away and going to her evening bag she took out her cigarette case and a tipped cigarette.

'So you don't remember your father at all?'

Tom shook his head.

'No. I was just a mistake. Some people are, aren't they? But if I was a mistake, which I assuredly was, I know it would be a greater one to try and find who I was meant to be, who my poor dead mother married. I know what he must have been like from what she *didn't* say about him. She was like someone who'd had a rotten time as a prisoner of war, she really wouldn't mention her marriage, and I don't blame her. So, I'm Tom O'Brien, and that's good enough for me, whatever it says there on Ma's passport. Maybe it will be different when I'm older, but I doubt it.'

'You are quite right, Tom. As I said: one should never go back to the past. It is the golden rule, never, ever go back.'

Florazel went over to the drinks tray, lighting the cigarette as she went. Tom replaced the passport and his mother's letter in the box, and after a few seconds followed this by taking out a small leather box which he held tightly as he walked towards her.

'Florazel?'

'Yes. Tom?'

She was now mixing them both one of her stunning cocktails.

'You know how much in love with you I am, don't you, Florazel?'

She looked up from her task, smiling.

'And I with you, Tom. We are both in love with each other. We know that, don't we?'

'Well, I wonder if you would marry me, Florazel?' Tom opened the top of the leather box and was gratified to see that the small diamond ring inside was just opulent enough to catch the lights far above them. 'Will you marry me, Florazel?'

Florazel stared first at the ring in the box, and then at Tom, his grey eyes so obviously full of the emotion of which he was speaking.

'No, Tom, I will not marry you.' She smiled. 'I will do

anything for you, but not that, I can never marry, not ever.'

Tom stared at her as she smiled apologetically.

'I don't like commitment, Tom. I don't like permanence. Now is the time I like. Tomorrow I might not like anything here, not even myself. We don't need rings and commitment. We have now and here, anything else is not worth thinking about, not worth sighing over.' Seeing the look of hurt on his face, she touched him lightly on his cheek. 'Cheer up, darling, it might be worse. I might say "yes"!'

Tom turned away feeling the most awful fool, and at the same time Bob's words came back to him from that early spring afternoon that now seemed like a century ago. '*She's a nymphomaniac, didn't you know, old boy? It's well known that Lady Florazel Compton devours younger men. It's her hobby.*'

'Hadn't you better go and change? We are entertaining in a private room downstairs tonight. So many more of my friends I want you to meet, darling.'

Later he heard Florazel saying laughingly to some friend, over the sound of the usual cocktail party chatter, 'You must come and meet my new toy, so handsome, such fun.'

Her words, lightly said, nevertheless had a horrid theatrical ring to them. They were false and he knew it, just flippant words that people use when they are at pains to appear lightweight and social, but now that he knew that Florazel did not want to commit herself, that he might well be just a passing fancy, her words seemed to have a cruel reality to them.

Filled with an overpowering desire to be on his own, away from all the inconsequential chatter, Tom slipped away from the party without bothering to collect Florazel, or even to tell her that he was leaving.

For the next few hours he walked around Mayfair, staring up at the lights in the elegant houses, looking at cars arriving and departing, their chauffeurs standing to attention, the maids in their black and white uniforms holding open the doors to allow the beautifully dressed guests to pass in or out. This was the world to which Florazel had introduced him. This was the world that he now inhabited. He had tasted of not one forbidden fruit but many. In a very few months he had grown used to the feel of good clothes, to eating exquisite food, to the constant attention of hotel staff, to chauffeurs and maids, valets and waiters. There was no going back now, and Tom knew it.

Bob was standing on the corner outside the Lyons teashop looking vaguely embarrassed as people do who are waiting for someone that they fear might not turn up. He shifted every now and then from foot to foot, and looked up and down the old street, noting how few people took a walk on Sunday afternoons, how the world and his wife seemed to disappear never to return, and at the same time remembering how long Sunday afternoon had been when he was a boy. He recalled how he had invented a friend with whom he would play imaginary games, games of which his friend would never tire – but the moment he caught sight of Alexandra being bowled along by the dogs, his face lit up and he forgot all about those lonely Sundays of childhood, and bounded forward, his hand outstretched for one of the tartan leads.

'Here, let me have a dog, Minty. I want a dog to walk too, you know.' He leaned down and patted the top of Rupert's head. 'He's a real gent, I can tell. He won't mind me taking charge of him, will he, Minty?'

Alexandra hesitated, about to tell him her real name, and then she stopped. It suddenly seemed better to stay being Minty, at least in Deanford, so much less confusing for everyone, including herself.

The green of the grass that day was a powdery green, as it would be, given the underlying chalk of the Downs, but the wild flowers did not seem to care that the lush green of the meadows far below was brighter than anything that surrounded them, any more than the birds that sang and flew past as Alexandra and Bob and the dogs attempted to run up the steep hills, only to stop out of breath, before turning to stare down the incline up which they had all come.

It was a rare feeling to be free of cooking and cleaning, to have the wind blow your hat off and to have to run back after it, to have Bob catch your hand to steady you as you stood on the crest of the topmost incline, and in turn for you both to catch up the spaniels and put them on their leads. It was deliciously satisfactory to walk slowly down to a nearby village, some few miles away from the still, Sundayness of Deanford, and order tea and toast at Ann's Pantry, not to mention sponge cake with a cream and jam filling, which suddenly seemed to both of them, what with the walking and the climbing, to be the first food they had eaten in days, so intense and individual were the tastes, so delicate the cups of tea, so friendly the service.

Up until then thoughts of love had not really entered Alexandra's head, and despite the usual adolescent anxieties over the exact way to wear her shoulder-length dark hair, or the advisability, or not, of sunbathing – something of which her grandmother had heartily disapproved – she had reconciled herself to realising that for her, as yet, the opposite sex was something about which she knew little and cared less. Her life at home had been too confined, altogether too regimented to allow for anything more than dreams, and any thoughts of romance had always to be put aside in favour of the practicalities of living.

Now was different. Now she was away from home, and she could see that Bob was already imagining that he was in love with her, and that was at the very least interesting, and at the very best exciting, because Bob was tall and handsome, and he had such an engaging manner that Alexandra soon realised that long before he came into sight, she was smiling just at the thought of him.

'I say, wasn't it ner-ner-nice that they let the dogs in?'

Although Alexandra had walked out of the café, closely followed by a deliriously happy Bob, she felt so carefree she now skipped one pace as children suddenly do. Seeing this Bob's heart too skipped a beat, and he knew instantly that he would love her all his life, and that no one else would do, that Minty was everything he could wish for in a girl, so different, so innocent of the false coquettish ways of other girls he had taken out.

'I must see you again, Minty. Please.'

They were standing by the back door to her basement flat. Alexandra looked away, not really wanting to see what Bob was feeling, not wanting to get there yet, wanting to keep everything as it had been that afternoon.

'I-I-I only have Sundays off, and then only really after mer-mer-midday, because I ler-ler-like to make sure that Mrs Smithers has her ler-ler-lunch laid on, that she doesn't feel lonely, especially on Sundays.'

'Does she feel lonely often?'

'She is going out to ler-ler-lunch next Sunday.'

'Then so are you, Minty.' Bob leaned forward and kissed her gently, lips closed. 'So are you.'

Seconds later he spun off down the street, whistling.

Mrs Smithers stared at Alexandra.

'This is becoming a bit of a habit, Minty. You have been going out so often with Mr Atkins over these last months, it won't be long before there are rumours running riot all over Deanford. I do hope that nothing is happening between you and Mr Atkins that might affect our little business, really I do.'

Alexandra, who was wearing a new evening dress bought for her by Bob, shrugged her shoulders lightly.

'If you'd rer-rer-rather I stayed behind . . .'

'Of course I would rather you stayed behind, but it is Saturday evening, and we have agreed recently that you are allowed Saturday off if we have no engagements in the house, so no more to be said, I don't suppose.' Mrs Smithers sniffed and shook the evening paper. 'I just hope that you don't bring trouble home, Minty dear. Maids so often do, in fact maids are famous for bringing trouble home.'

'I-I hope so ter-ter-too, ma'am!' Alexandra laughed lightly, and as she did so Mrs Smithers gave her a brief look over the top of her newspaper.

With the growing success of their little business, their relationship had changed a great deal, as it would. Even so, every so often, Alexandra delighted in saying 'ma'am', which she knew nowadays actually made Mrs Smithers feel vaguely uncomfortable.

But Mrs Smithers had said 'maids do bring trouble home' so often lately that Alexandra could not help teasing her a little. It was irresistible.

'Yer-yer-your supper's laid in the dining room, and Mr Ber-Ber-Bellasco is calling round at eight to ter-ter-take you for chatty bridge to Mr and Mrs Mitford's opposite; so you won't be wanting for distractions, as my grandmother used to say.'

Mrs Smithers shook the paper yet again.

'I dare say your grandmother was a woman with plenty of opinions, some of which were undoubtedly her own, Minty, but I had still rather you were at home here, even if I am not, most especially if I am not. No one to answer the telephone, and so on.'

'Mer-Mer-Mer-Mr Atkins wanted most especially to take me out, today being what it is, ma'am, with your per-permission, of course.'

Alexandra was now not just playing the contrite maid to the hilt but managing to look it too, while secretly enjoying it all the time.

'Mr Atkins should stick to taking you out on Sunday afternoons.'

'Well, he would have der-der-done, but seeing it was my birthday today . . .'

It was Alexandra's trump card, and she had played it at just the right moment, for in contrast to Alexandra, Mrs Smithers became instantly and genuinely contrite, insisting on pouring them both a sherry and toasting Minty's health, and ending by pressing a panic-stricken five-pound note into her maid's hand, a note which Alexandra promptly refused, knowing only too well that her employer needed it almost more than she did.

'Now off you go, Minty. And by the way, Mr Atkins has very fine taste. That dress is most fetching.'

Bob had brought the evening dress – well, it was not so much an evening dress as a cocktail dress – round by special delivery that morning. Its arrival had been a heart-stopping moment, for Alexandra had hardly woken when there was a knock at the basement door and she had opened it only to discover Bob, a cap on the back of his head, a cigarette stuck to the side of his mouth, a pile of boxes in his arms.

'Miss Minty Stamford? Morning to you, miss, I'm here to make a delivery for you from a Mr Atkins. He says to tell you he'll be round to fetch you in a chauffeured car at seven o'clock prompt, and he nicked your measurements when you was upstairs last Saturday doing tea for Lady Bobbity and her friends.'

'Ber-Ber-Bob! You shouldn't!'

From the first swanky box and startlingly white tissue paper had emerged a pale pink three-quarter-length dress, the bodice made of organza and decorated with three black bows; from the second box and yet more startlingly white tissue paper had come pale pink shoes and a matching clutch bag.

'Oh Ber-Ber-Bob . . .'

Bob, still glorying in the character of the errand boy, had been just about to back out of her flat again, when Alexandra reached up and kissed him extravagantly.

'Just as well I put me fag out, eh, Miss Stamford?'

They had both laughed, but what with Alexandra still being in her pyjamas, and Mrs Smithers, as if by sixth sense, calling down to her maid from the door above that led to the flat, Bob had been forced to flee.

It was only when he had reached the top step and had gone a few yards that he stopped and leaned against the black iron railings. Minty had really kissed him! She had really, really kissed him. She had kissed him as if she loved him. If Minty loved him, he was certain he would never need anything else.

Tom was meeting Bob once again for lunch. Bob was looking just the way Tom was feeling, on top of the world, the whole world outside the restaurant, where they were once more being tempted by ribs of beef in great silver dishes, roasted vegetables and what Bob insisted on calling 'lashings of thick dark brown gravy'.

'So, you're off to America, Tom O'Brien, and on the *Queen Mary*. You must be the luckiest devil alive, in love with a brilliant woman and sailing for the New World.'

'I suppose I must be.' Tom smiled ingenuously. He certainly could not think of anyone luckier than himself. 'How about you, Bob? How is the wonderful Minty?'

Bob smiled, and he sighed a sigh of such contentment and happiness that Tom, who had his fork raised, put it down momentarily and stared at him.

'Going that well, is it, Bob?'

'She is in love with me, and I with her.'

'But that is wonderful, my dear chap, wonderful.'

Bob looked at Tom, who now felt quite able to continue eating. Tom had changed so much since they had both met gardening, it was almost impossible to recognise him from the taciturn, roughly dressed young man with the slight country accent whom he had first taken to the pub. In the old days Tom would never have said 'my dear chap' or been able to cope with a wine list.

'So are you to propose? Will you marry?'

'No, I can't marry Minty, Tom, at least not yet.'

'Why? Because – because she's in service? Surely not? Will your parents not approve? To hell with their opinions, Bob, marry the girl you love.'

'No, it's not that. I know my parents will love her, she's kind and beautiful and innocent. No that is not why I can't marry her, at least not yet.'

'Then why?'

'National Service.'

Tom immediately put his fork down again and felt swamped by guilt. He was just about to suggest to Bob that he could ask Florazel to influence somebody to stop him having to do National Service, when he stopped, knowing instinctively that his friend would be repelled by the suggestion.

'You poor so-and-so.'

'And you. Have you had your call-up papers yet?'

'Yes, they chased me, right to the Ritz.'

They both laughed.

'And?'

'And I have been rejected.'

'For what reason – not the usual?'

'No, the unusual. TB gland. They don't like us tainted folks. Can't have people getting ill before they're shot, can they?'

'Ah, you have a nifty turn of phrase, old boy, you really do.' Bob looked amused and sober at the same time. 'So while I am falling to and square-bashing and all that, you will be sailing on the *Queen Mary* with the love of your life. Well, if that is not all the luck, I don't know it. You couldn't let me catch your TB, could you? Sniff, sniff, I could catch it if I tried hard enough, couldn't I?'

'You wouldn't want it, dear chap, really you wouldn't.'

'And when you get to New York? What then? Another round of luncheons and dinners, hiring a house on Long Island, the whirl of the social life, dancing your life away, that sort of thing?'

'No. At least I don't know. No, I – am going to start a business.'

Tom did not know why he had just said what he had said. He did not understand why he had suddenly stated something about which he had not even thought. It was really only a reaction to Bob's light sarcasm, and to the idea that he was some sort of gigolo just dancing his life away in the company of an older woman, but said it he had, and now that he had it seemed to him he had a strong feeling that was exactly what he *would* do. He could not spend the rest of his life socialising. It was not the kind of thing that a man would do. All of a sudden he felt ashamed that he had let Florazel get his papers passed not fit for active service. He determined he would make it up by making something of his life instead. More than that – he must.

'I say, what a cracking future you have, Tom. New York, America, and starting a business. The moment I get out of the Army, I will not only marry Minty, but we will join you in America, see if we don't, lucky devil that you are. You've already brought me luck, you'll bring me more, I know it.'

Early next morning, while Tom was having his hair cut at Trumper's, Florazel was busying herself putting the finishing touches to their packing. There was a mountain of luggage, as there always was when you sailed to New York. Florazel's own luggage had been made especially for her, large enough to take the most elaborate gowns, gowns that could be hung on hangers in vast trunks which opened like doors in a wardrobe and from which rails could be pulled forward so that the dresses did not crease.

Her maid had been busying herself with everything, both of them in that state of suspended excitement which comes with the prospect of a long sea journey, a change of scene, and social adventures to come, in another land.

There was a knock at the door of the suite. The maid went to open it. A messenger boy in a pillbox hat held out a silver tray on which was placed a card, and waited outside the door for a possible return message.

'A message for Lady Florazel Compton.'

Maria took the card and hurried back into the suite to present it to Florazel. It had a single name and a telephone number written on it. Florazel's mouth tightened and she paled as she saw the name, and then turned the card over and read the message on the back.

'Tell the bell boy— No, wait.'

She took one of her own cards and scribbled on the back.

'Give him this.'

When Maria returned Florazel was standing in the middle of the room looking wretched as she so often did when Tom was out and she found every minute seemed an hour.

'Maria, I must go downstairs and meet this lady, can you finish without me?'

'Of course, my lady. I will finish everything, my lady.'

Florazel gave a quick look at herself in the mirror, and then looked away. The very sight of that name on the card made her not just feel ugly, but look ugly. She turned to leave the suite, which now seemed strangely worn and shabby as hotel suites can do after a long stay. She picked up her handbag, which suddenly looked vulgar with its silly cipher in gold, and the beringed hand that picked it up, that too looked vulgar, the ring too big, the hand too soft and white, like someone else's hand, the hand of a person with whom you would not wish to become friends.

'Florazel.'

She might be much aged, as she would be, but her voice was almost precisely the same.

'Sally.'

Florazel kissed the aged cheek in a non-kissing manner, either side of the closely hatted, white-haired head.

'Would you like a glass of champagne? Champagne in the morning is good, don't you think?'

'Well, as a matter of fact,' Sally looked momentarily pleased, distracted. 'As a matter of fact, yes, I would.'

She paused, obviously feeling, in the face of this generosity, a little hampered, as if she could not continue until the wine had been served.

'Delicious. You are quite right, champagne in the morning can sometimes be just the thing, particularly when you are old.' She paused before starting again. 'The reason I have come to visit you after all these years, my dear, is because it has been brought to my attention that your newest beau is a young man who closely resembles someone . . .'

With her heart sinking Florazel sipped her champagne and listened to the old woman. Ever since she was very young she had always had a horror of older women calling her 'my dear'. For some reason the moment an older woman said 'my dear' you always knew that they were either about to tell you something you did not want to hear, or about to induce you to do something quite against your will. She already knew this morning was going to be no different, as with a sinking heart she realised that in some way the net was closing in on her affair with Tom, that Sally Hardwick had come to make a claim on her grandson.

The moment she had said 'my dear' Florazel knew instinctively that she would lay before Florazel the kind of 'either or' choices at which old women were so adept. Of course there would be no suggestion of blackmail, of that there was no need. Gerald her son had after all died, but her grandson now lived, and she could not, would not willingly look on while he went the same way as his poor father, leading a life of debauchery, pulled down by paper-thin social values, frittering away an existence of a life that depended only on the next party, the next invitation.

'How did you know it was him?' Florazel asked, eventually.

'How did *you*?'

'His mother's passport – maiden name, all that. And you?'

Florazel lit a cigarette and sat back, but her pretence at relaxation fooled neither of them.

'I saw you with him at Ascot, and I knew at once that Gerald had stamp-marked his only progeny. Can you imagine what it was like for an old woman seated on a bench on those green lawns to imagine that she was seeing her dead son coming towards her? Can you imagine what that was like?'

Florazel was silent. Ascot, dammit! And they had only gone on Ladies' Day, everything so crowded, people passing all the time, hats and laughter, champagne and strawberries, and yet with all that Sally Hardwick had still managed to recognise that Tom had to be Gerald's son.

'I knew at once that you must have, somehow, God alone knows how, Florazel, that you must have found Gerald's son. It didn't seem possible, and yet I knew it had to be. There are some fathers and some sons who look so alike it is like a punch in the stomach when you see them. My poor son, Gerald, was a weakling, we know that—'

'He was not a weakling, Sally, he was a monster.'

'If you say so, drink does destroy character I will admit, but I will also say this: I will not stand idly by while someone like you, Florazel, sets about the next generation.'

'Someone like me, Sally?'

'Yes, someone like you, Florazel. Whatever Gerald did to you is far into the past now. I may be old, may be dying, but I am not a fool. I know the kind of set in which you now move, and spending his time with people like you is no place for a young man. You know it, and I know it. You must end this affair before it is too late and the poor young man has gone in too deep. You must end this affair at once. If you do not, I will go to him myself.'

'I love him.'

'I'm sure you do, Florazel.' Sally nodded, but she went on, her voice now devoid of any particular emotion: 'But the simple truth is that you have loved before, many times, and you will love again.'

'This time is different.'

'Every time is different. You must give him up.'

'Or?'

Sally turned her faded green eyes on Florazel.

'Or else I will use my influence . . .'

'On?'

There was a small silence as Sally stared at Florazel.

'Proprietors of newspapers do so enjoy a campaign against someone new, you know. You have been very lucky so far – your reputation has been kept in the shadows. As I say –

so far, but only really on account of your brother. That protection can be swiftly removed. Do you really want to have to leave England, live the kind of bored and bitter existence that the Windsors now live? Be cut off from all that is familiar because doors everywhere will be closed to you—'

'As a matter of fact I am on my way to America even now,' Florazel interrupted flippantly.

'Yes, my dear, I am sure; but that is only exciting because you know that whenever you want you can, after all, come home. One should remind you that aside from death, the Romans' greatest punishment was exile. To have to live away from your friends and family, to hear only a foreign language spoken, reduces the most robust personality to a state of listlessness. I have seen the exiled English, in Florence, in Rome, in Paris, in the South of France; wherever they are they seem forever suspended in time. Always waiting: waiting for the English newspapers to arrive, waiting for English friends to visit, waiting for news of home. That very word – *home* – is surely the most emotive in the English language, and to be away from it means to be in a state of permanent limbo.'

Florazel was silent. It was true. She loved England, not because she was particularly patriotic but because in England she was after all the Duke of Somerton's sister, she was someone who was used to respect, deference, status. Once abroad she knew only too well she would be yet another ageing woman in search of entertainment, and perhaps, given Tom's youth, quite soon in search of another young lover. And too, as Sally Hardwick well knew, if Florazel became a victim of the British press, if she was made notorious, her already fragile reputation permanently destroyed, her brother would drop her, he was so old fashioned she imagined that he might even strike her name from the family bible.

'*Dragging the family name through the mud.*' How often she had heard that phrase when growing up. Relations forever distanced, confined to the lower echelons of Society, black-balled, doors shut against them for just that reason. No one, it seemed, stood by someone who dragged the family name through the mud. No one from a great family encouraged publicity. It was just not done.

'You can see the sense in what I am saying, can you not?'

Florazel stared at Sally. How she hated her! And the truth was she hated her all the more for being right.

'I can see what you are saying, yes.'

She stared down at the table in front of them, thinking in a dazed way that she could see everything that might happen as if it already had.

'Common sense, my dear, mere common sense. *Tempus fugit*. Time flies. You are getting older, you are still beautiful, but not young.'

'I was only young when your son first seduced me.'

'Exactly, then you know the danger and how much un-happiness it brought. My grandson is only young. You will give him up. You are too sensible not to.'

'Tom.'

He was looking so smart, so handsome, bursting with the kind of happiness that Florazel realised was heartbreaking in its lack of self-consciousness, its longing to share his joy with the rest of the world.

'At your service, my lady.' He kissed her hand, and turned his head. 'Like the cut?'

'Very fine, the finest haircut I have seen this morning. Tom.' She smiled, 'I want you to go on ahead to the ship, taking your luggage, in the first car, and make the suite ready for us. I will follow with Maria and my luggage in the second car. Here, take your passport and your tickets and reservations.' She touched him lightly on the shoulder to be sure of his attention, and pretended to frown. 'Now, you know how I like the rooms to look, Tom, you *will* be sure to make them look how I like?'

'Of course. White flowers, champagne in a bucket, et cetera.'

'Exactly. So, will you do this for me?'

'I will do anything for you, you know that.'

He leaned forward and kissed her as he always did, raising open eyes to heaven just a little, whereas Florazel closed hers, and they were still closed as he turned away.

'The excitement. New York, New York, it's a wonderful town!' Tom sang. 'I can't believe this is happening. We are on our way, at last we are on our way.'

Florazel turned away as he rang the service bell for a porter to come for his luggage.

'Off you go, Tom, off you go . . .'

'See you aboard, all aboard the *Q.M.*!'

He followed the porter out of the suite. Downstairs the old lady had gone, with a promise to return. Upstairs Florazel watched the love of her life stepping jauntily into the first of the waiting cars. She watched his dark head of hair, his tall slim body, and prayed that he would not turn, but he did. He turned and kissed his hand up to the window above him, knowing by some fine lover's sense that she was probably watching him. Florazel too turned, but away from the window, tears pouring down her face.

'My lady? My lady!'

Maria went to her mistress as she flung herself on the richly cushioned chintz sofa, sobbing.

'It's nothing, nothing.'

'If nothing, please why is my lady crying?'

'Because – I can't help myself.'

The maid put a comforting arm around her mistress, understanding all too well the exigencies of love.

'In Spain we say *he* who loves you, must hurt you. Also, I think, *she* who loves you, must hurt you.'

Downstairs the hall porter held the door open for Sally Hardwick. She stepped out into a London she no longer recognised. She had done her duty. She would swait to get in touch with her grandson. For the moment, the ending of his first affair would be shock enough.

A Rough Passage

Mrs Smithers glanced at Alexandra over the top of her cup of coffee and then carefully replaced the gold-decorated cup on its gold-decorated saucer and looked up at her former maid-of-all-work, now housekeeper-cum-business partner.

'I think you are a very wise person, Minty, to postpone marriage until after Robert comes out of the Army. National Service can change a man so greatly. Hasty marriages are not wise. The war exposed this, and now just look at the chaos we are enjoying. Divorce is becoming as usual as apple crumble, and as rampant as German measles.'

'Ber-Ber-Bob – Robert – wanted to get married straight away, ber-ber-but I don't think it would be a good idea. Ber-ber-besides I would not like to leave you, or Deanford, or the der-der-dogs. If we wait it will give us time to save up for a cottage here, somewhere near the Downs, because I never want to leave Deanford. It can only be good to wer-wer-wait, and it will be something I know you will want, won't you, Mrs Smithers?'

Mrs Smithers nodded. She was more than a little relieved, but anxious not to show it. Not that she thought that Minty would have left her in the lurch, because of course she knew that she would never do such a thing. A different sort of girl might, but Minty was not the average maid, and now that she was a housekeeper, and they were employing a daily lady to come in for the cleaning, now that the idea of the luncheons and dinners and At Homes were proving so popular with the older generation in Deanford, the idea of running it all – with someone else, or on her own – was not something to which she could look forward.

'So what is on the menu today, Minty?'

Alexandra glanced down at their appointment book.

'The two Misses Anderson, they are entertaining an all-ler-ler-ladies luncheon on behalf of their favourite charity.'

'Which is?'

'Der-Der-Dogs In Quarantine.'

'Oh yes, a dreadful business, so many of them die of heartbreak. Such a good idea of the dear ladies to organise dogs in these kennels to have regular visitors. I shall contribute something to it myself, I am afraid I always feel more for dogs than I perhaps should. Anybody at dinner?'

'No, we have no one at dinner, but you are invited to Mer-Mer-Major Cullington's for dinner and I am—'

'Chatty bridge, actually, Minty dear. The dear Major.' There was a small silence. 'You know he proposed marriage to me last week, Minty?'

Alexandra stared, startled, but determined not to show it, for after working for Mrs Smithers as long as she had, she was more than used to the idea that Mrs Smithers did not appreciate overt emotions of any kind.

'Really? Do you mer-mer-mind if I ask you whether you – whether you – accepted?'

'No, Minty dear. Like you, I thought it better to put off the whole idea until such time as we know how well we are doing. Security first, my dear, security first. I don't want to be supporting the Major until I am quite, quite sure that I have enough in the bank to do so.'

They both laughed.

'Besides,' Mrs Smithers went on. 'Besides, I have to tell you the idea of sharing my life with someone else is not something I particularly relish. It is all right to have beaux at my age, admirers certainly, but I certainly would not want to be at the behest of a member of the opposite sex again. They just can't help themselves, you know. They have to take control, and I couldn't countenance that, not at my age. At your age, it's different, but when one's older one is used to one's own way. No, it is best to keep the admirers on an end of a string, and let's face it, half the time, they enjoy it more like that.'

'Yes, I der-der-do understand.' Alexandra smiled. 'Perhaps this is the wrong time then to tell you that I myself am going out this evening, as a matter of fact.'

'Ah, Robert taking you to dinner, is he?'

Now that Bob was no longer a threat to their little business Mrs Smithers did not seem to mind talking about him quite openly.

'Ner-ner-no, well yes, but he is first taking me to the opera at Prentisbourne.'

'Do you mind telling me the title of the opera?'

'*La Ter*—' Alexandra hesitated. '*La Ter-Ter-Traviata.*'

'Ah. *La Traviata*. Mmm. A torrid tale if ever there was one; above all a warning to girls not to think that playing fast and loose can get you anywhere. Playing fast and loose always ends in tragedy.'

'Most especially if you have TB.'

'Ah yes, poor soul, poor Violetta coughing and spluttering, while at the same time singing fit to bust – heartbreaking! But we all love to believe in it, because we want to. Now be off with you, before I spoil it any more for you.'

It was evening dress for the opera, and so Alexandra was once more able to wear the dress that Bob had bought her for her birthday what now seemed an age ago, an age during which they had become unofficially engaged, putting off the awful moment when they met each other's parents, putting off the days of panic and recrimination, hurt and anxiety that weddings always seem to prompt.

'You look smashing. So glam. So – turn around. Oh and so beautiful,' Bob added softly.

'And you ler-ler-look as handsome as handsome does, Mr Atkins, soon no doubt to be Captain Atkins, or Colonel Atkins, or something.'

They both laughed, and minutes later stepped into the taxi that was due to take them to the local opera house.

Despite there being fewer in the audience who, like themselves, were younger, Alexandra experienced the overall feeling not of being out of place, or of joining a large assembly of a snobbish elite, but rather of mixing with people all of whom were determined to come looking their best, not for themselves, not to show off, but quite simply to honour the artists who were to present the opera.

From the moment the orchestra struck up the opening chords of the overture, Alexandra stilled. She had taken the precaution of listening to the music on a stack of Mrs Smithers's pre-war seventy-eight records, but the effect in an opera house was really rather different from that of an old wind-up gramophone. Besides, as she joked to Bob in the interval, it was such a relief not to have to change both the records and the needles.

During the second act, as the opera unfolded and the father made his entrance to plead to Violetta, a woman of bad repute, to give up his son, Alexandra remembered for the first time for months that she too had a father, albeit from whom she never heard, and it seemed to her that she could hear voices from the past, her grandmother's entreaties to Father to give up Kay Cullen, to find a girl from his own background, someone with whom he could settle down, a nice country girl.

'Poor old chap,' Bob said conversationally in the second interval, and Alexandra smiled. It was such a Bob thing to say, and because of that, for all sorts of reasons, she felt her heartache over her past ease. Bob had a way of making everything feel normal, and good, and settled.

The third act opened to gasps from the audience. The set had been magnified so that the characters seemed dwarfed by the tragedy of their situation; powerless to overcome the awfulness of parting, of love too late realised, unable to stop the awful advent of death.

The singing had just reached its crescendo as Alfredo realises that Violetta is not long for this world when the tenor stopped abruptly. The audience murmured as seconds later the orchestra too fell to silence, a silence finally followed by the sound of the tenor sobbing as he held the frail Violetta to him.

Finally the conductor turned to the audience and in courteous tones explained that the two singers had only just married that week and that in playing the part of Alfredo the tenor had quite simply been overcome by the moment. This was followed by a murmur, this time of appreciation, from all over the auditorium, and conciliatory applause, before the conductor once more raised his baton, the singers began again, and the opera finally continued to its inevitable, tragic conclusion.

If Alexandra had been moved by the opera itself, now she found herself equally moved by the situation on stage. Tears splashed unchecked onto her precious organdie-topped evening dress. So – so – so this was great love!

'I say, that's a lesson to snakes not to listen to one's father,' Bob joked as the curtain fell and he joined in the thunderous applause.

Alexandra, her face now hastily powdered, kept her head turned slightly away from him, knowing instinctively that Bob would not like it if he thought she had been crying.

'Something the matter, Minty?'

Bob held her to him as they sat together on her sofa later. Alexandra smiled, and shook her head.

'Ner-ner-no, of course not. It was a wonderful evening. Thank you so much.'

'I say, Italians do seem to have a corner in tragedy, don't they?'

Bob smiled. Alexandra nodded, her eyes not quite meeting his.

'Don't worry we shan't let it happen to us, darling. As soon as the old Nat. Service is over I will be back, bob, bob, bobbing along, and no father will stop me marrying you, I promise.'

He kissed her warmly and pasionately. Alexandra tried to return his feelings through their kiss, but knew that in some way she had failed, and worse than that she knew that Bob knew it.

'Last time I take you to the opera, young lady.'

'Ber-ber-because?'

'It's made you sad. Too sad.' He flicked her cheek affectionately. 'Doubtless you will cheer up soon. I'm leaving next week, so that should bring a smile back,' he added, careful to keep his tone flippant.

'Oh no, der-der-don't say that, I shall mer-mer-miss you so much.' Alexandra flung her arms around his neck. 'I shall miss you more than I can ever ter-ter-tell you.'

'I suppose we're right to wait so long?'

Bob looked down at her, a wistful tone overtaking his usual bustling cheerfulness.

'What else can we do? You ner-ner-know your parents won't hear of you marrying before you've been in the Army.

Der-der-different once I've proved myself to be a bit more than a maid-of-all-work maybe but at the moment—'

'You're as good as anyone. Just because your father has remarried and you have to make your own way in the world—'

'Jer-jer-just joking, but you know what I mean. I'm not exactly a catch, yet, but Mrs Smithers and I – we've got a good business going here, and she is going to make me a p-per-proper partner one of these days. So it's just as well to wait. It seems a long time now, but soon it will be over, the two years will be over, and we'll have a home of our own, which is unimaginable.'

Bob nodded but the look in his eyes was unchanged.

'I just don't want to lose you, Minty mine. I don't want to lose you to someone else while I'm away.'

'Why should you think that, Ber-ber-Bob? Not many per-per-people would per-per-put up with my hesitation, you know!' she ended joking.

Bob looked at her.

'You know I find your hesitation endearing; we've talked about that. No, I do – I worry that I will lose you when I'm away, lose you to someone else.'

'Don't be silly.'

'I lost you a little tonight, darling.'

'No, no, you didn't.'

'I did. Just for an hour or so, I lost you.' He flicked her cheek again. 'But now you're back with me. I wouldn't want it to happen again. People grow apart. The war's shown that. I don't want you to grow apart from me.'

'I shan't.'

Tom was waiting in the suite, a glass of champagne in his hand. The roses were all white, just the way Florazel liked them. The champagne was Veuve Clicquot, just the label she enjoyed, and one that he too had been enjoying for the past half-hour.

Outside the porthole windows the sun was shining, the sea sparkling. It would not be an exaggeration to say it seemed to him at that moment his heart would burst with happiness.

What had he done to deserve so much? He turned to go back into the bedroom and check that everything there too was just as Florazel liked it. He had already put his own clothes away. Now he imagined her moving swiftly and elegantly among her luggage. The vast, studded trunks, the soft leather of her hand luggage: it would soon be swamping the room, and she would be laughing and teasing him, and both of them looking forward to the excitements ahead.

Tom thought dreamily of her, as he always did when he was away from her for more than a few minutes. Everything about Florazel was amazing to him. Her air of distancing herself from the rest of the world, her smile that lit up her blue, blue eyes, the way her mouth curved at the corners, the sound of her laugh. He stroked the bedspread, imagining himself making love to her as the boat sailed off into the ocean blue, just the two of them in each other's arms on the ocean.

He looked around suddenly.

The boat was sailing off. My God the boat was sailing off, without Florazel.

Florazel!

What a stupid thing to do, to find yourself going to the door of your suite and about to call her name.

He put down his champagne glass and dashed through the door instead, flinging himself onto the stairs that led to the upper decks. Crowds were lining the sides of the ship, waving. They were all waving and cheering, but much as he searched among them, his eyes longing for the sight of her blonde hair, her beautiful face, there was no one among them who looked remotely like her.

'Florazel? Florazel? Where are you?'

He spun off down to their suite once more, to be greeted by a steward.

'Ah, there you are, sir. We was looking for you. A letter for you, to await arrival.' He pointed proudly to handwriting on the envelope that Tom recognised at once. 'And now you have arrived, you are arrived, and what is more, sir, you are here. So all is well.' He smiled.

Tom took the letter.

'Thank you,' he said. 'But I'm afraid that all is far from well. Lady Florazel has missed the boat, the ship, I think that she has missed boarding the ship.'

'I'm sorry to hear that, sir.'

'Thank you.'

The steward gave him a sympathetic look, and then hurried off as Tom tore open the envelope.

Tom darling [the letter inevitably began], *it has been wonderful. But the time has come to part. You to the New World, which you will love, I to pastures new. On the practical side I have left a large amount of cash for you with the ship's bursar, which you must use, if only to please me, and there is an account in New York at the Chase Manhattan Bank which I have opened in your name. Money enough I think to last you for a while. Please take it, because it is only what you deserve, Tom. There are so few words that can sum up the happiness that you have brought me in the last year, but happiness you have indeed brought me. Believe me. Great happiness. And I hope I have brought you happiness too, darling, but it can't go on. I have a corner in ending relationships, as you doubtless know, but always remember, that does not mean that I have not loved you.*

Florazel.

The ship plunged suddenly and so did Tom, forward onto the couch where, for the first time in his life, he found shameful tears coursing down his cheeks.

Once the spasm of grief had passed he lay for hours on the opulent sofa, his eyes sometimes closed, sometimes open, until it was dark outside; and then gradually came light – and then more light. Happily no one came to the suite, no one rang or knocked, so he could lie there pretending that he was in some way dead from the shock of Florazel's heartlessness. All he could hear in the distance was the sound of the ship's engines, and occasionally, people passing the outer door, some people laughing, some people talking, but such sounds as there were only confirmed his state of lonely isolation, of being bereft, of having nothing more for which to live. Florazel had been the centre of his whole life, his waking day, his closing night, and now she had cut him loose, thrown him off, made him feel worthless.

Finally, with the advent of morning and out of the darkness of his misery, he heard old Westrup's voice coming to him from the old days at Knighton Hall.

'Naught so dampening as self-pity, and you know what's worse than the damp of self-pity, young Tom? It's that in pitying thyself it leaves naught for anyone else to do, that's what's worse.'

Eventually, mercifully, Tom grew hungry, rang for breakfast, and began to curse Florazel's memory, and mock himself for feeling as he had. He had been a young fool, and she nothing but a lightweight. Lady Florazel Compton, able to throw off love as if a love such as they had enjoyed came along every five seconds, which possibly for someone like her, it did. Florazel could buy anyone. She had bought him, for God's sake. What had he heard her say about him that evening long ago? That he was her toy?

Well, it seemed that the toy having just been junked would now eat a hearty breakfast. He rang for the steward but when the poor man arrived Tom could face nothing except black coffee.

Bob was standing on Deanford station looking determinedly cheerful. He had already been home and said goodbye to his family, but saying goodbye to Minty was something altogether different. It was difficult, not dutiful.

'You take care of yourself, Minty, until I come bob, bob, bobbing along back to you. You will, won't you?'

Alexandra held his hand tightly.

'I shall mer-mer-miss you so.'

'I shall be too busy square-bashing to miss you for even a second, I hope. But I should appreciate it if you wrote nice long letters, to which I probably won't reply, of course. But I would like you to write jolly letters, all about Deanford and Mrs Smithers and the dogs—'

He stopped, looking away.

'Actually, I wish I hadn't said that. I can't wait to be coming home to you and the dogs, Mints. Don't stop thinking about me, will you?' he pleaded above the sound of the train arriving and, having kissed her, he jumped on to it, and then leaned out of the window the way Alexandra had so often seen troops do, waving and whistling, pretending cheer, when really they would probably give anything to be at home in front of the fire with a nice cup of tea and the radio playing.

'Bye!'

'Bye, darling! Bye!'

Alexandra repeatedly kissed her hand to Bob and ran beside his carriage until the train drew away from her, slowly at first, and then gathering speed with smoke furling and unfurling behind it reminding Alexandra of the untidy way-ward college scarf that Bob sometimes wore on their walks on the Downs.

Alexandra stood for some long minutes on the now empty station platform until the realisation came to her that the train would not be reappearing with Bob still on it, after which she turned slowly and walked back to number thirty-two, trying all the while to kick herself out of her lachrymose state.

Why did she think *she* was so different? Why did she imagine that *their* parting was more painful than someone else's parting? Why didn't she *realise* that people all over the world were busy parting from each other? Finally, why did she feel so strongly that she would never see Bob again? Answer: because *everyone* felt like that when they were saying goodbye. The act of saying goodbye was always and ever haunted by the words 'for ever'. It was normal. Just as Bob and she were *normal*. *Not* like the characters in the opera. They did not sing *arias* to each other, and have parents who made impassioned pleas. They were just normal. Bob would do his National Service, and eventually he would take her home and introduce her to his parents, they would buy a cottage with their savings, and he would come bob, bob, bobbing back to her, as he had promised her he would, and that was an end to it.

When she reached her flat she took off her coat, and ran upstairs in answer to Mrs Smithers's urgent call. Mind you, Mrs Smithers's calls were always urgent, but for once Alexandra was nothing if not grateful for their very urgency.

The following morning, having slept only fitfully, Tom found it necessary to eat a hearty breakfast, following which he went to the bedroom and slept through the day until evening started to fall. He awoke therefore to the almost dull notion that if he was not to do anything more dramatic, he must bath and dress, and sally forth for dinner.

He had never undertaken a long sea voyage before, but he

knew enough to understand that the more expensive the suite booked, the better placed your table in the dining room, which was why an hour later he found himself following a waiter away from the centre of the room to a table for two, at just the right angle to be served first, just the right position to command the maximum attention from the wine waiter.

The menu was long and in French, but thanks to Florazel, with the exception of some of the sauce names, it presented few problems for him. Thanks to her too he was up to ordering the correct wines for each course, but also thanks to her, dammit, he felt lonely and isolated, as one person seated at a table quite obviously set for two must always do. To add to his tension he found himself absurdly grateful for the orchestra playing, for every mouthful of the undoubtedly delicious food seemed to take an age, whereas had he been with Florazel he would have hardly noticed that he was eating, so busy would they have been, laughing and talking, gossiping and watching. Finally, feeling as if all eyes were upon him, which he knew could not be the case, he left before the dessert, defeated not just by the many courses, but by his still potent loneliness.

He started to wander the decks, smoking a cigarette and feeling the length of the evening ahead of him, miles of minutes and hours that seemed suddenly already unbearably long.

'This is the lone bachelor station, to lean on these rails you have to pay an entry fee of one Havana cigar, but membership lasts for the whole voyage.'

Tom turned to see the tip of a large cigar glowing in the darkness, the owner of which was standing smiling at him. The moment that Tom's grey eyes met Alfred Bodel's mischievous black ones, they instantly recognised in each other a kindred spirit.

Alfred promptly handed Tom a large cigar, which Tom lit

with great difficulty, his back to the wind. Finally they both leaned on the guard rails, puffing happily and staring out to sea, as if they had known and met each other in this fashion for months.

'How did you know I was a lone bachelor?' Tom asked after they had introduced themselves.

'Probably, my friend, because, like myself, you left before the dessert. Eating alone is a miserable business. Tomorrow we must make sure to lunch and dine together. Meanwhile, tell me which suite are you in?'

As Tom named his suite Alfred Bodel looked instantly impressed.

'Oh dear, so now is when I creep to you, is it not? Or would you prefer it if I just crawled?'

Tom smiled, about to explain that he had not actually paid for such a sumptuous suite from his own pocket, when he stopped.

'You can share my table,' he offered instead.

'Your table just has to be more comfortable than where I am, by the service door, courtesy of my berth in the bowels of the ship,' Alfred joked.

'I'm not sure I can finish this cigar . . .'

'Feeling a bit acey-deucey, huh?' Alfred took the cigar and threw it overboard. 'I smoke the damn things day and night, and have done since first grade. So.' He frowned and looked at Tom. 'Look, right now I have to go play chatty bridge with a group of dowagers. Want to come?'

'Certainly. I play bridge.'

'You do?'

'A bit.'

They walked together down the decks, already in step.

'The dear ladies, they do so love to lose to me, and really it's a pity to deprive them of their little pleasures, don't you agree? Tonight we are not playing for such stakes as would make your thick dark hair stand on end, so you may feel you can sit in when one of them finally leaves, exhausted from the pleasure of losing to me.'

To watch Alfred making his way towards the bridge table with the kind of easy swagger of a man who knows just what he is good at was something of an education for Tom.

'Lady Bilsey, may I introduce my good friend Tom O'Brien?'

'Oh Mr Bodel, I am sorry to say Lady Settington is not at all the thing and is lying down, and so unable to join us tonight. Shall you be able to find someone to partner you?'

Alfred shrugged his shoulders but, turning to Tom, he asked, as if it had only just occurred to him, 'I say, you don't happen by any chance to feel like chatty bridge tonight, do you, Mr O'Brien?'

Tom smiled. He did. Both ladies too smiled, delightedly. Tom was not so handsome that they had not noticed.

Tom had always had a fine card sense, as well he should growing up in stables and yards where incessant bad weather led to card games as easily as wine leads to love; and of course once Florazel had taught him bridge, which he had picked up in no time at all, they had become something of a formidable partnership around the quieter drawing rooms of Mayfair.

'Shall we go mad and play for – say a shilling a hundred?'

Alfred stared round the table at the other three, his eyes finally resting on Tom, who immediately guessed what his new friend was up to, and worse, what he might be. He had seen this little playlet re-enacted over and over again among the better-off grooms and hunt servants. The sharks always started low, casual, relaxed, waiting for the other players' blood to warm, for them to become excited by the play; they waited to find out how good they were, how much they remembered cards that had been played. And of course they never struck during the early games of poker or rubbers of bridge, but bided their time; once the other players had been lured, excited – 'fluffed up' old Westrup used to call it – then they moved in, and the poor lambs were shorn before they even knew they had been rounded up.

'Weren't we kind though?' Alfred put a friendly arm around Tom's shoulders. 'Weren't we just so kind, but really? We lost to them, and they felt ever so, ever so awful.' He stopped outside Tom's suite. 'Here, my friend, we must part, I to the bowels of the ship, and you to *Queen Mary*'s best.'

Tom looked embarrassed, and then, having opened the door, he turned to Alfred.

'Look, why don't you come in for a drink? No, more than that, why don't you move in with me? There's room enough for three people in here, let alone two. And I am on my own, as you know.'

'My dear chap, I couldn't possibly.'

'My dear chap, I'm sure you could!'

'Oh, very well, if you insist, I will hare off before you change your mind.'

They both laughed and not very much later Alfred arrived back at the door of the suite with a small suitcase and some hand luggage.

'The card sharp's luggage, you can spot it a mile off, see?' He pointed gaily at all the labels on the side of his case. 'Backwards and forwards we go, New York to London, London to New York, until winter comes when we go into hibernation, ready for the next season. Mind,' he went on affably, as he walked into the opulent drawing room, 'mind, we good guys never, ever cheat. No, we just win. Simple as that. Wow, what did you ever do to deserve this, my friend?' He looked round him in amazement at the gilt and the plush. 'Are you Lord O'Brien, or Duke O'Brien, or just a young millionaire?'

Tom shrugged his shoulders, momentarily playing with the idea of telling the truth and then rejecting it once again as he remembered that it was only a short time since he had palled up with Mr Alfred Bodel.

'It was a present, from a friend, in return for a favour. This voyage was a present, and no, I haven't a handle, I am just plain mister, like you.'

'Why do the British call a title a *handle*? I keep hearing the old biddies saying that so-and-so has a handle.'

Tom paused, thinking for a second.

'Because handles open doors?'

'We *are* going to be friends, you know that?' Alfred stated after they had both finished laughing.

'No,' Tom replied, after a second. 'No, Alfred, we're going to be more than that, we're – we're going to go *into* business together.'

Alfred stared at him.

'We are? But we have only known each other a few hours.'

Tom shrugged his shoulders.

'I believe in fate, don't you?'

'Only when it favours me, if it favours someone else I don't believe in it at all—'

'After all,' Tom continued ingenuously, ignoring him. 'After all, you can't spend your whole life fleecing, sorry playing cards with old ladies on liners, and I can't spend my whole life – in large suites on ocean liners.'

'No, not fleece, Tom, I don't fleece nice ladies, I stop them feeling *lonely*, in return for which I let them lose money. That's quite different.'

'First.' Tom went to the drinks tray. 'First we will have a drink. He who aspires to be a hero must drink brandy.' He seized a decanter and started to pour. 'Next we will make a plan. Open our eyes to the possibilities ahead of us in New York, where we will need contacts.' He handed Alfred a glass.

'Well, my friend, if we need contacts, no better way than to start on an ocean liner. People have affairs, make friends for life, leave each other, it all happens on ships.'

'You're right. Of course, it must do.'

'Believe me, I know. And now I come to think about it' – Alfred looked round him with an appraising eye – 'this suite is an admirable starting point for contacts, you know that? It's impressive. How about if we give a cocktail party here? Ask all the most influential people? It would be a start, wouldn't it? They won't wait to come, because—'

'Because we are two handsome young men, and ladies *like* handsome young men,' Tom finished for him.

'No, really?' Alfred murmured. 'I never noticed.'

'All we need is a few contacts in New York to start us up, and I'm sure we can land on our feet, start a business, start a new business.'

Alfred raised his eyebrows.

'You move fast, Tom O'Brien. But here's to it, my friend, here's to it.' There was a small silence as they drank. 'Yet. Tell me. I don't want to sound too practical, but once we have made our contacts, what kind of business might two beautiful young men like ourselves be good at, do you think?'

There was a long silence as they both mused, and drank.

'Selling something, certainly,' Tom ventured. 'After all, if you can sell yourselves you can sell anything, and I certainly think we can sell ourselves.'

'Oh yes, we are certainly beautiful at that, as we proved tonight! We sold ourselves so hard to those two dear old birds that they can't wait to fly back to the table for a good plucking.'

'And after all,' Tom went on, 'America is all about selling a life, that's what America has always been about, hasn't it? The new life, starting afresh and all that?'

'But where can we start? Where can we get ahead before the

rest of the competition? Something new, something that needs that overworked word: pizazz.'

Tom lit a cigarette and stared ahead of him, feeling elated, feeling free, his self-pity completely vanished. He was going to revenge himself on everyone, and the best revenge of all was success.

'Advertising, that's where we'd be good,' he stated, slowly. 'It's not new, but television advertising *is* new, and it needs people who are slick, and young, and we're both of those.'

'Yeah? This campaign brought to you by: Bodel O'Brien.' Tom tried it for sound.

'That's good. Certainly has a ring to it. You're right, Alfred. That's a brilliant idea. We'll set ourselves up as an advertising company. Slick, young, vibrant, but we won't bother with anything except television.'

'And what with your British savoir faire and my slick American savvy, here's betting we'll clean up in no time.'

Tom frowned.

'It will take a bit of self-sacrifice, Alfred, you know that?'

'Certainly. I'm quite prepared for that.'

'Starting tomorrow night.'

'That soon huh?'

'Yes. Starting tomorrow night, when *we* lose yet again, at the bridge table.'

Alfred groaned.

'But the dear ladies like losing to *me*, it gives them a cheap thrill.' He imitated one of the dowagers. ' "*Oh but you're so brilliant, Mr Bodel, how can any of us ladies possibly keep up with you?*" '

'These ladies have to become our friends, Alfred, not our victims.'

'Oh, very well.' Alfred shrugged theatrically. 'You're right, as it happens, because I happen to know that there is a widow of an oil well on board, and the widow of a motor-car company. Potential sponsors please call in at our suite?' He laughed, his eyes alight.

Tom went back to the drinks tray and collected the decanter.

'From tonight on, we are going to have to teach each other everything the other one knows. No holds barred. I shall begin by teaching you English.'

'OK. So what can I teach you?'

'American.'

'Done!'

'Hands across the sea?'

'Brandy, my friend, hands across the brandy.'

A Voyage of Discovery

Alexandra had written to her father asking if she could come to visit Lower Bridge Farm. She had carefully not asked if she could come 'home', which she thought might irritate Kay. It was some time before she received a reply, but when she did, it was from Kay making it quite clear that she, *Kay*, thought it was a nice idea for her to visit them, but she hoped that Alex would not be put off by the smell of paint as all the guest rooms were being redecorated, and all they could offer her in the way of a bed was the sitting-room sofa.

Alexandra stared at the letter, determined not to be irritated by its patronising tone. Shortly after she booked a room at the White Harte, and then sat down and wrote to her grandmother's friend, Janet Priddy, telling her that she would be coming to the White Harte, and would love to call in on her for tea, if or when it was convenient. She also wrote back to Kay saying more or less the same thing but that she would like to call in for dinner, if or when it was convenient. She knew that Kay would miss the underlying sarcasm and would feel only relief that she was not going to stay with them.

'So you're off to your homeland, far away from dear old Deanford, and then on to London to visit your cousins?'

Mrs Smithers was looking genuinely put out, and not

just because Alexandra was leaving her for a short holiday, but also because, as Alexandra well knew, she feared that Alexandra, once home, might not come back.

'I'll be back by Sunday evening next, smart as paint, wait till you see.'

'I shall miss you, Minty dear, even if I do have whatever her name is to look after me—'

'Mrs Cruddle—'

'Mrs Cruddle. Such a powerful woman – always seems about to break something, I don't know why. Not like you at all.'

'You ler-ler-like her, you know you der-der-do.'

Mrs Smithers leaned forward impulsively and kissed Alexandra on the cheek, a first for both of them.

'You take care, dear, and don't forget to leave me your hotel address.'

'It's on the pad by the drawing-room telephone, the White Harte. I can ber-ber-be reached at the dear old White Harte.'

'Do take care, dear.'

Alexandra put her head on one side.

'You have the Mer-major to think of now, Mrs Smithers, don't forget, you are due for chatty ber-ber-bridge on Saturday night.'

'Oh the Major, he is *such* a nuisance. He plays conventions I detest, and he makes mad bids, particularly once he's had a Scotch whisky or two, really he does.'

Mrs Smithers sighed, attempting to make Alexandra feel sorry for her, but Alexandra merely smiled and left.

Bob had taught Alexandra to drive and had loaned his car to her, so she was able to draw up outside the old coaching inn in some style, roof down, hair carefully concealed under a knotted scarf, luggage neatly packed.

She checked in, lunching on her own, imagining herself with Bob, imagining how they would laugh and talk, and try and guess the life stories of everyone else in the luncheon room. It made lunch pass quicker, pretending she was with Bob, picturing him sitting opposite her, his charm and bonhomie filling their corner of the room.

Driving first to have tea with Janet Priddy, before going on to see her father and Kay, was something she had long planned to do.

'Ah, Alexandra dear.'

Janet, like Alexandra, had grown older, but because Janet was much older than Alexandra, she had actually become quite old, which surprised her guest. She had never thought of Janet becoming older, as her grandmother had become older. She had thought of her going on to enjoy a form of eternal late middle age, always dressed in conventional tweed suits, seamed stockings quite straight, everything just so. However, the diamanté owl brooch on her lapel, which Alexandra remembered was always worn for lunches and teas, was unchanged, like the oak furniture in her front parlour, and the silvered Victorian teapot, always polished on a Monday afternoon, and the cat asleep in the window beside the pot plants.

Her talk was of the village, of deaths and births, or rather of more deaths, and fewer births, and was just succeeding in making Alexandra feel as if she had stepped back in time and was still wearing a smocked dress and long socks and sandals when she said, suddenly, 'You remember Mrs Laughton?'

Alexandra remembered her very well.

'Well, she died, dear. Did I tell you that? No? Well, she did, she died here on the farm, poor soul, in the cottage here; and the strangest thing happened, Alexandra. She only went and left me all her money.' Janet looked embarrassed. 'It's not as if I did anything except keep an eye on the old dear, but then she only upped and left me a small fortune. Of course I was so embarrassed, I couldn't accept it, not knowing that she had family, even though they never visited. They came to the funeral, of course.'

'Well, they wer-wer-wer-would.'

'And I could see that they were distressed about it, what with one thing and another.'

'Ab-ab-about the funeral?'

'No, not about the funeral, dear, no, no, about the money. So I told them they could have it all, all the money back, and I gave them all her – effects. But I did keep that.' She nodded towards a small porcelain ornament of a black and white cow with flowers beneath its feet. 'Seeing that I've been a farmer's wife all my life, I thought I would keep that, the cow, because she's pretty. I thought that was all right, seeing that she did leave me everything else and I did give it back to them. But they didn't much like it, I can tell you. I mean they didn't mind me making over the money to them, but they minded me keeping the cow. Even now they keep writing to me, asking for it back. And my lawyer, he keeps writing to them telling them that they're lucky to have what I gave them back, but it doesn't make any difference. At all events, I became so distressed by it all, I went to a lady who helps people with their . . . well, headaches and suchlike.' She smiled for the first time. 'Course I felt stupid at first, but now I quite enjoy it. She gives us games to play, and we sit in a circle and talk, and that. Yesterday she made us all imagine we were looking into a black pool of water, an oasis in a desert, and then she asked us what we could see in the water. Well, you can imagine all sorts came up, as it would. But me, guess who I saw in my oasis? Your grandmother.' Janet stopped, sighing. 'I still miss her, you know. We were friends for fifty years. Another cup of tea, dear?'

Alexandra handed her cup to her, and watched the tea being poured. It seemed to be coming out of the spout slower than the ticking of the old grandfather clock in the hall, so slow it could have been custard. Only half an hour of her visit had passed. She could not possibly leave before she had been there at least an hour. With a sudden rush of recognition she realised that the old way of life was too slow for her. She had been independent long enough now to be used to being always in a hurry, running everywhere from the moment she woke up to the moment she went to bed. Always trying to think of new ways to attract business to the house, to make the cuisine better, to accommodate the new tastes that were coming into vogue, even in sleepy Deanford.

'Shall I ter-ter-try imagining an oasis?' she asked, as the silence that had fallen threatened to extend and she had just given another nervous yawn. 'I could ter-ter-tell you what I see.'

'Yes, you do, dear, you'll be surprised at what you find, really you will. I tell you, some people saw things that you couldn't repeat in mixed company, really you couldn't. It made you wonder what sort of mind they had.'

Janet watched Alexandra with interest as she closed her eyes, and they both fell into yet another silence as Alexandra imagined herself riding through the desert towards the cool water of the oasis. In her mind she dismounted and went to the pool. She stared into the dark water. What she saw amazed her, and filled her with delighted warmth, so much so that she only, finally, opened her eyes very reluctantly.

'Well, come on, dear, what did you see?'

There was a long, long pause as Alexandra, still recalling what she had seen, waited for the warm feeling to subside, yet for some reason she could not quite understand it would not, or could not. The image that she had seen stayed on, and on, as clearly as anything she had ever known.

'I saw – myself. There were two of me. And we were both smiling at each other.'

She turned to Janet who put her teacup down and then

with the unmoving eyes of the old she stared at Alexandra for a few seconds looking strangely unsurprised.

'Well, you would, dear,' she said finally, in an almost satisfied voice. 'You would do.'

'Why? Why would I?'

'Why, because, Alexandra dear, you were a twin, you were born one of two. I dare say,' she went on, frowning, 'I dare say it must have been your sister that you saw, your poor dead twin sister.'

Alexandra stared at her, and Janet, realising at once the strength of her power over her, picked up her teacup and slowly sipped it, a sound that gathered in force to become a more than hearty noise in the silence that followed.

'I was a—'

'Twin, dear. One of two. Your mother died from what is known in medicine as toxic shock. Yes, it was the arrival of the second, unexpected baby that killed poor Laura. A girl like you, she was born dead, on account of your mother dying as she was born, and only half the weight of a normal baby. Of course none of the family spoke of it. Not at the time. Well, they wouldn't, would they? They didn't want everyone in the village turning round and blaming your grandmother, seeing that she was acting as a midwife, poor woman, the doctor not having arrived in time, except to sign the death certificates, of course.

'That's why your grandmother never wanted you to leave her side, never wanted you visiting Knighton Hall or your Millington relatives, none of that, she was always afraid that they might tell you something, or that questions might be asked and you might have been told, and would tell them. Of course they wouldn't have – they wouldn't have asked questions, no one did, or would, Lower Bridge Farm was too far away from everything not to have a life of its own, not to be a place where no one would ask questions. *I* knew of course, because she had to tell *someone*. But I kept mum; until now that is, because, well . . . you do, don't you? You stand by your friends. And your grandmother, well, she was a friend, and family too. But I always think that's why she gave in so easily when Kay came along, just left the house to her. It was as if the guilt of what she thought she had done to your father's first young wife, silly Laura, was still eating into her, making her ashamed – at the back of her mind, not the front of it, at the back. Always felt she could have done something more to save them both, the mother and that second baby.'

'Did my father know of this?'

'Not in too much detail, no, dear. Your grandmother hushed it all up, for her sake, and the poor doctor who always felt he could have been there. Besides, men can't deal with that kind of thing, and nor should they be asked to. No, the other baby, all that, it was just brushed under the carpet. This is our secret, just ours, yours and mine. What would be the point of bringing up the past, of raking over old miseries? No one could bring poor Laura back. It seems that she couldn't bear the thought of another delivery, you see, and no one knew there were two of you, as how would they, back then? But that is how it was, you see, Alexandra. That was what happened, and they buried them both in the same coffin, of course, and no more to be said. Now, would you like another cup of tea, and then I will show you round my new herbal, things are still coming along round here, you know. We may be old but we can still stoop to pick up a dibble.'

There was something so firm about Janet's manner, as there always had been, that Alexandra, dazed and speechless, found herself obediently drinking a second cup of tea, and then following her out to the courtyard garden. But when she eventually left her, it was without either of them once again referring to the subject of Laura and Alexandra's lost twin. Perhaps because of this Alexandra made up her mind to visit her mother's grave in the village churchyard. She had no flowers, and the shops in the village were shut, so she plucked some greenery from nearby shrubs, and some wild flowers from between the gravestones, and she twisted them into a small bouquet and laid them on her mother's grave.

Laura Millington Stamford. A beautiful young girl taken too young, always missed.

She *had* been taken too young. She *had* been beautiful, because although there had been no photographs of her at Knighton, Alexandra remembered the photograph that her father used to keep by his bedside.

Alexandra stood for a while willing herself to feel something, and yet knowing in her heart of hearts that if you have never known someone it is difficult to feel anything except regret on their behalf; tears such as she had shed at the opera would not come. Her mother and sister had died, but because she had never known them the way she had grown to know Violetta and Alfredo in the opera, her eyes were dry. For a second she even found herself wondering if Janet Priddy could have made everything up?

And yet she could not have made up the girl whom Alexandra had seen reflected in her imagined oasis, the smiling girl with the same long dark hair, the same shaped face, the same upturned nose as herself. Could she possibly have been some sort of imagined ghost of her dead sister that Janet had willed on her? Or was she just a figment of Alexandra's own imagination of which Janet had taken advantage? More than that, had she returned to Alexandra to tell her something? Was that why Alexandra had suddenly felt so warm, so wanted, so encouraged?

'I wish I had known you both, I know I should have loved you,' she said to the gravestone, after which she drove to Lower Bridge Farm.

*   *   *

'How are you, Pa?'

It seemed all right to address him in this way, since she was older, and he was older, and a father once more.

'Going along all right, thank you, Alexandra—'

'He's not, don't you believe it. He's got dreadful arthritis, in his wrists and his ankles,' Kay interrupted briskly, as if John Stamford could not hear what had been said. 'Any more of what we have been through this winter and he will have to sell the farm and go and live in a warmer climate. I keep telling him that. But your father does like to suffer in silence, one of the old sort. Gin and tonic?'

It was so strange to see Kay standing in a drawing room that had once been her childhood drawing room. To see her beside a drinks tray which was crowded with everything from gin and bottles of tonic water to decanters of sherry and Madeira, whisky and brandy. Grandmother had never drunk. Grandmother had tea. Grandmother had a glass of champagne at Christmas, and that was all.

'We haven't seen you here for so long, have we, John? When did we last see Alex?'

Kay carefully avoided the word 'home'. Alexandra was just about to say that she had written to her father regularly from Deanford, but, receiving no replies, she had quite given up when Kay, forgetting to pour anyone else a drink, or perhaps not caring if they had one or not, sat down and began drinking her gin and tonic very fast, as if it were medicine.

'Your father has missed you. He doesn't say as much, but he has. He has missed you,' Kay announced.

John Stamford remained silent, ignoring his wife, and staring across at Alexandra as if he was only now beginning to recognise who she was, as if she had changed so much that she was no longer recognisable to him.

'I have missed Lower Bridge Farm,' Alexandra stated, sounding prim, even to her own ears. 'But I have been

enjoying Deanford very much. I have a very good job now.'
She smiled.

Kay lit a cigarette.

'We're thinking of selling my cottage. The one you and
Mother-in-law occupied. If you're doing so well, why don't
you buy it?'

'It's not your cottage, dear—' John interrupted.

'It was always meant to be my cottage.' Kay paused as
Alexandra's father got up and wandered over to the drinks
table. Alexandra looked away as a silence fell. Happily,
Kay decided to fill it. 'Did you hear that mad woman Mrs
Laughton left all her money to Janet Priddy. The family were
furious. Of course they went hell for leather after her to get
back the money. And quite right too.'

'Janet gave it all back, Kay, you know she did.'

John was carefully mixing a drink for Alexandra and one
for himself.

Kay went on ruthlessly. 'Apparently Janet's gone round the
twist, so the village says, and not surprising. It was the strain
of the family setting the lawyers on to her.'

'Janet gave all the money back to the family, Kay,' John
repeated quietly as if to himself. At the same time he
shrugged his shoulders in Alexandra's direction. 'She only
took a little ornament for herself, that was all. She's a decent
woman, Kay. All she kept was just a little china ornament. I've
known Janet all my life, she would hardly accept a bunch of
parsley from anyone, let alone money. Proud as a peacock
she's always been.'

'She's a stupid old woman,' Kay finished.

'She may be a bit crusty on the outside, but she's a sweet
person inside,' John persisted.

A silence followed broken only by Kay lighting another
cigarette.

'By the way, Alex, congratulations.'

Alexandra looked at Kay, surprised, knowing she could not possibly know about Bob.

'Congratulations. Your stammer is much better—'

Her father pointed a sudden indignant finger at Kay.

'She does not have a stammer, Kay. She has a slight hesitation.'

'I-er-I-er-I-er—' Alexandra started, feeling as if she was floating above them both, somewhere near the ceiling, feeling as if she had shed the weight of a thousand years, feeling as if she had just been born. 'I-er ther-think it is much better,' she agreed, realising suddenly that it had improved, almost without her realising it. 'Much better.'

Her father beamed at Alexandra, and the look in his eyes was more proud than the day he won the cup at the agricultural show.

'Just as well, I kept telling John you will never get a husband with a stammer like that.'

Kay went to the gramophone and put on some band music. This seemed to offer John the opportunity he needed, because as he bent over to hand Alexandra a drink, he whispered, 'Pear Tree Cottage, the cottage, is in your name, to do with what you will, your grandmother made sure of that. It was hers to give you, not Kay's, whatever she says.'

'What was that you said?'

Kay turned sharply.

'I was just remembering the first time Alexandra had a proper drink, before a Christmas party at the Chisholms'.'

'Oh those Chisholms, what a mess. Such a mess they've made of everything.'

Alexandra stared at Kay. She had given up trying to write to Frances, and although she had telephoned them before she left Deanford, for some reason their response to hearing from her had been more than discouraging. It had been as if they had never known her.

'The Chisholms are about to go under, have been for some time. They are at their wits' end,' Kay announced to the room at large. 'They have built far too many boxes for their hirelings, and of course what has happened now? Their yard is half empty. Serves them right for being so greedy. I tried to tell them, everyone tried to tell them, but would they listen?'

John resumed his place in his favourite armchair and stared ahead of him as Kay went on relentlessly shredding the neighbourhood above the sound of a second-rate band. At that moment it seemed to his daughter that John Stamford was like an old bulldog, strong in aspect, but perhaps essentially gentle as bulldogs are, needing only for someone to understand them, wanting to be hugged and petted.

'I suppose we'd better go in to dinner,' Kay announced reluctantly, as the clock struck seven.

Dinner was served by a new, younger woman, and she certainly did not have Mavis's touch with pastry, or anything else for that matter. Nevertheless the dinner was delicious, because all the produce came from the farm, and yet Alexandra could not wait to leave, could not wait to drive off to the old coaching inn, be on her own, think everything through.

'You should have stayed with us, really you should,' her father protested.

'I would not want to put Kay out, not with little Arthur teething and everything, and Kay having the decorators in.'

'*Little Arthur's History Book*, remember that? Your grand-mother liked to read you that,' her father mused.

They both smiled.

'Sorry you missed seeing the little chap, but you know . . . bedtime is bedtime, and poor Kay is pregnant again, probably why she's a bit scratchy.'

'It's been lovely, thank you, Pa.'

'Come again soon, won't you, Alexandra?'

He leaned forward and slipped her something in an envelope.

'The key to Pear Tree Cottage. We got the tenant out at last, and it is yours whatever Kay says; and it was always meant to be yours. Sell it, do what you want with it, it is yours. You understand?'

'Of course.'

She gave her father a quick peck on the cheek and fled down the front steps to her car. On the way back to the inn she paused yet again outside the churchyard, but because it was dark she did not get out of the car, but only wondered why it was that the past sometimes seemed more complicated, more dangerous, more threatening than the future might possibly be?

And then the answer came to her. It was because there was nothing you could do about it. What was it that Mrs Chisholm had used to say to her? 'Just kick on, just kick on.'

Sweet and Low

As soon as the ship docked, on Alfred's advice, Tom booked them both into the Plaza for a few nights. Equally soon, within hours, Tom found that a whole new love by the name of New York had taken over his life. Just to walk with Alfred down the spring-lit streets with the skyscrapers towering above him, to feel the exuberance of the place, was more than a tonic, it was a lifeline. Here was something not just beckoning to him, but pulling him forcefully towards it: not just a new life, but also a new way of being. Here he could learn to be a new person, someone who did not have to be grateful, who did not have to aspire to a new or different class, or have a particular accent. He had to do only one thing. He had to succeed.

With the money that Florazel had left in a New York account for him, with his new wardrobe and his new business partner, he was certain that he had only to work hard and life would reward him. But first they had to find an apartment, not to mention business premises.

Alfred whistled incredulously, sweet and low, when Tom told him the amount of capital that they now had at their disposal.

'This woman must have done more than love you, Thomas O'Brien, she must have adored you, my friend.'

'Not really,' Tom stated, after a few seconds. 'No, what she felt for me, was . . . I don't know: what do rich, older women feel for you when they enjoy you and then tire of you?'

'Not having your gorgeous looks, I couldn't say. I've never had that privilege, Thomas, my son.'

'In that case, don't let's go in to it, shall we?'

Tom looked uncomfortable, and felt ashamed.

Every time he looked back at his relationship he felt shattered at how much he had loved Florazel, ashamed at just how much he had believed that she loved him. Embarrassed at how one part of him had believed and yet not believed Bob Atkins's warning that she was a woman of a certain reputation, managing to persuade himself that every other man had meant less to her than himself, that what they had was something out of this world, a love that few could have enjoyed, or might ever know.

'I was young, in some ways,' he muttered finally to Alfred who was still staring at him with an over-interested expression. 'I was young, and – very stupid, and finally very hurt.'

'She must have known that, Thomas, that's why she's made it up to you, funding you this way, that is making it up to you, and some. How, though, am *I* going to make it up to you, Tom? I can't match your investment.'

It was Alfred's turn to look suddenly helpless and vulnerable.

'You don't have to, Al. In all sincerity, you don't have to make anything up to me. Your friendship is more than enough. We will work together, and we will grow rich together, and . . .' Tom paused.

'There's *more*?'

'Yes, at least – no, that is enough, for the moment. No your friendship, as I have just said, is more than enough. I honestly think if you had not been standing smoking that sick-making cigar of yours by the ship's rail that night, if you hadn't have joked with me when you did, such was my foolish despair, I might well have thrown myself over.'

Alfred whistled again.

'That bad, huh?'

'That bad.' Tom nodded. 'So now, Alfred Bodel and Thomas O'Brien are going into business together and we're going to be a formidable duo, do you know that?'

'Is that all? A mere nothing, my friend.'

'No, there is one more thing.'

'Yes, my friend?'

'With your help I shall fulfil my one ambition.'

'Which is?'

'To go back and buy Knighton Hall.'

'Knighton Hall, huh? Is that where the Queen lives? Might not she mind?' Alfred joked.

'No, the Queen does not live at Knighton Hall, but a man by the name of James Millington does.'

'And?'

'And . . .' Tom paused. 'It has long been my dream to stand in the hall of that house and watch him go down the front steps and drive off down that drive, and know that I have booted him out, the way he booted me out, and I don't think I will be happy until I have done just that.'

'That bad, eh, Thomas? The old worm of revenge eating into you, is it? Made a hole right through you, has it?'

Tom smiled although his eyes remained less than amused.

'Yes, my friend,' he said, mimicking Alfred back to him. 'Quite that bad. And I'm afraid to say it is not something that will go away.'

Alfred nodded.

'Well,' he said judiciously, 'there is much we can say on the subject of revenge, but little that has not been said before. For myself becoming eaten up with a desire to pay someone back is not something in which I wish to indulge.'

'Goody goody.'

'Nothing of the sort, no. It is simply because I love life too much. Like enjoying myself far too much. Don't want to miss the sunrises or the sunsets of my life; and I always think that if I were preoccupied by some feeling such as you have, understandable as it is, I would fail to notice the beauty of what lay around me. But if you are intent on getting your own back . . .' He shrugged his shoulders. 'Well, in Italy they say revenge is like lying on a garden pea, and no amount of feather mattresses thrown on top of it will ever stop you feeling its hard little presence in the small of your back.'

'No,' Tom agreed, after a while. 'There isn't a mattress made that will stop me feeling what I feel for James Millington, until I can do back what he did to me.'

'Well, all to the good, I suppose. Make you work harder and faster to achieve what you want.'

'And you? What do you want?'

'Me?' Alfred laughed. 'My tastes are simple my friend. All I want out of life is a beautiful girl, a fast boat, and a house on Long Island, that will do for me, you can keep the rest.'

He clapped his arm around Tom's shoulders.

'Onwards and upwards, my friend, onwards and upwards.'

Alexandra was standing at the window of the cottage that she now knew was hers. As she did so she remembered how her grandmother had sat, day after day, in that same room, unmoving, declining to go on living. She opened the door with the key that her father had surreptitiously slipped to her with such a set expression, as if he knew that he would have to pay for his action, but thought it quite worth it.

She would sell the place, if only because she knew that her father would expect her to do so. He would not want her living too near to himself and Kay; he would not want her to witness his daily humiliations at the hands of his new wife; he would want to think that he had done something for her, helped her to a more secure future.

The idea of how much the cottage might fetch only came to Alexandra slowly, once she had shelved the memories of herself, now seeming so much younger, so naïve compared to how she was now. These were swiftly followed by a resolve to spend what the sale would bring. Once Bob was out of the Army they really could be married. But first she had to go to London, to visit her Millington cousins.

The address to which she had been directed by Tasha Millington was well away from the normal stamping grounds of the kind of people that Jessamine and Cyrene would have been brought up to believe that they were. The flat was just one of hundreds in a large, dull, badly painted square. Outside what had once been grand privately owned houses were a few shabby cars, alongside which Alexandra now carefuly parked Bob's car. She stepped out onto the pavement and from there up to the badly painted front door with its row of bells beside which names were scrawled in a mixture of pens and handwritings. Beside the topmost bell was written 'Millington'. She rang the bell for a few seconds, and then, seeing that there was no hall porter, she pushed the front door open and was instantly assailed by the smell of dull cooking, as dull as the paintwork within, the taste doubtless as dreary as the stair carpet.

'Ah, there you are, dear Alexandra.'

Alexandra had been called Minty for so long now whenever anyone said '*Alexandra*' she was hard put not to look behind her to see whom it might be that the person was addressing.

Tasha leaned forward and kissed her warmly on both cheeks.

'My dear, dear, Alexandra, so lovely to see you after all this time. We have lost touch for so long I honestly had the idea that we might never see you again, as we have not seen so many of our friends.' She stopped, a sad expression coming into her eyes. 'You know how it is when one is down on one's luck: so few people want to know one any more. It is quite shattering how few people want to know one, once the ball is over, as it were. Still, you certainly discover who your true friends are. Come in, come in. The girls will be back from their little jobs soon.'

Alexandra followed Tasha into the sitting room, and immediately felt a pang of nostalgia for so much of the furniture and fittings, which had once seen more glamorous days, was now set about the little yellow painted room. The button-backed chair that had once stood in the corner of Tasha's elaborate bedroom at Knighton Hall, the wing chair that had once been in the library, the silver boxes that had been scattered about tables in the saloon at Knighton: they were all there. But now that they were all crowded into one little top-floor London flat, they had a disconsolate air, as if they were so many passengers in a crowded train carriage, unused to and unwilling to being huddled together in a close situation.

'Will you have a sherry, Alexandra?'

Alexandra nodded. In the old days Tasha always said she loathed sherry and only drank champagne and French wine. She had obviously decanted some cheap sherry into one of the old decanters and was now pouring it with the same care that Janet Priddy had poured Alexandra's tea from her silvered teapot.

'Cheers!' There was a pause. Tasha frowned. 'So funny to say that, but everyone round here does, you know!'

'Cheers.'

They both sipped at their tiny, cheap glasses, and fell to silence, and as they did so Alexandra found herself hoping against hope that Jessamine and Cyrene would be coming back from their work soon, that there would be some other distraction, because she had never really had much to do with Tasha, and when she did have, it was always to listen. She remembered how much Tasha had enjoyed talking about her clothes. She remembered how she had enjoyed walking about her dressing room trying on hats and jackets and evening tops and every other kind of paraphernalia, but now that there were no such things, and she would have no dressing room, it seemed that Tasha had run out of subjects.

'I've just been to see my father and Kay,' Alexandra finally stated.

'Oh yes? I've never heard from them, you know, not since the divorce. Well, I never did anyway except at Christmas, but certainly not now.'

Tasha sighed and taking out a cheap packet of small cigarettes from a worn handbag, she lit one.

'But there you are, once you are a divorcee, even if you are the innocent party, you find yourself ostracised.'

It was terrible to see the bitter look in Tasha's eyes and watch how slowly she smoked her cheap cigarette, and notice how now that she could no longer afford to have her hair styled by a top hairdresser, it sat too flat and too square on her head, and how grey it was compared to the colour it had been before. Her dress too was cheap and there was a ladder in one of her stockings that she had stopped with red nail varnish, which looked strange.

'Ah, there they are!'

Tasha sprang to her feet as if she knew that Alexandra was having as much trouble as she in keeping up a conversation, so changed were her circumstances.

Jessamine and Cyrene walked into the sitting room looking as different from their mother as it was possible to be. In contrast to Tasha they were dressed to the nines in the latest fashions: long full coats with three-quarter sleeves, worn with long gloves and small hats from under which showed short elfin-styled hair; seamed stockings, high heels and crocodile handbags completed their elegance.

While Alexandra was by no means shabbily dressed, her life at Deanford would never require her to look as her cousins did now, older and more sophisticated than she would have thought possible, particularly given their mother's appearance. They made her feel as shabby as Tasha must feel set beside her daughters.

'Why, Alexandra, how lovely to see you.'

'Alexandra.'

They both kissed her, smelling strongly of French scent, and as they did so Alexandra noted how beautifully made up they were, and how long and red their immaculately varnished nails, once they had removed their fine expensive suede gloves.

'Mummy given you a sherry, has she? Bless her, she is good, isn't she?'

They both removed their coats and sat down, leaning their backs against the faded chintz of the chairs while their mother fussed round them, bringing them glasses of sherry and consoling them with the idea that they had after all come to the end of a long hard day, and that they must now relax and let their mother take over.

Alexandra stared at them. She knew that after the dreadful incident of Jessamine throwing her drink all over Jennifer, that they had been cut off without a penny by her uncle; that he now didn't mind what happened to them, because when it first happened they had both written to tell her so, after which she had not heard from them, except, inevitably, from Tasha at Christmas.

What she did not know was how they came to be dressed as they were, how they came to be so sophisticted, so elegantly turned out: but for a change of address card, she would long ago have lost touch with them.

'I shall just pop out to the kitchen and warm up some cutlets for us all.'

Tasha left the room and Jessmine watched her dully.

'Not cutlets again, can't she learn to do anything but grill?' She looked at Alexandra and remembering her cooking she smiled. 'Couldn't you take over?'

Alexandra smiled.

'I could, if you like.'

'It's all right, she's only joking,' Cyrene put in quickly.

They all three sipped their drinks rather too fast, and then sighed.

'So how's sleepy old Deanford?'

'It's fun. We're very busy at the moment. We do lunches and dinners, it's hard work, but it's all going very well.'

'Good show.' Jessamine leaned forward and reached into her mother's handbag. Pinching her packet of cigarettes, she lit one, swiftly followed by Cyrene. They both puffed together for a second or two, inhaling sharply and efficiently.

'Yes, but what do you do when you're not cooking and so on?'

'Nothing really, except I have a sort of fiancé now. He's called Bob.'

'Oh I say. Well done.'

'Let's see the ring?'

'He hasn't bought me one yet—'

'Too poor, is he? What a shame.'

'Goodness no, he's not poor, just young. We're only starting out. He's doing his National Service.'

'Doesn't stop him being rich.'

'How much does this old bag in Deanford pay you?'

When Alexandra told them they both made shocked noises.

'Is that all?'

'Mean old bag.'

'It's all she can afford at the moment. Her husband's company went bankrupt.'

'Never mind what she tells you, she should be paying you acres more than that. You'll have to come to London. You'll get much more than that in London.'

'I don't think I could at the moment.'

'You can hardly have your hair done for that.'

'We could hardly have our nails done for that.'

Tasha came into the sitting room carrying a tray with which she staggered to the window. She laid it on a pre-prepared table.

'Here we are, darlings, a nice mixed grill, and then some cheddar and biscuits.'

They all sat round the small table feeling and looking absurdly self-conscious, as if Alexandra's advent had forced them to remember their former circumstances, the long dining table at Knighton, the library where the drinks had been served, the butler who had served them.

'How's Douro?' Alexandra asked brightly.

'Oh, Douro is fine—'

'Don't listen to Mummy, he's a mess.' Jessamine snorted lightly.

'He drinks a little too much,' Tasha conceded. 'I say, Alexandra' – she leaned forward quickly, too obviously trying to steer the subject away from Douro – 'if you don't mind me saying so, it's lovely to hear that your nervous hesitation has disappeared. You must be very happy in your new life, for it to disappear like that.'

'Yes – yes I suppose I am.'

'Did you do anything special?'

'In a way.'

Tasha looked interested while her daughters merely went on eating diligently, as if they were used to her trying to turn the attention away from Douro Partridge.

'Yes, I found out about my mother, and how I had a twin sister who died after I was born, when my mother died, and from then on for some reason – I don't know why, my stammer started to really go. It was as if it solved something, which it obviously did.'

They all stared at her, fascinated, while Tasha pushed her plate away from her as if she could stand her own cooking less than anyone.

'We always did wonder, Jamie and I – well, *all* of us did wonder what exactly happened to poor Laura.'

'Well that's what happened. My grandmother had to do the delivery, and she delivered me, and none of them knew about the second baby, but when she arrived, my mother was already dead, the shock apparently having killed her, but. Well. Anyway. That's all in the past. Like my hesitation, I hope, it's all in the past.'

Alexandra smiled.

'Only wish Douro was,' Jessamine stated gloomily, returning to what was obviously her favourite subject.

'Douro can't keep a proper job for more than five seconds, so we all have to keep *him*, worse luck,' Cyrene moaned.

'Don't talk about Mummy's new husband like that, Cyrene,' Tasha begged her. 'He does his best, really he does.'

'I didn't know you had married him, Aunt Tasha? How lovely.'

'She didn't,' Cyrene put in quickly. 'Douro married her, and a dratted nuisance he's proved to be.'

'Please, Cyrene, Douro is a very sweet person, and you both always used to like him, in the old days.'

'No, I didn't like him. I always thought he was a dratted nuisance then, at Knighton, if you really want to know. I thought he was a dratted nuisance full stop.'

'What does he do?' Alexandra asked Tasha, trying to ignore the other two and look sympathetic.

'He's working in a meat-packing place adding up little bits of meat.'

Jessamine stared hard at her mother across the table as if it was her fault.

'He's quite quick with figures, and suchlike, because of the Army; and the pay is very good.'

'He gets paid in one week what we get paid in one day, and he thinks that's good. He's pathetic, he really is.'

Alexandra stared at her plate. She did not know why but she had imagined that their fall in fortunes might change her cousins.

Now they both sighed, pushed their plates away from them and lit cigarettes as Alexandra dabbed her lips with her napkin, yet another small embroidered relic from the old days at Knighton. She had spent the past hour avoiding a thought that would keep occurring, a thought that would not go away, but now was difficult to reject wholly.

She remembered Bob once staring at an over-opulent car outside a house in Deanford and how he had said, 'Money that quick never comes from anything good, Mints. Mark my words. Never.'

Jessamine and Cyrene were too well dressed, their wrists decorated with bracelets made of fool's gold that jangled with each movement that they made, the expression in their eyes defiant and guarded. They were obviously making money quickly, but perhaps not from anything that they would care to talk about at dinner.

The rest of the dinner passed quickly, principally because Jessamine and Cyrene were obviously keen to have an early night.

'Can I help you wash up, Aunt Tasha?'

'Sweet of you, Alexandra, but no, really. Just wish I could offer you a bed for the night. Sorry you missed Douro, he won't be back until after midnight.'

'Thank God she can't,' Jessamine told her mother. 'It's overcrowded enough in here.'

'Thank you so much. It's been lovely seeing you all again.'

Alexandra could not have said who she felt was gladder to see the back of her – her aunt or her cousins. They quite obviously felt as if they had done their duty by her, and could not wait for her to go, so that they could get their clothes off, enjoy a hot bath, and see what tomorrow would bring.

'We escort businessmen who are in London,' Cyrene confided when she walked Alexandra quickly down the many stairs to the street. 'Jessamine's right, you could do it too. It's easy-peasy work, really it is. You just have to be well brought up and have dinner or lunch with these old codgers. You know, turn up smartly dressed, be decorative and amusing. Nothing more to it than that.'

The light from the lamp caught Cyrene's face as she finished speaking, highlighting the dead look to her eyes, and at the same time her childish words caught at Alexandra's heart.

'It's very kind of you, Cy, but I think I really must try to make a go of Deanford first.'

Cyrene nodded, not really paying much attention, her eyes drifting down the road to where an expensive sports car was being parked.

'Well, anyway. Don't forget: give us a ring if you change your mind. It's perfectly respectable. The old Colonel who runs it used to be in the Army with Douro. He's not bad, and he does pay. God knows what he wrings out of the old codgers though.'

A moment later she was gone, leaving Alexandra to drive off, wanting to leave behind the dreary square, the dark of London, determined to make Deanford by the early hours. The further she drove from the great city, the more she felt peace returning to her as she thought with relief of her own life, of dear Mrs Smithers and the old ladies who came to the house and were so lively and fun, and of course she thought of Bob, and how much they were both looking forward to his coming home on leave, and how he was going to take her to meet his parents at last.

She also amused herself thinking of Bob's letters to her, letters that he always decorated with funny drawings such as: *The Colonel trying to light his cigarette in a gale, Sergeant Gumley's gaiters, Me assembling a firearm.*

Bob had loved reading Rupert Brooke's poems, loved the old churches in the villages that were set so sedately at the foot of the Downs, loved simple things like taking tea at Ann's Pantry. Most of all she thought about how Bob had brought normality into her life, not just stopped the loneliness, but taken Alexandra away from all the dreary family complications, seeming to have run her off into a dear, decent life, up the hills and fields with the dogs chasing after them, run off the greyness that sometimes descended on her when her speech problem grew tiring and tiresome. But he had made everything seem right, and she mentally kissed her hand to him as she had kissed her hand to his departing train.

It was a long journey, but when she finally arrived outside the old Regency house in the old Regency square, she truly felt as if she was coming home, and that was before she opened the door to the basement and, bending down, allowed the dogs to jump into her arms. It was then that she realised that neither Jessamine nor Cyrene had referred to their beloved pets, not even when their mother had left the room, and was safely out of earshot. The dogs were obviously quite dead to Jessamine and Cyrene, along with so much.

'You're back early, Minty dear.'

Mrs Smithers looked delighted and surprised, but curious.

Alexandra nodded.

'Am I?' she joked, looking around about her as if she

hadn't realised quite where she was. 'Well, so I am. I wonder what happened?'

'Not enough to keep you in London, at any rate?'

'Oh, quite enough.' Alexandra put her head on one side. 'Quite enough. But not enough of what I would enjoy, so I came home.'

'I'm glad that Deanford still has its attractions.' Mrs Smithers turned towards her drawing room. 'By the way, a letter came for you, but I didn't think it worthwhile sending on. I kept it here, until you came back.'

Alexandra stared at the unknown handwriting, and then at the postmark.

It was from Bob's village, someone in the village had written to her. She opened the letter and turned it over, looking with interest at the signature. She turned the sheet of paper back, and as she did so, inexplicably, she thought she could see the set of Bob's handsome head and hear his voice, saying, 'Don't worry, Mints, your Bob will come bob, bob, bobbing back to you.'

Dear Miss Stamford,

We have never met, but I feel I do know you because Bob told me so much about you, before he had to go away on his National Service. The reason I am writing to you is because I have to impart tragic news, and knowing how he felt about you, although not yet engaged, thought you should know, felt that you ought to know, that poor young Bob was killed last week caught in cross fire on an exercise . . .

'Oh my dear, I am so sorry . . .'

Alexandra could hear Mrs Smithers's voice somewhere, but she could not see her face because everything inside her head had gone still and dead.

'Sit down, dear, sit down, I will fetch some brandy.'

*   *   *

Alexandra sat in the pew of the old church staring dully ahead of her at the altar. If she could wish anything more than that Bob had not been killed she would wish that he had not died in an utterly futile accident.

She had never met Bob's parents, had no status, so had seated herself at the back of the church. As a consequence, since she had arrived early, she was eventually passed by everyone.

'That's Lady Florazel Compton,' the woman next to her murmured as a tall, elegant blonde woman was escorted up the aisle to her seat at the top. 'She would be representing the Duke, on account of his being abroad at the moment, in Morocco. And that's the manager, Mr . . .'

The woman went on murmuring names as Alexandra sat remembering how Bob had swung through the basement door of a Saturday evening, or a Sunday afternoon, his face alight with that marvellous love of life that only the innocent of heart can ever quite achieve. She remembered how he had stood on the station looking suddenly so young and vulnerable saying, 'I can't wait to be coming home to you and the dogs, Mints.'

She knelt forward suddenly, sinking her head in her hands, trying to pray – despite the woman beside her keeping up her wretched murmurings – and remained kneeling until the organ started to play the entrance music and the coffin, held aloft on young, broad shoulders, passed slowly by, at which point Alexandra forced herself to look at it, trying to make sense of its reality.

Bob was not lying silenced in some wooden box, he was just away, sure to come back to her soon; and just as soon she would be flying into his arms and they would go walking on the Downs, and on the bright days to come they would take picnics, simple sandwiches and fruit and bottles of beer, and the flowers would sway and the larks rise singing, and there would be no Army, no bullets, just peace and love and beauty, and some time during tea he would be sure to quote their favourite lines from Rupert Brooke's 'The Great Lover'.

> *These have I loved:*
> *White plates and cups, clean-gleaming,*
> *Ringed with blue lines; and feathery, faery dust;*
> *Wet roofs, beneath the lamp-light; the strong crust*
> *Of friendly bread; and many tasting food;*
> *Rainbows; and the blue bitter smoke of wood;*
> *And radiant raindrops couching in cool flowers;*
> *And flowers themselves, that sway through sunny hours,*
> *Dreaming of moths that drink them under the moon.*

Then the sounds changed and despite the noise of the congregation rising, Alexandra was sure she could hear Bob's voice, not saying the poem, but saying, '*I just don't want to lose you again, Minty mine.*'

Now Alexandra had lost him, but not for an hour, for ever.

Later, as the rest of the congregation filed out after the coffin and she remained trying to pray, rather than remember, a hand touched her lightly on the arm.

'I'm sorry to disturb you, but I'm poor Bob's friend – Tom O'Brien, I am his old landlady, Mrs Posnet? After Tom left so suddenly, his friend Bob used to call round sometimes, and then it became a kind of a habit with him. I thought I recognised you from a photograph Bob showed me when he was home, before he went off to the Army – you know.'

Alexandra looked up at the face beneath the black veiled hat, and then stood up.

'How do you do?' she said, shaking the woman's gloved hand, but for some reason not letting go of it.

'I wrote to Tom. He's in America now, you know. He will be ever so cut up, I know that. You changed young Bob, you know. He stopped being such a jack-the-lad after he'd met you, became more settled in himself. Such a tragedy.' Her eyes were sad and mournful. 'He was ever such a character was young Bob. I can't believe he's gone. We must keep in touch. Really, we must. You'll not have anyone who knew him as well as we knew him, here in his home town. It will be a comfort to you, being that you are so far away from where he grew up.'

'I don't know what to do with his car – '

Alexandra heard her voice rising on a stifled sob and found herself still clinging to this unknown woman's hand in a desperate effort not to cry.

Mrs Posnet nodded, understanding, practical.

'You could keep it until you hear different.'

'No, I think I'd better leave it with you, really. You could have someone take it to his parents.'

'If that's what you want.'

Alexandra nodded, turning away, finally letting go of the poor woman's hand.

'I couldn't keep it,' she said from deep within the grey-black fog that was surrounding her. 'It wouldn't be right.'

She walked out into the churchyard outside. The burial was private, only family to attend. She walked down the road and drove Mrs Posnet to her house, locking the car and leaving the keys with her.

'We'll be in touch, won't we?'

'You know where I live, love. Any time.'

Alexandra nodded and, turning, she walked off to the station. The truth was that it was almost a relief to be rid of the car. Unbearable to drive it again, knowing that its owner would never come back. She started to run down the road to the future which seemed suddenly darker than it had ever been.

*   *   *

Tom stared at Alfred and for a few seconds he felt filled with gratitude to *him*, for thanks to Al's contacts they had already made faster progress than he would have thought possible. Inviting several of their card-playing older lady friends to tea at the Plaza had proved more than fruitful, it had proved to be a bonanza, particularly since several of them had major shareholdings in their husbands' companies.

'I do so love the idea of backing some sort of theatre in the afternoon, Mr O'Brien. You know, for us ladies there is nothing to watch on television in the afternoon, when we want to enjoy a quiet siesta, but nothing. If my poor dead husband were alive now I know that he would be taking his company in just such a direction as you are saying now. He would want his oil to oil the wheels of television. He *loved* the theatre. He wanted to be an actor, but of course it was out of the question, what with the company making forty million a week, or was it a day. At any rate, too much for his father to be able to entrust the business to any but a son. Still, my husband always hankered, and let's face it, most of us do have our dreams.'

Alfred smiled, and excused himself from the table, but not before he had passed Tom's chair making that same familiar, sweet, low whistle, which had now become their signal to each other when they knew they were on to something good: the prospect of a calm sea, and a good breeze that would bring them into port with plenty to trade.

'My friend Martha Sachs, I know she would be interested in joining in. She just loves theatre too, and of course she knows so many people in the clothing business. It would be of great interest to her, I am sure.'

Tom turned his full attention on the two ladies delicately sipping their tea. He could not believe that business could be that simple. That by being in the right place at the right time,

you really could succeed, but it seemed this was true. More
than that, it seemed it was particularly true in America, and
more than true in New York. He looked round at the rest
of the company taking tea. Salvador Dali was at one table,
easily recognisable. Gregory Peck at another, just as easily
recognisable. Tom O'Brien at his table, not recognisable to
anyone, *and* Alfred Bodel – both of them soon to be so, if he
had anything to do with it.

'Now, you leave it to us, young man,' the more powerful of
the ladies was saying in that particularly comfortable tone that
rich women use when they know they are on not just to a good
business idea, but the on-going company of two attractive
young men. 'As soon as you have opened up the New York
branch of your company, we will be ready to back you. We are
all quite excited about this, you know. We women can make a
difference to the quality of life in America, and what is more
we are determined on doing so. Quite determined. The men
have held sway for too long in tele- vision. We want something
on in the afternoons that *we* enjoy.'

Alfred returned and Tom and he escorted the two ladies to
their limousines, kissing their hands in the European manner
which they seemed to enjoy inordinately.

'Outrageous.'

'So mannerly.'

Alfred looked after what amounted to a departing motor-
cade and sighed with deep contentment.

'Do you know something, my friend? I like those old dolls
better and better each time I see them. They have charm and
manners, and they want nothing from us that we can't give
them—'

'They want afternoon television, sponsored by them.'

They both turned back to the Plaza, and the doors were
instantly opened to them, as they were now everywhere they
went – whether it was a table at 21, or at Sardi's.

'We should really toast the old *Queen*, don't you think?' Alfred suggested later, as he leaned forward over the dinner table in the main dining room. 'After all, if it weren't for the old *Queen* we would never have met, would we?'

Tom hesitated, disinclined to be anything but truthful, since they both knew it was really owing to Florazel that they were where they were, at any rate at that moment. He certainly owed everything to Florazel, but then remembering how she had thrown him away so callously, he raised his glass.

'Yes, you're right. Let's drink to the *Queen Mary*!'

They touched glasses and drank, and once again Alfred gave his sweet low whistle, which made Tom smile.

Part Three

THE HOUR

Home Chats

In some ways Mrs Smithers was a great deal tougher than Alexandra, her comments certainly more pithy, but most of all she was less sympathetic to women of her own age. This puzzled Alexandra sometimes, most particularly when it was someone she knew who had booked a luncheon or a dinner.

'Not Lydia Passmore! We don't want her, do we? Surely we're not so hard put as to need to cater to Lydia Passmore's whims?'

Alexandra looked up from her bookings list surprised by Mrs Smithers's tone. Lydia Passmore was a little older, a great deal more frail, and perhaps a little more vaguely desperate than most of the ladies who used the house for socialising.

'She seems a very nice lady.'

'You did not know Lydia Passmore when she was young. She was always such a flirt, such a show-off, never had any time for anyone. Now of course she's down on her luck, so it's all different, I suppose.'

Alexandra put her head on one side. It was over a year since Bob's death, and although the extreme sensitivity that goes with the first state of mourning had passed, she still found unkindness of any sort shocked her. Doubtless it was inevitable when a light went out in your life that you woke up not just to your own darkness, but to that of other people's, and certainly Mrs Passmore had evoked a sense of protectiveness in her, for she had none of the assumed grandeur and snooty ways of some of the ladies of the town.

'Mrs Passmore's just giving a lunch here for a couple of younger people. Relatives, I think.'

'I dare say they both think she is wealthy.' She gave a short laugh. 'Poor deluded creatures.'

Alexandra smiled.

'Could be. On the other hand they might just like having lunch with her.'

Mrs Smithers sniffed and started to take herself off to the comfort of her upstairs rooms, rooms that she could still reach without growing out of breath, rooms where she could set out her card tables and entertain the Major and others.

'Mark my words, if you had known Lydia Passmore when I knew her, you might not want to serve her lunch, Minty,' she called over her shoulder as she left the room.

Alexandra shrugged her shoulders, checked the dining room, made certain that Jane, the young girl who now helped at the table, was quite sure of her duties, and, since Jane was busy, went to answer the front door in her stead.

Mrs Passmore might have been a flirt and a show-off when she was young, but nowadays she was a fragile old lady with a heartbreaking, valiant sort of air, and clothes that had once been smart and fashionable but were now a little faded, a little shiny, a little sad.

'Mrs John Passmore, I booked some months ago.'

'Yes, Mrs Passmore, of course, how nice to see you, do come in.'

'Have my young guests arrived yet?'

She stared up at Alexandra with faded grey eyes.

'Not yet, Mrs Passmore, no, but I expect they'll be here

very soon. It's not yet one o'clock, so I dare say they're on their way.'

Mrs Passmore nodded.

'I dare say,' she agreed, and followed Alexandra upstairs.

Once in the drawing room Mrs Passmore glanced anxiously at the clock as if to make sure that it was true, that it was not yet one o'clock.

'Sherry?'

'Oh my dear, should we?'

'Of course, you must have a winter warmer, mustn't you?'

Alexandra loved the way the ladies who lunched and dined always said 'should we?' and then happily bolted down their sherries, as if once they had Alexandra's approval they felt quite free to drink as much as they wanted, or perhaps even more, which they very often did.

'It's my niece and her husband, that's who's coming, that's whom I invited today. My only relatives, you know, but I am so looking forward to seeing them. They have been abroad for some years, but are now back in London. So looking forward to it, I remember her as a little girl you know. So sweet and charming, and not at all a nuisance.'

After two schooners of sherry, when the hands of the drawing-room clock were pointing to quarter to two, it was really rather obvious that Mrs Passmore's guests had either forgotten or decided not to be bothered with their elderly relative.

'I wonder what happened to them . . .' Mrs Passmore glanced for the fiftieth time at the clock, as if willing it not to be telling the truth. 'Do you think they put down the wrong day? Do you think they forgot?'

'Perhaps there is a message – a message at home, perhaps there is a message at home?'

'Oh no dear, I know there isn't.' Mrs Passmore glanced up hopelessly at Alexandra. 'There isn't a telephone, let alone a message box at my lodgings, dear, that's how I know there isn't a message, and can't be.'

'Why don't we all have lunch, anyway?' Alexandra asked brightly. 'After all, everything is cooked and ready, we might as well all enjoy it, don't you think?'

Mrs Passmore shook her head and put her empty glass down on a side table.

'Very kind of you, dear, but I don't think I feel I could eat anything, not now. I was so looking forward to this, you know. So looking forward to it.'

She sat down very suddenly and Alexandra went to her at once as she took out a handkerchief and blew her nose delicately making no sound.

'I'm sure there is some explanation. Their car might be broken down; something delayed them.'

'Oh yes, dear, there is an explanation, I know there is, and I'll tell you *what* it is. The explanation is that no one wants to know about the old. When you're old you're a nuisance to yourself, and to everyone else, believe me, really you are. I know.'

Alexandra patted her shoulder.

'I dare say, but don't you think you should eat lunch, even so? It would do you good. I'll eat lunch with you, and so will Jane, we'll all sit down together and have a jolly lunch, and what's more I will make sure we give you a refund, after such a horrid disappointment.'

'Give Lydia Passmore a refund! Over my dead body.'

Mrs Smithers was looking quite furious. Alexandra stared at her, half amazed by her reaction, and half shocked.

'I will pay for it, out of my own pocket, Mrs S., promise. It will be down to me, all of it, including Jane. Only fair, after all.'

'More fool you,' Mrs Smithers stated, but she sat down

322

rather suddenly, and Alexandra, thinking discretion the better part of valour, went to leave the room.

'Don't go,' she said, after a short pause. 'I suppose you're right. The young are awfully cruel. It was cruel not to let Lydia know, I will admit.' She paused again. 'And really, I suppose I should stop taking it out on Lydia, just because she stole my beau from me.'

Alexandra bit her lip. She might have known. So much in Deanford was down to the past, things that had happened forty years before, never to be forgotten, sometimes never to be forgiven.

'I know you must think me cruel, but Lydia stole Pip from me.' An unusually tender look came into Mrs Smithers's eyes. 'Pip was the love of my life – Pip Passmore. Died in the war, finally, dismantling a bomb. He was handsome and charming, and do you know? I still miss him. We were so in love, but his parents didn't approve, or was it mine? I can't now quite remember. Perhaps it was both?' She paused. 'No, well, perhaps – no, I have to admit it, it must have been mine. My mother, you know, she wanted something better for me. But when did a mother not want something better for her daughter?' For a second she sounded almost bitter. 'At any rate Pip married Lydia, on the rebound everyone said, but it was the start of the war when everyone was marrying everyone, because we all thought we were going to be killed, and then of course he *was* killed.'

Alexandra stared. Somehow she had never thought of Mrs Smithers having been the romantic type; she'd always had the impression that Mrs S. considered husbands to be a mere convenience, good at providing amply for their wives – or not, as the case might be – but not up to much else.

'I'm so sorry.'

Alexandra sat down beside her, and once again she took an old hand into hers, and looked into eyes that were no longer so bright as she would wish them to be, or they might long to be. As Mrs Chisholm had once said to her, there were two rules in life. One was that when talking to someone of twenty it was best to address them as if they were seventy, and to those who were seventy as if they were twenty. At that moment Mrs Smithers was quite definitely twenty.

Mrs Smithers looked contrite.

'I shouldn't hold out against Lydia, should I, Minty? I mean it was all so long ago, I should be kind now we are all so old.'

Alexandra said nothing, and at that moment Jane knocked at the drawing-room door.

'I'm just off now, Miss Minty, all right?'

'Yes, Jane, yes of course. Goodnight.'

'Letter for you, Miss Minty.'

Alexandra stared down at the letter in her hand, dreading to open it, convinced as always that, despite the airmail stamp, it must be bad news.

'Shall I open it for you, dear?' Mrs Smithers took it, as she so often did with letters nowadays, and stared at it. 'It's from America. Since you don't know anyone in America, shall I read it for you?'

'Would you?'

There was a long silence, and then Mrs Smithers looked up from a quick perusal of the letter.

'It's all right, dear, it's not too sad. A bit, but not too. It's from a friend of poor Bob's, someone living in New York. And when he comes to England, he would like to meet you. It will not be for some while yet,' she finished, sounding relieved, because their little business was now flourishing, and with hardly a day passing without some sort of booking they both knew they could ill spare Alexandra from the house. 'Not until the spring. He will be over then, and would like to meet you.'

Alexandra took the letter now, and started to read it,

feeling as she always did that she should be stronger, and yet knowing that she was not, and perhaps never would be. The mere arrival of a letter, the mention of someone else of the same name, a myriad things, and suddenly the fog of sadness would return and she would once more begin to struggle from day to day as if on crutches, finding getting up in the morning as difficult as going to sleep.

As if realising this, feeling ashamed and wanting to make it up to her, Mrs Smithers said gently, 'I tell you what, Minty dear. I'll ask Lydia Passmore to tea next week, because if what you seem to think is true, and she is a bit lonely, it might make her feel less so. We might make it a regular thing. She might even play bridge with the Major's friend, he's always looking for a partner.'

In the event when she finally read the letter for herself Alexandra found that, despite it being typewritten on office paper and headed BODEL O'BRIEN with a secretary's initials at the top, it was nothing if not courteous in tone.

> *Dear Miss Stamford,*
>
> *I understood from my old landlady, Mrs Posnet, whom it seems you visited last month, that you were unofficially engaged to my late friend Bob Atkins. I hope it does not seem presumptuous, but when I come to London next spring I should very much like to meet you and talk over old times. Besides Muriel Posnet there is no one I know who knew Bob, of whom I have to say I was very fond. I was, as you must have been, devastated by his death. I do hope that this will prove possible. Please send Mrs Posnet my regards.*
>
>

Yours sincerely,
Thomas O'Brien

After due consideration Alexandra allowed a few days to elapse before she sat down to write a handwritten letter on the very same writing paper that had finally proved to be the inspiration for their business.

> *Dear Mr O'Brien,*
> *Thank you for your letter. It would be very nice to meet you. Bob talked about you often. I am seeing Mrs Posnet next month. I will send her your regards and wait to hear from you when you come to London next spring.*
> *Yours sincerely,*

She signed herself Minty Stamford because that was what was on the envelope, and that was how she knew Bob would have referred to her, as 'Minty' or 'Mints'. Then she determinedly forgot all about the letter, put it out of her mind, simply because that was her only way of coping with her ever-present sadness, to push everything firmly from her mind, just concentrate on the day-to-day details of running the business. Besides, she had money now from the sale of her cottage, a sale that the lawyer had hinted had irritated her stepmother to boiling point, and it was high time she spent it. However, she did not buy a cottage as she and Bob had planned, she bought the house next door.

'Is that wise, Minty dear?'

For some reason Mrs Smithers always said that when she secretly really rather approved of whatever was being mooted.

'We can do the same thing next door as we are doing here, only a little differently.'

'Oh yes, and how would that be, Minty dear?'

'Well, I thought we should make the first-floor drawing room over to bridge playing, little tables always ready, that sort of thing. And some of the upper rooms, we can turn into suites like yours, can't we?'

Mrs Smithers stopped playing Patience and looked up.

'You're a glutton for punishment, aren't you?'

'Not really, it's just I like what we're doing, and I think it's needed.'

'You're going to come a cropper, you know that? You have an endlessly bleeding heart when it comes to old people. I do believe it all must have started with your grandmother. It marked you for life. Just don't expect people to like you better for trying to be kind to them, will you? If you want to make an enemy, the saying goes, help someone.'

'How do you mean?'

'Well, in the event that some of the older ladies or gentlemen who come and live with us next door, or just visit here on their high days and holidays, if they leave you a legacy, or even just a pair of etchings, the town will be on to you like a shot. You've lived here long enough to know that. Now we have not one, but two houses, the town will just think you're after their money, not trying to make them happy and comfortable. You know how it is. People can be unkind to a degree.'

'I already thought of that.' Alexandra laughed. 'What an embarrassment that could be. But you're quite right to mention it. I shall ask any residents who come to live next door to sign something that will guarantee they leave their money away from me, to their favourite charity. It will be a condition.'

'You are, Minty – what is it that American said in that film you took me to the other day? – ah yes, you are one cute kid!'

Alexandra smiled. She was glad that Mrs Smithers approved. She was glad to have a new challenge. She was glad that the sun was shining outside. She was just sorry she was feeling so tired; and that was all before Christmas arrived and she felt she had to make sure to round up all the lonely and neglected in the town for what Mrs Smithers called, sighing deeply, 'Minty's big bash'. She nevertheless seemed to enjoy it inordinately, even down to dancing with the dreaded Major until the rest of the guests had gone, after which he was sent on his way in no uncertain terms, as if he had been forcing her to dance and she the most reluctant of party-goers, and only there from duty.

'You know I don't think she's ever going to marry me,' he said to Alexandra as they parted at the door this particular Christmas.

Alexandra watched him climbing down the steps to the pavement, before weaving his way back to his own house in the next-door square, and sighed. Most unfortunately for the poor old Major she had the feeling that he was right. Mrs Smithers valued her freedom and her business far too much to take on another husband.

Later, Alexandra lay on her bed with her two dogs on her feet and thought over the unlikely turn her life had taken. She stroked the tops of the dogs' heads and wondered how everyone else spent their Christmases – not running about after Mrs Smithers and her guests, and waiting for their favourite conjuror to arrive to play magic tricks before Christmas tea. She knew what her presents under the tree would be, they would be just like last year. There would be at least a half-dozen pairs of knitted gloves, some with different coloured finger tops. There would be chocolates, various, and pull-on woollen hats, some of which she would have to oblige the donors by wearing when she shopped in the town. There would be scarves, also knitted and woollen, and there would be some bars of soap and tins of talcum powder. She rolled over on her side and buried her face in her pillows. She was very lucky. She was loved, and she was lucky – if rather over-endowed with hand-knitted gloves.

Mrs Smithers stared at Alexandra.

'I'm not terribly certain about the colour of those gloves. A trifle light, wouldn't you say, even for the time of year, Minty?'

Alexandra stared down at her light-coloured suede gloves. She had thought them really rather fetching; now however she was filled with doubt, and went back to the drawing-room mirror to stare at herself. There was no doubt about it, she did look chic, but perhaps Mrs Smithers was right about the gloves. She had to admit that going to Brighton on the train and buying the smartest and most expensive outfits she could find had cheered her out of her winter blues in a way that she would not have thought possible.

'Oh I think they're all right,' she said, addressing herself rather than Mrs Smithers in the mirror. 'Apparently they're absolutely the thing in London, lighter-coloured gloves, really they are.'

She stared appreciatively at the pleated skirt and simple, fitted jacket with scarf collar in which she had chosen to travel, and pulled her chic close-fitting hat down with her gloved hands. She looked and felt an attractive young woman again, something which she had not felt for far too long.

'That suiting looks very twenties in style,' Mrs Smithers went on ruthlessly, as if determined to remain coldly objective about Alexandra's transformation. 'I remember people wearing suits just like that when I was growing up. I hope you didn't pay too much for it. I must have a trunk full of outfits like that in the attic.'

Alexandra turned and smiled brightly and determinedly at Mrs Smithers, because she was not fooling her for an instant.

'You're going to be fine while I'm away,' she told her firmly, ignoring her remarks. 'Everyone is going to be putting all hands to the pump, and there will be nothing more for you to do than you do normally. You'll see, really you will.'

'I just don't see why you have to go away for the whole week—'

'Because,' said Alexandra with sudden and rare passion, 'Because I need to get *away* for a little. You must understand I have not been away from here for so *long*. I mean I hardly know what it is like not to be looking into the appointment book, not to be planning meals, supervising the builders next door, or reminding Jane that we need new tea towels.' She took Mrs Smithers's hands in hers. 'Now repeat after me: *"Minty is coming back soon, Minty is coming back soon."*'

Mrs Smithers did not find this in the least bit amusing, but merely turned her head away like a sulky child and sniffed.

'At least we have got Lydia Passmore playing bridge,' she said. 'At least there is that.'

Alexandra ignored her, picked up her handbag and headed for the door. In her mind's eye she could see her new car, the open road, a plush hotel where she would have to do nothing for herself. In other words she could see freedom from wool and chatty bridge, from Mrs Smithers and Jane. Just for a few days she was going to walk about London and no one would know her, no one would care if she was wearing the woolly hats or gloves they had knitted her for Christmas, or had put out the ornament they had given her for her birthday. Just for once she would be able to upset no one but herself, care only to do what she wanted to do, and pass people who didn't know who she was or where she was going, and were less than curious.

'I will telephone to you tonight when I reach London,' she called over her shoulder, but Mrs Smithers did not reply, determined on becoming a martyr to Alexandra's selfish desire for a short holiday.

'Bye, Jane!'

She opened the kitchen door and stared in. Jane was polishing silver, but also looking sulky, as if Alexandra's absence was going to give her a great deal more work, which it wasn't, since she had found a temporary replacement through a local agency.

'Mrs Cruddle is just feeding the dogs, and then she will be up to take over. She won't be more than ten minutes.'

Jane pretended not to hear. Alexandra closed the door with a sigh. She had no idea that taking a week off could cause so much trouble, or prove to her how much she herself was needed.

She swung through the door to her car, her proudest, newest purchase and drove off in it with her hat pulled firmly down, and the roof gaily open. She had packed all her new clothes into new luggage, and was so determined to enjoy herself that it occurred to her that if the end of the world was announced, it could not destroy her mood.

The speed with which Bodel O'Brien Advertising Inc. had taken off had surprised even the partners. It semed that once you had doors open to you in New York, once great wealth in the shape of the optimistic and agreeable widows of huge corporations decided to back you, the world was certainly not your oyster, the world was, as Alfred put it after success seemed certain, 'One hell of a pearl, my friend, one hell of a pearl, that is what the world has turned into for us.'

Tom might have turned his back on romance in favour of escorting beautiful models and actresses, all of whom could not wait to be associated with the company, but Alfred had all too predictably fallen in love with the daughter of a chic Long Island banker. It took some time to persuade her father that Alfred Bodel was everything he could want in a future son-in-law, but persuade him Alfred finally did, which meant that on a fine sunny Saturday morning Tom found himself acting as best man to his best friend, wishing him all the luck in the world, while knowing that Alfred and Scottie would really not need it. They already had it. The luck was they had met, and they had fallen in love, and now they were married. Who needed more luck than that?

The weddings of those close to you, however, have a way of concentrating the mind, and having – together with four hundred other guests – waved Alfred and Scottie off on their honeymoon, Tom turned his mind to returning to England. He had already written to Mrs Posnet to warn her he intended on returning for a fortnight's holiday, and now it seemed there was no better time to do it than the present.

'I knew you would be back,' his old landlady told him with a smile when Tom walked into her kitchen looking and feeling like a stranger compared to the boy who had left it for the Duke's glasshouses and gardens what seemed like half a century before. 'I knew you would be back, and I knew you would be different, but I also knew the kind of different you would be.'

Tom leaned forward and kissed her on the cheek, which made her blush, before he swung her round a couple of times.

'I have bought you so many presents,' he told her. 'So many presents from New York. You are going to be the belle of the town.'

'How do you know I'm not that already?' Mrs Posnet pointed proudly towards her small, narrow hall. 'It's tuppence to talk to me now I have a telephone, young man, if not threepence.'

Tom laughed.

'You'll be even more the belle of the town, put it that way.'

He had bought her a taffeta petticoat that crackled and swayed to go under an evening skirt, a spring hat with ribbons and flowers, and a bottle of scent from Bergdorf Goodman that had somehow miraculously stayed unbroken.

'You're spoiling me,' Mrs Posnet told him, delighted, and she tried on the hat even though it looked a little strange with the clothes she was wearing. 'Now, enough of that, sit down and I will make you tea, and I've baked a cake for your coming, and some home-made biscuits.'

Tom ate his cake dutifully and with relish, drank his tea, and felt quite a lad again, despite his smart clothes and urbane transatlantic manners and accent.

'So you're a millionaire are you now, Tom O'Brien?'

'Not quite, but something like,' he admitted. 'Just by chance, I met Alfred Bodel on the *Queen Mary* – and just by chance we met these old dears and they backed us to go into television, sponsoring afternoon theatre, that sort of thing. In America, you see, unlike here, Mrs P., the women have their say. Some people say they hold complete sway. Anyway, the thing took off very quickly, and in a very short space of time, there we were, a success. You know what I found out though, Mrs P.?'

Mrs Posnet eyed him with interest. He had changed so much that despite what she had said she felt she hardly knew Tom O'Brien now from the wordless boy who had lodged with her.

'I have found that it is easier to be a success than a failure, that is what I have found.'

In her turn Mrs Posnet must have found this remark a little conceited because she ignored it and then felt it incumbent on her to put Tom down, to remind him from where she shrewdly knew his good luck had originated.

'You know Lady Florazel still comes down to stay here at her brother's house, don't you? She even comes here for tea now and then, likes to talk over old times.'

If Tom had looked conceited in her eyes before, now he looked young, stricken, almost helpless at hearing Florazel's name mentioned, and since he got up to leave very shortly after, Mrs Posnet was sure that she had put her foot in it, which indeed she had. Perhaps to make up for this she changed the subject, but only slightly.

'You are going to look up that poor Bob Atkins's girl, aren't you, Tom?'

Tom paused by the door. He wanted nothing more than to hotfoot it away from his old lodgings, before by some dreadful chance Florazel turned up. He wished he hadn't decided to visit his old landlady. He even found himself wishing to God he hadn't come back to England, especially if the price he had to pay was seeing Florazel again.

Since he had sailed for America he had been at pains to have only the most light-hearted of affairs, had taken care not to let his heart become involved, never wishing to go through that same humiliating, despairing heartbreak he had suffered over Florazel. He was determined that he was not about to break that resolution, for he was all too aware that once the heart had been damaged, you never quite knew what would happen. It was not time to go, so much as time to flee.

'I have already telephoned Miss Stamford's hotel,' he told Mrs Posnet. 'We are due to have a drink together tomorrow lunchtime. At Claridge's.'

Mrs Posnet frowned.

'I'm not sure that Claridge's Hotel would be quite the right place for Miss Stamford, Tom, really I'm not. She is a simple sort of girl, quite home-spun in some ways, you know. Very pretty, but never London smart. You wouldn't want to make her feel ill at ease, would you? Just because you're a rich boy now doesn't mean that everyone else is as well off as you, young man.'

'She sounded all right about it on the telephone.'

Tom was fairly legging it back to his car now, almost panic-struck.

'Well,' Mrs Posnet agreed, following him and shrugging her shoulders. 'I dare say if she sounded all right about it, it will be all right.' She caught Tom by the arm. 'But you're not to hurt her feelings. You know what I mean? Not to laugh at her, or condescend to her in a way that could hurt. She's been hurt enough by poor Bob Atkins's death. Still not herself, I wouldn't have said, even after however long it has been.'

'Listen, if I still miss Bob, she must do so much more, I realise that.'

'Well, never mind that. Just you mind your manners as far as Miss Stamford is concerned, young man, and thank you for the hat and everything, you shouldn't have, but I'm glad you did!'

Tom nodded, waved to her from the window of his hired car, and drove off too fast.

Certainly Mrs Posnet had said enough, there had been enough warning in her eyes to make him feel that meeting Miss Minty Stamford was not going to be exactly the glam date of all time. But at least he was only meeting her for a drink, and at least it was in London.

Alexandra had never been to Claridge's for a drink before, so she was immediately impressed by the ambience, which was civilised, old-fashioned and full of the kind of quiet class she had only ever read about in magazines. She had not meant to arrive before Thomas O'Brien, but once it was clear that she had, she made up her mind to enjoy herself.

'I don't think I will order yet, as I am expecting someone,' she told the waiter as he put down some nuts in a bowl. 'The worst of it is,' she confided, 'I have no idea what he looks like. Would you know what a Mr Thomas O'Brien looks like? He is staying here, I think.'

The waiter looked round.

'He's just coming in now, miss, that's him over there, I think.'

But it wasn't, it was another Mr O'Brien, also staying. They both laughed, and parted, and Alexandra sat down once again now feeling even more isolated and not a little foolish, despite the fact that it was only just twelve-thirty.

'I will page him for you, if you like – Miss er?'

'Stamford. But no need, really. I'm early. Silly of me. Taxi ride was much shorter than I expected.'

'Very well, miss, but I will inform that gentleman over there. He will tell you when your Mr O'Brien, Mr Thomas O'Brien whom he looks after at dinner, arrives. He will bring him over to you, to avoid any more embarrassment.'

Alexandra looked away. She was wishing to goodness that she had never agreed to meet poor Bob's friend when Tom came into the room. He looked around, and eyeing a glamorous, smartly dressed young woman seated at a nearby table immediately dismissed the idea that it could be Minty Stamford, since Mrs Posnet had after all described her as 'home-spun'. He sat down, looking round for a waiter, instead of which the maître d'hôtel came to his side.

'Mr O'Brien, I think you will find your guest is waiting over there for you.' He politely indicated the same young woman that Tom had decided was not Minty Stamford.

Tom stood up and walked over to Alexandra's table. She looked up at him and smiled.

'Thomas O'Brien?'

He nodded wordlessly, staring down at her.

'Yes,' he answered, finally.

Alexandra cleared her throat and held out her hand.

'How nice to meet Bob's friend at last. I'm Minty Stamford – well, I'm not, actually.'

'You're not? Really?'

'Well I am, but my real name is actually Alexandra. As you probably know Bob knew me as "Minty", but I'm really Alexandra, that's my real name,' she finished in a rush.

Tom smiled and sat down feeling an odd sense of relief, as if a yoke had been lifted from his shoulders, as if he had been given a second chance. *Minty* had been Bob's girlfriend, but this young woman was *not* Minty. She was Alexandra, and he realised that this albeit small fact of a name nevertheless freed him from instantly associating this beautiful girl in her close-fitting suit with its pleated skirt and rounded collar from the Minty that Bob had always been going on about. This girl looked altogether different from the maid-of-all-work that he had imagined.

'Are you all right?' Alexandra asked and she could not help staring, and not just because he was staring at her, but because she saw something in his eyes that she knew she had seen before. She frowned.

'It sounds stupid, but I feel we've met before, but of course we couldn't have . . .' Her voice tailed off, but she was still frowning.

'I don't think we have,' Tom put in far too quickly, and he sat down, at last. 'But I have the same feeling, I feel as if we have met before, perhaps because – I have heard so much about you.'

He could hear his voice saying the words, but felt that it was someone else speaking them, or speaking them for him, because actually his eyes were doing all the speaking, and they were saying: '*I love your long dark hair, and your blue eyes, and the way your head is carried at such a brave, proud angle, as if you are always ready and waiting to take on the world. And I love your beautiful hands, which are not feline but feminine, and the way you are smiling now is making my heart miss a beat, which it really hasn't done in such a long while I had forgotten that it actually could.*'

'I didn't dare order a drink, it looks a bit fast, sitting on your own,' she was saying, half apologetically as if she didn't really expect him to pay for a drink for her.

Tom smiled.

'Let's have a bottle of champagne. After all, we have heard so much about each other. And you know how it is when . . .'

337

He was about to say, 'You have heard so much about someone from a friend,' but, not wanting to bring up the subject of poor Bob, he went on, 'Well, I do feel I know you, that I already know you, and even though we haven't met before, here we are meeting at last, and that does deserve at least a bottle of champagne.'

They drank their champagne too quickly of course, as people always do when they know they have been instantly set alight by each other, and as they did so the subject of Bob seemed to have become forbidden territory, a name that neither of them wanted to utter; because they both knew instinctively it was a part of something that was the past. At that moment Bob was no longer anything to do with them, and certainly nothing to do with what they knew was happening now. No matter what happened next, the moment that Tom came up to her table Alexandra had become quite sure that the past had become irrelevant, and what was more, perhaps they both knew it.

'You've very different from how I imagined, actually,' Alexandra stated several times, in between everything else they were or were not saying, because inevitably, as happens, they found they were still talking about everything and nothing while still staring at each other, still sure they had met before, that somehow if they could only remember where, it would all come back to them, and they would be able to click their fingers and say, as people do, 'Of course! Yes, of course, *that's* where we met,' because that feeling of having always known each other just would not go away.

But in the event they did not snap their fingers at each other, instead they went into lunch, which Tom had not thought for one moment that he would be doing with Minty, but which he now realised he could not wait to do with Alexandra, and after lunch, he took her upstairs to his suite, and they started to kiss and then make love, leaving a trail of

338

clothes across the expensive carpet. It was not something Alexandra ever thought she would do with someone she did not know, but since she felt she had always known him, it seemed perfect. And the truth was it was perfect, and when they walked out into Brook Street a few hours later it seemed to Alexandra that London had never seemed so sparkling, the shop windows so glamorous, the people that they passed so fascinating.

'How about if I take you to a cartoon cinema. Do you like Donald Duck and Mickey Mouse?'

Alexandra had grown up old, as so many solitary, only children do, not just because she was always with older people but because when she was with them she was expected to be old, and talk about old things. And of course just recently she had been with the really quite old, and it was not that she did not like and respect them, but now suddenly she was with Tom, and he was her generation, not old like Mrs Smithers or the Major. So she let him catch her hand and steer her towards a cartoon cinema where they sat for several hours in a haze, pretending to watch cartoons, when in reality all they could remember was making love, and that was all that they now wanted to do. Everything that interrupted the kissing and the love was now irrelevant, timeserving, an interruption.

'You'll move into my hotel, you'll be with me here, won't you?' Tom gestured round the suite. 'It's big enough – you'll come here, won't you?'

Alexandra was lying, tousled, languorous, her expression dreamy as she looked at Tom's suntanned back, and marvelled at what had happened to her in the previous hours.

'Whatever you say . . .'

'I do say.' Tom turned and looked at her. 'Where are you staying?'

'The Ritz.'

339

He reacted to this as if she had said something tactless, as if she had mentioned Bob.

He paused before saying, 'OK, so where are your things? I mean which suite are they in?'

'I'm not in a suite, not like this. Just a single room and bathroom.'

'I'll ring them, and you can tell them to send your luggage round here.'

'I should go and pack—'

'No, no. I don't want you going back there. I'll pick up the tab, you just tell them to pack up your things, they'll send them on.'

'I wouldn't want them to pack for me!'

'Hotels do it all the time.'

'No, but—'

'No. No, no "no, buts", just tell them to send your things.'

He asked to be put through to the Ritz and held out the telephone to Alexandra who did as asked, frowning. She replaced the receiver. She wanted to know why she was not allowed back to her hotel, but something stopped her from asking, something telling her that this was enemy territory, that such a question would break the spell, and she really did not want that.

The next two days they walked around London hand in hand, strolled in the parks, went to the cinema again, lunched, dined, danced to the orchestra downstairs, went back to the suite, made love, and Alexandra was in heaven, but it wasn't until she heard a snatch of *La Traviata* on the radio as they were dressing to go down for dinner that the reality dawned on her.

So this was love! And once again she remembered Bob flicking her cheek and saying '*I lost you a little tonight*,' and her trying to deny it, but realising that it was true, that he had lost her, if only for a minute or two.

'What's the matter?'

Tom was standing over her.

'Nothing.'

'Something.'

Alexandra looked up at him with sad eyes.

'Yes, actually, something.'

'Can I help?'

'I don't think so.'

She couldn't say what she now knew to be true, that she had thought she loved Bob, and she had – but not like this. This really was love.

This was the tenor breaking down in a passion of tears because he so identified with Violetta dying in his arms, when the arms held the woman he loved in reality. This was love that knew that the impossible could happen, that you could lose love, and never ever find it again.

Tom took her hands and pulled her to her feet, and taking her head he kissed her forehead gently.

'I'm kissing away whatever you are thinking. You are not to think it again, do you hear?'

Alexandra closed her eyes briefly before opening them again. She did not want to say what she knew to be true, which was that try as he might, Tom could not kiss away that particular thought. It was just a fact.

Florazel had been visiting Mrs Posnet, which she sometimes did when she was staying at her brother's estate, all part of what she called her 'basket of scones' duties, since many years before Mrs Posnet had used to work for the Duke as a housekeeper, and the family always prided themselves on not losing touch.

This particular visit Mrs Posnet was looking and sounding strangely glamorous, petticoat rustling, smelling strongly of expensive French scent.

'Have you been on holiday, Mrs Posnet?'

Florazel smiled encouragingly, her beautiful blue eyes crinkling appreciatively, because she was always curious about people.

'No, Lady Florazel, no, I have not been on holiday, I have been visited by a certain young gentleman newly returned from America. He's the one who's on holiday. Come back to see his old landlady.'

She started colouring, as she remembered the scandal attached to Tom O'Brien's sudden departure, and how Lady Florazel had paid up his rent for him and, rumour had it, lived with him in fine style for a long time.

Florazel knew at once to whom she was referring, but she said no more, as neither of them would expect her to do. She had long ago regretted throwing Tom O'Brien over in such a hasty way, as if what that stupid old woman had said counted in the least. What would it have mattered if she had dragged the family name through the mud? But now the stupid old woman had died, she was quite sure that throwing Tom over had been a mistake. He had been the love of her life, and she was quite sure that she had been the love of his, and such love did not, alas, come along with a snap of the fingers.

Of course she had been so-called in love since Tom. She was not someone who was ever content not to have an affair on the go, but the men who had followed Tom O'Brien had been less than satisfactory. They had been handsome, some of them, amusing, some of them, but none of them had done for her what he had done, and there was no denying this. She remembered their long affair, and how they had lived in such bliss – really there was no other word for it – at the Ritz, how she had turned him into an elegant, fashionable man about town, how much money she had lavished on him, both during the affair and after it. How she had sent a large sum to start him off in New York, how guilt had made her feel that she should endow him with enough funds to start him over again.

But that was a long time ago, or seemed a long time ago, and now the realisation that Tom was back in England was exhilarating. More than that, she realised he really rather owed her now. She realised this because she knew, from what Mrs Posnet was saying about his having made such a success of his advertising company in New York, that Tom must have made a go of everything except perhaps love, because Mrs Posnet also mentioned that he was still a bachelor. So all in all she was very grateful that she had visited Mrs Posnet.

Florazel smiled her really rather pretty cat-like smile, and she left Mrs Posnet as soon as she could, which was very shortly afterwards, so shortly afterwards that Mrs Posnet had the strangest feeling that she had said something wrong. She just couldn't put her finger on what it was. Something. But what? Something, certainly. She went upstairs and removed her new taffeta petticoat from under her felt skirt, feeling somehow ashamed that she had worn it for Lady Florazel's visit.

Meanwhile Florazel drove to London in her new Bentley Continental feeling quite certain that the time might have come to pick up where she had left off with Tom O'Brien. After all, he had loved her with a passion, and now surely she had only to snap her fingers and he would do so again?

Once back at her new London flat Florazel started to ring around the smartest hotels, starting naturally with the Ritz, and finally finishing with Claridge's, which she had imagined might be just a little staid for Tom. How wrong she proved to be.

She left a message for him. The hall porter put it in the relevant place, and when Tom and Alexandra checked in after dinner and the theatre later that evening he handed it to Tom. *Come to the Ritz for a drink tomorrow lunchtime, the*

downstairs bar, will you? I long to see you, if only for old times' sake.
FLORAZEL.

'Something interesting?'

Tom shook his head and threw the note into a nearby wastepaper basket.

'No,' he said. 'No, not really, just someone who's a bit of a menace.'

He smiled at Alexandra, and kissed her quickly on the cheek. He too wanted to see Florazel, if only to write her a cheque, to repay her for the start she had given him, and to tell her that he was grateful to her for throwing him over, that he had met someone else. It would be just a drink after all, just a drink and then he would be back with Alexandra. As he asked for their key Alexandra glanced back at the wastepaper basket wondering why Tom had thrown the note away quite so quickly.

The Devil's Comedy

The following morning Tom and Alexandra parted, neither making it particularly clear where they were going, but arranging to meet back at the hotel after lunch, where love would most definitely be on the menu.

Alexandra, filled with love and wonder for the happiness she had enjoyed for the past days, went to Bond Street where she bought Tom a beautiful pair of enamelled cuff-links. She had never bought a man a present before, at least not a present that was not for a birthday or Christmas. It seemed almost shocking. The assistant seemed to understand her vague embarrassment and was sympathetic, wrapping the present in exquisite paper and making sure that the smart sticker on the box proclaimed the jeweller's name.

Tom went shopping for Alexandra. He went to a myriad places: to Halcyon Days, where he bought her an exquisite marble jar and a woman's hand holding a mirror with a pearl ring on one finger. He then went to Harrods where he bought her a matching pearl ring and earrings, and then, almost satiated, but not quite, he bought her a dozen LPs of the kind of music he now knew that she loved.

And so it was that loaded down with the gifts that he

wanted to give his beloved Alexandra, he went to the down-stairs bar of the Ritz, to meet Florazel.

As soon as he saw her he remembered just how much he had loved her, and just how much she had hurt him, and his feelings were torn between both extremes, but as he set down his carrier bags beside the chair which she indicated, he remembered that how he was feeling was how he *had* felt but no longer.

Now was different. Now he had found Alexandra.

'Tom.'

She smiled, crinkling her eyes at him.

'Florazel.'

'You're different. So much a man.'

'You're not, still so much a woman.'

She immediately took that as a compliment, but then her eyes dropped to the carrier bags with their smart labels and gift-wrapped contents, and since Tom was making no obvious move to hand one, or any of them to her, a light frowning look came into the beautiful blue eyes, and she knew at once. Or at least she guessed that the presents were intended for someone else, that he must believe he was in love with someone else, not Florazel, and she was immediately glad that she had done as she had, that on leaving Mrs Posnet's house she had driven to London and telephoned round, not just to the smart hotels, but to a friend of a friend who had been at school with one of the gossip columnists, a paid public-school snitch who liked to earn his corn by passing on tidbits, which so many of them did.

Alexandra was meeting Jessamine and Cyrene for lunch. They were both rather silenced by her new look.

'Wow, you look like the cat's pyjamas, Alexandra Stamford. Really, twice the thing, if not three times.'

Jessamine stared at her smart suit, her suede gloves and elegant shoes.

'What happened to the home-made look, dear coz?'

'I chucked it for the London look.'

Both girls stared at her now, closely. They could see that she had changed, and not just because of her clothes.

'Shopping at smart shops too.'

Now they both stared at her small, chic parcel, so obviously a present for someone.

'Nice present to yourself?'

'Not exactly.'

They were all sipping drinks, and eyeing each other, wondering which way the lunch would go, how much they would tell each other, or how much they would not tell each other.

Alexandra leaned forward, and dropping her voice she confided with a smile and a small fond look towards the parcel.

'It's a present for the new man in my life.'

It was a cheap way to describe what she felt for Tom, but it was the kind of phrase her cousins would understand.

'Oh, who?'

'Do tell.'

She paused, not quite willing, but not quite unwilling either.

'He's called Tom O'Brien. And he was a friend of my late fiancé and he wrote to me, ages ago, and we met this week – and, well, it seems that we've fallen in love.'

There was a short silence.

'We knew a Tom O'Brien,' Cyrene said slowly, frowning. 'You knew a Tom O'Brien, at Knighton. Remember?'

Alexandra shook her head.

'Yes, you do remember. Remember "*the oik*"?'

'I remember you talking about him, but I never met him, no, I don't remember him.'

347

For some reason she could not name Alexandra felt her mouth going dry. It was something to do with the way the girls were staring at her, something to do with the way the girls were watching her so closely, as if they were waiting.

'He was tall, dark and handsome. Very handsome, but you know – common.'

'I expect there are literally hundreds of tall, dark, handsome Tom O'Briens in this world—'

Jessamine picked up a copy of the newspaper beside her handbag, and opened it rather officiously as if about to make an important announcement. Alexandra watched her, saying nothing, but not liking the expression on her face.

'Here. That's him. That's the oik. Used to be our groom until Daddy discovered him in one of the barns without a stitch on and had to boot him out. Bad boy O'Brien, that's him.'

She turned the newspaper towards Alexandra.

The piece was headed: *'New Love for Old?'*

Lady Florazel Compton, voted the débutante of the year during her Season, has remet a former love, one Thomas O'Brien, co-founder of Bodel O'Brien Inc., New York and London. Fingers are crossing for the ill-starred Duke's daughter, everyone hoping that Cupid will finally hold sway and she will be hacking it up the aisle very soon. 'I can't comment at the moment. Let's say it's all going really rather well,' my source was coyly told by Lady Florazel. Let's hope so indeed. Lady Florazel has been a footloose filly for far too long.

Alexandra had read the piece all too quickly, now she read the piece again all too slowly, and then she looked across at Jessamine.

'Yes, that's him,' she admitted. 'That's Tom O'Ber-Ber-Brien.'

The girls were silenced.

'Oh dear, we could have warned you.' For once in her life Cyrene looked genuinely upset. 'He was always such a bad boy. Always flirting with us in the stables, always on the lookout for himself.'

Alexandra stared around the restaurant blankly. She had been taken for one great ride. She had thrown herself at the Millingtons' former groom, the oik, and now he was obviously intent on hacking off with this Lady Florazel Compton, whoever she was when she was at home. God, how could she have been so stupid?

'I say, er, would you mind if I don't have anything mer-mer-more? It's all been a ber-ber-bit of a shock. I-er think I will just go back to the-the hotel.'

She swallowed hard, tried to smile, and left.

Jessamine stared after her.

'What a thing to happen.'

Cyrene sighed.

'It would have to be the oik, wouldn't it? Trust her to fall for him.'

Tom stared at Florazel. She was still crinkling her eyes at him, but it was not having much effect, because her mouth was telling him something that he realised was still so painful to her.

'How could I have gone on with you, knowing as I did that I had told you such terrible things about – about Gerald Hardwick, once I realised that . . .'

She paused, waiting for maximum effect.

'That he was my father.'

She stared at him, stunned.

'You knew? You knew all the time that I had run off with Gerald and that he was your father?'

Tom shook his head and lit a cigarette.

'No, as a matter of fact I didn't know, I only found out a few weeks ago. You see my partner, Alfred Bodel, he was getting married, and in the States, very wisely, before you marry, you have to have a blood test, so that you know what is what about your blood as far as having children is concerned. So seeing Al going through all this, I decided to try and find out about my own background. I confess I was interested, particularly once I had received a much delayed notification from England that my grandmother had died, leaving me a large bequest, which thanks to lazy English lawyers falling behind in their work and being unable to trace me, had only just come to light. Of course from there the trail inevitably led back to Gerald, and to a whole new set of questions about my mother. Why had she taken a job so near to the Millingtons of all people? Guilt perhaps? They say you always return to the scene of the crime and she must have believed that she in some way caused Laura Millington's death, however inadvertently.'

Florazel was looking vaguely bored now. Sally Hardwick had died shortly after their meeting. They had never liked each other. It was not a subject she wished to discuss. She turned her attention back to Tom, not wanting to remember Sally and her threats.

'So that's how I realised that I had as it were, shared the same mistress as the late, and I gather, very unlamented Gerald Hardwick – my father,' Tom finished.

'I never wanted you to know. But the morning we were leaving for America Gerald's mother turned up and she wanted to see you, but I didn't want you to know about the past, didn't want everything spoilt for us.'

Tom looked at Florazel, feeling patient but unsympathetic, not believing her. Of course he would have liked to have known his grandmother, but since it was too late, he had every idea that keeping Sally Hardwick from Tom had not been Florazel's only motivation. She would not have wanted the old lady to tell him about Florazel's past, a past that she had kept so carefully hidden from him, for like all women who did what they wanted when they wanted with little regard to the outcome, Florazel had obviously fondly believed that poor Tom O'Brien had known nothing of her previous lovers, had perhaps always imagined that Tom lived in a state of complete innocence, thinking that Florazel enjoyed only one brief unhappy affair before finding love with him.

'Florazel.' He smiled at her. She was still stunning, but she was nothing compared to Alexandra. Certainly she was more beautiful, yards more sophisticated, but what was more than obvious to him now – Florazel was devious. 'Florazel, you know you remind me of a dog?'

Florazel's eyes narrowed.

'Quite a rich dog, I hope,' she snapped.

'You know the way a dog hides its head under a tablecloth fondly thinking that you can't see the rest of its body?' Tom continued inexorably. 'That is what you remind me of when you speak about the past – because you know and I know that you are not telling me the whole truth.'

'I suppose I should feel grateful that you didn't say a bitch hiding its head under a table.'

Tom leaned forward and took his wallet out of the breast pocket of his suit.

'I have always meant to pay you back, and now I can.'

He placed an envelope on the table in front of them both. Florazel stared at it, and then him. He was being fair and honest, and honourable, and he was insulting her too, and they both knew it.

'Oh Tom, but how sweet of you. But don't think this is the last you will hear about us, will you?'

Florazel's beautiful blue eyes crinkled yet again. It should have acted as a warning to Tom, but it did not.

*   *   *

Alexandra ran towards Claridge's with only one aim in mind, to pack up and leave as soon as was perfectly possible. She did not know what to do about the bill, but since the manager had reassured her that the suite was booked in Mr O'Brien's name and therefore the account would be paid by him, she had to believe him.

She drove through the early afternoon until she reached Deanford at last. The call of the seagulls was always the first thing that seemed to come to her, long before she saw the sea, or the white tops of the waves, or the pier stretching out to sea, as if reaching out to invite the fish to play on its decks, fish that no one ever seemed to catch in any kind of numbers.

'Oh, so you're back.' Mrs Smithers looked vaguely irritated as people do when their game of Patience is interrupted. 'Mrs Cruddle won't like that. Mrs Cruddle and Jane are managing really rather well.'

Alexandra nodded, knowing without being told that things had already changed while she was away.

'Oh dear,' she said eventually. 'Well, why don't we keep her on for a few days, until we have made up our minds about everything.'

Mrs Smithers looked up sharply from her cards as if she had guessed that there was some inner struggle going on.

'So what's to be done?'

Alexandra thought for a moment.

'I thought I would go next door, and work on the house there. I'll take the dogs with me, she won't mind if I take the dogs, I don't suppose.'

'As long as you tell her.'

'Of course.'

Alexandra started to turn on her heel. Mrs Smithers did not look up this time.

'Enjoy London, did you?'

'Yes, I did.'

'Quite an experience after Deanford, I should imagine.'

'Quite an experience,' Alexandra agreed.

'But not so good that you wanted to stay. Missed old Deanford, I expect,' she added comfortably.

Alexandra, already halfway out of the room and on her way to the basement to collect her dogs, called back, 'That's right.'

But Mrs Smithers had looked up from her cards once again.

'By the way, you may be glad to hear that I was right about Lydia Passmore. She has not changed one bit.'

Curiosity forced Alexandra to be drawn back into the room as Mrs Smithers knew very well that she would be.

'Yes, she has not changed an iota. Kindness does not pay with those sorts of women, Minty, really it does not. I should have listened to myself.' Mrs Smithers paused. 'She has only pinched the Major from me this time, as a bridge-playing partner. She has, she has pinched the Major. Leopards do not change their spots, Minty, remember that. Not ever. People do not change.' She sighed with some satisfaction, and returned to her game.

No one who has ever gone through the heartbreak of dis-illusion can ever forget what they have experienced. Happily however, no one can quite remember just how sharp the pain, once it fades. It is as if not just the whole heart, but the whole body is being twisted in opposite directions, as if all emotion has been battered out of it, leaving only a shell out of which the possessor stares with disinterest at the passing parade that is known as life, but in which they are now quite certain they can no longer be involved.

Alexandra wandered round number thirty-three with her

dogs on leads, shivering with the cold. She could remember, only six short days ago, how proud she was of finishing the first of the bedroom suites, how proud she had been of her purchase of some bridge tables to set about the first-floor drawing room, but she could not feel those emotions any more. It was not just love that had fled and hidden its face, it seemed to her that it was life itself, her life that had fled. Everything seemed not just cold and sad, but dead. As if the people who would be occupying the rooms were already dead, and she with them.

Tom returned to the hotel with his packages feeling coldly satisfied. He had seen Florazel, he had seen that she was still Florazel, and he knew that the boy that he had been who had loved her did so no longer, and the man that he was could not do so any more.

'Ah, sir?'

Tom turned and, having collected his key, smiled back at the hall porter. Nice fellow, old-fashioned sort with gentle, good manners, not obsequious, just right. Now, however, the look in his eyes was a little cautious, even sorrowful, as if he had to tell Tom something that he might not like.

'The lady who was staying,' he said tactfully, 'your wife,' he added firmly, both of them knowing that the old-fashioned rules still pertained, that the old hotels, if no one else, still maintained their standards. 'She left an hour or so ago. Left this for you.'

He handed Tom a small package. Tom looked at it, and then hurried towards the lift, knowing but not wanting to know what he would find when he went to his suite.

He found no letter, but he found no clothes either, no trace of Alexandra. He put down all his carefully chosen presents and stared around him. She had left the wardrobe doors open as if to prove that everything she owned was gone. He turned to the small package and started to open it, knowing that she must have chosen whatever it was with care, for he could already see from the way that she dressed that she had taste.

He stared at the cufflinks. They were exquisite and expensive, but since Alexandra was gone, they were just heartbreaking.

'Mrs P.?'

'Yes.'

Mrs Posnet was answering the telephone in the vague, distant and distrusting manner that Tom had noticed everyone new to the telephone answered it – as if it was about to explode, or tell them something that they would not like.

'It's Tom O'Brien.'

'Yes.'

'I, er, wondered if you have Alexandra Stamford's address. I seem to have lost it.'

'You mean Minty that was? Yes, I have her address, yes.'

'Could you give it to me?'

'Yes.'

She put the telephone down, and Tom could hear her footsteps crossing the tiled kitchen floor, and then recrossing it.

'I shall be some time since my book is in the scullery.'

There was a much longer pause, more footsteps, each of which seemed to Tom to be taking more time than he had taken to fly across the Atlantic. Finally the receiver was picked up again.

'Yes. I have it here, Tom. It is thirty-two Queen Alexandra Square, Deanford. No, I tell a lie. She sent me a card a few weeks back. No, it is thirty-two and thirty-three Queen Alexandra Square. They seemed to have named the square after her,' she joked.

'Thank you Mrs P. And – thank you. Goodbye.'

Mrs Posnet stared at the telephone with some satisfaction. She did not mind people calling her. She just did not ever want the expense of having to call them. She would not call Miss Stamford. Cost too much money, that would.

Alexandra stepped back and stared at the suite to which she had just finished adding the final touches. It was very pretty and chintzy, just right for Deanford, but with some seaside touches, like a striped rug on the floor by the bed, and a picture of children with buckets and spades over the chimneypiece.

She had made excuses to Mrs Smithers because she did not want to face going back to her basement at number thirty-two. For some reason going back to the basement meant that the door would be closing on her London days for ever, and she could not quite face that, instead she had made up her mind to stay the night where she was. The house was warming up, and in some ways so was she. The horror of the day had begun to fade a little. Perhaps it was the view of the sea from the windows, the heartbreakingly beautiful sky seeming to Alexandra to be making fun of human feelings, seeming to be telling her that a love affair gone wrong was just that, a love affair gone wrong, nothing more. She would get better, because she had to; finally everyone had to.

She set a table in front of the fire that she had lit in the still empty drawing room, and placed the only large armchair in front of it. She made herself a drink, happily to hand on the improvised drinks table, and promptly fell fast asleep.

She was awoken by the sound of voices. One of them that of Mrs Smithers saying, 'The bell doesn't work, you see. We're only just doing this place up. But you'll find her at the top of the stairs I expect, busying herself as usual.'

The front door closed and there was the unmistakable sound of male feet on the stairs. For some reason she did not understand, as the dogs barked and she nearly knocked her drink flying, Alexandra positioned herself behind the winged chair, hastily pulling her long hair back into their side combs, pulling down her skirt, doing up the top button of her blouse.

'What are you doing here?' she asked into the growing darkness of the old, tall-ceilinged room with its decorative plasterwork and air of having been, like herself, only just awoken.

'I have come to fetch you back, Alexandra.'

'Back?'

'Yes, back. You know what I mean. I have come to fetch you back.'

'I don't want to be fetched back,' she retorted, and she turned to switch on the table lamp beside the fireplace, but it wasn't working yet so they remained as they were in the gradually darkening room.

'Yes, you do. You know you want to be fetched back.'

'For what reason?'

'To be with me.'

'I don't want to be with you. Haven't you had enough women to date? Why do you want me as well?'

'I admit—'

Tom walked forward a few steps.

'You just stay right where you are. This is my house and I don't want you near me, not now, not ever.'

'I won't move a muscle, if you will only tell me why you ran off the way you did.'

'You read newspapers, don't you?'

'No. At least not since I met you. Been too preoccupied,' he said, trying to lighten the atmosphere.

'Well, I had lunch with my Millington cousins, and they do

read newspapers, and they showed me the item about you and Lady Florazel whatsit; and they told me all about how you were sacked for being found with a girl in a barn, by my uncle.'

Tom stared at her.

'I don't know what you're talking about. Well, at least I do.' He paused. 'You're a – *Millington*? Of Knighton Hall? James Millington is your – uncle?'

'My mother was James Millington's sister. She died when I was born, but I used to stay at Knighton. When you worked there I was staying, but we never met. If we had, I might have known you for what you are; it might have saved me from making a fool of myself over you.'

Tom sighed.

'Mr Millington never found me in a barn with a girl. I found him in the barn, with *his* girl, now his wife. I found him with Jennifer Langley-Ancram. I was on my bike, going to fetch old Westrup his cough medicine when I heard a noise. To tell you the truth I thought a cow had locked itself in there—' He stopped. 'Now I come to think of it, a cow had, but not the kind that gives milk.'

Alexandra did not smile. The reason she did not smile was not because the remark was not apt but because she knew, right down in her deepest heart, that Tom might actually be telling the truth. It fitted in with everything she knew about Jennifer and her uncle, about everything that had happened at Knighton. She had always heard Jessamine and Cyrene joking and laughing about the handsome groom they called the oik, planning some new way to flirt with him.

'I don't mind that you're a Millington, so you mustn't mind if I'm whatever I'm meant to be – oh yes, a Hardwick – except I am not. I am actually Thomas O'Brien of New York, and Long Island, and from now on, occasionally Claridge's.'

Alexandra was silent.

'So on to today. What happened today so particularly that made you run away the way you did?'

Tom had cautiously put in a few more steps, but he was still a long way from Alexandra behind her winged chair.

'What happened today was that I saw the item about you and Florazel, the person you were meant to be meeting for your so-called "business drink". My cousins showed me the item about you and *Lady* Florazel, about how you were about to become engaged.'

Tom closed his eyes momentarily and sighed. Oh dear God. Of course, what was why when he had left Florazel she had seemed to have a positive gleam in her eye. She had always laughed about Fleet Street, about how easy it was to use the gossip columns to discomfort your enemies, how you just had to use some paid ex-public-school snitch to plant something, while you yourself distanced yourself from the item.

'There is no truth in whatever you read. I admit I didn't tell you about going to see Florazel, simply because I didn't want to upset you.' He stopped, realising that to his shame he was now sounding rather too like Florazel. He started again. 'No, that's not true. I just thought that since Florazel no longer mattered to me, that she needn't matter to you.'

He was closer to Alexandra now, and had her whole attention; so much so that it seemed to him that she had not noticed.

'Florazel would have posted that piece in whatever gossip column it was. Nothing to do with reality, nothing to do with anything but her making mischief, wanting history to repeat itself, since my father ran off with her when she was young.'

Alexandra stared at Tom.

'How do you know?'

'I have known for some time. But since our affair was

long, long over, and I believe that as far as the past is concerned the buck stops here, it didn't seem to matter. It was a temporary, wounding embarrassment, and then I realised it really had nothing to do with anything. She had run off with him, had the briefest of relationships, and then run away from him. He had died. All that was their business, not mine. Finally I felt it should mean nothing to me, must not mean anything to me and, truthfully, now it doesn't.'

Alexandra stared at him and then past him, bewildered by so much information, yet longing to believe him.

'Oh darling, I brought you so many presents this morning – I ran back to the hotel with them so longing for you – and I found you gone. Do you know what it felt like not to find you? It felt as if I was dying. You are the person I have been longing to meet all my life – and I could have done. We must have passed within a few yards of each other dozens of times at Knighton, but never quite seen each other, because we were not meant to meet until now. But now we have met – we know what we know. The past few days surely have proved that. Haven't you felt that this was all meant, that we were supposed to be together, and that if we pass on each other now, for whatever reason, that we will be passing up on love for ever? It doesn't happen twice in a lifetime. And it won't. I know it, and I think you do too.'

He was so close to her now, so near that he could have put out his arms and pulled her to him, but instead he pointed past her to the curtainless windows.

'Look at that beautiful sky, look at the sunset reaching out to meet the dark of the sky. Do you know what that is called?'

'No—' She turned

'It's called the magic hour, because myth says that this is the magic hour of the day and if two people embrace, just as the sky meets the sun's setting before it gets dark, they will always be together.'

Tom held out his arms to her. Alexandra turned from the sky which was just beginning to touch the orange of the sunset and, not willing to risk her happiness ever again, she went quickly into them.

Epilogue

Tom had longed to see James Millington humiliated, longed to see him handing over the keys to Knighton Hall, James a ruined man at last, but he never did.

Not that Jennifer Langley-Ancram did not ruin James, because, inevitably, and really rather satisfyingly, she did: over-spending on the house, and socialising to such an extent that Millington lost his touch on the stock exchange and eventually all his fortune.

While Tom did not feel sorry for him when he heard the news, at the same time he had no desire to snub him by buying Knighton from him, his impending Long Island wedding to Alexandra bringing with it, as it would do, good sense and a generous attitude.

Their wedding was not the highlight of the following summer season, but it certainly caused a stir in Deanford, not least because so many of its residents had been invited, at the bridegroom's expense, to attend. Naturally Mrs Cruddle and Jane, who had taken over the running of the houses from the bride, could not attend, but they were well content with the photographs which Mrs Smithers and her entourage brought back.

The black and white images showed an elegant bride

in a decorous dress of white chiffon, high-waisted and falling to the back in a long train, the cap sleeves of which were braid-edged. Her long, dark hair was caught up in an elegant figure of eight from the back of which sprang yards of netting topped with fresh white flowers. In her short-gloved white hands she carried one long stem of white lily. The honeymoon was spent in the Bahamas, but the following anniversaries were all spent in England, not at Knighton Hall, but at Claridge's; which, as the happy couple would acknowledge for the rest of their lives, had in truth been somewhat of a fairy godmother to their romance – never adding, as perhaps they should have done, that other godparent to love: the Magic Hour.

If you enjoyed The Magic Hour, *look out for Charlotte Bingham's next novel,* Friday's Child.

Charlotte Bingham would like to invite you to visit her website at www.charlottebingham.com